"The Feast of Saint Dionysus" by Robert Silverberg—Another world had claimed his fellow astronauts in blood sacrifice. Now would he pay a terrible price or find his own private epiphany among Earth's desert sands?

"Sticks" by Karl Edward Wagner—Haunted by a vision of horror found in an old farmhouse, he incorporated it into his art, little realizing that his own macabre images might prove the catalyst for doom. . . .

"Fear is a Business" by Theodore Sturgeon—He had made his fortune inventing tales of invaders from the stars, attracting a cult of followers who believed his every word. Everything was just fine until the day his fictions became reality. . . .

These are just a few of the tales included in this chilling collection that takes you from the world of the everyday to the inescapable domain of—

CULTS OF HORROR

READ THESE BLOOD-FREEZING

DAW Horror Anthologies:

VAMPS Edited by Martin H. Greenberg and Charles G. Waugh. Terrifying tales of those irresistible ladies of the night—vampires!

HOUSE SHUDDERS Edited by Martin H. Greenberg and Charles G. Waugh. Fiendish chillers about haunted houses.

HUNGER FOR HORROR Edited by Robert Adams, Martin H. Greenberg and Pamela Crippen Adams. A devilish stew from the master chefs of horror.

RED JACK Edited by Martin H. Greenberg, Charles G. Waugh and Frank D. McSherry, Jr. The 100th anniversary collection of Jack the Ripper tales.

PHANTOMS Edited by Martin H. Greenberg and Rosalind M. Greenberg. Original tales of terror—from the Phantom of the Paris Opera to the dark side of New York's fashion scene to a soap opera cursed by a ghostly doom.

DEVIL WORSHIPERS Edited by Martin H. Greenberg and Charles G. Waugh. They are the dwellers in darkness, the people of the night, with a hunger for evil that will never be sated!

CULTS OF HORROR

Edited by
Martin H. Greenberg and
Charles G. Waugh

DAW BOOKS, INC.
DONALD A. WOLLHEIM, PUBLISHER

375 Hudson Street, New York, NY 10014

Cover art by Jim Warren

DAW Book Collectors No. 826

First Printing, August 1990

1 2 3 4 5 6 7 8 9

PRINTED IN THE U.S.A.

ACKNOWLEDGMENTS

TABLE OF CONTENTS

INTRODUCTION

The Killer Cults

Frank D. McSherry Jr.

"Poison your children!" thundered the Man of God.

And they heard and obeyed.

"Kill yourselves!" shrieked the Man of God.

And they heard and obeyed—

It sounds like a slasher movie. It is, actually, a macabre reality. On the hot afternoon of November 18, 1978, Reverend Jim Jones, a fundamentalist preacher who told his followers to call him Father (sometimes he told them he was Jesus Christ, sometimes Lenin or Buddha; Jones got a little confused about who he was now and then), ordered his followers to kill themselves. Obediently, they fed poison to their babies and lined up for their own; a few who broke and ran were shot down. By evening, more than nine hundred bodies lay lifeless, literally carpeting with corpses the neat fields and barracks of the religious commune they had carved out of the green jungles of Guatemala. Even the dogs had been killed; the Man of God had left nothing living behind him. The death rate at Jonestown, after four years of worship of the God who taught: Thou shalt not kill, actually exceeded a hundred percent: Reverend Jones ordered People's Temple member Larry Layton to kill several people who were not members of the commune, including U. S. Congressman Leo J. Ryan (Democrat, California), a lady trying to escape from the communel, and several reporters.

Layton heard and obeyed.

A cult. A cult of horror.

Why did these people obey such orders?

Psychiatrists say that the cultists—the True Believers—put a person, usually a charismatic leader type, literally in place of their conscience. They must therefore believe anything he tells them no matter how false it may be, and do anything he orders them to do. "I got to do it!" Larry Layton cried. "Father told me to do it!"

And if the charismatic leader is insane? If his orders are (in the strictly medical sense of the term) symptoms of a mental illness?

Cults of horror—

The Jonestown group lasted only four years. The Cult of the Assassins, set in the walled fortress of Alamut in the high mountains of Asia, lasted for two centuries as a power in the Middle East. Its founder, the Old Man of the Mountain, defied the Crusaders and the Saracen leader, Saladin, by using opium to make his band of killers believe that their drug-induced fantasies of Allah's Paradise were real. In 1276 Hulagu, a grandson of Genghis Khan, took Alamut by storm and broke the cult's power forever.

Cults themselves, of all kinds, are still with us today. They include Devil-worshiping cults (one of whom murdered two Mexican policemen, a boy, and an American medical student in religious rites near Matamoros, Mexico, in April 1989; the Order, alleged militant arm of the Aryan Nations, an anti-black, anti-Semitic, neo-Nazi group who believes Anglo-Saxons are the descendants of the Lost Tribes of Israel (I am not making this up) and ten of whose members were convicted in December 1985 for the murder of talk show host Alan Berg and robberies netting $4 million dollars; religious groups who do not believe in blood transfusions or contagious diseases or medical treatment—and many more; watch your daily newspaper.

The stories included here colorfully demonstrate how varied these dangerous groups can be. The shadowy worship and sacrifice of voodoo is represented in Leslie Charteris' "The Questing Tycoon," in which the Robin Hood of modern crime finds unexpected evil in the dark mountains of Haiti; in Jack London's vivid story, "The Scarlet One," an explorer on Guadalcanal finds a native cult worshiping something frightening indeed, that may have come to the island from beyond the stars; in modern New York a slick evangelist preys on the fears and gullibility of his followers in Theodore Sturgeon's "Fear Is A Business." Karl Edward Wagner's prize-winning tale "Sticks" reveals a cult that has lasted, secret and sinister, for centuries in Massachusetts; Edward Hoch's long-lived detective, Simon Ark, investigates murder among the pain-worshiping sect of Penitentes among the appropriately named Sangre di Cristo (Blood of Christ) mountains of the American Southwest—and more. . . .

These stories are meant to thrill, to keep you in suspense—just to provide entertainment.

But if these stories about cultists and their characteristics tell you enough to provide a little advance warning when you need it, then you may get an unexpected dividend on your investment in these hours of entertainment.

The fortune—or, perhaps, even the life—you save may be your own.

THE FEAST OF SAINT DIONYSUS

by Robert Silverberg

Sleepers, awake. Sleep is separateness; the cave of solitude is the cave of dreams, the cave of the passive spectator. To be awake is to participate, carnally and not in fantasy, in the feast; the great communion.

—NORMAN O. BROWN: *Love's Body*

This is the dawn of the day of the Feast. Oxenshuer knows roughly what to expect, for he has spied on the children at their catechisms, he has had hints from some of the adults, he has spoken at length with the high priest of this strange apocalyptic city; and yet, for all his patiently gathered knowledge, he really knows nothing at all of today's event. What will happen? They will come for him: Matt, who has been appointed his brother, and Will and Nick, who are his sponsors. They will lead him through the labyrinth to the place of the saint, to the god-house at the city's core. They will give him wine until he is glutted, until his cheeks and chin drip with it and his robe is stained with red. And he and Matt will struggle, will have a contest of some sort, a wrestling match, an agon: whether real or symbolic, he does not yet know. Before the whole community they will contend. What else, what else? There will be hymns to the saint, to the god—god and saint, both are one, Dionysus and Jesus, each an aspect of the other. Each a manifestation of the divinity we carry within us, so the Speaker has said. Jesus and Dionysus, Dionysus and Jesus, god and saint, saint and god, what do the terms matter? He has heard the people singing:

This is the god who burns like fire
This is the god whose name is music
This is the god whose soul is wine

Fire. Music. Wine. The healing fire, the joining fire, in which all things will be made one. By its leaping blaze he will drink and drink and drink, dance and dance and dance. Maybe there will be some sort of sexual event—an orgy perhaps, for sex and religion are closely bound among these people: a communion of the flesh opening the way toward communality of spirit.

I go to the god's house and his fire consumes me
I cry the god's name and his thunder deafens me
I take the god's cup and his wine dissolves me

And then? And then? How can he possibly know what will happen, until it has happened? "You will enter into the ocean of Christ," they have told him. An ocean? Here in the Mojave Desert? Well, a figurative ocean, a metaphorical ocean. All is metaphor here. "Dionysus will carry you to Jesus," they say. Go, child, swim out to God. Jesus waits. The saint, the mad saint, the boozy old god who is their saint, the mad saintly god who abolishes walls and makes all things one, will lead you to bliss, dear John, dear tired John. Give your soul gladly to Dionysus the Saint. Make yourself whole in his blessed fire. You've been divided too long. How can you lie dead on Mars and still walk alive on Earth?

Heal yourself, John. This is the day.

From Los Angeles the old San Bernardino Freeway rolls eastward through the plastic suburbs, through Alhambra and Azusa, past the Covina Hills branch of Forest Lawn Memorial Parks, past the mushroom sprawl of San Bernardino, which is becoming a little Los Angeles, but not so little. The highway pushes onward into the desert like a flat gray cincture holding the dry brown hills asunder. This was the road by which John Oxenshuer finally chose to make his escape. He had had no particular destination in mind but was seeking only a parched place, a sandy place, a place where he could be alone: he needed to recreate, in what might well be his last weeks of life, certain aspects of barren Mars. After considering a number of possibilities he fastened upon this route, attracted to it by the way the freeway seemed to lose itself in the desert north of the Salton Sea. Even in this overcivilized epoch a man could easily disappear there.

Late one November afternoon, two weeks past his fortieth birthday, he closed his rented apartment on Hollywood Boulevard. Taking leave of no one, he drove unhurriedly toward the freeway entrance. There he surrendered control to the electronic highway net, which seized his car and pulled it into the traffic flow. The net governed him as far as Covina; when he saw Forest Lawn's statuary-speckled hilltop coming up on his right, he readied himself to resume driving. A mile beyond the vast cemetery a blinking sign told him he was on his own, and he took the wheel. The car continued to slice inland at the same mechanical velocity of 140 kilometers per hour. With each moment the recent past dropped from him, bit by bit.

Can you drown in the desert? Let's give it a try, God. I'll make a bargain with You. You let me drown out there. All right? And I'll give myself to You. Let me sink into the sand, let me bathe in it, let it wash Mars out of my soul, let it drown me, God, let it drown me. Free me from Mars and I'm yours, God. Is it a deal? Drown me in the desert and I'll surrender at last. I'll surrender.

At twilight he was in Banning. Some gesture of farewell to civilization seemed suddenly appropriate, and he risked stopping to have dinner at a small Mexican restaurant. It was crowded with families enjoying a night out, which made Oxenshuer fear he would be recognized. Look, someone would cry, there's the Mars astronaut, there's the one who came back! But of course no one spotted him. He had grown a bushy, sandy moustache that nearly obliterated his thin, tense lips. His body, lean and wide-shouldered, no longer had an astronaut's springy erectness; in the nineteen months since his return from the red planet he had begun to stoop a little, to cultivate a roundedness of the upper back, as if some leaden weight beneath his breastbone were tugging him forward and downward. Besides, spacemen are quickly forgotten. How long had anyone remembered the names of the heroic lunar teams of his youth? Borman, Lovell, and Anders. Armstrong, Aldrin, and Collins. Scott, Irwin, and Worden. Each of them had had a few gaudy weeks of fame, and then they had disappeared into the blurred pages of the almanac—all, perhaps, except Armstrong; children learned about him at school. His one small step: he would become a figure of myth, up there with Columbus and Magellan. But the others? Forgotten. Yes. Yesterday's heroes. Oxenshuer, Richardson, and Vogel. Who? Oxenshuer, Richardson, and Vogel. That's Oxenshuer right over there, eating tamales and enchiladas, drinking a bottle of Double-X. He's the one who came back. Had some sort of breakdown and left his wife. Yes. That's a funny name. Oxenshuer. Yes. He's the one who came back. What about the other two? They died. Where did they die, Daddy? They died on Mars, but Oxenshuer came back. What were their names again? Richardson and Vogel. They died. Oh. On Mars. And Oxenshuer didn't. What were their names again?

Unrecognized, safely forgotten, Oxenshuer finished his meal and returned to the freeway. Night had come by this time. The moon was nearly full; the mountains, clearly outlined against the darkness, glistened with a coppery sheen. There is no moonlight on Mars except the feeble, hasty glow of Phobos, dancing in and out of eclipse on its nervous journey from west to east. He had found Phobos disturbing; nor had he cared for fluttery Deimos, starlike, a tiny rocketing point of light. Oxenshuer drove onward, leaving the zone of urban sprawl behind, entering the true desert, pockmarked here and there by resort towns: Palm Springs, Twentynine Palms, Desert Hot Springs. Beckoning billboards summoned him to the torpid pleasures of whirlpool baths and saunas. These temptations he ignored without difficulty. Dryness was what he sought.

Once he was east of Indio he began looking for a place to abandon the car; but he was still too close to the southern boundaries of Joshua Tree National Monument, and he did not want to make camp this near to any area that might be patrolled by park rangers. So he kept driving until the moon was high and he was deep into the Chuckwalla country, with nothing much except sand dunes and mountains and dry lakebeds between him and the Arizona border. In a stretch where the land seemed relatively flat he slowed the car almost to an idle, killed his lights, and swerved gently off the road, following a vague northeasterly course; he gripped the wheel tightly as he jounced over the rough, crunchy terrain. Half a kilometer from the highway Oxenshuer came to a shallow sloping basin, the dry bed of some ancient lake. He eased down into it until he could no longer see the long yellow tracks of headlights on the road, and knew he must be below the line of sight of any passing vehicle. After turning off the engine, he locked the car—a strange prissiness here, in the midst of nowhere!—took his backpack from the trunk, slipped his arms through the shoulder straps, and, without looking back, began to walk into the emptiness that lay to the north.

As he walked he composed a letter he would never send. *Dear Claire, I wish I had been able to say goodbye to you before I left Los Angeles. I regretted only that:*

leaving town without telling you. But I was afraid to call. I draw back from you. You say you hold no grudge against me over Dave's death, you say it couldn't possibly have been my fault, and of course you're right. And yet I don't dare face you, Claire. Why is that? Because I left your husband's body on Mars and the guilt of that is choking me? But a body is only a shell, Claire. Dave's body isn't Dave, and there wasn't anything I could do for Dave. What is it, then, that comes between us? Is it my love, Claire, my guilty love for my friend's widow? Eh? That love is salt in my wounds, that love is sand in my throat, Claire. Claire. Claire. I can never tell you any of this, Claire. I never will. Goodbye. Pray for me. Will you pray?

His years of grueling NASA training for Mars served him well now. Powered by ancient disciplines, he moved swiftly, feeling no strain even with forty-five pounds on his back. He had no trouble with the uneven footing. The sharp chill in the air did not bother him, though he wore only light clothing—slacks and shirt and a flimsy cotton vest. The solitude, far from oppressing him, was actually a source of energy: a couple of hundred kilometers away in Los Angeles it might be the ninth decade of the twentieth century, but this was a prehistoric realm, timeless, unscarred by man, and his spirit expanded in his self-imposed isolation. Conceivably every footprint he made was the first human touch this land had felt. That gray, pervasive sense of guilt, heavy on him since his return from Mars, held less weight for him here beyond civilization's edge.

This wasteland was the closest he could come to attaining Mars on Earth. Not really close enough, for too many things broke the illusion: the great gleaming scarred moon, and the succulent terrestrial vegetation, and the tug of Earth's gravity, and the faint white glow on the leftward horizon that he imagined emanated from the cities of the coastal strip. But it was as close to Mars in flavor as he could manage. The Peruvian desert would have been better, only he had no way of getting to Peru.

An approximation. It would suffice.

A trek of at least a dozen kilometers left him still unfatigued, but he decided, shortly after midnight, to settle down for the night. The site he chose was a small level quadrangle bounded on the north and south by spiky, ominous cacti—chollas and prickly pears—and on the east by a maze of scrubby mesquite; to the west, a broad alluvial fan of tumbled pebbles descended from the nearby hills. Moonlight, raking the area sharply, highlighted every contrast of contour: the shadows of cacti were unfathomable inky pits and the tracks of small animals—lizard and kangaroo rats—were steep-walled canyons in the sand. As he slung his pack to the ground two startled rats, browsing in the mesquite, noticed him belatedly and leaped for cover in wild, desperate bounds, frantic but delicate. Oxenshuer smiled at them.

On the twentieth day of the mission Richardson and Vogel went out, as planned, for the longest extravehicular on the schedule, the ninety-kilometer crawler jaunt to the Gulliver site. "Goddamned well about time," Dave Vogel had muttered when the EVA okay had at last come floating up, time-lagged and crackly, out of far-off Mission Control. All during the eight-month journey from Earth, while the brick-red face of Mars was swelling patiently in their portholes, they had argued about the timing of the big Marswalk—pursuing an argument that had begun six months before launch date. Vogel, insisting that the expedition was the mission's most important scientific project, had wanted to do it first, to get it done and out of the way before mishaps might befall them and force them to scrub it. No matter that the timetable decreed it for Day 20. The timetable was too conservative. "We can overrule Mission Control," Vogel said. "If they don't like it, let them reprimand us when we get home." Bud Richardson, though, wouldn't go along. "Houston knows best," he kept saying. He always took the side of authority. "First we have to get used to working on Mars, Dave. First we ought to do the routine stuff close by the landing site, while we're getting acclimated. What's our hurry? We've got to stay here a month until the return window opens, anyway. Why breach the schedule? The scientists know what they're doing, and they want us to do everything in its proper order,'' Richardson said. Vogel, stubborn, eager, seething, thought he would find an ally in Oxenshuer. ''You vote with me, John. Don't tell me *you* give a crap about Mission Control! Two against one and Bud will have to give in.'' But Oxenshuer, oddly, took Richardson's side. He hesitated to deviate from the schedule. He wouldn't be making the long extravehicular himself in any case; he had drawn the short straw, he was the man who'd be keeping close to the ship all the time. How then could he vote to alter the carefully designed schedule and send Richardson off, against his will, on a risky and perhaps ill-timed adventure? ''No,'' Oxenshuer said. ''Sorry, Dave, it isn't my place to decide such things.'' Vogel appealed anyway to Mission Control, and Mission Control said, ''Wait till Day 20, fellows.'' On Day 20 Richardson and Vogel suited up and went out. It was the ninth EVA of the mission, but the first that would take anyone more than a couple of kilometers from the ship.

Oxenshuer monitored his departing companions from his safe niche in the control cabin. The small video screen showed him the path of their crawler as it diminished into the somber red plain. You're well named, rusty old Mars. The blood of fallen soldiers stains your soil. Your hills are the color of the flames that lick conquered cities. Jouncing westward across Solis Lacus, Vogel kept up a running commentary. ''Lots of dead nothing out here, Johnny. It's as bad as the Moon. A prettier color, though. Are you reading me?'' ''I'm reading you,'' Oxenshuer said. The crawler was like a submarine mounted on giant preposterous wheels. Joggle, joggle, joggle, skirting craters and ravines, ridges and scarps. Pausing now and then so Richardson could pop a geological specimen or two into the gunny sack. Then onward, westward, westward. Heading bumpily toward the site where the unmanned Ares IV Mars Lander, almost a decade earlier, had scraped some Martian microorganisms out of the ground with the Gulliver sampling device.

* * *

"Gulliver" is a culture chamber that inoculates itself with a sample of soil. The sample is obtained by two 7½-meter lengths of kite line wound on small projectiles. When the projectiles are fired, the lines unwind and fall to the ground. A small motor inside the chamber then reels them in, together with adhering soil particles. The chamber contains a growth medium whose organic nutrients are labeled with radioactive carbon. When the medium is inoculated with soil, the accompanying microorganisms metabolize the organic compounds and release radioactive carbon dioxide. This diffuses to the window of a Geiger counter, where the radioactivity is measured. Growth of the microbes causes the rate of carbon dioxide production to increase exponentially with time—an indication that the gas is being formed biologically. Provision is also made for the injection, during the run, of a solution containing a metabolic poison which can be used to confirm the biological origin of the carbon dioxide and to analyze the nature of the metabolic reactions.

* * *

All afternoon the crawler traversed the plain, and the sky deepened from dark purple to utter black, and the untwinkling stars, which on Mars are visible even by day, became more brilliant with the passing hours, and Phobos came streaking by, and then came little hovering Deimos. Oxenshuer, wandering around the ship, took readings on this and that and watched his screen and listened to Dave Vogel's chatter, and Mission Control offered a comment every little while. And during these hours the Martian temperature began its nightly slide down the Centigrade ladder. A thousand kilometers away an inversion of thermal gradients unexpectedly developed, creating fierce currents in the tenuous Martian atmosphere, ripping gouts of red sand loose from the hills, driving wild scarlet clouds eastward toward the Gulliver site. As the sandstorm increased in intensity, the scanner satellites in orbit around Mars detected it and relayed pictures of it to Earth, and after the normal transmission lag it was duly noted at Mission Control as a potential hazard to the men in the crawler; but somehow—the NASA hearings did not succeed in fixing blame for this inexplicable communications failure—no one passed the necessary warning along to the three astronauts on Mars. Two hours after he had finished his solitary dinner aboard the ship, Oxenshuer heard Vogel say, "Okay, Johnny, we've finally reached the Gulliver site, and as soon as we have our lighting system set up we'll get out and see what the hell we have here." Then the sandstorm struck in full fury. Oxenshuer heard nothing more from either of his companions.

Making camp for the night, he took first from his pack his operations beacon, one of his NASA souvenirs. By the sleek instrument's cool, inexhaustible green light he laid out his bedroll in the flattest, least pebbly place he could find; then, discovering himself far from sleepy, Oxenshuer set about assembling his solar still. Although he had no idea how long he would stay in the desert—a week, a month, a year, forever—he had brought perhaps a month's supply of food concentrates with him, but no water other than a single canteen's worth, to tide him through thirst on this first night. He could not count on finding wells or streams here, any more than he had on Mars, and, unlike the kangaroo rats, capable of living indefinitely on nothing but dried seeds, producing water metabolically by the oxidation of carbohydrates, he would not be able to dispense entirely with fresh water. But the solar still would see him through.

He began to dig.

Methodically he shaped a conical hole a meter in diameter, half a meter deep, and put a wide-mouthed two-liter jug at its deepest point. He collected pieces of cactus, breaking off slabs of prickly pear but ignoring the stiletto-spined chollas, and placed these along the slopes of the hole. Then he lined the hole with a sheet of clear plastic film, weighting it by rocks in such a way that the plastic came in contact with the soil only at the hole's rim and hung suspended a few centimeters above the cactus pieces and the jug. The job took him twenty minutes. Solar energy would do the rest: as sunlight passed through the plastic into the soil and the plant material, water would evaporate, condense in droplets on the underside of the plastic, and trickle into the jug. With cactus as juicy as this, he might be able to count on a liter a day of sweet water out of each hole he dug. The still was emergency gear developed for use on Mars; it hadn't done anyone any good there, but Oxenshuer had no fears of running dry in this far more hospitable desert.

Enough. He shucked his pants and crawled into his sleeping bag. At last he was where he wanted to be: enclosed, protected, yet at the same time alone, unsurrounded, cut off from his past in a world of dryness.

He could not yet sleep; his mind ticked too actively. Images out of the last few years floated insistently through it and had to be purged, one by one. To begin with, his wife's face. (Wife? I have no wife. Not now.) He was having difficulty remembering Lenore's features, the shape of her nose, the turn of her lips, but a general sense of her existence still burdened him. How long had they been married? Eleven years, was it? Twelve? The anniversary? March 30, 31? He was sure he had loved her once. What had happened? Why had he recoiled from her touch?

——No, please don't do that. I don't want to yet.

——You've been home three months, John.

Her sad green eyes. Her tender smile. A stranger, now. His ex-wife's face turned to mist and the mist congealed into the face of Claire Vogel. A sharper image: dark glittering eyes, the narrow mouth, thin cheeks framed by loose streamers of unbound black hair. The widow Vogel, dignified in her grief, trying to console him.

——I'm sorry, Claire. They just disappeared, is all. There wasn't anything I could do.

——John, John, it wasn't your fault. Don't let it get you like this.

——I couldn't even find the bodies. I wanted to look for them, but it was all sand everywhere—sand, dust, the craters, confusion; no signal, no landmarks—no way, Claire, no way.

——It's all right, John. What do the bodies matter? You did your best. I know you did.

Her words offered comfort but no absolution from guilt. Her embrace—light, chaste—merely troubled him. The pressure of her heavy breasts against him made him tremble. He remembered Dave Vogel, halfway to Mars, speaking lovingly of Claire's breasts. Her jugs, he called them. "Boy, I'd like to have my hands on my lady's jugs right this minute!" And Bud Richardson, more annoyed than amused, telling him to cut it out, to stop stirring up fantasies that couldn't be satisfied for another year or more.

Claire vanished from his mind, driven out by a blaze of flashbulbs. The hovercameras, hanging in midair, scanning him from every angle. The taut, earnest faces of the newsmen, digging deep for human interest. See the lone survivor of the Mars expedition. See his tortured eyes! See his gaunt cheeks! "There's the President himself, folks, giving John Oxenshuer a great big welcome back to Earth! What thoughts must be going through this man's mind, the only human being to walk the sands of an alien world and return to our old down-to-Earth planet! How keenly he must feel the tragedy of the two lost astronauts he left behind up there! There he goes now, there goes John Oxenshuer, disappearing into the debriefing chamber—"

Yes, the debriefings. Colonel Schmidt, Dr. Harkness, Commander Thompson, Dr. Burdette, Dr. Horowitz, milking him for data. Their voices carefully gentle, their manner informal, their eyes all the same betraying their singlemindedness.

——Once again, please, Captain Oxenshuer. You lost the signal, right, and then the backup line refused to check out, you couldn't get any telemetry at all. And then?

——And then I took a directional fix, I did a thermal scan and tripled the infrared, I rigged an extension lifeline to the sample-collector and went outside looking for them. But the collector's range was only ten kilometers. And the dust storm was too much. The dust storm. Too damned much. I went five hundred meters and you ordered me back into the ship. Didn't want to go back, but you ordered me.

——We didn't want to lose you too, John.

——But maybe it wasn't too late, even then. Maybe.

—There was no way you could have reached them in a short-range vehicle.

—I would have figured some way of recharging it. If only you had let me. If only the sand hadn't been flying around like that. If. Only.

—I think we've covered the point fully.

—Yes. May we go over some of the topographical data now, Captain Oxenshuer?

—Please. Please. Some other time.

It was three days before they realized what sort of shape he was in. They still thought he was the old John Oxenshuer, the one who had amused himself during the training period by reversing the inputs on his landing simulator, just for the hell of it, the one who had surreptitiously turned on the unsuspecting Secretary of Defense just before a Houston press conference, the one who had sung bawdy carols at a pious Christmas party for the families of the astronauts in '86. Now, seeing him darkened and turned in on himself, they concluded eventually that he had been transformed by Mars, and they sent him, finally, the chief psychiatric team, Mendelson and McChesney.

—How long have you felt this way, Captain?

—I don't know. Since they died. Since I took off for Earth. Since I entered Earth's atmosphere. I don't know. Maybe it started earlier. Maybe it was always like this.

—What are the usual symptoms of the disturbance?

—Not wanting to see anybody. Not wanting to talk to anybody. Not wanting to be with anybody. Especially myself. I'm so goddamned sick of my own company.

—And what are your plans now?

—Just to live quietly and grope my way back to normal.

—Would you say it was the length of the voyage that upset you most, or the amount of time you had to spend in solitude on the homeward leg, or your distress over the deaths of—

—Look, how would I know?

—Who'd know better?

—Hey, I don't believe in either of you, you know? You're figments. Go away. Vanish.

—We understand you're putting in for retirement and a maximum-disability pension, Captain.

—Where'd you hear that? It's a stinking lie. I'm going to be okay before long. I'll be back on active duty before Christmas, you got that?

—Of course, Captain.

—Go. Disappear. Who needs you?

—John, John, it wasn't your fault. Don't let it get you like this.

—I couldn't even find their bodies. I wanted to look for them, but it was all sand everywhere—sand, dust, the craters, confusion; no signal, no landmarks—no way, Claire, no way.

The images were breaking up, dwindling, going. He saw scattered glints of light slowly whirling overhead, the kaleidoscope of the heavens, the whole astronomical psychedelia swaying and cavorting, and then the sky calmed, and then only Claire's face remained, Claire and the minute red disk of Mars. The events of the nineteen months contracted to a single star-bright point of time, and became as nothing, and were gone. Silence and darkness enveloped him. Lying tense and rigid on the desert floor, he stared up defiantly at Mars, and closed his eyes, and wiped the red disk from the screen of his mind, and slowly, gradually, reluctantly, he surrendered himself to sleep.

Voices woke him. Males voices, quiet and deep, discussing him in an indistinct buzz. He hovered a moment on the border between dream and reality, uncertain of his perceptions and unsure of his proper response; then his military reflexes took over and he snapped into instant wakefulness, blinking his eyes open, sitting up in one quick move, rising to a standing position in the next, poising his body to defend itself.

He took stock. Sunrise was maybe half an hour away; the tips of the mountains to the west were stained with early pinkness. Thin mist shrouded the low-lying land. Three men stood just beyond the place where he had mounted his beacon. The shortest one was as tall as he, and they were desert-tanned, heavyset, strong and capable-looking. They wore their hair long and their beards full; they were oddly dressed, shepherd-style, in loose belted robes of light green muslin or linen. Although their expressions were open and friendly and they did not seem to be armed, Oxenshuer was troubled by awareness of his vulnerability in this emptiness, and he found menace in their presence. Their intrusion on his isolation angered him. He stared at them warily, rocking on the balls of his feet.

One, bigger than the others, a massive, thick-cheeked, blue-eyed man, said, "Easy. Easy, now. You look all ready to fight."

"Who are you? What do you want?"

"Just came to find out if you were okay. You lost?'

Oxenshuer indicated his neat camp, his backpack, his bedroll. "Do I seem lost?"

"You're a long way from anywhere," said the man closest to Oxenshuer, one with shaggy yellow hair and a cast in one eye.

"Am I? I thought it was just a short hike from the road."

The three men began to laugh. "You don't know *where* the hell you are, do you?" said the squint-eyed one. And the third one, dark-bearded, hawk-featured, said, "Look over thataway." He pointed behind Oxenshuer, to the north. Slowly, half anticipating trickery, Oxenshuer turned. Last night, in the moonlit darkness, the land had seemed level and empty in that direction, but now he beheld two steeply rising mesas a few hundred meters apart, and in the opening between them he saw a low wooden palisade, and behind the palisade the flat-roofed tops of buildings were visible, tinted orange-pink by the spreading touch of dawn. A settlement out here? But the map showed nothing, and, from the looks of it, that was a town of some two or three thousand people. He wondered if he had somehow been transported by magic during the night to some deeper part of the desert. But no: there was his solar still, there was the mesquite patch, there were last night's prickly pears. Frowning, Oxenshuer said, "What is that place in there?"

"The City of the Word of God," said the hawk-faced one calmly.

"You're lucky," said the squint-eyed one. "You've been brought to us almost in time for the Feast of Saint Dionysus. When all men are made one. When every ill is healed."

Oxenshuer understood. Religious fanatics. A secret retreat in the desert. The state was full of apocalyptic cults, more and more of them now that the end of the century was only about ten years away and millenary fears were mounting. He scowled. He had a native Easterner's innate distaste for Californian irrationality. Reaching into the reservoir of his own decaying Catholicism, he said thinly, "Don't you mean Saint *Dionysius?* With an *i?* Dionysus was the Greek god of wine."

"Dionysus," said the big blue-eyed man. "Dionysius is somebody else, some Frenchman. We've heard of him. Dionysus is who we mean." He put forth his hand. "My name's Matt, Mr. Oxenshuer. If you stay for the Feast, I'll stand brother to you. How's that?"

The sound of his name jolted him. "You've heard of me?"

"Heard of you? Well, not exactly. We looked in your wallet."

"We ought to go now," said the squint-eyed one. "Don't want to miss breakfast."

"Thanks," Oxenshuer said, "but I think I'll pass up the invitation. I came out here to get away from people for a little while."

"So did we," Matt said.

"You've been called," said Squint-eye hoarsely. "Don't you realize that, man? You've been called to our city. It wasn't any accident you came here."

"No?"

"There aren't any accidents," said Hawk-face. "Not ever. Not in the breast of Jesus, not ever a one. What's written is written. You were called, Mr. Oxenshuer. Can you say no?" He put his hand lightly on Oxenshuer's arm. "Come to our city. Come to the Feast. Look, why do you want to be afraid?"

"I'm not afraid. I'm just looking to be alone."

"We'll let you be alone, if that's what you want," Hawk-face told him. "Won't we, Matt? Won't we, Will? But you can't say no to our city. To our saint. To Jesus. Come along, now. Will, you carry his pack. Let him walk into the city without a burden." Hawk-face's sharp, forbidding features were softened by the glow of his fervor. His dark eyes gleamed. A strange, persuasive warmth leaped from him to Oxenshuer. "You won't say no. You won't. Come sing with us. Come to the Feast. Well?"

"Well?" Matt asked also.

"To lay down your burden," said squint-eyed Will. "To join the singing. Well? Well?"

"I'll go with you," Oxenshuer said at length. "But I'll carry my own pack."

They moved to one side and waited in silence while he assembled his belongings. In ten minutes everything was in order. Kneeling, adjusting the straps of his pack, he nodded and looked up. The early sun was full on the city now, and its rooftops were bright with a golden radiance. Light seemed to stream upward from them; the entire desert appeared to blaze in that luminous flow.

"All right," Oxenshuer said, rising and shouldering his pack. "Let's go." But he remained where he stood, staring ahead. He felt the city's golden luminosity as a fiery tangible force on his cheeks, like the outpouring of heat from a crucible of molten metal. With Matt leading the way the three men walked ahead, single file, moving fast. Will, the squint-eyed one, bringing up the rear, paused to look back questioningly at Oxenshuer, who was still standing entranced by the sight of that supernal brilliance. "Coming," Oxenshuer murmured. Matching the pace of the others, he followed them briskly over the parched, sandy wastes toward the City of the Word of God.

There are places in the coastal desert of Peru where no rainfall has ever been recorded. On the Paracas Peninsula, about eleven miles south of the port of Pisco, the red sand is absolutely bare of all vegetation: not a leaf, not a living thing; no stream enters the ocean nearby. The nearest human habitation is several miles away where wells tap underground water and a few sedges line the beach. There is no more arid area in the western hemisphere; it is the epitome of loneliness and desolation. The psychological landscape of Paracas is much the same as that of Mars. John Oxenshuer, Dave Vogel, and Bud Richardson spent three weeks camping there in the winter of 1987, testing their emergency gear and familiarizing themselves with the emotional texture of the Martian environment. Beneath the sands of the peninsula are found the desiccated bodies of an ancient people unknown to history, together with some of the most magnificent textiles that the world has ever seen. Natives seeking salable artifacts have rifled the necropolis of Paracas, and now the bones of its occupants lie scattered on the surface, and the winds alternately cover and uncover fragments of the coarser fabrics, discarded by the diggers, still soft and strong after nearly two millennia.

Vultures circle high over the Mojave. They would pick the bones of anyone who had died here. There are no vultures on Mars. Dead men become mummies, not skeletons, for nothing decays on Mars. What has died on Mars remains buried in the sand, invulnerable to time, imperishable, eternal. Perhaps archaeologists, bound on a futile but inevitable search for the remains of the lost races of old Mars, will find the withered bodies of Dave Vogel and Bud Richardson in a mound of red soil, ten thousand years from now.

At close range the city seemed less magical. It was laid out in the form of a bull's-eye, its curving streets set in concentric rings behind the blunt-topped little palisade, evidently purely symbolic in purpose, that rimmed its circumference between the mesas. The buildings were squat stucco affairs of five or six rooms, unpretentious and undistinguished, all of them similar if not identical in style: pastel-hued structures of the sort found everywhere in southern California. They seemed to be twenty or thirty years old and in generally shabby condition; they were set close together and close to the street, with no gardens and no garages. Wide avenues leading inward pierced the rings of buildings every few hundred meters. This seemed to be entirely a residential district, but no people were in sight, either at windows or on the streets, nor were there any parked cars; it was like a movie set, clean and empty and artificial. Oxenshuer's footfalls echoed loudly. The silence and surreal emptiness troubled him. Only an occasional child's tricycle, casually abandoned outside a house, gave evidence of recent human presence.

As they approached the core of the city, Oxenshuer saw that the avenues were narrowing and then giving way to a labyrinthine tangle of smaller streets, as intricate a maze as could be found in any of the old towns of Europe; the bewildering pattern seemed deliberate and carefully designed, perhaps for the sake of shielding the central section and making it a place apart from the antiseptic, prosaic zone of houses in the outer rings. The buildings lining the streets of the maze had an institutional character: they were three and four stories high, built of red brick, with few windows and pinched, unwelcoming entrances. They had the look of nineteenth-century hotels; possibly they were warehouses and meeting halls and places of some municipal nature. All were deserted. No commercial establishments were visible—no shops, no restaurants, no banks, no loan companies, no theaters, no newsstands. Such things were forbidden, maybe, in a theocracy such as Oxenshuer suspected this place to be. The city plainly had not evolved in any helter-skelter free enterprise fashion, but had been planned down to its last alleyway for the exclusive use of a communal order whose members were beyond the bourgeois needs of an ordinary town.

Matt led them surefootedly into the maze, infallibly choosing connecting points that carried them steadily deeper toward the center. He twisted and turned abruptly through juncture after juncture, never once doubling back on his track. At last they stepped through one passageway barely wide enough for Oxenshuer's pack, and he found himself in a plaza of unexpected size and grandeur. It was a vast open space, roomy enough for several thousand people, paved with cobbles that glittered in the harsh desert sunlight. On the right was a colossal building two stories high that ran the entire length of the plaza, at least three hundred meters; it looked as bleak as a barracks, a dreary utilitarian thing of clapboard and aluminum siding painted a dingy drab green, but all down its plaza side were tall, radiant stained-glass windows, as incongruous as pink gardenias blooming on a scrub oak. A towering metal cross rising high over the middle of the pointed roof settled all doubts: this was the city's church. Facing it across the plaza was an equally immense building, no less unsightly, built to the same plan but evidently secular, for its windows were plain and it bore no cross. At the far side of the plaza, opposite the place where they had entered it, stood a much smaller structure of dark stone in an implausible Gothic style, all vaults and turrets and arches. Pointing to each building in turn, Matt said, "Over there's the house of the god. On this side's the dining hall. Straight ahead, the little one, that's the house of the Speaker. You'll meet him at breakfast. Let's go eat."

. . .Captain Oxenshuer and Major Vogel, who will spend the next year and a half together in the sardine-can environment of their spaceship as they make their round-trip journey to Mars and back, are no strangers to each other. Born on the same day—November 4, 1949—in Reading, Pennsylvania, they grew up together, attending the same elementary and high schools as classmates and sharing a dormitory room as undergraduates at Princeton. They dated many of the same girls; it was Captain Oxenshuer who introduced Major Vogel to his future wife, the former Claire Barnes, in 1973. "You might say he stole her from me," the tall, slender astronaut likes to tell interviewers, grinning to show he holds no malice over the incident. In a sense Major Vogel returned the compliment, for Captain Oxenshuer has been married since March 30, 1978, to the major's first cousin, the former Lenore Reiser, whom he met at his friend's wedding reception. After receiving advanced scientific degrees—Captain Oxenshuer in meteorology and celestial mechanics, Major Vogel in geology and space navigations—they enrolled together in the space program in the spring of 1979 and shortly afterward were chosen as members of the original 36-man group of trainees for the first manned flight to the red planet. According to their fellow astronauts, they quickly distinguished themselves for their fast and imaginative responses to stress situations, for their extraordinarily deft teamwork, and

also for their shared love of high-spirited pranks and gags, which got them into trouble more than once with sober-sided NASA officials. Despite occasional reprimands, they were regarded as obvious choices for the initial Mars voyage, for which their selection was announced on March 18, 1985. Colonel Walter ("Bud") Richardson, named that day as command pilot for the Mars mission, cannot claim to share the lifelong bonds of companionship that link Captain Oxenshuer and Major Vogel, but he has been closely associated with them in the astronaut program for the past ten years and long ago established himself as their most intimate friend. Colonel Richardson, the third of this country's three musketeers of interplanetary exploration, was born in Omaha, Nebraska, on the 5th of June, 1948. He hoped to become an astronaut from earliest childhood onward, and . . .

They crossed the plaza to the dining hall. Just within the entrance was a dark-walled low-ceilinged vestibule; a pair of swinging doors gave access to the dining rooms beyond. Through windows set in the doors Oxenshuer could glimpse dimly lit vastnesses to the left and the right, in which great numbers of solemn people, all clad in the same sort of flowing robes as his three companions, sat at long bare wooden tables and passed serving bowls around. Nick told Oxenshuer to drop his pack and leave it in the vestibule; no one would bother it, he said. As they started to go in, a boy of ten erupted explosively out of the left-hand doorway, nearly colliding with Oxenshuer. The boy halted just barely in time, backed up a couple of paces, stared with shameless curiosity into Oxenshuer's face, and, grinning broadly, pointed to Oxenshuer's bare chin and stroked his own as if to indicate that it was odd to see a man without a beard. Matt caught the boy by the shoulders and pulled him against his chest; Oxenshuer thought he was going to shake him, to chastise him for such irreverence, but no, Matt gave the boy an affectionate hug, swung him far overhead, and tenderly set him down. The boy clasped Matt's powerful forearms briefly and went springing through the right-hand door.

"Your son?" Oxenshuer asked.

"Nephew. I've got two hundred nephews. Every man in this town's my brother, right? So every boy's my nephew."

——If I could have just a few moments for one or two questions, Captain Oxenshuer.

——Provided it's really just a few moments. I'm due at Mission Control at O-eight-thirty, and—

——I'll confine myself, then, to the one topic of greatest relevance to our readers. What are your feelings about the Deity, Captain? Do you, as an astronaut soon to depart for Mars, believe in the existence of God?

——My biographical poop sheet will tell you that I've been known to go to Mass now and then.

——Yes, of course, we realize you're a practicing member of the Catholic faith, but, well, Captain, it's widely understood that for some astronauts religious observance is more of a public-relations matter than a matter of genuine spiritual urgings. Meaning no offense, Captain, we're trying to ascertain the actual nature of your relationship, if any, to the Divine Presence, rather than—

——All right. You're asking a complicated question and I don't see how I can give an easy answer. If you're asking whether I literally believe in the Father, Son, and Holy Ghost, whether I think Jesus came down from heaven for our salvation and was crucified for us and was buried and on the third day rose again and ascended into heaven, I'd have to say no. Not except in the loosest metaphorical sense. But I do believe—ah—suppose we say I believe in the existence of an organizing force in the universe, a power of sublime reason that makes everything hang together, an underlying principle of rightness. Which we can call God for lack of a better name. And which I reach toward, when I feel I need to, by way of the Roman Church, because that's how I was raised.

——That's an extremely abstract philosophy, Captain.

——Abstract. Yes.

——That's an extremely rationalistic approach. Would you say that your brand of cool rationalism is characteristic of the entire astronaut group?

—I can't speak for the whole group. We didn't come out of a single mold. We've got some all-American boys who go to church every Sunday and think that God himself is listening in person to every word they say, and we've got a couple of atheists, though I won't tell you who, and we've got guys who just don't care one way or the other. And I can tell you we've got a few real mystics, too, some out-and-out guru types. Don't let the uniforms and haircuts fool you. Why, there are times when I feel the pull of mysticism myself.

—In what way?

—I'm not sure. I get a sense of being on the edge of some sort of cosmic breakthrough. An awareness that there may be real forces just beyond my reach, not abstractions but actual functioning dynamic entities, which I could attune myself to if I only knew how to find the key. You feel stuff like that when you go into space, no matter how much of a rationalist you think you are. I've felt it four or five times, on training flights, on orbital missions. I want to feel it again. I want to break through. I want to reach God, am I making myself clear? I want to reach God.

—But you say you don't literally believe in Him Captain. That sounds contradictory to me.

—Does it really?

—It does, sir.

—Well, if it does, I don't apologize. I don't have to think straight all the time. I'm entitled to a few contradictions. I'm capable of holding a couple of diametrically opposed beliefs. Look, if I want to flirt with madness a little, what's it to you?

—Madness, Captain?

—Madness. Yes. That's exactly what it is, friend. There are times when Johnny Oxenshuer is tired of being so goddamned sane. You can quote me on that. Did you get it straight? There are times when Johnny Oxenshuer is tired of being so goddamned sane. But don't print it until I've blasted off for Mars, you hear me? I don't want to get bumped from this mission for incipient schizophrenia. I want to go. Maybe I'll find God out there this time, you know? And maybe I won't. But I want to go.

—I think I understand what you're saying, sir. God bless you, Captain Oxenshuer. A safe voyage to you.

—Sure. Thanks. Was I of any help?

* * *

Hardly anyone glanced up at him, only a few of the children, as Matt led him down the long aisle toward the table on the platform at the back of the hall. The people here appeared to be extraordinarily self-contained, as if they were in possession of some wondrous secret from which he would be forever excluded, and the passing of the serving bowls seemed far more interesting to them than the stranger in their midst. The smell of scrambled eggs dominated the great room. That heavy greasy odor seemed to expand and rise until it squeezed out all the air. Oxenshuer found himself choking and gagging. Panic seized him. He had never imagined he could be thrown into terror by the smell of scrambled eggs. "This way," Matt called. "Steady on, man. You all right?" Finally they reached the raised table. Here sat only men, dignified and serene of mien, probably the elders of the community. At the head of the table was one who had the unmistakable look of a high priest. He was well past seventy—or eighty or ninety—and his strong-featured leathery face was seamed and gullied; his eyes were keen and intense, managing to convey both a fierce tenacity and an all-encompassing warm humanity. Small-bodied, lithe, weighing at most one hundred pounds, he sat ferociously erect, a formidably commanding little man. A metallic embellishment of the collar of his robe was, perhaps, the badge of his status. Leaning over him, Matt said in exaggeratedly clear, loud tones, "This here's John. I'd like to stand brother to him when the Feast comes, if I can. John, this here's our Speaker."

Oxenshuer had met popes and presidents and secretaries-general, and, armored by his own standing as a celebrity, had never fallen into foolish awe-kindled embarrassment. But here he was no celebrity, he was no one at all, a stranger, an outsider, and he found himself lost before the Speaker. Mute, he waited for help. The old man said, his voice as melodious and as resonant as a cello, "Will you join our meal, John? Be welcome in our city."

Two of the elders made room on the bench. Oxenshuer sat at the Speaker's left hand; Matt sat beside him. Two girls of about fourteen brought settings: a plastic dish, a knife, a fork, a spoon, a cup. Matt served him: scrambled eggs, toast, sausages. All about him the clamor of eating went on. The Speaker's plate was empty. Oxenshuer fought back nausea and forced himself to attack the eggs. "We take all our meals together," said the Speaker. "This is a closely knit community, unlike any community I know on Earth." One of the serving girls said pleasantly, "Excuse me, brother" and, reaching over Oxenshuer's shoulder, filled his cup with red wine. Wine for breakfast? They worship Dionysus here, Oxenshuer remembered.

The Speaker said, "We'll house you. We'll feed you. We'll love you. We'll lead you to God. That's why you're here, isn't it? To get closer to Him, eh? To enter into the ocean of Christ."

—What do you want to be when you grow up, Johnny?

—An astronaut, ma'am. I want to be the first man to fly to Mars.

No. He had never said any such thing.

Later in the morning he moved into Matt's house, on the perimeter of the city, overlooking one of the mesas. The house was merely a small green box, clapboard outside, flimsy beaverboard partitions inside: a sitting room, three bedrooms, a bathroom. No kitchen or dining room. ("We take all our meals together.") The walls were bare: no ikons, no crucifixes, no religious paraphernalia of any kind. No television, no radio, hardly any personal possessions at all in evidence: a dozen worn books and magazines, some spare robes and extra boots in a closet, little more than that. Matt's wife was a small, quiet woman in her late thirties, soft-eyed, submissive, dwarfed by her burly husband. Her name was Jean. There were three children, a boy of about twelve and two girls, maybe nine and seven. The boy had had a room of his own; he moved uncomplainingly in with his sisters, who doubled up in one bed to provide one for him, and Oxenshuer took the boy's room. Matt told the children their guest's name, but it drew no response from them. Obviously they had never heard of him. Were they even aware that a spaceship from Earth had lately journeyed to Mars? Probably not. He found that refreshing: for years Oxenshuer had had to cope with children paralyzed with astonishment at finding themselves in the presence of a genuine astronaut. Here he could shed the burdens of fame.

He realized he had not been told his host's last name. Somehow it seemed too late to ask Matt directly, now. When one of the little girls came wandering into his room he asked her, "What's your name?"

"Toby," she said, showing a gap-toothed mouth.

"Toby what?"

"Toby. Just Toby."

No surnames in this community? All right. Why bother with surnames in a place where everyone knows everyone else? Travel light, brethren, travel light, strip away the excess baggage.

Matt walked in and said, "At council tonight I'll officially apply to stand brother to you. It's just a formality. They've never turned an application down."

"What's involved, actually?"

"It's hard to explain until you know our ways better. It means I'm, well, your spokesman, your guide through our rituals."

"A kind of sponsor?"

"Well, sponsor's the wrong word. Will and Nick will be your sponsors. That's a different level of brotherhood, lower, not as close. I'll be something like your godfather, I guess, that's as near as I can come to the idea. Unless you don't want me to be. I never consulted you. Do you want me to stand brother to you, John?"

It was an impossible question. Oxenshuer had no way to evaluate any of this. Feeling dishonest, he said, "It would be a great honor, Matt."

"You have any real brothers?" Matt asked. "Flesh kin?"

"No. A sister in Ohio." Oxenshuer thought a moment. "There once was a man who was like a brother to me. Knew him since childhood. As close as makes no difference. A brother, yes."

"What happened to him?"

"He died. In an accident. A long way from here."

"Terrible sorry," Matt said. "I've got five brothers.

Three of them outside; I haven't heard from them in years. And two right here in the city. You'll meet them. They'll accept you as kin. Everyone will. What did you think of the Speaker?"

"A marvelous old man. I'd like to talk with him again."

"You'll talk plenty with him. He's my father, you know."

Oxenshuer tried to imagine this huge man springing from the seed of the spare-bodied, compactly built Speaker and could not make the connection. He decided Matt must be speaking metaphorically again. "You mean, the way that boy was your nephew?"

"He's my true father," Matt said. "I'm flesh of his flesh." He went to the window. It was open about eight centimeters at the bottom. "Too cold for you in here, John?"

"It's fine."

"Gets cold sometimes, these winter nights."

Matt stood silent, seemingly sizing Oxenshuer up. Then he said, "Say, you ever do any wrestling?"

"A little. In college."

"That's good."

"Why do you ask?"

"One of the things brothers do here, part of the ritual. We wrestle some. Especially the day of the Feast. It's important in the worship. I wouldn't want to hurt you any when we do. You and me, John, we'll do some wrestling before long, just to practice up for the Feast, okay? Okay?"

They let him go anywhere he pleased. Alone, he wandered through the city's labyrinth, that incredible tangle of downtown streets, in early afternoon. The maze was cunningly constructed, one street winding into another so marvelously that the buildings were drawn tightly together and the bright desert sun could barely penetrate; Oxenshuer walked in shadow much of the way. The twisting mazy passages baffled him. The purpose of this part of the city seemed clearly symbolic: everyone who dwelt here was compelled to pass through these coiling, interlacing streets in order to get from the commonplace residential quarter, where people lived in isolated family groupings, to the dining hall, where the entire community together took the sacrament of food, and to the church, where redemption and salvation were to be had. Only when purged of error and doubt, only when familiar with the one true way (or was there more than one way through the maze? Oxenshuer wondered) could one attain the harmony of communality. He was still uninitiated, an outlander; wander as he would, dance tirelessly from street to cloistered street, he would never get there unaided.

He thought it would be less difficult than it had first seemed to find his way from Matt's house to the inner plaza, but he was wrong: the narrow, meandering streets misled him, so that he sometimes moved away from the plaza when he thought he was going toward it, and, after pursuing one series of corridors and intersections for fifteen minutes, he realized that he had merely returned himself to one of the residential streets on the edge of the maze. Intently he tried again. An astronaut trained to maneuver safely through the trackless wastes of Mars ought to be able to get about in one small city. Watch for landmarks, Johnny. Follow the pattern of the shadows. He clamped his lips, concentrated, plotted a course. As he prowled he occasionally saw faces peering briefly at him out of the upper windows of the austere warehouselike buildings that flanked the streets. Were they smiling? He came to one group of streets that seemed familiar to him, and went in and in, until he entered an alleyway closed at both ends, from which the only exit was a slit barely wide enough for a man if he held his breath and slipped through sideways. Just beyond, the metal cross of the church stood outlined against the sky, encouraging him: he was nearly to the end of the maze. He went through the slit and found himself in a cul-de-sac; five minutes of close inspection revealed no way to go on. He retraced his steps and sought another route.

One of the bigger buildings in the labyrinth was evidently a school. He could hear the high, clear voices of children chanting mysterious hymns. The melodies were conventional seesaws of piety, but the words were strange:

Bring us together. Lead us to the ocean.
Help us to swim. Give us to drink.
Wine in my heart today,
Blood in my throat today,
Fire in my soul today,
All praise, O God, to thee.

Sweet treble voices, making the bizarre words sound all the more grotesque. Blood in my throat today. Unreal city. How can it exist? Where does the food come from? Where does the wine come from? What do they use for money? What do the people do with themselves all day? They have electricity: what fuel keeps the generator running? They have running water. Are they hooked into a public-utility district's pipelines, and if so why isn't this place on my map? Fire in my soul today. Wine in my heart today. What are these feasts, who are these saints? This is the god who burns like fire. This is the god whose name is music. This is the god whose soul is wine. You were called, Mr. Oxenshuer. Can you say no? You can't say no to our city. To our saint. To Jesus. Come along, now?

Where's the way out of here?

Three times a day, the whole population of the city went on foot from their houses through the labyrinth to the dining hall. There appeared to be at least half a dozen ways of reaching the central plaza, but, though he studied the route carefully each time, Oxenshuer was unable to keep it straight in his mind. The food was simple and nourishing, and there was plenty of it. Wine flowed freely at every meal. Young boys and girls did the serving, jubilantly hauling huge platters of food from the kitchen; Oxenshuer had no idea who did the cooking, but he supposed the task would rotate among the women of the community. (The men had other chores. The city, Oxenshuer learned, had been built entirely by the freely contributed labor of its own inhabitants. Several new houses were under construction now. And there were irrigated fields beyond the mesas.) Seating in the dining hall was random at the long tables, but people generally seemed to come together in nuclear-family groupings.

Oxenshuer met Matt's two brothers, Jim and Ernie, both smaller men than Matt but powerfully built. Ernie gave Oxenshuer a hug—a quick, warm, impulsive gesture. "Brother," he said. "Brother! Brother!"

The Speaker received Oxenshuer in the study of his residence on the plaza, a dark ground-floor room whose walls were covered to ceiling height with shelves of books. Most people here affected a casual hayseed manner, an easy, drawling, rural simplicity of speech, that implied little interest in intellectual things, but the Speaker's books ran heavily to abstruse philosophical and theological themes, and they looked as though they had all been read many times. Those books confirmed Oxenshuer's first fragmentary impression of the Speaker: that this was a man of supple, well-stocked mind, sophisticated, complex. The Speaker offered Oxenshuer a cup of cool, tart wine. They drank in silence. When he had nearly drained his cup, the old man calmly hurled the dregs to the glossy slate floor. "An offering to Dionysus," he explained.

"But you're Christians here," said Oxenshuer.

"Yes, of course we're Christian! But we have our own calendar of saints. We worship Jesus in the guise of Dionysus and Dionysus in the guise of Jesus. Others might call us pagans, I suppose. But where there's Christ, is there not Christianity?" The Speaker laughed. "Are you a Christian, John?"

"I suppose. I was baptized. I was confirmed. I've taken communion. I've been to confession now and then."

"You're of the Roman faith?"

"More that faith than any other," Oxenshuer said.

"You believe in God?"

"In an abstract way."

"And in Jesus Christ?"

"I don't know," said Oxenshuer uncomfortably. "In a literal sense, no. I mean, I suppose there was a prophet in Palestine named Jesus, and the Romans nailed him up, but I've never taken the rest of the story too seriously. I can accept Jesus as a symbol, though. As a metaphor of love. God's love."

"A metaphor for *all* love," the Speaker said. "The love of God for mankind. The love of mankind for God. The love of man and woman, the love of parent and child, the love of brother and brother, every kind of love there is. Jesus is love's spirit. God is love. That's what we believe here. Through communal ecstasies we are reminded of the new commandment He gave unto us. That ye love one another. And as it says in Romans, Love is the fulfilling of the law. We follow His teachings; therefore we are Christians."

"Even though you worship Dionysus as a saint?"

"Especially so. We believe that in the divine madnesses of Dionysus we come closer to Him than other Christians are capable of coming. Through revelry, through singing, through the pleasures of the flesh, through ecstasy, through union with one another in body and in soul—through these we break out of our isolation and become one with Him. In the life to come we shall all be one. But first we must live this life and share in the creation of love, which is Jesus, which is God. Our goal is to make all beings one with Jesus, so that we become droplets in the ocean of love which is God, giving up our individual selves."

"This sounds Hindu to me, almost. Or Buddhist."

"Jesus is Buddha. Buddha is Jesus."

"Neither of them taught a religion of revelry."

"Dionysus did. We make our own synthesis of spiritual commandments. And so we see no virtue in self-denial, since that is the contradiction of love. What is held to be virtue by other Christians is sin to us. And vice versa, I would suppose."

"What about the doctrine of the virgin birth? What about the virginity of Jesus himself? The whole notion of purity through restraint and asceticism?"

"Those concepts are not part of our belief, friend John."

"But you do recognize the concept of sin?"

"The sins we deplore," said the Speaker, "are such things as coldness, selfishness, aloofness, envy, maliciousness, all those things that hold one man apart from another. We punish the sinful by engulfing them in love.

But we recognize no sins that arise out of love itself or out of excess of love. Since the world, especially the Christian world, finds our principles hateful and dangerous, we have chosen to withdraw from that world."

"How long have you been out here?" Oxenshuer asked.

"Many years. No one bothers us. Few strangers come to us. You are the first in a very long time."

"Why did you have me brought to your city?"

"We knew you were sent to us," the Speaker said.

At night there were wild, frenzied gatherings in certain tall, windowless buildings in the depths of the labyrinth. He was never allowed to take part. The dancing, the singing, the drinking, whatever else went on, these things were not yet for him. Wait till the Feast, they told him, wait till the Feast, then you'll be invited to join us. So he spent his evenings alone. Some nights he would stay home with the children. No babysitters were needed in this city, but he became one anyway, playing simple dice games with the girls, tossing a ball back and forth with the boy, telling them stories as they fell asleep. He told them of his flight to Mars, spoke of watching the red world grow larger every day, describing the landing, the alien feel of the place, the iron-red sands, the tiny glinting moons. They listened silently, perhaps fascinated, perhaps not at all interested: he suspected they thought he was making it all up. He never said anything about the fate of his companions.

Some nights he would stroll through town, street after quiet street, drifting in what he pretended was a random way toward the downtown maze. Standing near the perimeter of the labyrinth—even now he could not find his way around in it after dark, and feared getting lost if he went in too deep—he would listen to the distant sounds of the celebration, the drumming, the chanting, the simple, repetitive hymns:

This is the god who burns like fire
This is the god whose name is music
This is the god whose soul is wine

And he would also hear them sing:

Tell the saint to heat my heart
Tell the saint to give me breath
Tell the saint to quench my thirst

And this:

Leaping shouting singing stamping
Rising climbing flying soaring
Melting joining loving blazing
Singing soaring joining loving

Some nights he would walk to the edge of the desert, hiking out a few hundred meters into it, drawing a bleak pleasure from the solitude, the crunch of sand beneath his boots, the knife-blade coldness of the air, the forlorn gnarled cacti, the timorous kangaroo rats, even the occasional scorpion. Crouching on some gritty hummock, looking up through the cold brilliant stars to the red dot of Mars, he would think of Dave Vogel, would think of Bud Richardson, would think of Claire, and of himself, who he had been, what he had lost. Once, he remembered, he had been a high-spirited man who laughed easily, expressed affection readily and openly, enjoyed joking, drinking, running, swimming—all the active, outgoing things. Leaping shouting singing stamping. Rising climbing flying soaring. And then this deadness had come over him, this zombie absence of response, this icy shell. Mars had stolen him from himself. Why? The guilt? The guilt, the guilt, the guilt—he had lost himself in guilt. And now he was lost in the desert. This implausible town. These rites, this cult. Wine and shouting. He had no idea how long he had been here. Was Christmas approaching? Possibly it was only a few days away. Blue plastic Yule trees were sprouting in front of the department stores on Wilshire Boulevard. Jolly red Santas pacing the sidewalk. Tinsel and glitter. Christmas might be an appropriate time for the Feast of St. Dionysus. The Saturnalia revived. Would the Feast come soon? He anticipated it with fear and eagerness.

Later in the evening, when the last of the wine was gone and the singing was over, Matt and Jean would return, flushed wine-drenched, happy, and through the thin partition separating Oxenshuer's room from theirs would come the sounds of love, the titanic poundings of their embraces, far into the night.

——Astronauts are supposed to be sane, Dave.

——Are they? Are they really, Johnny?

——Of course they are.

——Are *you* sane?

——I'm sane as hell, Dave.

——Yes. Yes. I'll bet you think you are.

——Don't you think I'm sane?

——Oh, sure, you're sane, Johnny. Saner than you need to be. If anybody asked me to name him one sane man, I'd say John Oxenshuer. But you're not all that sane. And you've got the potential to become very crazy.

——Thanks.

——I mean it as a compliment.

——What about you? You aren't sane?

——I'm a madman, Johnny. And getting madder all the time.

——Suppose NASA finds out that Dave Vogel's a madman?

——They won't, my friend. They know I'm one hell of an astronaut, and so by definition I'm sane. They don't know what's inside me. They can't. By definition, they wouldn't be NASA bureaucrats if they could tell what's inside a man.

——They know you're sane because you're an astronaut?

——Of course, Johnny. What does an astronaut know about the irrational? What sort of capacity for ecstasy does he have, anyway? He trains for ten years, he jogs in a centrifuge, he drills with computers, he runs a thousand simulations before he dares to sneeze, he thinks in spaceman jargon, he goes to church on Sundays and doesn't pray, he turns himself into a machine so he can run the damnedest machines anybody ever thought up. And to outsiders he looks deader than a banker, deader than a stockbroker, deader than a sales manager. Look at him, with his 1975 haircut and his 1965 uniform. Can a man like that even know what a mystic experience *is?* Well, some of us are really like that. They fit the official astronaut image. Sometimes I think you do, Johnny, or at least that you want to. But not me. Look, I'm a yogi. Yogis train for decades so they can have a glimpse of the All. They subject their bodies to crazy disciplines. They learn highly specialized techniques. A yogi and an astronaut aren't all that far apart, man. What I do, it's not so different from what a yogi does, and it's for the same reason. It's so we can catch sight of the White Light. Look at you, laughing! But I mean it, Johnny. When that big fist knocks me into orbit, when I see the whole world hanging out there, it's a wild moment for me, it's ecstasy, it's nirvana. I live for those moments. They make all the NASA crap worthwhile. Those are breakthrough moments, when I get into an entirely new realm. That's the only reason I'm in this. And you know something? I think it's the same with you, whether you know it or not. A mystic thing, Johnny, a crazy thing, that powers us, that drives us on. The yoga of space. One day you'll find out. One day you'll see yourself for the madman you really are. You'll open up to all the wild forces inside you, the lunatic drives that sent you to NASA. You'll find out you weren't just a machine after all, you weren't just a stockbroker in a fancy costume, you'll find out you're a yogi, a holy man, an ecstatic. And you'll see what a trip you're on, you'll see that controlled madness is the only true secret and that you've always known the Way. And you'll set aside everything that's left of your old straight self. You'll give yourself up completely to forces you can't understand and don't want to understand. And you'll love it, Johnny. You'll love it.

When he had stayed in the city about three weeks—it seemed to him that it had been about three weeks, though perhaps it had been two or four—he decided to leave. The decision was nothing that came upon him suddenly; it had always been in the back of his mind that he did not want to be here, and gradually that feeling came to dominate him. Nick had promised him solitude while he was in the city, if he wanted it, and indeed he had had solitude enough—no one bothering him, no one making demands on him, the city functioning perfectly well without any contribution from him. But it was the wrong kind of solitude. To be alone in the midst of several thousand people was worse than camping by himself in the desert. True, Matt had promised him that after the Feast he would no longer be alone. Yet Oxenshuer wondered if he really wanted to stay there long enough to experience the mysteries of the Feast and the oneness that presumably would follow it. The Speaker spoke of giving up all pain as one enters the all-encompassing body of Jesus. What would he actually give up, though—his pain or his identity? Could he lose one without losing the other? Perhaps it was best to avoid all that and return to his original plan of going off by himself in the wilderness.

One evening after Matt and Jean had set out for the downtown revels, Oxenshuer quietly took his pack from the closet. He checked all his gear, filled his canteen, and said good night to the children. They looked at him strangely, as if wondering why he was putting on his pack just to go for a walk, but they asked no questions. He went up the broad avenue toward the palisade, passed through the unlocked gate, and in ten minutes was in the desert, moving steadily away from the City of the Word of God.

It was a cold, clear night, very dark, the stars almost painfully bright, Mars very much in evidence. He walked roughly eastward, through choppy countryside badly cut by ravines, and soon the mesas that flanked the city were out of sight. He had hoped to cover eight or ten kilometers before making camp, but the ravines made the hike hard going; when he had been out no more than an hour, one of his boots began to chafe him and a muscle in his left leg sprang a cramp. He decided he would do well to halt. He picked a campsite near a stray patch of Joshua trees that stood like grotesque sentinels, stiff-armed and bristly, along the rim of a deep gully. The wind rose suddenly and swept across the desert flats, agitating their angular branches violently. It seemed to Oxenshuer that those booming gusts were blowing him the sounds of singing from the nearby city:

I go to the god's house and his fire consumes me
I cry the god's name and his thunder deafens me
I take the god's cup and his wine dissolves me

He thought of Matt and Jean, and Ernie who had called him brother, and the Speaker who had offered him love and shelter, and Nick and Will, his sponsors. He retraced in his mind the windings of the labyrinth until he grew dizzy. It was impossible, he told himself, to hear the singing from this place. He was at least three or four kilometers away. He prepared his campsite and unrolled his sleeping bag. But it was too early for sleep; he lay wide awake, listening to the wind, counting the stars, playing back the chants of the city in his head. Occasionally he dozed, but only for fitful intervals, easily broken. Tomorrow, he thought, he would cover twenty-five or thirty kilometers, going almost to the foothills of the mountains to the east, and he would set up half a dozen solar stills and settle down for a leisurely reexamination of all that had befallen him.

The hours slipped by slowly. About three in the morning he decided he was not going to be able to sleep, and he got up, dressed, paced along the gully's edge. A sound came to him: soft, almost a throbbing purr. He saw a light in the distance. A second light. The sound redoubled, one purr overlaid by another. Then a third light, farther away. All three lights in motion. He recognized the purring sounds now: the engines of dune cycles. Travelers crossing the desert in the middle of the night? The headlights of the cycles swung in wide circular orbits around him. A search party from the city? Why else would they be driving like that, cutting off arcs of desert in so systematic a way?

Yes. Voices. "John? Jo-ohn! Yo, John!"

Looking for him. But the desert was immense; the searchers were still far off. He need only take his gear and hunker down in the gully, and they would pass him by.

"Yo, John! Jo-ohn!"

Matt's voice.

Oxenshuer walked down the slope of the gully, paused a moment in its depths, and, surprising himself, started to scramble up the gully's far side. There he stood in silence a few minutes, watching the circling dune cycles, listening to the calls of the searchers. It still seemed to him that the wind was bringing him the songs of the city people. This is the god who burns like fire. This is the god whose name is music. Jesus waits. The saint will lead you to bliss, dear tired John. Yes. Yes. At last he cupped his hands to his mouth and shouted, "Yo! Here I am! Yo!"

Two of the cycles halted immediately; the third, swinging out far to the left, stopped a little afterward. Oxenshuer waited for a reply, but none came.

"Yo!" he called again. "Over here, Matt! Here!"

He heard the purring start up. Headlights were in motion once more, the beams traversing the desert and coming to rest on him. The cycles approached. Oxenshuer recrossed the gully, collected his gear, and was waiting again on the cityward side when the searchers reached him. Matt, Nick, Will.

"Spending a night out?" Matt asked. The odor of wine was strong on his breath.

"Guess so."

"We got a little worried when you didn't come back by midnight. Thought you might have stumbled into a dry wash and hurt yourself some. Wasn't any cause for alarm, though, looks like." He glanced at Oxenshuer's pack, but made no comment. "Long as you're all right, I guess we can leave you finish what you were doing. See you in the morning, okay?"

He turned away. Oxenshuer watched the men mount their cycles.

"Wait," he said.

Matt looked around.

"I'm all finished out here," Oxenshuer said. "I'd appreciate a lift back to the city."

"It's a matter of wholeness," the Speaker said. "In the beginning, mankind was all one. We were in contact.

The communion of soul to soul. But then it all fell apart. *'In Adam's Fall we sinnéd all,'* remember? And that Fall, that original sin, John, it was a falling apart, a falling away from one another, a falling into the evil of strife. When we were in Eden we were more than simply one family, we were one being, one universal entity; and we came forth from Eden as individuals, Adam and Eve, Cain and Abel. The original universal being broken into pieces. Here, John, we seek to put the pieces back together. Do you follow me?''

''But how is it done?'' Oxenshuer asked.

''By allowing Dionysus to lead us to Jesus,'' the old man said. ''And in the saint's holy frenzy to create unity out of opposites. We bring the hostile tribes together. We bring the contending brothers together. We bring man and woman together.''

Oxenshuer shrugged. ''You talk only in metaphors and parables.''

''There's no other way.''

''What's your method? What's your underlying principle?''

''Our underlying principle is mystic ecstasy. Our method is to partake of the flesh of the god, and of his blood.''

''It sounds very familiar. Take; eat. This is my body. This is my blood. Is your Feast a High Mass?''

The Speaker chuckled. ''In a sense. We've made our synthesis between paganism and orthodox Christianity, and we've tried to move backward from the symbolic ritual to the literal act. Do you know where Christianity went astray? The same place all other religions have become derailed. The point at which spiritual experience was replaced by rote worship. Look at your lamas, twirling their prayer wheels. Look at your Jews, muttering about Pharaoh in a language they've forgotten. Look at your Christians, lining up at the communion rail for a wafer and a gulp of wine, and never once feeling the terror and splendor of knowing that they're eating their god! Religion becomes doctrine too soon. It becomes professions of faith, formulas, talismans, emptiness. 'I believe in God the Father Almighty, creator of heaven and earth, and in Jesus Christ his only son, our Lord, who was conceived by the Holy Spirit, born of the Virgin Mary—' Words. Only words. We don't believe, John, that religious worship consists in reciting narrative accounts of ancient history. We want it to be real. We want to *see* our god. We want to *taste* our god. We want to *become* our god."

"How?"

"Do you know anything about the ancient cults of Dionysus?"

"Only that they were wild and bloody, with plenty of drinking and revelry and maybe human sacrifices."

"Yes. Human sacrifices," the Speaker said. "But before the human sacrifices came the divine sacrifices, the god who dies, the god who gives up his life for his people. In the prehistoric Dionysiac cults the god himself was torn apart and eaten; he was the central figure in a mystic rite of destruction in which his ecstatic worshipers feasted on his raw flesh, a sacramental meal enabling them to be made full of the god and take on blessedness, while the dead god became the scapegoat for man's sins. And then the god was reborn and all things were made one by his rebirth. So in Greece, so in Asia Minor, priests of Dionysus were ripped to pieces as surrogates for the god, and the worshipers partook of blood and meat in cannibalistic feasts of love, and in more civilized times animals were sacrificed in place of men, and still later, when the religion of Jesus replaced the various Dionysiac religions, bread and wine came to serve as the instruments of communion, metaphors for the flesh and blood of the god. On the symbolic level it was all the same. To devour the god. To achieve contact with the god in the most direct way. To experience the rapture of the ecstatic state, when one is possessed by the god. To unite that which society has forced asunder. To break down all boundaries. To rip off all shackles. To yield to our saint, our mad saint, the drunken god who is our saint, the mad saintly god who abolishes walls and makes all things one. Yes, John? We integrate through disintegration. We dissolve in the great ocean. We burn in the great fire. Yes,

John? Give your soul gladly to Dionysus the Saint, John. Make yourself whole in his blessed fire. You've been divided too long." The Speaker's eyes had taken on a terrifying gleam. "Yes, John? Yes? Yes?"

In the dining hall one night Oxenshuer drinks much too much wine. The thirst comes upon him gradually and unexpectedly; at the beginning of the meal he simply sips as he eats, in his usual way, but the more he drinks, the more dry his throat becomes, until by the time the meat course is on the table he is reaching compulsively for the carafe every few minutes, filling his cup, draining it, filling, draining, filling, draining. He becomes giddy and boisterous; someone at the table begins a hymn, and Oxenshuer joins in, though he is unsure of the words and keeps losing the melody. Those about him laugh, clap him on the back, sing even louder, beckoning to him, encouraging him to sing with them. Ernie and Matt match him drink for drink, and now whenever his cup is empty they fill it before he has a chance to. A serving girl brings a full carafe. He feels a prickling in his earlobes and the tip of his nose, feels a band of warmth across his chest and shoulders, and realizes he is getting drunk, but he allows it to happen. Dionysus reigns here. He has been sober long enough. And it has occurred to him that his drunkenness perhaps will inspire them to admit him to the night's revels.

But that does not happen. Dinner ends. The Speaker and the other old men who sit at his table file from the hall; it is the signal for the rest to leave. Oxenshuer stands. Falters. Reels. Recovers. Laughs. Links arms with Matt and Ernie. "Brothers," he says. "Brothers!" They go from the hall together, but outside, in the great cobbled plaza, Matt says to him, "You better not go wandering in the desert tonight, man, or you break your neck for sure." So he is still excluded. He goes back through the labyrinth with Matt and Jean to their house, and they help him into his room and give him a jug of wine in case he still feels the thirst, and then they leave him. Oxenshuer sprawls on his bed. His head is spinning. Matt's boy looks in and asks if everything's all right.

"Yes," Oxenshuer tells him. "I just need to lie down some." He feels embarrassed over being so helplessly intoxicated, but he reminds himself that in this city of Dionysus no one need apologize for taking too much wine. He closes his eyes and waits for a little stability to return.

In the darkness a vision comes to him: the death of Dave Vogel. With strange brilliant clarity Oxenshuer sees the landscape of Mars spread out on the screen of his mind, low snubby hills sloping down to broad crater-pocked plains, gnarled desolate boulders, purple sky, red gritty particles blowing about. The extravehicular crawler well along on its journey westward toward the Gulliver site, Richardson driving, Vogel busy taking pictures, operating the myriad sensors, leaning into the microphone to describe everything he sees. They are at the Gulliver site now, preparing to leave the crawler, when they are surprised by the sudden onset of the sandstorm. Without warning the sky is red with billowing capes of sand, driving down on them like snowflakes in a blizzard. In the first furious moment of the storm the vehicle is engulfed; within minutes sand is piled a meter high on the crawler's domed transparent roof; they can see nothing, and the sandfall steadily deepens as the storm gains in intensity.

Richardson grabs the controls, but the wheels of the crawler will not grip. "I've never seen anything like this," Vogel mutters. The vehicle has extendible perceptors on stalks, but when Vogel pushes them out to their full reach he finds that they are even then hidden by the sand. The crawlers' eyes are blinded; its antennae are buried. They are drowning in sand. Whole dunes are descending on them. "I've never seen anything like this," Vogel says again. "You can't imagine it, Johnny. It hasn't been going on five minutes and we must be under three or four meters of sand already." The crawler's engine strains to free them. "Johnny? I can't hear you, Johnny. Come in, Johnny." All is silent on the ship-to-crawler transmission belt. "Hey, Houston," Vogel says, "we've got this goddamned sandstorm going, and I seem to have lost contact with the ship. Can you raise him for us?" Houston does not reply. "Mission Control, are you reading me?'' Vogel asks. He still has some idea of setting up a crawler-to-Earth-to-ship relay, but slowly it occurs to him that he has lost contact with Earth as well. All transmissions have ceased. Sweating suddenly in his spacesuit, Vogel shouts into the microphone, jiggles controls, plugs in the fail-safe communications banks, only to find that everything has failed; sand has invaded the crawler and holds them in a deadly blanket. ''Impossible,'' Richardson says. ''Since when is sand an insulator for radio waves?'' Vogel shrugs. ''It isn't a matter of insulation, dummy. It's a matter of total systems breakdown. I don't know why.'' They must be ten meters underneath the sand now. Entombed.

Vogel pounds on the hatch, thinking that if they can get out of the crawler somehow they can dig their way to the surface through the loose sand, and then—and then what? Walk back, ninety kilometers, to the ship? Their suits carry thirty-six-hour breathing supplies. They would have to average two and a half kilometers an hour, over ragged cratered country, in order to get there in time; and with this storm raging, their chances of surviving long enough to hike a single kilometer are dismal. Nor does Oxenshuer have a back-up crawler in which he could come out to rescue them, even if he knew their plight; there is only the flimsy little one-man vehicle that they use for short-range geological field trips in the vicinity of the ship.

''You know what?'' Vogel says. ''We're dead men, Bud.'' Richardson shakes his head vehemently. ''Don't talk garbage. We'll wait out the storm, and then we'll get the hell out of here. Meanwhile we better just pray.'' There is no conviction in his voice, however. How will they know when the storm is over? Already they lie deep below the new surface of the Martian plain, and everything is snug and tranquil where they are. Tons of sand hold the crawler's hatch shut. There is no escape. Vogel is right: they are dead men. The only remaining question is one of time. Shall they wait for the crawler's air supply to exhaust itself, or shall they take some more immediate step to hasten the inevitable end, going out honorably and quickly and without pain?

Here Oxenshuer's vision falters. He does not know how the trapped men chose to handle the choreography of their deaths. He knows only that whatever their decision was, it must have been reached without bitterness or panic, and that the manner of their departure was calm. The vision fades. He lies alone in the dark. The last of the drunkenness has burned itself from his mind.

"Come on," Matt said. "Let's do some wrestling."

It was a crisp winter morning, not cold, a day of clear hard light. Matt took him downtown, and for the first time Oxenshuer entered one of the tall brick-faced buildings of the labyrinth streets. Inside was a large bare gymnasium, unheated, with bleak yellow walls and threadbare purple mats on the floor. Will and Nick were already there. Their voices echoed in the cavernous room. Quickly Matt stripped down to his undershorts. He looked even bigger naked than clothed; his muscles were thick and rounded, his chest was formidably deep, his thighs were pillars. A dense covering of fair curly hair sprouted everywhere on him, even his back and shoulders. He stood at least two meters tall and must have weighed close to 110 kilos. Oxenshuer, tall but not nearly so tall as Matt, well built but at least twenty kilos lighter, felt himself badly outmatched. He was quick and agile, at any rate: perhaps those qualities would serve him. He tossed his clothing aside.

Matt looked him over closely. "Not bad," he said. "Could use a little more meat on the bones."

"Got to fatten him up some for the Feast, I guess," Will said. He grinned amiably. The three men laughed; the remark seemed less funny to Oxenshuer.

Matt signaled to Nick, who took a flask of wine from a locker and handed it to him. Matt uncorked it, drank deep, and passed the flask to Oxenshuer. It was different from the usual table stuff: thicker, sweeter, almost a sacramental wine. Oxenshuer gulped it down. Then they went to the center mat.

They hunkered into crouches and circled each other tentatively, outstretched arms probing for an opening. Oxenshuer made the first move. He slipped in quickly, finding Matt surprisingly slow on his guard and unsophisticated in defensive technique. Nevertheless, the big man was able to break Oxenshuer's hold with one fierce toss of his body, shaking him off easily and sending him sprawling violently backward. Again they circled. Matt seemed willing to allow Oxenshuer every initiative. Warily Oxenshuer advanced, feinted toward Matt's shoulders, seized an arm instead; but Matt placidly ignored the gambit and somehow pivoted so that Oxenshuer was caught in the momentum of his own onslaught, thrown off balance, vulnerable to a bear hug. Matt forced him to the floor. For thirty seconds or so Oxenshuer stubbornly resisted him, arching his body; then Matt pinned him. They rolled apart and Nick proffered the wine again. Oxenshuer drank, gasping between pulls. "You've got good moves," Matt told him. But he took the second fall even more quickly, and the third with not very much greater effort. "Don't worry," Will murmured to Oxenshuer as they left the gym. "The day of the Feast, the saint will guide you against him."

Every night, now, he drinks heavily, until his face is flushed and his mind is dizzied. Matt, Will, and Nick are always close beside him, seeing to it that his cup never stays dry for long. The wine makes him hazy and groggy, and frequently he has visions as he lies in a stupor on his bed, recovering. He sees Claire Vogel's face glowing in the dark, and the sight of her wrings his heart with love. He engages in long, dreamlike imaginary dialogues with the Speaker on the nature of ecstatic communion. He sees himself dancing in the god-house with the other city folk, dancing himself to exhaustion and ecstasy. He is even visited by St. Dionysus. The saint has a youthful and oddly innocent appearance, with a heavy belly, plump thighs, curling golden hair, a flowing golden beard; he looks like a rejuvenated Santa Claus. "Come," he says softly. "Let's go to the ocean." He takes Oxenshuer's hand and they drift through the silent dark streets, toward the desert, across the swirling dunes, floating in the night, until they reach a broad-bosomed sea, moonlight blazing on its surface like cold white fire. What sea is this? The saint says, "This is the sea that brought you to the world, the undying sea that carries every mortal into life. Why do you ever leave the sea? Here. Step into it with me.'' Oxenshuer enters. The water is warm, comforting, oddly viscous. He gives himself to it, ankle-deep, thigh-deep; he hears a low murmuring song rising from the gentle waves, and he feels all sorrow going from him, all pain, all sense of himself as a being apart from others. Bathers bob on the breast of the sea. Look: Dave Vogel is here, and Claire, and his parents, and his grandparents, and thousands more whom he does not know; millions, even, a horde stretching far out from shore; all the progeny of Adam, even Adam himself, yes, and Mother Eve, her soft pink body aglow in the water. ''Rest,'' the saint whispers. ''Drift. Float. Surrender. Sleep. Give yourself to the ocean, dear John.'' Oxenshuer asks if he will find God in this ocean. The saint replies, ''God *is* the ocean. And God is within you. He always has been. The ocean is God. You are God. I am God. God is everywhere, John, and we are His indivisible atoms. God is everywhere. But before all else, God is within you.''

What does the Speaker say? The Speaker speaks Freudian wisdom. Within us all, he says, there dwells a force, an entity—call it the unconscious; it's as good a name as any—that from its hiding place dominates and controls our lives, though its workings are mysterious and opaque to us. A god within our skulls. We have lost contact with that god, the Speaker says; we are unable to reach it or to comprehend its powers, and so we are divided against ourselves, cut off from the chief source of our strength and cut off, too, from one another: the god that is within me no longer has a way to reach the god that is within you, though you and I both came out of the same primordial ocean, out of that sea of divine unconsciousness in which all being is one. If we could tap that force, the Speaker says, if we could make contact with that hidden god, if we could make it rise into consciousness or allow ourselves to submerge into the realm of unconsciousness, the split in our souls would be healed and we would at last have full access to our godhood. Who knows what kind of creatures we would become then? We would speak, mind to mind. We would travel through space or time, merely by willing it. We would work miracles. The errors of the past could be undone; the patterns of old griefs could be rewoven. We might be able to do anything, the Speaker says, once we have reached that hidden god and transformed ourselves into the gods we were meant to be. Anything. Anything. Anything.

This is the dawn of the day of the Feast. All night long the drums and incantations have resounded through the city. He has been alone in the house, for not even the children were there; everyone was dancing in the plaza, and only he, the uninitiated, remained excluded from the revels. Much of the night he could not sleep. He thought of using wine to lull himself, but he feared the visions the wine might bring, and let the flask be. Now it is early morning, and he must have slept, for he finds himself fluttering up from slumber, but he does not remember having slipped down into it. He sits up. He hears footsteps, someone moving through the house. "John? You awake, John?" Matt's voice. "In here," Oxenshuer calls.

They enter his room: Matt, Will, Nick. Their robes are spotted with splashes of red wine, and their faces are gaunt, eyes red-rimmed and unnaturally bright; plainly they have been up all night. Beneath their fatigue, though, Oxenshuer perceives exhilaration. They are high, very high, almost in an ecstatic state already, and it is only the dawn of the day of the Feast. He sees that their fingers are trembling. Their bodies are tense with expectation.

"We've come for you," Matt says. "Here. Put this on."

He tosses Oxenshuer a robe similar to theirs. All this time Oxenshuer has continued to wear his mundane clothes in the city, making him a marked man, a conspicuous outsider. Naked, he gets out of bed and picks up his undershorts, but Matt shakes his head. Today, he says, only robes are worn. Oxenshuer nods and pulls the robe over his bare body. When he is robed he steps forward; Matt solemnly embraces him, a strong warm hug, and then Will and Nick do the same. The four men leave the house. The long shadows of dawn stretch across the avenue that leads to the labyrinth; the mountains beyond the city are tipped with red. Far ahead, where the avenue gives way to the narrower streets, a tongue of black smoke can be seen licking the sky. The reverberations of the music batter the sides of the buildings. Oxenshuer feels a strange onrush of confidence, and is certain he could negotiate the labyrinth unaided this morning. As they reach its outer border he is actually walking ahead of the others. But sudden confusion confounds him, an inability to distinguish one winding street from another comes over him, and he drops back in silence, allowing Matt to take the lead.

Ten minutes later they reach the plaza.

It presents a crowded, chaotic scene. All the city folk are there, some dancing, some singing, some beating on drums or blowing into trumpets, some lying sprawled in exhaustion. Despite the chill in the air, many robes hang open, and more than a few of the citizens have discarded their clothing entirely. Children run about, squealing and playing tag. Along the front of the dining hall a series of wine barrels has been installed, and the wine gushes freely from the spigots, drenching those who thrust cups forward or simply push their lips to the flow. To the rear, before the house of the Speaker, a wooden platform has sprouted, and the Speaker and the city elders sit enthroned upon it. A gigantic bonfire has been kindled in the center of the plaza, fed by logs from an immense woodpile—hauled no doubt from some storehouse in the labyrinth—that occupies some twenty square meters. The heat of this blaze is tremendous, and it is the smoke from the bonfire that Oxenshuer was able to see from the city's edge.

His arrival in the plaza serves as a signal. Within moments, all is still. The music dies away; the dancing stops; the singers grow quiet; no one moves. Oxenshuer, flanked by his sponsors, Nick and Will, and preceded by his brother, Matt, advances uneasily toward the throne of the Speaker. The old man rises and makes a gesture, evidently a blessing. "Dionysus receive you into His bosom," the Speaker says, his resonant voice traveling far across the plaza. "Drink, and let the saint heal your soul. Drink, and let the holy ocean engulf you. Drink. Drink."

"Drink," Matt says, and guides him toward the barrels. A girl of about fourteen, naked, sweat-shiny, wine-soaked, hands him a cup. Oxenshuer fills it and puts it to his lips. It is the thick sweet wine, the sacramental wine, that he had had on the morning he had practiced wrestling with Matt. It slides easily down his throat; he reaches for more, and then for more when that is gone.

At a signal from the Speaker, the music begins again. The frenzied dancing resumes. Three naked men hurl more logs on the fire and it blazes up ferociously, sending sparks nearly as high as the tip of the cross above the church. Nick and Will and Matt lead Oxenshuer into a circle of dancers who are moving in a whirling, dizzying step around the fire, shouting, chanting, stamping against the cobbles, flinging their arms aloft. At first Oxenshuer is put off by the uninhibited corybantic motions and finds himself self-conscious about imitating them, but as the wine reaches his brain, he sheds all embarrassment and prances with as much gusto as the others: he ceases to be a spectator of himself and becomes fully a participant. Whirl. Stamp. Fling. Shout. Whirl. Stamp. Fling. Shout. The dance centrifuges his mind; pools of blood collect at the walls of his skull and flush the convolutions of his cerebellum as he spins. The heat of the fire makes his skin glow. He sings:

Tell the saint to heat my heart
Tell the saint to give me breath
Tell the saint to quench my thirst

Thirst. When he has been dancing so long that his breath is fire in his throat, he staggers out of the circle and helps himself freely at a spigot. His greed for the thick wine astonishes him. It is as if he has been parched for centuries, every cell of his body shrunken and withered, and only the wine can restore him.

Back to the circle again. His head throbs; his bare feet slap the cobbles; his arms claw the sky. This is the god whose name is music. This is the god whose soul is wine.

There are ninety or a hundred people in the central circle of dancers now, and other circles have formed in the corners of the plaza, so that the entire square is a nest of dazzling interlocking vortices of motion. He is being drawn into these vortices, sucked out of himself; he is losing all sense of himself as a discrete individual entity.

Leaping shouting singing stamping
Rising climbing flying soaring
Melting joining loving blazing
Singing soaring joining loving

"Come," Matt murmurs. "It's time for us to do some wrestling."

He discovers that they have constructed a wrestling pit in the far corner of the plaza, over in front of the church. It is square: four low wooden borders, about ten meters long on each side, filled with the coarse sand of the desert. The Speaker has shifted his lofty seat so that he now faces the pit; everyone else is crowded around the place of the wrestling, and all dancing has once again stopped. The crowd opens to admit Matt and Oxenshuer. Not far from the pit Matt shucks his robe; his powerful naked body glistens with sweat. Oxenshuer, after only a moment's hesitation, strips also. They advance toward the entrance of the pit. Before they enter, a boy brings them each a flask of wine. Oxenshuer, already feeling wobbly and hazy from drink, wonders what more wine will do to his physical coordination, but he takes the flask and drinks from it in great gulping swigs. In moments it is empty. A young girl offers him another. "Just take a few sips," Matt advises. "In honor of the god." Oxenshuer does as he is told. Matt is sipping from a second flask too; without warning, Matt grins and flings the contents of his flask over Oxenshuer. Instantly Oxenshuer retaliates. A great cheer goes up; both men are soaked with the sticky red wine. Matt laughs heartily and claps Oxenshuer on the back. They enter the wrestling pit.

Wine in my heart today,
Blood in my throat today,

Fire in my soul today,
All praise, O God, to thee.

They circle each other warily. Brother against brother. Romulus and Remus, Cain and Abel, Osiris and Set: the ancient ritual, the timeless conflict. Neither man offers. Oxenshuer feels heavy with wine, his brain clotted, and yet a strange lightness also possesses him each time he puts his foot down against the sand the contact gives him a little jolt of ecstasy. He is excitingly aware of being alive, mobile, vigorous. The sensation grows and possesses him, and he rushes forward suddenly, seizes Matt, tries to force him down. They struggle in almost motionless rigidity. Matt will not fall, but his counterthrust is unavailing against Oxenshuer. They stand locked, body against sweat-slick, wine-drenched body, and after perhaps two minutes of intense tension they give up their holds by unvoiced agreement, backing away trembling from each other. They circle again. Brother. Brother. Abel. Cain. Oxenshuer crouches. Extends his hands, groping for a hold. Again they leap toward each other. Again they grapple and freeze. This time Matt's arms pass like bands around Oxenshuer, and he tries to lift Oxenshuer from the ground and hurl him down. Oxenshuer does not budge. Veins swell in Matt's forehead and, Oxenshuer suspects, in his own. Faces grow crimson. Muscles throb with sustained effort. Matt gasps, loosens his grip, tries to step back; instantly Oxenshuer steps to one side of the bigger man, catches his arm, pulls him close. Once more they hug. Each in turn, they sway but do not topple. Wine and exertion blur Oxenshuer's vision; he is intoxicated with strain. Heaving, grabbing, twisting, shoving, he goes round and round the pit with Matt, until abruptly he experiences a dimming of perception, a sharp moment of blackout, and when his senses return to him he is stunned to find himself wrestling not with Matt but with Dave Vogel. Childhood friend, rival in love, comrade in space. Vogel, closer to him than any brother of the flesh, now here in the pit with him: thin sandy hair, snub nose, heavy brows, thick-muscled shoulders. "Dave!" Oxenshuer cries. "Oh, Christ, Dave!

Dave!'' He throws his arms around the other man. Vogel gives him a mild smile and tumbles to the floor of the pit. ''Dave!'' Oxenshuer shouts, falling on him. ''How did you get here, Dave?'' He covers Vogel's body with his own. He embraces him with a terrible grip. He murmurs Vogel's name, whispering in wonder, and lets a thousand questions tumble out. Does Vogel reply? Oxenshuer is not certain. He thinks he hears answers, but they do not match the questions. Then Oxenshuer feels fingers tapping his back. ''Okay, John,'' Will is saying. ''You've pinned him fair and square. It's all over. Get up, man.''

''Here, I'll give you a hand,'' says Nick.

In confusion Oxenshuer rises. Matt lies sprawled in the sand, gasping for breath, rubbing the side of his neck, nevertheless still grinning. ''That was one hell of a press,'' Matt says. ''That something you learned in college?''

''Do we wrestle another fall now?'' Oxenshuer asks.

''No need. We go to the god-house now,'' Will tells him. They help Matt up. Flasks of wine are brought to them; Oxenshuer gulps greedily. The four of them leave the pit, pass through the open crowd, and walk toward the church.

Oxenshuer has never been in here before. Except for a sort of altar at the far end, the huge building is wholly empty: no pews, no chairs, no chapels, no pulpit, no choir. A mysterious light filters through the stained-glass windows and suffuses the vast open interior space. The Speaker has already arrived; he stands before the altar. Oxenshuer, at a whispered command from Matt, kneels in front of him. Matt kneels at Oxenshuer's left; Nick and Will drop down behind them. Organ music, ghostly, ethereal, begins to filter from concealed grillworks. The congregation is assembling; Oxenshuer hears the rustle of people behind him, coughs, some murmuring. The familiar hymns soon echo through the church.

I go to the god's house and his fire consumes me
I cry the god's name and his thunder deafens me
I take the god's cup and his wine dissolves me

Wine. The Speaker offers Oxenshuer a golden chalice. Oxenshuer sips. A different wine: cold, thin. Behind him a new hymn commences, one that he has never heard before, in a language he does not understand. Greek? The rhythms are angular and fierce; this is the music of the Bacchantes, this is an Orphic song, alien and frightening at first, then oddly comforting. Oxenshuer is barely conscious. He comprehends nothing. They are offering him communion. A wafer on a silver dish: dark bread, crisp, incised with an unfamiliar symbol. Take; eat. This is my body. This is my blood. More wine. Figures moving around him, other communicants coming forward. He is losing all sense of time and place. He is departing from the physical dimension and drifting across the breast of an ocean, a great warm sea, a gentle undulating sea that bears him easily and gladly. He is aware of light, warmth, hugeness, weightlessness; but he is aware of nothing tangible. The wine. The wafer. A drug in the wine, perhaps? He slides from the world and into the universe. This is my body. This is my blood. This is the experience of wholeness and unity. I take the god's cup and his wine dissolves me. How calm it is here. How empty. There's no one here, not even me. And everything radiates a pure warm light. I float. I go forth. I. I. I. John Oxenshuer. John Oxenshuer does not exist. John Oxenshuer is the universe. The universe is John Oxenshuer. This is the god whose soul is wine. This is the god whose name is music. This is the god who burns like fire. Sweet flame of oblivion. The cosmos is expanding like a balloon. Growing. Growing. Go, child, swim out to God. Jesus waits. The saint, the mad saint, the boozy old god who is a saint, will lead you to bliss, dear John. Make yourself whole. Make yourself into nothingness. I go to the god's house and his fire consumes me. Go. Go. Go. I cry the god's name and his thunder deafens me. *Dionysus! Dionysus!*

All things dissolve. All things become one.

This is Mars. Oxenshuer, running his ship on manual, lets it dance lightly down the final five hundred meters to the touchdown site, gently adjusting the yaw and pitch, moving serenely through the swirling red clouds that his rockets are kicking free. Contact light. Engine stop. Engine arm, off.

—All right, Houston, I've landed at Gulliver Base.

His signal streaks across space. Patiently he waits out the lag and gets his reply from Mission Control at last:

—Roger. Are you ready for systems checkout prior to EVA?

—Getting started on it right now, Houston.

He runs through his routines quickly, with the assurance born of total familiarity. All is well aboard the ship; its elegant mechanical brain ticks beautifully and flawlessly. Now Oxenshuer wriggles into his backpack, struggling a little with the cumbersome life-support system; putting it on without any fellow astronauts to help him is more of a chore than he expected, even under the light Martian gravity. He checks out his primary oxygen supply, his ventilating system, his water support loop, his communications system. Helmeted and gloved and fully sealed, he exists now within a totally self-sufficient pocket universe. Unshipping his power shovel, he tests its compressed-air supply. All systems go.

—Do I have a go for cabin depressurization, Houston?

—You are go for cabin depress, John. It's all yours. Go for cabin depress.

He gives the signal and waits for the pressure to bleed down. Dials flutter. At last he can open the hatch. "We have a go for EVA, John." He hoists his power shovel to his shoulder and makes his way carefully down the ladder. Boots bite into red sand. It is midday on Mars in this longitude, and the purple sky has a warm auburn glow. Oxenshuer approaches the burial mound. He is pleased to discover that he has relatively little excavating to do; the force of his rockets during the descent has stripped much of the overburden from his friends' tomb. Swiftly he sets the shovel in place and begins to cut away the remaining sand. Within minutes the glistening dome of the crawler is visible in several places. Now Oxenshuer works more delicately, scraping with care until he has revealed the entire dome. He flashes his light through it and sees the bodies of Vogel and Richardson. They are unhelmeted and their suits are open: casual dress, the best outfit for dying. Vogel sits at the crawler's controls; Richardson lies just behind him on the floor of the vehicle. Their faces are dry, almost fleshless, but their features are still expressive, and Oxenshuer realizes that they must have died peaceful deaths, accepting the end in tranquillity. Patiently he works to lift the crawler's dome. At length the catch yields and the dome swings upward. Oxenshuer climbs in, slips his arms around Dave Vogel's body, and draws it out of the spacesuit. So light: a mummy, an effigy. Vogel seems to have no weight at all. Easily Oxenshuer carries the parched corpse over to the ship. With Vogel in his arms he ascends the ladder. Within, he breaks out the flag-sheathed plastic container NASA has provided and tenderly wraps it around the body. He stows Vogel safely in the ship's hold. Then he returns to the crawler to get Bud Richardson. Within an hour the entire job is done.

——Mission accomplished, Houston.

The landing capsule plummets perfectly into the Pacific. The recovery ship, only three kilometers away, makes for the scene while the helicopters move into position over the bobbing spaceship. Frogmen come forth to secure the flotation collar: the old, old routine. In no time at all the hatch is open. Oxenshuer emerges. The helicopter closest to the capsule lowers its recovery basket; Oxenshuer disappears into the capsule, returning a moment later with Vogel's shrouded body, which he passes across to the swimmers. They load it into the basket and it goes up to the helicopter. Richardson's body follows, and then Oxenshuer himself.

The President is waiting on the deck of the recovery ship. With him are the two widows, black-garbed, dry-eyed, standing straight and firm. The President offers Oxenshuer a warm grin and grips his hand.

——A beautiful job, Captain Oxenshuer. The whole world is grateful to you.

——Thank you, sir.

Oxenshuer embraces the widows. Richardson's wife

first: a hug and some soft murmurs of consolation. Then he draws Claire close, conscious of the television cameras. Chastely he squeezes her. Chastely he presses his cheek briefly to hers.

—I had to bring him back, Claire. I couldn't rest until I recovered those bodies.

—You didn't need to, John.

—I did it for you.

He smiles at her. Her eyes are bright and loving.

There is a ceremony on deck. The President bestows posthumous medals on Richardson and Vogel. Oxenshuer wonders whether the medals will be attached to the bodies, like morgue tags, but no, he gives them to the widows. Then Oxenshuer receives a medal for his dramatic return to Mars. The President makes a little speech. Oxenshuer pretends to listen, but his eyes are on Claire more often than not.

With Claire sitting beside him, he sets forth once more out of Los Angeles via the San Bernardino Freeway, eastward through the plastic suburbs, through Alhambra and Azusa, past the Covina Hills Forest Lawn, through San Bernardino and Banning and Indio, out into the desert. It is a bright late-winter day, and recent rains have greened the hills and coaxed the cacti into bloom. He keeps a sharp watch for landmarks: flatlands, dry lakes.

—I think this is the place. In fact, I'm sure of it.

He leaves the freeway and guides the car northeastward. Yes, no doubt of it: there's the ancient lakebed, and there's his abandoned automobile, looking ancient also, rusted and corroded, its hood up, its wheels and engine stripped by scavengers long ago. He parks this car beside it, gets out, dons his backpack. He beckons to Claire.

—Let's go. We've got some hiking ahead of us.

She smiles timidly at him. She leaves the car and presses herself lightly against him, touching her lips to his. He begins to tremble.

—Claire. Oh, God, Claire.

—How far do we have to walk?

—Hours.

He gears his pace to hers. If necessary, they will camp overnight and go on into the city tomorrow, but he hopes they can get there before sundown. Claire is a strong hiker, and he is confident she can cover the distance in five or six hours, but there is always the possibility that he will fail to find the twin mesas. He has no compass points, no maps, nothing but his own intuitive sense of the city's location to guide him. They walk steadily northward. Neither of them says very much. Every half hour they pause to rest; he puts down his pack and she hands him the canteen. The air is mild and fragrant. Jackrabbits boldly accompany them. Blossoms are everywhere. Oxenshuer, transfigured by love, wants to leap and soar.

——We ought to be seeing those mesas soon.

——I hope so. I'm starting to get tired, John.

——We can stop and make camp if you like.

——No. No. Let's keep going. It can't be much farther, can it?''

They keep going. Oxenshuer calculates they have covered twelve or thirteen kilometers already. Even allowing for some straying from course, they should be getting at least a glimpse of the mesas by this time, and it troubles him that they are not in view. If he fails to find them in the next half-hour, he will make camp, for he wants to avoid hiking after sundown.

Suddenly they breast a rise in the desert and the mesas come into view, two steep wedges of rock, dark gray against the sand. The shadows of late afternoon partially cloak them, but there is no mistaking them.

——There they are, Claire. Out there.

——Can you see the city?

——Not from this distance. We've come around from the side, somehow. But we'll be there before very long.

At a faster pace, now, they head down the gentle slope and into the flats. The mesas dominate the scene. Oxenshuer's heart pounds, not entirely from the strain of carrying his pack. Ahead wait Matt and Jean, Will and Nick, the Speaker, the god-house, the labyrinth. They will welcome Claire as his woman; they will give them a small house on the edge of the city; they will initiate her into their rites. Soon. Soon. The mesas draw near.

——Where's the city, John?

——Between the mesas.

——I don't see it.

——You can't really see it from the front. All that's visible is the palisade, and when you get very close you can see some rooftops above it.

——But I don't even see the palisade, John. There's just an open space between the mesas.

——A shadow effect. The eye is easily tricked.

But it does seem odd to him. At twilight, yes, many deceptions are possible; nevertheless he has the clear impression from there that there *is* nothing but open space between the mesas. Can these be the wrong mesas? Hardly. Their shape is distinctive and unique; he could never confuse those two jutting slabs with other formations. The city, then? Where has the city gone? With each step he takes he grows more perturbed. He tries to hide his uneasiness from Claire, but she is tense, edgy, almost panicky now, repeatedly asking him what has happened, whether they are lost. He reassures her as best he can. This is the right place, he tells her. Perhaps it's an optical illusion that the city is invisible, or perhaps some other kind of illusion, the work of the city folk.

——Does that mean they might not want us, John? And they're hiding their city from us?''

——I don't know, Claire.

——I'm frightened.

——Don't be. We'll have all the answers in just a few minutes.

When they are about five hundred meters from the face of the mesas, Claire's control breaks. She whimpers and darks forward, sprinting through the cacti toward the opening between the mesas. He calls out to her, tells her to wait for him, but she runs on, vanishing into the deepening shadows. Hampered by his unwieldy pack, he stumbles after her, gasping for breath. He sees her disappear between the mesas. Weak and dizzy, he follows her path, and in a short while comes to the mouth of the canyon.

There is no city.

He does not see Claire.

He calls her name. Only mocking echoes respond. In wonder he penetrates the canyon, looking up at the steep sides of the mesas, remembering streets, avenues, houses.

—Claire?

No one. Nothing. And now night is coming. He picks his way over the rocky, uneven ground until he reaches the far end of the canyon. He looks back at the mesas, and outward at the desert, and he sees no one. The city has swallowed her and the city is gone.

—Claire! Claire!

Silence.

He drops his pack wearily, sits for a long while, finally lays out his bedroll. He slips into it but does not sleep; he waits out the night, and when dawn comes he searches again for Claire, but there is no trace of her. All right. All right. He yields. He will ask no questions. He shoulders his pack and begins the long trek back to the highway.

By mid-morning he reaches his car. He looks back at the desert, ablaze with moonlight. Then he gets in and drives away.

He enters his apartment on Hollywood Boulevard. From here, so many months ago, he first set out for the desert; now all has come round to the beginning again. A thick layer of dust covers the cheap utilitarian furniture. The air is musty. All the blinds are closed. He wanders aimlessly from hallway to living room, from living room to bedroom, from bedroom to kitchen, from kitchen to hallway. He kicks off his boots and sprawls out on the threadbare living-room carpet, face down, eyes closed. So tired. So drained. I'll rest a bit.

"John?"

It is the Speaker's voice.

"Let me alone," Oxenshuer says. "I've lost her. I've lost you. I think I've lost myself."

"You're wrong. Come to us, John."

"I did. You weren't there."

"Come now. Can't you feel the city calling you? The Feast is over. It's time to settle down among us."

"I couldn't find you."

"You were still lost in dreams then. Come now. Come. The saint calls you. Jesus calls you. Claire calls you."

"Claire?"

"Claire," he says.

Slowly Oxenshuer gets to his feet. He crosses the room and pulls the blinds open. This window faces Hollywood Boulevard; but, looking out, he sees only the red plains of Mars, eroded and cratered, glowing in purple noonlight. Vogel and Richardson are out there, waving to him. Smiling. Beckoning. The faceplates of their helmets glitter by the cold gleam of the stars. Come on, they call to him. We're waiting for you. Oxenshuer returns their greeting and walks to another window. He sees a lifeless wasteland here too. Mars again, or is it only the Mojave Desert? He is unable to tell. All is dry, all is desolate, all is beautiful with the serene transcendent beauty of desolation. He sees Claire in the middle distance. Her back is to him; she is moving at a steady, confident pace toward the twin mesas. Between the mesas lies the City of the Word of God, golden and radiant in the warm sunlight. Oxenshuer nods. This is the right moment. He will go to her. He will go to the city. The Feast of St. Dionysus is over, and the city calls to him.

Bring us together. Lead us to the ocean.
Help us to swim. Give us to drink.
Wine in my heart today,
Blood in my throat today,
Fire in my soul today,
All praise, O God, to thee.

Oxenshuer runs in long loping strides. He sees the mesas, he sees the city's palisade. The sound of far-off chanting throbs in his ears. "This way, brother!" Matt shouts. "Hurry, John!" Claire cries. He runs. He stumbles, and recovers, and runs again. Wine in my heart today. Fire in my soul today. "God is everywhere," the saint tells him. "But before all else, God is within you."

The desert is a sea, the great warm cradling ocean, the undying mother-sea of all things, and Oxenshuer enters it gladly, and drifts, and floats, and lets it take hold of him and carry him wherever it will.

DEVILS IN THE DUST

by Arthur J. Burks

CHAPTER I
Children of Darkness

The old weatherbeaten church built by our grandfathers was a place of utter gloom. No electric lights; only lanterns, candles, kerosene lamps, showered strange radiance on the moaning congregation. Our shadows were grotesque, demoniac, leaping upon the walls. Our people listened to the ranting of Marmer Hovis, the fanatic lay-preacher.

I sat stiffly holding the hand of Norma Drake. When Marmer Hovis had finished his shouting we were to marry. I, Kelcey Fayne, was at last to have my childhood sweetheart as my wife . . . at last before dusty death overtook us.

"Listen!" shrieked Hovis, his hair wild in his eyes, his face streaked with dirty sweat. "Listen how they suffer—your own dumb brutes."

The sad moaning of our people ceased. For a few seconds the congregation ceased swaying. The sound Hovis mentioned came through the night to us all. Like the whirring of the dust-wind which, it seemed, would never stop. Pitiful whickering of horses. Mournful lowing of cattle. In my mind's eye I could see them, standing stark and bony on skylines formed by the awful, desolate dunes, crying to their beast-gods. Never to us! They must have known us—helpless brutes like themselves—impotent to serve them. Water and food? We had neither. Their ribs arched like curved sabers stretching hairy parchment skins.

"Oh, God," I breathed, "will this storm of horror never pass from us?"

Norma Drake and I—we approached the spieler when the congregation left. Outside the stark church the wind was rising higher and higher, shrieking, roaring like flame.

I looked to my left. Little ripples of dust sifted through the cracks in the old building, flowing like water over the floor. My heart sank, drowned in dust. I had thought that the dust would come no more; that there could be none left in whatever place of horror it had first risen.

"Marry us!" I snapped at Hovis. "I will give you your fee later."

His face clouded. His eyes darkened, flashing with anger.

"Would you take a woman in hell?" he demanded. "Would you beget children in the midst of this evil plague of dust?"

I almost struck him. I trembled with desire to fasten my trembling fingers in his throat.

"Marry us, Hovis," I cried, "or by the living God. . . !"

I choked. Hovis answered:

"Thou shalt not take the Name of thy Lord in vain!"

"Marry us!" I repeated, raving. "How do you know the plague of dust will not pass? You have peopled the dust with devils! Why should you fill my people with greater fear?"

"You think I do not know?" he shouted. "Come to the window. Look! See for yourself!"

I went with him; looked out to the west, the direction

whence the wind always came. And there, high against the night, high up under the roof of dark sky, sweeping the tortured earth with ebon skirts, there spread such a wall of abysmal horror as even stricken County Carlson had never known. I stared at the curling shape of it. It bowed over at the crest, like a vast sea billow rolling. The sound of it was as a flight of destroying locusts—a deadly muted, softly slithering roar.

"You knew somehow!" I accused Hovis. "I do not believe in your professed gift of prophecy. But marry us now—"

Well, he made us man and wife at the brink of hell. I turned and looked back at him standing at the church door. He was peering after us, grinning, washing his hands with air. He shouted after us:

"Remember, the Devil is in the dust! Satan seeks his own through the plague he has brought to sinners!"

Had I stayed I must surely have closed with him, battered his leering, grinning face to a pulp. My whole body was burnt with desire to tear him. Held in my big, gnarled hand, Norma's hand trembled. It was so terribly, woefully thin. There had been so little to eat and drink weeks on end. Now—nothing. Our wedding supper—the only guest would be famine.

"I'm afraid," whispered Norma.

"I will protect you," I told her, "against anything that comes!"

Even as I spoke, a flash of lightning tore through the sky-veil of dust. The roaring of the wind! The lightning showed us the black wall of the roaring dust storm, ebon across the night. It showed the doom cloud circling to encompass us in a whirling maelstrom. And the flame crackling from the dust struck the church. Great tongues of flames leaped high.

Aghast, I looked. I thought that through the dancing flames I could see Marmer Hovis, red-garbed in destroying fire. Marmer Hovis with horns and a tail; with the black beard of Mephisto, grinning satanically as he washed his bloody hands with air. Then the fancy, Devil in the dust—Devil of the flame. Dust of disintegrating earth.

"Come, Norma," I said. "We have only two miles to go."

We walked with the wind and dust in our faces. I had a car. Now it was buried beneath a sand dune which indicated the spot—no more. For weeks there had been no money for gas, no water to waste. Yes, there were horses—so gaunt with starvation that they could scarcely stand, whickering like pitifully broken children hungry for crusts of bread.

We walked, and held hands, staggering like dizzy drunkards.

"Kelcey?" said Norma, there beside me. Her voice came faintly through the wind which whipped her worn ragged garments tightly against her thin legs.

"Yes?" I said.

"Your face," she said. "I saw it in the lightning flash. It was covered with sweat, and something else, Kelcey."

"Yes, what?"

"Dust like a mask. I scarcely knew you, Kelcey! It is heavy in my clothes. It's bigger than ever. Too big. I am afraid!"

"We'll manage somehow," I told her, though I was not sure.

We stopped within a quarter mile of home, the rambling farmhouse where Norma had always lived, now like a wooden mausoleum. We stopped because a new sound came down the wind: the ululation of hunting dogs. Dogs gone wild as wolves.

Dust was already banked before the door when we reached it. Norma and I looked at each other. I saw terror in her eyes.

CHAPTER II
Whispers in the Wind

And the new terror? Simply this: We had battled almost an hour to walk those two miles home, and I had no home. The dust at last had reached my land. It was banking high like snow in a bitter winter, on the leeward side of the house. The blackness of the night was almost absolute.

I had the feeling that my house, low of roof, would be buried, under the fine dust before morning. It would be like being buried alive in a mighty coffin of many rooms.

Norma entered with me. We closed the door. The dust on the sill grated as I forced the door open, and the sound was like the squeaking of many mice.

Wind tugged at the shingles, caught under the eaves, tried to rip the house apart. We had to shout to make ourselves heard.

Norma's face was very white. She darted small glances this way and that. I followed them, noting what she noted; that in spite of the packing in the cracks, little dunes of silt sifted across the floor from the western walls, hammered through every microscopic crevice.

"Hadn't you better do something for your horses and cattle, Kelcey?" said Norma.

I shook my head.

"Listen!" I said. "Do you hear horses whickering? Or cattle lowing?"

She listened. Our meeting eyes were filled with misery. Neither sound of horse nor cow could be heard. We understood the worst; that nothing remained alive on my farm, save ourselves.

The smaller creatures, ducks, chickens, pigs, were all eaten—the last of them yesterday. My parents had been with me up to four days ago. Both had died, their lungs choked by dust-pneumonia.

They were buried behind this house in which they had been married. A few of my neighbors had come to help. There had been no funeral ceremony. Eerie shadows seemed to creep in on us as the oil-lamp flickered. They darted away before gleaming lamp-light. Now, as though demons realized that there was nothing to fear, they were coming back.

We stood, facing each other. I took Norma in my arms. I could hear her heart beating against mine. I loved her to the depths of my being, as she loved me.

"I'm afraid, Kelcey," she whispered.

"Don't be," I said. "We've been through dust storms

before. When this has passed we'll mortgage the farm, re-stock it, begin again—"

Outside there suddenly sounded a weird chorus of howling.

Norma's eyes grew big. We knew the meaning of those sounds. They were the baying of the homeless dogs of the country, creatures gaunt, terrible, many of them mad, perhaps. Masterless dogs, foraging now for food. The ululations died.

"They've found the dead horses and cows," I told Norma.

We listened, scarcely daring to breathe, as snarling hunger sounds from the ghastly night. I could see, in fancy, the dust in their hair being shaken off; I could see a score of dogs, all the same wolf-brown color because of the dust in their coats.

I lifted my head to listen. There was a scratching sound at the door, a thin whining.

Norma shivered. I knew, then, as Norma did, that the hungry dogs had gathered in packs; that but for the locked door they must enter and tear us limb by limb—even old Bunt, my own dog, who had always loved me.

I went to the door to make sure of the fastening.

I peered out a window, into whirling black murk. Two balls of flame looked at me, two more, two, and yet other two. There were many dogs at the door. One saw me. Two eyes leaped at the window like arrows.

A gaunt beast struck the glass. It splintered.

The beast dropped soundless, into the growling dust outside. His slaver smeared the windowpane. The slaver turned to dust as fine silt was hammered into it by the wind.

God, the terror that gripped me! Norma and I—prisoners in a mausoleum indeed. I knew why: my animals had been so gaunt, so skinny from lack of water and food that they had been slight food indeed for the dogs.

I paced back to Norma. She did not need to ask me anything. She knew. I searched the room for a cudgel. I found an ancient, knobbed walking stick which had belonged to my grandfather, a mighty weapon. My rifle would not serve, because dust would clog the bore.

The club must suffice, in case the dogs smashed through the windows.

Then, in the midst of terror, the light flickered and went out. There was no kerosene left. I might have lighted a fire in the potbellied stove, but there was no wood, save only the furniture. We sat very still. The bedroom, to which I had hoped one day to take my bride, became, oddly enough, a place of horror.

I could almost hear Hovis, chuckling softly to himself.

Norma stifled a scream.

I saw them—two pairs of glowing eyes against the western window, two gaunt heads of dogs with lolling tongues trying to look in, scenting us, eager to savor the flesh of our bodies.

I was thinking now, strangely, of something else, for to the west of the house I heard other dogs howling. Were the dogs seeking the bodies of my father and mother? They had been buried without coffins in shallow graves because no coffins were procurable, even if there had been money with which to buy.

I wonder what made Norma say what she next said?

"I feel them close to us, Kelcey. Your father and mother! I can feel them in the room with us trying to tell us something."

I shivered at that. It was a strange comment to my own thoughts. Maybe my parents were close because the dogs were near to uncovering them? Now that Norma had spoken I felt it, too.

A voice seemed to whisper to me through the sound of the storm. My mother's voice:

"Leave us in the house where we were wed, my son. Then go with your bride . . ."

And my father added:

"Quarter the wind, Kelcey; quarter the wind! If Norma lives you will yet find happiness. Never here, my son; not in this desert."

Decision filled me with queer exaltation.

"Norma," I said, "lock yourself in here. I shall not go far, but there is something that must be done. Wait until I call. Don't be afraid of the dogs even though you hear them snarling and think that they attack me!"

I caught up the cudgel. I went to the outer door, swung it back with all my strength; held it until the drifting silt formed a stop to hold it open. I had scarcely done that, when a black shape, only less black then the night itself, hurtled at me. My eyes, used to darkness, were keen because of Norma's need of protection.

I struck with all my might. I heard bone crush as the dog crashed to the silt. I knew it was dead. Two others charged, leaped, and were slain. Then my mouth gritty with flying sand, I clutched the knobbed stick and circled the house going to the graves of my parents.

A tumbling, milling mass of creatures boiled about it.

In time! I saw dogs straining at a white garment—her white shroud—a sheet. Mad as the dogs themselves, I smashed in among them, striking with the stick, laying about me.

Both graves had been opened.

I dragged Mother home first, shutting the door after I had placed her on the floor in a dark corner. I worked with feverish haste. I went back for Father. The dogs had uncovered him. They snarled over him, a mass of writhing flesh. I was glad that I could not see too well.

I took Father to the house, dragging him with my left hand, fighting off the famished dogs with my right. Had I lost the stick they would have pulled me down. The dust from their coats stifled my nostrils. Three times I stopped, stood astride the corpse, brained dogs with the heavy stick.

I placed Father beside Mother. I was sickened at what had already happened to him. I shut the door. The dogs that were left leaped against the door. I called Norma out. We piled the meager furniture across the corner—a barricade. Norma asked no questions. I found matches, when I did not think any were left.

I fired the furniture; said to Norma: "Now we quarter the wind."

CHAPTER III
Marmer Hovis

I caught up a strip of canvas that had been used to pack the space between the bottom of the door and the sill, and strung it around my neck, so that it hung above my hips like a sling for a broken arm. I fastened a handkerchief about Norma's mouth, one about my own. The fire was rising, would soon disclose to Norma those whom I had placed in the corner, side by side. She must not see them. I would see them to the very end of my days.

I had cheated the dogs. Their bony bodies crashed against the walls, against the windows. I gripped my stick fiercely.

At the door I told Norma not to look back. I helped her knot the sling across my back, so that she faced to my left. Her back would be to the hammer and drive of the wind.

Now I had both hands free to use my stick; need not worry about losing Norma.

I pushed the door open. The dogs charged. I shouted at them, in savage exultation. The door shut behind me. I stood there, fighting the dogs.

Eerie lights came through the windows, painting ghastly, unreal pictures against the fall of silt which whipped over the roof of the house like drifting snow. Already the silt had piled up almost level with the windows. When it had, then the charging dogs could have driven their weight straight through. In my mind's eye I could see them, crashing glass to the floor, hunting us through the house with slobbering jaws.

I would fight them off now until the boards behind me were hot against the flesh of my beloved.

Whence had all the dogs come? I had not known there were so many in all the countryside. But then it came to me: they had started drifting with the dust-storm, trying to head it. They must have gathered ahead of the dust tempest for many miles, maybe all the miles the dust had traveled.

And dog packs, then, were probably trying to drag

people down ten, fifteen, twenty miles from here, if they, too, had drifted before the wind and the black dust.

"It's getting hot, Kelcey," Norma shouted in my ears.

"All right, we're going, Norma," I said. "Be brave. Resolve to live. Hold fast to me. Before God, I'll get us both out of this horror. We travel south, dear. Watch the dogs behind us. Put your face against my neck, so that I shall know every minute that you are loving me."

"Yes, Kelcey," she answered.

I surged into the thick of the dog pack. Hunger, thirst, had no effect on me now. I was fighting for life, and for love. Without love, life would not be worth having. If Norma died . . .

I shouted to her.

"Breathe through the handkerchief. Take care that it does not slip down. Clear its outside with your palm whenever you begin to choke."

I struck with savage fury. I felt bones break before the slash of my cudgel. The living tore the fallen. The dogs had reverted to the ways of their ancient ancestors, the wolves. They destroyed their own kind with cannibalistic fury. I knocked down more, and more. The rank odor of their thick blood was in my nostrils.

I looked back. Dimly, redly lurid through the curtains of dust, I could see the flames from the farmhouse, rising into black night. Pennants of flame, wind-blown, seemed to lie flat against the ground. Prowling dogs, black shapes against the blood-red glow, raced like ghostly shadows, driven mad by the smells which came out of the burning house.

Despite all the horror, I sighed with relief. My handkerchief slipped. Each breath sucked silt into my mouth, dry as dust already. I clenched my teeth.

Now, keeping the wind against my right cheek—driven sand and silt were ripping the very skin from my face—I set out to the south. If we fled before the wind we could never reach the end of it. If we traveled across it, there *must* be an end somewhere. Ten miles, even fifty—I could do fifty for the sake of my beloved if only she could endure the hunger and thirst that long.

She was so woefully light. I scarcely felt her weight.

My heart hammered with hope. I did not mind the loss of her home or of mine. Never again, in any case, could we live in either place remembering so much of sorrow and heartache.

I listened to the sounds.

The roaring of the wind; vast formless roaring, with all the fury of flaming hell in it. The drifting sand and silt reached to the very sky. If it did not cease by morning we could not even tell night from day. No light could pierce the flowing plague of dust. Dust filled every fiber of my clothing. My ears were clogged with it. I gouged at my ears; I must hear for protection's sake.

Dust on the ground eddied about my shoe-tops, as though I traveled through dry quicksand. It was like swimming in a strange kind of water in which one could barely breathe.

Through the cataclysmic devils' drone of the storm came other clamorous sounds. More dogs, everywhere, though I knew I heard only those to the west, shrill yelping coming to me down the wind. To the east the dogs might be within a few feet of me not knowing we passed. The dust-filled wind would carry no scent other than that of dry earth. So I kept my streaming eyes to the left. Now and then dogs attacked. I brained one, or two, or three, and went on. I licked my dry lips. I thought of something: their blood could be drunk, would sustain life. But not yet—oh, God, not yet—for they had eaten human flesh, many of them. There was a limit to which one might plumb the depths of horror, yet remain sane.

Other sounds—the lamentations of men and of women. Sometimes the glow of lamps in farmhouses, were women wailed, over their dead, perhaps.

I thought of Marmer Hovis, rubbing his hands and avidly grinning behind me. Devils in the dust, he had said! I felt, somehow, that he was the Devil himself, riding the dust, directing yet other devils.

Did he laugh and chuckle, hearing the lamentations of those who feared the black wings of the dust as they feared nothing else on earth or under it? I could feel his presence everywhere except in front of me where I could see him rubbing his hands and chuckling.

Hours passed. Maybe they were minutes which seemed like hours. I did not know. My skin was dust. Blinding, torturing dust filmed over my streaming eyes.

I heard, often, the shrill, birdlike cries of women. Others were doing as I did, quartering the wind with their women, seeking escape from the horror of the storm. Had father and mother, loving their neighbor as themselves, bidden them, also, to "quarter the wind"? I did not know.

But this I did know: terror stalked among those who took part in the exodus to the south. Not dogs or wolves, not anything natural! It was always the young girls who screamed through the storm.

I came on one such girl, drifting like a phantom of dust through the dark. She fought with another apparition. I saw dust-powdered hands rip at her clothing, tear it from her: saw her fair skin become dust even as it was bared. Her dusty, loosened hair flung out on the wind, and she screamed continually.

I saw the other shadow clutch her, bear her back, fumbling at her body with his right hand. His left hand clutched her throat so that she could not scream again.

The two shadows fell. I needed all of my strength to save my Norma. But I could not pass when such devil's work was happening in the storm. I lunged forward. Above the girl the figure moved, a movement of horror. Once his left hand thrust out and a thin, piping scream came forth.

I scarcely paused in my stumbling, swift stride, thinking even as I lifted my cudgel:

"What shall I do with the girl?"

I struck.

A man's skull cracked—no dusty phantom.

I looked down at the skinny woman—a stranger. But I saw the marks of the man's hand on her dust-grimed throat. I saw that her head rolled oddly. I stooped, while Norma clung, trying to see.

"Shut your eyes, beloved," I cried to her.

Then I straightened. The girl's neck was broken. Flying dust already covering her. To baffle the dogs—

I laughed hoarsely. I strode on, turned back for a moment, turned the man over, rubbed the dust from his face.

He was Marmer Hovis!

I was glad, now, that I had stopped to slay him. I grabbed at his collar, dragged him to a little height swept bare of dust by the wind—where the blowing sand would not bury him quickly; where the girl would not, even in death, be near him. So I left him, to be meat for the dogs.

Then I went on, glad in what I had done.

An hour passed—or perhaps a minute—when once more, I came upon a girl. There was the man, too. The whole nightmare, if such a scene in such a ghastly setting could be anything but delusion, was the same as the first instance. The girl's clothing ripped off. Her scream. The hand at her throat. Two bodies, tightly locked, falling to the soft ground inches deep in silt, dropped here by the wind out of hell.

Once more I struck, but this time to save the girl's life. She screamed, rose, and ran staggering into the storm, drifting with it, very soon lost instantly to sight. There was madness in her eyes. Terror of myself as she vanished. She had seen Norma on my back. To her I must have been another foul demon of the storm. Devils in the dust!

Again I turned a dead man on his back. I stumbled back, dazed with fright, stricken with supernatural fear.

For the second man was Marmer Hovis likewise! It couldn't be, yet there it was, the lay-preacher—the dead prophet of the dust.

Marmer Hovis! Marmer Hovis!

Satan? Or were these two I had slain his imps, torturing the crazed victims of their storm? Now terror gripped me, for I remembered how, joining Norma to me in marriage, he had licked his red lips when he had looked at her.

I stumbled, staggered on. Norma's arms clung like dead stalks about my bowed neck. She was so light—but her weight crushed me so, that I stumbled.

Once again I struck and slew, and the girl vanished fleeing before the wind. And the dead man was Hovis! Perhaps I was mad, utterly, completely mad. The howling storm seemed to chant mockingly the name of the spieler who prophesied punishment for our sins. Was this ghastly punishment? Torture for all sinners in thought or deed?

"Marmer Hovis! Marmer Hovis!"

And Norma screamed. I felt her being dragged away from me while her thin legs clutched my waist. As though hard hands tugged at her—tugged so savagely that I was dragged backward.

CHAPTER IV
Devils in the Dust

I turned, mad as the dogs. The sling in which I had carried my beloved was broken. I heard her scream dying away. I whirled, the club lifted, red lust to kill in my heart. There was a devil's troupe of Marmer Hovises behind us; how many behind the dust screen I had no way of knowing.

They all looked the same. I suppose I must have looked like them, too. They had no resemblance to anything human. If they wore clothing, all their garments were dust. The wind whipped powdery dust from them when they moved, so that they looked like men of dust disintegrating. As I look back at the horror now I wonder how I saw so much in the dark with my tortured eyes. Much, perhaps, I saw with the eyes of terror, exaggerated beyond all words to express.

Marmer Hovis—Norma! But no, never Norma . . . my beloved—!

A half dozen dust-devils were taking her from me. She was kicking, screaming. The handkerchief came off her mouth. Her face was white where it had covered her. Her mouth was open; she screamed. They passed her back among them.

Two came toward me with a rope. Two carried guns. Their faces writhed with murderous malice. If they could be called faces, for they, too, were formed of dust. Only the eyes seemed alive, moist and muddy. Mouths that opened to scream foul oaths as Norma was passed back, further and further away from me while she kicked and screamed.

If I did not follow I would never know her when—if we met again. Nor would she know me. We had passed through the storm as strange, ghastly dirt creatures, all looking alike. But I would know Marmer Hovis anywhere, and the demons were Marmer Hovis or his carbon copies. They had tortured many women; now they were seeking Norma whom, I swore to myself, they should not have.

I think in those awful moments, with the wind howling madly, the dust thicker and thicker, choking eyes and throat, I became a superman, though my genius ran to destruction. Three men, now, were between Norma and me. Three men held my kicking bride.

I lifted my stick. One of the automatics spoke flatly. I saw the red flare, though the storm all but muffled the sound of it. I flung myself flat. The bullet passed over me. I rolled in the dust, and rose to my feet, my stick lifted. I struck. I struck so quickly that no human being could have dodged. I struck with all my power, and my power was great in the defense of my love.

Now more of her white flesh could be seen, because she was fighting madly, and leaving her clothing in their hands.

I heard the dull crunch of the stick against the skull of the first. He went down. I saw his skull cracked open—a hole into which I could have placed the edge of my palm. He was still as I jumped over him.

Another weapon spoke. As it spoke it disappeared from the hand of the man who carried it, exploding in his fist because its bore had been clogged with dust. He yelled in agony. The man with the rope hurled it. But I jumped into the wind; the rope followed the wind, and so it missed me. I struck savagely.

Dust powdered from the head of the man with the rope when my stick crashed. My hands held the stick as with fingers of steel. I dared not lose it.

Two men closed with me, trying to twist the clubbed

stick from my hand. One succeeded. But no sooner had he grasped it than I was upon him, kicking, biting. The taste of his blood—God help me!—was like wine on my lips. I would, but for Norma, have drunk his blood like a vampire, for it was moist.

I remembered, then, that I was a man, not a fiend, and spat forth the blood. I think I was screaming—a ghastly figure. I doubt, even now, if Norma knew which of us was her man. If I had the stick she would know. Now another held it. I got it from him, turned, struck harder than before.

"Norma! Norma!" I screamed.

The men screamed, too, but their words were unintelligible in the chaotic maelstrom, as my words must have been meaningless. It was hellish, like a nightmare.

Devils? Imps?

God only knew, if God Himself could see through the heart of the driven dust.

But I was seeing Marmer Hovis everywhere, in every face. Even the face of Norma became his face. Only her bared flesh was white—but even as I looked it became dusty, black, like the others.

A stunning blow struck the back of my head. I fell. I felt a rope about my neck; struggled up, was yanked forward, failing on my face. Many hands laid hold of the rope; began to drag me. Looking for a tree, I supposed, in order to watch me choke out life dangling from a limb.

Even while being dragged I clung to the stick. When they paused, I managed to struggle to my feet. I hurled myself along the rope. It loosened, so that those who dragged me whirled to see why. I crashed into them swinging my stick. Two went down.

Norma, ahead of me, was being dimmed, erased by the screens and walls of the storm. God, I had to get to her!

I screamed:

"Marmer Hovis! Marmer Hovis!"

The men answered me with demoniac laughter. One of them shouted and I thought he said: "The spieler cannot help you now!"

As though I wanted his help! I wanted my fingers about his neck, about all his necks, choking breath from the throats of Marmer Hovis and all his imps.

I had slain several. Now if I lost Norma I would wander the rest of my life through the storm. I must follow the storm to wherever it blew, slaying, one after the other, the devils in the dust.

I was more than a little mad. I knew that those whom I had slain had risen again as soon as I had left them. The dogs could not feed on the bodies of the undead. They could not harry the supernatural unless they themselves were demon hounds of hell.

I was sobbing, sucking the dust into my throat where it became gritty, horrible slime.

I could barely see Norma. But I had freed myself from the rope. I could not cease sobbing, but I could hurry after, as I did, my club flailing. I must have looked, as I felt, a very incarnation of terror.

The others, to me, were not things of this earth or above it. Below? Perhaps. Who knows? Maybe Marmer Hovis had been right. Maybe he was trying now to make his words come true—

"Norma! Norma!"

Somehow, she worked free of her captors. She was almost naked. She came running toward me. Her hands touched me. She peered into my face.

"Are you Kelcey?" she asked.

Her dirt rimmed eyes were wide with terror.

"Kelcey," I said.

"Prove it," she cried.

"Remember the slaver of the dog upon the window of our house where I took you as bride?"

Then she knew me. I put her behind me, fought the demons, or men. They saw, then, that she wished to be with me. Some drew away. Others slogged along beside me, out of reach of the stick. One more, after covering Norma with my outer garment—sand and dust hammered at my bare torso like needles driven by invisible guns—I fastened her against me with the sling.

The others staggered. They kept their distance. And

finally, somehow, I lost them. We continued dragging our racked bodies through the endless storm.

We must have traveled many miles. It must have been within two hours of daylight. I spoke to Norma hoarsely.

"I can't go much further. You can't walk. Maybe we can find a farmhouse."

I felt her shudder against me.

"I'd rather die than enter any farmhouse," she said. "I am afraid. If we stop, let's lie down, tight in each other's arms. Let the dust cover us."

Weary, broken, bleeding, I wanted to do that. I wanted to die.

It would be so easy. Just to lie down, with our heads toward the wind, our garments wrapped around us. To await the end, our arms about each other. It would be an easy death.

I gasped.

"Let's Norma."

Without motion, merely lying there close together, it seemed that we were still moving, for the dirt under us moved, squirmed, twisted, shaken as though we bedded on a tangle of countless writhing snakes. Above us the sky moved. We were still, and though it seemed that we moved, it was the screaming wind of night and the dust that moved.

With each cough more dirt sucked into my lungs. Norma was coughing, too. I turned her against me, put my lips against her. Her lips . . . it was like kissing the dry dirt on which we lay, panting.

I would at that moment have given anything in this world, life itself, to have known the glory of Norma's kisses, as I had known that glory since we had acknowledged love. It was that compelling desire, I think, which made me insist that we stand once more. I could scarcely move. Every bone and muscle cried protest in agony.

But I got Norma on my back again, the handkerchief in place over her mouth. I covered my own mouth with my left hand. My right held the stick which I would never relinquish.

Down the screaming wind came the cries of women.

Down the wind came the hunting howls of the scourging dogs.

I stumbled on.

"We will not stop," I said, "as long as there is breath of life in my body. I must see your face again, kiss your dear lips once more."

"We must keep going," she said.

Hours passed. I did not stop, knowing that if I did I could not go on. My body was a living flame, flayed by the driven dirt. It ground into the wounds it had already made—so many that all my body was one open sore at which the wind imps were stabbing with metal barbs.

On and on, without end.

Finally, a glimmer of light to my left. At last dawn was breaking. But another hour passed, and it was no brighter. We had stumbled and staggered into dim daylight, and there was, really, no change at all. Pilgrims lost in hell, easier for the devils of the dust to find.

CHAPTER V
Muddy River

All that day, while the storm raged and shrieked, we traveled, quartering the wind. I did not stop once. I swear it. I knew that we had long since passed any landmark I could possibly know. My knowledge of the country in this direction was very slight, for I had loved the land of my fathers and had clung to it tightly. During those ghastly hours, I only knew that I progressed at all by the wire fences which marked the boundaries of what had once been farms.

Now and then I would strike against the barbed wire. It would score and sear my flesh; bring me to a standstill. Then, slowly, painfully—telling myself that I hadn't stopped of my own free will—I would tear wire from post, and stumble on.

Sometimes we saw houses, black through the smother of dirt.

Now and again there were coursing dogs. Once we traveled behind a herd of mournfully lowing cattle, headed across the wind as we were headed. They were attacked by dogs, and stampeded down the wind, so we lost them. I was glad that in traveling with the storm which must slay them, they took the dogs with them—the dogs they would feed one by one as they were dragged down.

For hours, now, Norma had been a dead weight on my back, but I knew she lived because her body was warm against mine. I would have sworn that we traveled due south, for the course of the wind was not changed.

Was there never to be an end? Were we to travel through eternity, as no man and wife, even in purgatory, had traveled on honeymoon? Only to die at long last because the mountains of moving, roaring dust reached to the very end of the world?

Doggedly I told myself that this could not be so. Did I not see a glimmering of light, far ahead? I thought that I did.

Then I was sure that, for a few minutes, I saw the blood-red round disk of the sun opposite my right hand. I had traveled through the day, bearing with me the burden I loved. My tongue hung out coated thick with black dust. I could not close my mouth. My tongue was thrice its normal size. I could not speak the name of my beloved, though I whispered it in my heart:

"Norma! Norma!"

I spoke to Norma deep in my soul, because I had lost all faith in God. But one thing had gone with me, through hell; the words of my dead father, bidding me "quarter the wind." Would there be no end?

Yes, thank God! Thank Siva, the many-armed destroyer! Or Vishnu, the preserver! Or any gods there were.

The dust was thinning! No longer a mountain through which one thrust like a burrowing mole. No longer a river of dust across the floor of which one walked like a weighted diver with clogging, heavy shoes on his feet!

I could not even croak.

I was afraid, terribly afraid now that I might still stumble and fall. As though the thought had fathered the fact, I did fall, and buried my dry, cracked face in the dust. I struggled—God, how I struggled!—to rise. Norma did not move, did not know that I fell, nor that I stood erect once more.

But she was still warm on my back, folded up, crouched in a knot.

Would I reach safety, beyond the hell dust, only to find that my beloved had died? I sobbed inside me. The sobs could not get through my swollen lips. But I heard my own sobs, bubbling, stirring inside me, so that I trembled inwardly as though filled with bees. That thought made me laugh wildly, hysterically. The hysterical laughter still sounded like the droning of bees within the walls of my chest.

I saw people!

To right and left, people quartering the wind. Strong, gaunt women. Bony, hard-handed men. All of them looked like Marmer Hovis. There were many men without women, who I knew had not come into the storm without them. The farmers of our country did not thus desert their wives.

There were no children. The children had been lost in the storm; never found again. The women—well, what of those men I had slain? The man Marmer Hovises?

I cursed savagely, remembering. There was a taste as of dried blood in my mouth. My chest hummed with fierce oaths.

I stumbled past many carcasses of cattle and horses. All faced down the wind. The dogs had picked them clean of flesh. They had been at the very edge of the storm—now I could see the shapes of dunes and hills—but had died, as perhaps we would die.

Where were the dogs? In my dream forever, I must hear their phantom howls whirled against the wall high sky, as they sought through dusty veils for living flesh on which to feast.

Then, I was through! Was it strange that although I had breathed, eaten, drank dust I fell on my face and kissed the soil? Rather, that I touched Mother Earth with my swollen tongue which protruded between cracked, blubbery lips. Strange enough, but stranger things came out of the storm which howled behind us.

Men and women—ten times as many men as women—figures of earth, marching, converging toward a winding stream that glistened in the dying sun.

I saw the stream; thought it part of a dream. I knew that if I fell but once more I could not rise again.

I reached the stream. I fell into it, face foremost. I wanted to writhe and twist and roll in it.

But there was Norma. I loosed her, let her down, a dead weight although so pitifully light.

Her nostrils quivered. I brushed her face with my hands.

I could not know that she breathed. I glanced about me. Men and women were stripping off their clothing, sliding into the muddy stream like white snakes whose heads and shoulders were dirt—dirt which had been hammered into their flesh by the wind.

The storm behind us still writhed upward to the sky. It roared as it had roared, as it promised to roar without end.

I stripped off what little was left of Norma's clothing. I stripped off my own.

I pushed her into the stream until only her face was above it. I watched the water turn her dark skin to muddy brown and white. I let my own thirsty body drink the water.

God knows how I did it, but I managed to desist from drinking, while I held her mouth open, and dribbled water into it with my hand. I did not know what I had done with my stick. It no longer seemed to matter.

Norma stirred and moaned; opened her eyes. They were as blue as the sky above us. She lifted her head, saw the water, sighed, and croaked:

"Drink, Kelcey!"

I tried to drink. Water dribbled past my swollen tongue, so that my parched throat seemed to suck my hand dry.

Hours passed. I did not feel the pain of my broken body. Such pain would pass. I gloried in lying in the soft ooze of the stream, while the water flowed sluggishly over me; and Norma's body was close, wet against mine.

Then, when some of those who had been of the exodus came to us to say that a fire had been kindled, I managed to sit; managed to lift Norma from the stream; managed somehow to clothe us both with our dusty rags. The messenger said:

"Reverend Hovis commands us all to the fire, under that big tree, to render thanks to God for deliverance."

Marmer Hovis!

Things came flooding back. I said nothing to Norma. She did not, apparently, remember the horror which was hers when we had been captured, back there in the storm.

I lifted Norma. Like two old people, bent and broken, walking in sleep, we went to the fire.

Marmer Hovis had found a box somewhere to serve as a pulpit. I stared at him. His face was expressionless, immobile. He did not move as he waited for us to gather around him. He stood laving his hands with air.

"Move closer, that you may hear!" were his first words, "for the storm is still near so you cannot easily hear me."

I stared at him.

Two dirty, knotted handkerchiefs were bound like blood-soaked bandages about his head. Blood had come through them. I knew it was blood, though it looked like mud that had dried.

He washed his hands with air. I thought of Pontius Pilate, who gave the Son of Man to the mob to be crucified:

"Give me water that I may wash my hands of the Man."

Those were not the exact words, but . . . I thought of Judas, who had hanged himself on a thorn tree. I rose to my feet; screamed at Marmer Hovis.

"You! You!" I screamed. "Where are your imps? Where are the fiends you brought to Carlson County? It was you, Marmer Hovis, who frightened us into fleeing from the storm's judgment; you who wanted the women and girls to be separated from husbands, brothers, sweethearts!" I glared about wildly. "How many of you men know what happened to your women in the storm—back there? Speak, Marmer Hovis! Before we hang you to the tree behind you."

The men heard, stirred, began murmuring. The face

of Marmer Hovis, which he had cleaned in the stream, was dirty-white. His hand went to his head. I screamed again:

"Hold him! If the wound on his head was made with a club, I made it! I show you the man who tortured many of your women; the false prophet whose imps out of hell maltreated yet others! Show your wound, Marmer Hovis! Show us your broken head!"

But he would not. He looked as though he were ready to flee. They charged him then—the silent, wifeless, sisterless men. They ripped off the bandage. Under it was a mark that only a club could have made.

Einer Svenson, a big Swede neighbor of mine, wept loudly:

"We were hunting the fiends who tortured our women. We thought you, Kelcey Fayne, were one of them, until Norma went to you. You killed two of us, thinking we were the devils. But there is no punishment, for those men had lost their wives; perhaps they had preferred to die."

My hands were the first to touch the neck of Marmer Hovis when they brought the rope.

He confessed.

There were twenty of his fiends back there in the storm. With so many strangers among us how would they be known? He told us their names.

Then we hanged him to the tree. While his body dangled, before his kicking feet were still, Einer Svenson told off a dozen men to stand guard at the edge of the storm. They asked each newcomer who came to give his name; to prove himself.

Norma slept. She did not know. For a little while I lay down beside her. There were many others lying silently around us. I watched the swaying of Hovis' body in the wind before I went to sleep.

It was dawn when I wakened. Others—several others—looking very much like their leader, swung from the tree.

I gathered Norma in my arms, and walked with her down stream. We came to a ford and crossed. I did not look back once. We walked out into sunlight, determined never to leave the stream which gave us life, until we came to some town, or village, where life could start again.

My body would be scarred, but my sores would heal. Norma was gaunt and thin, but food and drink would make her figure round again.

Her eyes were haunted. Her body often trembled, as her mind remembered horror. Her lips kept shaping a name.

"Marmer Hovis! Marmer Hovis!"

Why did he do what he did, he and his imps? Why did they all look alike?

I knew both answers, but all I did then was to soothe Norma. I would not tell her.

It was not only madness brought on by our terror in the dust storm. Not only delusion that peopled the dust storm with Marmer Hovises. Not only nightmare hallucination, though that had its part.

There were, indeed, many of his kind with Hovis. And all did seem alike because of the dust. Fanatics who, under his teaching, had delved too deeply into old, forbidden religions, violent religions wherein the tenets of sadism, brutality and horror became fundamentals of faith.

I was glad I killed some of them; that others were hanged. No more would they torture and slay our women. It was a good thing when their evil bodies became one with the dust.

And it was good to turn our backs against the horror, leaving it behind forever; good to face whatever might lie before us, together, hand in hand.

THE QUESTING TYCOON

by Leslie Charteris

It was intolerably hot in Port-au-Prince; for the capital city of Haiti lies at the back of a bay, a gullet twenty miles deep beyond which the opening jaws of land extend a hundred and twenty miles still farther to the west and northwest, walled in by steep high hills, and thus perfectly sheltered from every normal shift of the trade winds which temper the climate of most parts of the Antilles. The geography which made it one of the finest natural harbors in the Caribbean had doubtless appealed strongly to the French buccaneers who founded the original settlement; but three centuries later, with the wings of Pan American Airways to replace the sails of a frigate, a no less authentic pirate could be excused for being more interested in escaping from the sweltering heat pocket than in dallying to admire the anchorage.

As soon as Simon Templar had completed his errands in the town, he climbed into the jeep he had borrowed and headed back up into the hills.

Knowing what to expect of Port-au-Prince at that time

of year, he had passed up the ambitious new hotels of the capital in favor of the natural air-conditioning of the Châtelet des Fleurs, an unpretentious but comfortable inn operated by an American whom he had met on a previous visit, only about fifteen miles out of the city but five thousand feet above the sea-level heat. He could feel it getting cooler as the road climbed, and in a surprisingly short time it was like being in another latitude. But the scenery did not seem to become any milder to correspond with the relief of temperature: the same brazen sun bathed rugged brownish slopes with few trees to soften their parched contours. Most of the houses he passed, whether a peasant's one-room cottage or an occasional expensive château, were built of irregular blocks of the same native stone, so that they had an air of being literally carved out of the landscape; but sometimes in a sudden valley or clinging to a distant hillside there would be a palm-thatched cabin of rough raw timbers that looked as if it had been transplanted straight from Africa. And indisputably transplanted from Africa were the straggling files of ebony people, most of them women, a few plutocrats adding their own weight to the already fantastic burdens of incredibly powerful little donkeys, but the majority laden fabulously themselves with great baskets balanced on their heads, who bustled cheerfully along the rough shoulders of the road.

He came into the little town of Pétionville, drove past the pleasant grass-lawned square dominated by the very French-looking white church, and headed on up the corkscrew highway towards Kenscoff. And six kilometers further on he met Sibao.

As he rounded one of the innumerable curves he saw a little crowd collected, much as some fascinating obstruction would create a knot in a busy string of ants. Unlike other groups that he had passed before where a few individuals from one of the ant-lines would fall out by the wayside to rest and gossip, this cluster had a focal point and an air of gravity and concern that made him think first of an automobile accident, although there was no car or truck in sight. He slowed up automatically, trying to see what it was all about as he went by, like almost any normal traveller; but when he glimpsed the unmistakable bright color of fresh blood he pulled over and stopped, which perhaps few drivers on that road would have troubled to do.

The chocolate-skinned young woman whom the others were gathered around had a six-inch gash in the calf of one leg. From the gestures and pantomime of her companions rather than the few basic French word-sounds which his ear could pick out of their excited jabber of Creole, he concluded that a loose stone had rolled under her foot as she walked, taking it from under her and causing her to slip sideways down off the shoulder, where another sharp pointed stone happened to stick out at exactly the right place and angle to slash her like a crude dagger. The mechanics of the accident were not really important, but it was an ugly wound, and the primitive first-aid efforts of the spectators had not been able to stanch the bleeding.

Simon saw from the tint of the blood that no artery had been cut. He made a pressure bandage with his handkerchief and two strips ripped from the tail of his shirt; but it was obvious that a few stitches would be necessary for a proper repair. He picked the girl up and carried her to the jeep.

"Nous allons chercher un médecin," he said; and he must have been understood, for there was no protest over the abduction as he turned the jeep around and headed back towards Pétionville.

The doctor whom he located was learning English and was anxious to practise it. He contrived to keep Simon around while he cleaned and sewed up and dressed the cut, and then conveniently mentioned his fee. Simon paid it, although the young woman tried to protest, and helped her back into the jeep.

His good-Samaritan gesture seemed to have become slightly harder to break off than it had been to get into; but with nothing but time on his hands he was cheerfully resigned to letting it work itself out.

"Where were you going?" he asked in French, and she pointed up the road.

"Là-haut."

The reply was given with a curious dignity, but without presumption. He was not sure at what point he had begun to feel that she was not quite an ordinary peasant girl. She wore the same faded and formless kind of cotton dress, perhaps cleaner than some, but not cleaner than all the others, for it was not uncommon for them to be spotless. Her figure was slimmer and shapelier than most, and her features had a patrician mould that reminded him of ancient Egyptian carvings. They had remained mask-like and detached throughout the ministrations of the doctor, although Simon knew that some of it must have hurt like hell.

He drove up again to the place where he had found her. Two other older women were sitting there, and they greeted her as the jeep stopped. She smiled and answered, proudly displaying the new white bandage on her leg. She started to get out.

He saw that there were three baskets by the roadside where the two women had waited. He stopped her, and said: "You should not walk far today, especially with a load. I can take you all the way."

"Vous êtes très gentil.'

She spoke French very stiffly and shyly and correctly, like a child remembering lessons. Then she spoke fluently to the other women in Creole, and they hoisted the third basket between them and put it in the back of the jeep. Her shoes were still on top of its miscellany of fruits and vegetables, according to the custom of the country, which regards shoes as too valuable to be worn out with mere tramping from place to place, especially over rough rocky paths.

Simon drove all the way to the Châtelet des Fleurs, where the road seems to end, but she pointed ahead and said: *"Plus loin."*

He drove on around the inn. Not very far beyond it the pavement ended, but a navigable trail meandered on still further and higher towards the background peaks. He expected it to become impassable at every turn, but it teased him on for several minutes and still hadn't petered out when a house suddenly came in sight, built out of rock and perched like a fragment of a medieval castle on a promontory a little above them. A rutted driveway branched off and slanted up to it, and the young woman pointed again.

"La maison-là."

It was not a mansion in size, but on the other hand it was certainly no native peasant's cottage.

"Merci beaucoup," she said in her stilted schoolgirl French, as the jeep stopped in front of it.

"De rien," he murmured amiably, and went around to life out the heavy basket.

A man came out on to the verandah, and she spoke rapidly in Creole, obviously explaining about her accident and how she came to be chauffeured to the door. As Simon looked up, the man came down to meet him, holding out his hand.

"Please don't bother with that," he said. "I've got a handy man who'll take care of it. You've done enough for Sibao already. Won't you come in and have a drink? My name's Theron Netlord."

Simon Templar could not help looking a little surprised. For Mr. Netlord was not only a white man, but he was unmistakably an American; and Simon had some vague recollection of his name.

II

It can be assumed that the birth of the girl who was later to be called Sibao took place under the very best auspices, for her father was the *houngan* of an *houmfort* in a valley that could be seen from the house where Simon had taken her, which in terms of a more familiar religion than voodoo would be the equivalent of the vicar of a parish church; and her mother was not only a *mambo* in her own right, but also an occasional communicant of the church in Pétionville. But after the elaborate precautionary rituals with which her birth was surrounded, the child grew up just like any of the other naked children of the hills, until she was nearly seven.

At that time, she woke up one morning and said: "Mama, I saw Uncle Zande trying to fly, but he dived into the ground."

Her mother thought nothing of this until the evening, when word came that Uncle Zande, who was laying tile on the roof of a building in Léogane, had stumbled off it and broken his neck. After that much attention was paid to her dreams, but the things that they prophesied were not always so easy to interpret until after they happened.

Two years later her grandfather fell sick with a burning fever, and his children and grandchildren gathered around to see him die. But the young girl went to him and caressed his forehead, and at that moment the sweating and shivering stopped, and the fever left him and he began to mend. After that there were others who asked for her touch, and many of them affirmed that they experienced extraordinary relief.

At least it was evident that she was entitled to admission to the *houmfort* without further probation. One night, with a red bandanna on her head and gay handkerchiefs knotted around her neck and arms, with a bouquet in one hand and a crucifix in the other, she sat in a chair between her four sponsors and watched the *hounsis-canzo*, the student priests, dance before her. Then her father took her by the hand to the President of the congregation, and she recited her first voodoo oath:

"*Je jure, je jure,* I swear, to respect the powers of the *mystères de Guinée*, to respect the powers of the *houngan*, of the President of the Society, and the powers of all those on whom these powers are conferred."

And after she had made all her salutations and prostrations, and had herself been raised shoulder high and applauded, they withdrew and left her before the altar to receive whatever revelation the spirits might vouchsafe to her.

At thirteen she was a young woman, long-legged and comely, with a proud yet supple walk and prematurely steady eyes that gazed so gravely at those whom she noticed that they seemed never to rest on a person's face but to look through into the thoughts behind it. She went faithfully to school and learned what she was told to, including a smattering of the absurdly involved and illogical version of her native tongue which they called "French"; but when her father stated that her energy could be better devoted to helping to feed the family, she ended her formal education without complaint.

There were three young men who watched her one evening as she picked pigeon peas among the bushes that her father had planted, and who were more interested by the grace of her body than by any tales they may have heard of her supernatural gifts. As the brief mountain twilight darkened they came to seize her; but she knew what was in their minds, and ran. As the one penitent survivor told it, a cloud suddenly swallowed her: they blundered after her in the fog, following the sounds of her flight: then they saw her shadow almost within reach, and leapt to the capture, but the ground vanished from under their feet. The bodies of two of them were found at the precipice; and the third lived, though with a broken back, only because a tree caught him on the way down.

Her father knew then that she was more than qualified to become an *hounsis-canzo,* and she told him that she was ready. He took her to the *houmfort* and set in motion the elaborate seven-day ritual of purification and initiation, instructing her in all the mysteries himself. For her *loa,* or personal patron deity, she had chosen Erzulie; and in the baptismal ceremony of the fifth day she received the name of Sibao, the mystic mountain ride where Erzulie mates with the Supreme Gods, the legendary place of eternal love and fertility. And when the *houngan* made the invocation, the goddess showed her favor by possessing Sibao, who uttered prophecies and admonitions in a language that only *houngans* can interpret, and with the hands and mouth of Sibao accepted and ate of the sacrificial white pigeons and white rice; and the *houngan* was filled with pride as he chanted:

"Les Saints mandés mangés.
Genoux-terre!
Parce que gnou loa nan govi pas capab mangé,
Ou gaingnin pour mangé pour li!"

Thereafter she hoed the patches of vegetables that her father cultivated as before, and helped to grate manioc, and carried water from the spring, and went back and forth to market, like all the other young women; but the tale of her powers grew slowly and surely, and it would have been a reckless man who dared to molest her.

Then Theron Netlord came to Kenscoff, and presently heard of her through the inquiries that he made. He sent word that he would like her to work in his house; and because he offered wages that would much more than pay for a substitute to do her work at home, she accepted. She was then seventeen.

"A rather remarkable girl," said Netlord, who had told Simon some of these things. "Believe me, to some of the people around here, she's almost like a living saint."

Simon just managed not to blink at the word.

"Won't that accident this afternoon shake her pedestal a bit?" he asked.

"Does a bishop lose face if he trips over something and breaks a leg?" Netlord retorted. "Besides, *you* happened. Just when she needed help, you drove by, picked her up, took her to the doctor, and then brought her here. What would you say were the odds against her being so lucky? And then tell me why it doesn't still look as if *something* was taking special care of her!"

He was a big thick-shouldered man who looked as forceful as the way he talked. He had iron-grey hair and metallic grey eyes, a blunt nose, a square thrusting jaw, and the kind of lips that even look muscular. You had an inevitable impression of him at the first glance; and without hesitation you would have guessed him to be a man who had reached the top ranks of some competitive business, and who had bulled his way up there with ruthless disregard for whatever obstructions might have to be trodden down or jostled aside. And trite as the physiognomy must seem, in this instance you would have been absolutely right.

Theron Netlord had made a fortune from the manufacture of bargain-priced lingerie.

The incongruity of this will only amuse those who know little about the clothing industry. It would be natural for the uninitiated to think of the trade in fragile feminine frotheries as being carried on by fragile, feminine and frothy types, but in fact, at the wholesale manufacturing level it is as tough and cut-throat a business as any legitimate operation in the modern world. And even in a business which has always been somewhat notorious for lack of tenderness towards its employees, Mr. Netlord had been a perennial source of ammunition for socialistic agitators. His longstanding vendetta against organized labor was an epic of its kind; and he had been named in one Congressional investigation as the man who, with a combination of gangster tactics and an ice-pick eye for loopholes in union contracts and government regulations, had come closest in the last decade to running an old-fashioned sweatshop. It was from casually remembered references to such things in the newspapers that Simon had identified the name.

"Do you live here permanently?" Simon asked in a conversational way.

"I've been here for a while, and I'm staying a while," Netlord answered equivocally. "I like the rum. How do you like it?"

"It's strictly ambrosial."

"You can get fine rum in the States, like that Lemon Hart from Jamaica, but you have to come here to drink Barbancourt. They don't make enough to export."

"I can think of worse reasons for coming here. But I might want something more to hold me indefinitely."

Netlord chuckled.

"Of course you would. I was kidding. So do I. I'll never retire. I *like* being in business. It's my sport, my hobby, and my recreation. I've spent more than a year all around the Caribbean, having what everyone would say was a nice long vacation. Nuts. My mind hasn't been off business for a single day."

"They tell me there's a great future in the area."

"And I'm looking for the future. There's none left in America. At the bottom, you've got your employees demanding more wages and pension funds for less work every year. At the top, you've got a damned paternalistic Government taxing your profits to the bone to pay for all its utopian projects at home and abroad. The man who's trying to literally mind his own business is in the middle, in a squeeze that wrings all the incentive out of him. I'm sick of bucking that set-up."

"What's wrong with Puerto Rico? You can get a tax exemption there if you bring in an employing industry."

"Sure. But the Puerto Ricans are getting spoiled, and the cost of labor is shooting up. In a few more years they'll have it as expensive and as organized as it is back home."

"So you're investigating Haiti because the labor is cheaper?"

"It's still so cheap that you could starve to death trying to sell machinery. Go visit one of the factories where they're making wooden salad bowls, for instance. The only power tool they use is a lathe. And where does the power come from? From a man who spends the whole day cranking a big wheel. Why? Because all he costs is one dollar a day—and that's cheaper than you can operate a motor, let alone amortizing the initial cost of it!"

"Then what's the catch?"

"This being a foreign country: your product hits a tariff wall when you try to import it into the States, and the duty will knock you silly."

"Things are tough all over," Simon remarked sympathetically.

The other's sinewy lips flexed in a tight grin.

"Any problem is tough till you lick it. Coming here showed me how to lick this one—but you'd never guess how!"

"I give up."

"I'm sorry, I'm not telling. May I fix your drink?"

Simon glanced at his watch and shook his head.

"Thanks, but I should be on my way." He put down his glass and stood up. "I'm glad I needn't worry about you getting ulcers, though."

Netlord laughed comfortably, and walked with him out on to the front verandah.

"I hope getting Sibao back here didn't bring you too far out of your way."

"No, I'm staying just a little below you, at the Châtelet des Fleurs."

"Then we'll probably run into each other." Netlord put out his hand. "It was nice talking to you, Mr.——"

"Templar. Simon Templar."

The big man's powerful grip held on to Simon's.

"You're not—by any chance—that fellow they call the Saint?"

"Yes." The Saint smiled. "But I'm just a tourist."

He disengaged himself pleasantly; but as he went down the steps he could feel Netlord's eyes on his back, and remembered that for one instant he had seen in them the kind of fear from which murder is born.

III

In telling so many stories of Simon Templar, the chronicler runs a risk of becoming unduly preoccupied with the reactions of various characters to the discovery that they have met the Saint, and it may fairly be observed that there is a definite limit to the possible variety of these responses. One of the most obvious of them was the shock to a guilty conscience which could open a momentary crack in an otherwise impenetrable mask. Yet in this case it was of vital importance.

If Theron Netlord had not betrayed himself for that fleeting second, and the Saint had not been sharply aware of it, Simon might have quickly dismissed the panty potentate from his mind; and then there might have been no story to tell at all.

Instead of which, Simon only waited to make more inquiries about Mr. Netlord until he was able to corner his host, Atherton Lee, alone in the bar that night.

He had an easy gambit by casually relating the incident of Sibao.

"Theron Netlord? Oh, yes, I know him," Lee said. "He stayed here for a while before he rented that house up on the hill. He still drops in sometimes for a drink and a yarn."

"One of the original rugged individualists, isn't he?" Simon remarked.

"Did he give you his big tirade about wages and taxes?"

"I got the synopsis, anyway."

"Yes, he's a personality all right. At least he doesn't make any bones about where he stands. What beats me is how a fellow of that type could get all wrapped up in voodoo."

Simon did not actually choke and splutter over his drink because he was not given to such demonstrations, but he felt as close to it as he was ever likely to.

"He what?"

"Didn't he get on to that subject? I guess you didn't stay very long."

"Only for one drink."

"He's really sold on it. That's how he originally came up here. He'd seen the voodoo dances they put on in the tourist spots down in Port-au-Prince, but he knew they were just a night-club show. He was looking for the McCoy. Well, we sent the word around, as we do sometimes for guests who're interested, and a bunch from around here came up and put on a show in the patio. They don't do any of the real sacred ceremonies, of course, but they're a lot more authentic than the professionals in town. Netlord lapped it up; but it was just an appetizer to him. He wanted to get right into the fraternity and find out what it was all about."

"What for?"

"He said he was thinking of writing a book about it. But half the time he talks as if he really believed in it. He says that the trouble with Western civilization is that it's too practical—it's never had enough time to develop its spiritual potential."

"Are you pulling my leg or is he pulling yours?"

"I'm not kidding. He rented that house, anyway, and set out to get himself accepted by the natives. He took lessons in Creole so that he could talk to them, and he speaks it a hell of a lot better than I do—and I've lived here a hell of a long time. He hired that girl Sibao just because she's the daughter of the local *houngan*, and she's been instructing him and sponsoring him for the *houmfort*. It's all very serious and legitimate. He told me some time ago that he'd been initiated as a junior member, or whatever they call it, but he's planning to take the full course and become a graduate witch-doctor."

"Can he do that? I mean, can a white man qualify?"

"Haitians are very broad-minded," Atherton Lee said gently. "There's no color bar here."

Simon broodingly chain-lighted another cigarette.

"He must be dreaming up something new and frightful for the underwear market," he murmured. "Maybe he's planning to top those perfumes that are supposed to contain mysterious smells that drive the male sniffer mad with desire. Next season he'll come out with a negligee with a genuine voodoo spell woven in, guaranteed to give the matron of a girls' reformatory more sex appeal than Cleopatra."

But the strange combination of fear and menace that he had caught in Theron Netlord's eyes came back to him with added vividness, and he knew that a puzzle confronted him that could not be dismissed with any amusing flippancy. There had to be a true answer, and it had to be of unimaginable ugliness: therefore he had to find it, or he would be haunted for ever after by the thought of the evil he might have prevented.

To find the answer, however, was much easier to resolve than to do. He wrestled with it for half the night, pacing up and down his room; but when he finally gave up and lay down to sleep, he had to admit that his brain had only carried him around in as many circles as his feet, and gotten him just as close to nowhere.

In the morning, as he was about to leave his room, something white on the floor caught his eye. It was an envelope that had been slipped under the door. He picked it up. It was sealed, but there was no writing on it. It was stiff to his touch, as if it contained some kind of card, but it was curiously heavy.

He opened it. Folded in a sheet of paper was a piece of thin bright metal, about three inches by two, which looked as if it might have been cut from an ordinary tin can, flattened out and with the edges neatly turned under so that they would not be sharp. On it had been hammered an intricate symmetrical design.

Basically, a heart. The inside of the heart filled with a

precise network of vertical and horizontal lines, with a single dot in the center of each little square that they formed. The outline of the heart trimmed with a regularly scalloped edge, like a doily, with a similar dot in each of the scallops. Impaled on a mast rising from the upper V of the heart, a crest like an ornate letter M, with a star above and below it. Two curlicues like skeletal wings swooping out, one from each shoulder of the heart, and two smaller curlicues tufting from the bottom point of the heart, on either side of another sort of vertical mast projecting down from the point and ending in another star—like an infinitely stylized and painstaking doodle.

On the paper that wrapped it was written, in a careful childish script:

Pour vous protéger.
Merci.
Sibao

Simon went on down to the dining room and found Atherton Lee having breakfast.

"This isn't Valentine's Day in Haiti, is it?" asked the Saint.

Lee shook his head.

"Or anywhere else that I know of. That's sometime in February."

"Well, anyhow, I got a valentine."

Simon showed him the rectangle of embossed metal.

"It's native work," Lee said. "But what is it?"

"That's what I thought you could tell me."

"I never saw anything quite like it."

The waiter was bringing Simon a glass of orange juice. He stood frozen in the act of putting it down, his eyes fixed on the piece of tin and widening slowly. The glass rattled on his service plate.

Lee glanced up at him.

"Do you know what it is?"

"Vêver," the man said.

He put the orange juice down and stepped back, still staring.

Simon did not know the word. He looked inquiringly

at his host, who shrugged helplessly and handed the token back.

"What's that?"

"*Vêver,*" said the waiter. "Of Maîtresse Erzulie."

"Erzulie is the top voodoo goddess," Lee explained. "I guess that's her symbol, or some sort of charm."

"If you get good way, very good," said the waiter obscurely. "If you no should have, very bad."

"I believe I dig you, Alphonse," said the Saint. "And you don't have to worry about me. I got it the good way." He showed Lee the paper that had enclosed it. "It was slid under my door sometime this morning. I guess coming from her makes it pretty special."

"Congratulations," Lee said. "I'm glad you're officially protected. Is there anything you particularly need to be protected from?"

Simon dropped the little plaque into the breast pocket of his shirt.

"First off, I'd like to be protected from the heat of Port-au-Prince. I'm afraid I've got to go back down there. May I borrow the jeep again?"

"Of course. But we can send down for anything you want."

"I hardly think they'd let you bring back the Public Library," said the Saint. "I'm going to wade through everything they've got on the subject of voodoo. No, I'm not going to take it up like Netlord. But I'm just crazy enough myself to lie awake wondering what's in it for him."

He found plenty of material to study—so much, in fact, that instead of being frustrated by a paucity of information he was almost discouraged by its abundance. He had assumed, like any average man, that voodoo was a primitive cult that would have a correspondingly simple theology and ritual: he soon discovered that it was astonishingly complex and formalized. Obviously he wasn't going to master it all in one short day's study. However, that wasn't necessarily the objective. He didn't have to write a thesis on it, or even pass an examination. He was only looking for something, anything, that would give him a clue to what Theron Netlord was seeking.

He browsed through books until one o'clock, went out to lunch, and returned to read some more. The trouble was that he didn't know what he was looking for. All he could do was expose himself to as many ideas as possible, and hope that the same one would catch his attention as must have caught Netlord's.

And when the answer did strike him, it was so far-fetched and monstrous that he could not believe he was on the right track. He thought it would make an interesting plot for a story, but could not accept it for himself. He felt an exasperating lack of accomplishment when the library closed for the day and he had to drive back up again to Kenscoff.

He headed straight for the bar of Châtelet des Fleurs and the long relaxing drink that he had looked forward to all the way up. The waiter who was on duty brought him a note with his drink.

Dear Mr. Templar,

I'm sorry your visit yesterday had to be so short. If it wouldn't bore you too much, I should enjoy another meeting. Could you come to dinner tonight? Just send word by the bearer.

Sincerely,
Theron Netlord

Simon glanced up.

"Is someone still waiting for an answer?"

"Yes, sir. Outside."

The Saint pulled out his pen and scribbled at the foot of the note:

Thanks. I'll be with you about 7.

S.T.

He decided, practically in the same instant in which the irresponsible impulse occurred to him, against signing himself with the little haloed stick figure which he had made famous. As he handed the note back to the waiter he reflected that, in the circumstances, his mere acceptance was bravado enough.

IV

There were drums beating somewhere in the hills, faint and faroff, calling and answering each other from different directions, their sound wandering and echoing through the night so that it was impossible ever to be certain just where a particular tattoo had come from. It reached inside Netlord's house as a kind of vague vibration, like the endless thin chorus of nocturnal insects, which was so persistent that the ear learned to filter it out and for long stretches would be quite deaf to it, and then, in a lull in the conversation, with an infinitesimal retuning of attention, it would come back in a startling crescendo.

Theron Netlord caught the Saint listening at one of those moments, and said, "They're having a *brûler zin* tonight."

"What's that?"

"The big voodoo festive ceremony which climaxes most of the special rites. Dancing, litanies, invocation, possession by *loas,* more dances, sacrifice, more invocations and possessions, more dancing. It won't begin until much later. Right now they're just telling each other about it, warming up and getting in the mood."

Simon had been there for more than an hour, and this was the first time there had been any mention of voodoo.

Netlord had made himself a good if somewhat overpowering host. He mixed excellent rum cocktails, but without offering his guest the choice of anything else. He made stimulating conversation, salted with recurrent gibes at bureaucratic government and the Welfare State, but he held the floor so energetically that it was almost impossible to take advantage of the provocative openings he offered.

Simon had not seen Sibao again. Netlord had opened the door himself, and the cocktail makings were already on a side table in the living room. There had been subdued rustlings and clinkings behind a screen that almost closed a dark alcove at the far end of room, but no servant announced dinner: presently Netlord had announced it himself and led the way around the screen and switched on a light, revealing a damask-covered table set for two and burdened additionally with chafing dishes, from which he himself served rice, asparagus, and a savory chicken stew rather like *coq au vin*. It was during one of the dialogue breaks induced by eating that Netlord had caught Simon listening to the drums.

"*Brûler*—that means 'burn,' " said the Saint. "But what is *zin?*"

"The *zin* is a special earthenware pot. It stands on a tripod, and a fire is lighted under it. The *mambo* kills a sacrificial chicken by sticking her finger down into its mouth and tearing its throat open." Netlord took a hearty mouthful of stew. "She sprinkles blood and feathers in various places, and the plucked hens go into the pot with some corn. There's a chant:

'Hounsis là yo, levez, nous domi trope:
Hounsis là yo, levez, pour nous laver yeux nous:
Gadè qui l'heu li yé.'

Later on she serves the boiling food right into the bare hands of the *hounsis*. Sometimes they put their bare feet in the flames too. It doesn't hurt them. The pots are left on the fire till they get red hot and crack, and everyone shouts *'Zin yo craqués!'* "

"It sounds like a big moment," said the Saint gravely. "If I could understand half of it."

"You mean you didn't get very far with your researches today?"

Simon felt the involuntary contraction of his stomach muscles, but he was able to control his hands so that there was no check in the smooth flow of what he was doing.

"How did you know about my researches?" he asked, as if he were only amused to have them mentioned.

"I dropped in to see Atherton Lee this morning, and asked after you. He told me where you'd gone. He said he'd told you about my interest in voodoo, and he supposed you were getting primed for an argument. I must admit, that encouraged me to hope you'd accept my invitation tonight."

The Saint thought that that might well qualify among the great understatements of the decade, but he did not let himself show it. After their first reflex leap his pulses ran like cool clockwork.

"I didn't find out too much," he said, "except that voodoo is a lot more complicated than I imagined. I thought it was just a few primitive superstitions that the slaves brought with them from Africa."

"Of course, some of it came from Dahomey. But how did it get there? The voodoo story of the Creation ties up with the myths of ancient Egypt. The Basin of Damballah—that's a sort of font at the foot of a voodoo altar—is obviously related to the blood trough at the foot of a Mayan altar. Their magic uses the Pentacle—the same mystic figure that medieval European magicians believed in. If you know anything about it, you can find links with eighteenth-century Masonry in some of their rituals, and even the design of the *vêvers*——"

"Those are the sacred drawings that are supposed to summon the gods to take possession of their devotees, aren't they? I read about them."

"Yes, when the *houngan* draws them by dripping ashes and corn meal from his fingers, with the proper invocation. And doesn't that remind you of the sacred sand paintings of the Navajos? Do you see how all those roots must go back to a common source that's older than any written history?"

Netlord stared at the Saint challengingly, in one of those rare pauses where he waited for an answer.

Simon's fingertips touched the hard shape of the little tin plaque that was still in his shirt pocket, but he decided against showing it, and again he checked the bet.

"I saw a drawing of the *vêver* of Erzulie in a book," he said. "Somehow it made me think of Catholic symbols connected with the Virgin Mary—with the heart, the stars, and the 'M' over it."

"Why not? Voodoo is pantheistic. The Church is against voodoo, not voodoo against the Church. Part of the purification prescribed for anyone who's being initiated as a *hounsis-canzo* is to go to church and make confession. Jesus Christ and the Virgin Mary are regarded as powerful intermediaries to the highest gods. Part of the litany they'll chant tonight at the *brûler zin* goes: *Grâce, Marie, Grâce, Marie Grâce, Grâce, Marie Grâce, Jésus, par-donnez-nous!*''

''Seriously?''

''The invocation of Legba Atibon calls on St. Anthony of Padua: *Par pouvoir St.-Antoine de Padoue.* And take the invocation of my own patron, Ogoun Feraille. It begins: *Par pouvoir St.-Jacques Majeur* . . .''

''Isn't that blasphemy?'' said the Saint. ''I mean, a kind of deliberate sacrilege, like they're supposed to use in a Black Mass, to win the favor of devils by defiling something holy?''

Netlord's fist crashed on the table like a thunderclap.

''No, it isn't! The truth can't be blasphemous. Sacrilege is a sin invented by bigots to try to keep God under contract to their own exclusive club. As if supernatural facts could be alerted by human name-calling! There are a hundred sects all claiming to be the only true Christianity, and Christianity is only one of thousands of religions, all claiming to have the only genuine divine revelation. But the real truth is bigger than any one of them and includes them all!''

''I'm sorry,'' said the Saint. ''I forgot that you were a convert.''

''Lee told you that, of course. I don't deny it.'' The metallic grey eyes probed the Saint like knives. ''I suppose you think I'm crazy.''

''I'd rather say I was puzzled.''

''Because you wouldn't expect a man like me to have any time for mysticism.''

''Maybe.''

Netlord poured some more wine.

''That's where you show your own limitations. The whole trouble with Western civilization is that it's blind in one eye. It doesn't believe in anything that can't be weighed and measured or reduced to a mathematical or chemical formula. It thinks it knows all the answers because it invented airplanes and television and hydrogen bombs. It thinks other cultures were backward because they fooled around with levitation and telepathy and raising the dead instead of killing the living. Well, some mighty clever people were living in Asia and Africa and Central America, thousands of years before Europeans crawled out of their caves. What makes you so sure that they didn't discover things that you don't understand?"

"I'm not so sure, but—"

"Do you know why I got ahead of everybody else in business? Because I never wore a blinker over one eye. If anyone said he could do anything, I never said 'That's impossible.' I said 'Show me how.' I don't care who I learn from, a college professor or a ditch-digger, a Chinaman or a nigger—so long as I can use what he knows."

The Saint finished eating and picked up his glass.

"And you think you'll find something in voodoo you can use?"

"I have found it. Do you know what it is?"

Simon waited to be told, but apparently it was not another of Netlord's rhetorical questions. When it was clear that a reply was expected, he said: "Why should I?"

"That's what you were trying to find out at the Public Library."

"I suppose I can admit that," Simon said mildly. "I'm a seeker for knowledge, too."

"I was afraid you would be, Templar, as soon as I heard your name. Not knowing who you were, I'd talked a little too much last night. It wouldn't have mattered with anyone else, but as the Saint you'd be curious about me. You'd have to ask questions. Lee would tell you about my interest in voodoo. Then you'd try to find out what I could use voodoo for. I knew all that when I asked you to come here tonight."

"And I knew you knew all that when I accepted."

"Put your cards on the table, then. What did your reading tell you?"

Simon felt unwontedly stupid. Perhaps because he had let Netlord do most of the talking, he must have done more than his own share of eating and drinking. Now it was an effort to keep up the verbal swordplay.

"It wasn't too much help," he said. "The mythology of voodoo was quite fascinating, but I couldn't see a guy like you getting a large charge out of spiritual trimmings.

You'd want something that meant power, or money, or both. And the books I got hold of today didn't have much factual material about the darker side of voodoo—the angles that I've seen played up in lurid fiction."

"Don't stop now."

The Saint felt as if he lifted a slender blade once more against a remorseless bludgeon.

"Of course," he said, and meant to say it lightly, "you might really have union and government trouble if it got out that Netlord Underwear was being made by American zombies."

"So you guessed it," Netlord said.

V

Simon Templar stared.

He had a sensation of utter unreality, as if at some point he had slipped from wakeful life into a nightmare without being aware of the moment when he fell asleep. A separate part of his brain seemed to hear his own voice at a distance.

"You really believe in zombies?"

"That isn't a matter of belief. I've seen them. A zombie prepared and served this dinner. That's why he was ordered not to let you see him."

"Now I really need the cliché: this I have got to see!"

"I'm afraid he's left for the night," Netlord said matter-of-factly.

"But you know how to make 'em?"

"Not yet. He belongs to the *houngan* But I shall know before the sun comes up tomorrow. In a little while I shall go down to the *houmfort*, and the *houngan* will admit me to the last mysteries. The *brûler zin* afterwards is to celebrate that."

"Congratulations. What did you have to do to rate this?"

"I've promised to marry his daughter, Sibao."

Simon felt as if he had passed beyond the capacity for surprise. A soft blanket of cotton wool was folding around his mind.

"Do you mean that?"

"Don't be absurd. As soon as I know all I need to, I can do without both of them."

"But suppose they resent that."

"Let me tell you something. Voodoo is a very practical kind of insurance. When a member is properly initiated, certain parts of a sacrifice and certain things from his body go into a little urn called the *pot de tête*, and after that the vulnerable element of his soul stays in the urn, which stays in the *houmfort.*"

"Just like a safe deposit."

"And so, no one can lay an evil spell on him."

"Unless they can get hold of his *pot de tête.*"

"So you see how easily I can destroy them if I act first."

The Saint moved his head as if to shake and clear it. It was like trying to shake a ton weight.

"It's very good of you to tell me all this," he articulated mechanically. "But what makes you so confidential?"

"I had to know how you'd respond to my idea when you knew it. Now you must tell me, truthfully."

"I think it stinks."

"Suppose you knew that I had creatures working for me, in a factory—zombies, who'd give me back all the money they'd nominally have to earn, except the bare minimum required for food and lodging. What would you do?"

"Report it to some authority that could stop you."

"That mightn't be so easy. A court that didn't believe in zombies couldn't stop people voluntarily giving me money."

"In that case," Simon answered deliberately, "I might just have to kill you."

Netlord sighed heavily.

"I expected that too," he said. "I only wanted to be sure. That's why I took steps in advance to be able to control you."

The Saint had known it for some indefinite time. He was conscious of his body sitting in a chair, but it did not seem to belong to him.

"You bastard," he said. "So you managed to feed me

some kind of dope. But you're really crazy if you think that'll help you."

Theron Netlord put a hand in his coat pocket and took out a small automatic. He leveled it at the Saint's chest, resting his forearm on the table.

"It's very simple," he said calmly. "I could kill you now, and easily account for your disappearance. But I like the idea of having you work for me. As a zombie, you could retain many of your unusual abilities. So I could kill you, and, after I've learned a little more tonight, restore you to living death. But that would impair your usefulness in certain ways. So I'd rather apply what I know already, if I can, and make you my creature without harming you physically."

"That's certainly considerate of you," Simon scoffed.

He didn't know what unquenchable spark of defiance gave him the will to keep up the hopeless bluff. He seemed to have no contact with any muscles below his neck. But as long as he didn't try to move, and fail, Netlord couldn't be sure of that.

"The drug is only to relax you," Netlord said. "Now look at this."

He dipped his left hand in the ashtray beside him, and quickly began drawing a pattern with his fingertips on the white tablecloth—a design of crisscross diagonal lines with other vertical lines rising through the diamonds they formed, the verticals tipped with stars and curlicues, more than anything like the picture of an ornate wrought-iron gate. And as he drew it he intoned in a strange chanting voice:

"Par pouvoir St.-Jacques Majeur, Ogoun Badagris nèg Baguidi, Bago. Ogoun Feraille nèg fer, nèg feraille, nèg tagnifer nago, Ogoun batala, nèg, nèg Ossagne malor, ossangne aquiquan Ossange agouelingui. Jupiter tonnerre, nèg blabla, nèg cloncoun, nèg vantè-m pas fie'm. . . . Aocher nago, aocher nago, aocher nago!"

The voice had risen, ending on a kind of muted shout, and there was a blaze of fanatic excitement in Netlord's dilated eyes.

Simon wanted to laugh. He said: "What's that—a sequel to the Hutsut Song?" Or he said: "I prefer *'Twas brillig and the slithy toves.' "* Or perhaps he said neither, for the thoughts and the ludicrousness and the laugh were suddenly chilled and empty, and it was like a hollowness and a darkness, like stepping into nothingness and a quicksand opening under his feet, sucking him down, only it was the mind that went down, the lines of the wrought-iron gate pattern shimmering and blinding before his eyes, and a black horror such as he had never known rising around him.

Out of some untouched reserve of will power he wrung the strength to clear his vision again for a moment, and to shape words that he knew came out, even though they came through stiff clumsy lips.

"Then I'll have to kill you right now," he said.

He tried to get up. He had to try now. He couldn't pretend any longer that he was immobile from choice. His limbs felt like lead. His body was encased in invisible concrete. The triumphant fascinated face of Theron Netlord blurred in his sight.

The commands of his brain went out along nerves that swallowed them in enveloping numbness. His mind was drowning in the swelling dreadful dark. He thought: "Sibao, your Maîtresse Erzulie must be the weak sister in this league."

And suddenly, he moved.

As if taut wire had snapped, he moved. He was on his feet. Uncertainly, like a thawing out, like a painful return of circulation, he felt connections with his body linking up again. He saw the exultation in Netlord's face crumple into rage and incredulous terror.

"Fooled you, didn't I?" said the Saint croakily. "You must still need some coaching on your hex technique."

Netlord moved his hand a little, rather carefully, and his knuckle whitened on the trigger of the automatic. The range was point-blank.

Simon's eardrums rang with the shot, and something struck him a stunning blinding blow over the heart. He had an impression of being hurled backwards as if by the blow of a giant fist; and then with no recollection of falling he knew that he was lying on the floor, half under the table, and he had no strength to move any more.

VI

Theron Netlord rose from his chair and looked down, shaken by the pounding of his own heart. He had done many brutal things in his life, but he had never killed anyone before. It had been surprisingly easy to do, and he had been quite deliberate about it. It was only afterwards that the shock shook him, with his first understanding of the new loneliness into which he had irrevocably stepped, the apartness from all other men that only murderers know.

Then a whisper and a stir of movement caught his eye and ear together, and he turned his head and saw Sibao. She wore the white dress and the white handkerchief on her head, and the necklaces of threaded seeds and grain, that were prescribed for the ceremony that night.

"What are you doing here?" he snarled in Creole. "I said I would meet you at the *houmfort.*"

"I felt there was need for me."

She knelt by the Saint, touching him with her sensitive hands. Netlord put the gun in his pocket and turned to the sideboard. He uncorked a bottle of rum, poured some into a glass, and drank.

Sibao stood before him again.

"Why did you want to kill him?"

"He was—he was a bad man. A thief."

"He was good."

"No, he was clever." Netlord had had no time to prepare for questions. He was improvising wildly, aware of the hollowness of his invention and trying to bolster it with truculence. "He must have been waiting for a chance to meet you. If that had not happened, he would have found another way. He came to rob me."

"What could he steal?"

Netlord pulled out his wallet, and took from it a thick pad of currency. He showed it to her.

"He knew I had this. He would have killed me for it." There were twenty-five crisp hundred-dollar bills, an incredible fortune by the standards of a Haitian peasant, but only the amount of pocket money that Netlord normally carried and would have felt undressed without. The girl's dark velvet eyes rested on it, and he was quick to see more possibilities. "It was a present I was going to give to you and your father tonight." Money was the strongest argument he had ever known. He went on with new-found confidence: "Here, take it now."

She held the money submissively.

"But what about—him?"

"We must not risk trouble with the police. Later we will take care of him, in our own way. . . . But we must go now, or we shall be late."

He took her compellingly by the arm, but for a moment she still held back.

"You know that when you enter the *sobagui* to be cleansed, your *loa*, who sees all things, will know if there is any untruth in your heart."

"I have nothing to fear." He was sure of it now. There was nothing in voodoo that scared him. It was simply a craft that he had set out to master, as he had mastered everything else that he made up his mind to. He would use it on others, but it could do nothing to him. "Come along, they are waiting for us."

Simon heard their voices before the last extinguishing wave of darkness rolled over him.

VII

He woke up with a start, feeling cramped and bruised from lying on the floor. Memory came back to him in full flood as he sat up. He looked down at his shirt. There was a black-rimmed hole in it, and even a grey scorch of powder around that. But when he examined his chest, there was no hole and no blood, only a pronounced soreness over the ribs. From his breast pocket he drew out the metal plaque with the *vêver* of Erzulie. The bullet had scarred and bent it, but it had struck at an angle and glanced off without even scratching him, tearing another hole in the shirt under his arm.

The Saint gazed at the twisted piece of tin with an uncanny tingle feathering his spine.

Sibao must have known he was unhurt when she touched him. Yet she seemed to have kept the knowledge to herself. Why?

He hoisted himself experimentally to his feet. He knew that he had first been drugged, then over that lowered resistance almost completed mesmerized; coming on top of that, the deadened impact of the bullet must have knocked him out, as a punch over the heart could knock out an already groggy boxer. But now all the effects seemed to have worn off together, leaving only a tender spot on his chest and an insignificant muzziness in his head. By his watch, he had been out for about two hours.

The house was full of the silence of emptiness. He went through a door to the kitchen, ran some water, and bathed his face. The only other sound there was the ticking of a cheap clock.

Netlord had said that only the two of them were in the house. And Netlord had gone—with Sibao.

Gone to something that everything in the Saint's philosophy must refuse to believe. But things had happened to himself already that night which he could only think of incredulously. And incredulity would not alter them, or make them less true.

He went back through the living room and out on to the front verandah. Ridge beyond ridge, the mysterious hills fell away from before him under a full yellow moon that dimmed the stars; and there was no jeep in the driveway at his feet.

The drums still pulsed through the night, but they were no longer scattered. They were gathered together, blending in unison and counterpoint, but the acoustical tricks of the mountains still masked their location. Their muttering swelled and receded with chance shifts of air, and the echoes of it came from all around the horizon, so that the whole world seemed to throb softly with it.

There was plenty of light for him to walk down to the Châtelet des Fleurs.

He found Atherton Lee and the waiter starting to put out the lights in the bar. The innkeeper looked at him in a rather startled way.

"Why—what happened?" Lee asked.

Simon sat up at the counter and lighted a cigarette.

"Pour me a Barbancourt," he said defensively, "and tell me why you think anything happened."

"Netlord brought the jeep back. He told me he'd taken you to the airport—you'd had some news which made you suddenly decide to catch the night plane to Miami, and you just had time to make it. He was coming back tomorrow to pick up your things and send them after you."

"Oh, that," said the Saint blandly. "When the plane came through, it turned out to have filled up at Ciudad Trujillo. I couldn't get on. So I changed my mind again. I ran into someone downtown who gave me a lift back."

He couldn't say: "Netlord thought he'd just murdered me, and he was laying the foundation for me to disappear without being missed." Somehow, it sounded so ridiculous, even with a bullet hole in his shirt. And if he were pressed for details, he would have to say: "He was trying to put some kind of hex on me, or make me a zombie." That would be assured of a great reception. And then the police would have to be brought in. Perhaps Haiti was the only country on earth where a policeman might feel obliged to listen seriously to such a story; but the police were still the police. And just at those times when most people automatically turn to the police, Simon Templar's instinct was to avoid them.

What would have to be settled now between him and Theron Netlord, he would settle himself, in his own way.

The waiter, closing windows and emptying ashtrays, was singing to himself under his breath:

"Moin pralé nan Sibao,
Chaché, chaché, lolé-o——"

"What's that?" Simon asked sharply.

"Just Haitian song, sir."

"What does it mean?"

"It mean, *I will go to Sibao*—that holy place in voodoo, sir. *I take oil for lamp,* it say. *If you eat food of Legba you will have to die.*

'Si ou mangé mangé Legba
Ti ga çon onà mouri, oui.
Moin pralé nan Sibao——' "

"After spending an evening with Netlord, you should know all about that," Atherton Lee said.

Simon downed his drink and stretched out a yawn.

"You're right. I've had enough of it for one night," he said. "I'd better let you go on closing up—I'm ready to hit the sack myself."

But he lay awake for a long time, stretched out on his bed in the moonlight. Was Theron Netlord merely insane, or was there even the most fantastic possibility that he might be able to make use of things that modern materialistic science did not understand? Would it work on Americans, in America? Simon remembered that one of the books he had read referred to a certain American evangelist as *un houngan insuffisamment instruit;* and it was a known fact that that man controlled property worth millions, and that his followers turned over all their earnings to him, for which he gave them only food, shelter, and sermons. Such things *had* happened, and were as unsatisfactory to explain away as flying saucers. . . .

The ceaseless mutter of the distant drums mocked him till he fell asleep.

"Si ou mangé mangé Legba
Ti ga çon onà mouri, oui!"

He awoke and still heard the song. The moonlight had given way to the grey light of dawn, and the first thing he was conscious of was a fragile unfamiliar stillness left void because the drums were at last silent. But the voice went on—a flat, lifeless, distorted voice that was nevertheless recognizable in a way that sent icy filaments crawling over his scalp.

"Moin pralé nan Sibao,
Moin pralé nan Sibao,
Moin pralé nan Sibao,
Chaché, chaché, lolé-o . . ."

His window overlooked the road that curved up past the inn, and he was there while the song still drifted up to it. The two of them stood directly beneath him—Netlord, and the slender black girl dressed all in white. The girl looked up and saw Simon, as if she had expected to. She raised one hand and solemnly made a pattern in the air, a shape that somehow blended the outlines of a heart and an ornate letter M, quickly and intricately, and her lips moved with it.

It was curiously like a benediction.

Then she turned to the man beside her, as she might have turned to a child.

"*Venez,*" she said.

The tycoon also looked up, before he obediently followed her. But there was no recognition, no expression at all, in the grey face that had once been so ruthless and domineering; and all at once Simon knew why Theron Netlord would be no problem to him or to anyone, any more.

THE PEACEMAKER

by Gardner Dozois

Roy had dreamed of the sea, as he often did. When he woke up that morning, the wind was sighing through the trees outside with a sound like the restless murmuring of surf, and for a moment he thought that he was home, back in the tidy brick house by the beach, with everything that had happened undone, and hope opened hotly inside him, like a wound.

"Mom?" he said. He sat up, straightening his legs, expecting his feet to touch the warm mass that was his dog Toby. Toby always slept curled at the foot of his bed, but already everything was breaking up and changing, slipping away, and he blinked through sleep-gummed eyes at the thin blue light coming in through the attic window, felt the hardness of the old Army cot under him, and realized that he wasn't home, that there was no home anymore, that for him there could never be a home again.

He pushed the blankets aside and stood up. It was bitterly cold in the big attic room—winter was dying hard, the most terrible winter he could remember—and the rough wood planing burned his feet like ice, but he couldn't stay in bed anymore, not now.

None of the other kids were awake yet; he threaded his way through the other cots—accidently bumping against one of them so that its occupant tossed and moaned and began to snore in a higher register—and groped through cavernous shadows to the single high window. He was just tall enough to reach it, if he stood on tiptoe. He forced the window open, the old wood of its frame groaning in protest, plaster dust puffing, and shivered as the cold dawn wind poured inward, hitting him in the face, tugging with ghostly fingers at his hair, sweeping past him to rush through the rest of the stuffy attic like a restless child set free to play.

The wind smelled of pine resin and wet earth, not of salt flats and tides, and the bird-sound that rode in on that wind was the burbling of wrens and the squawking of bluejays, not the raucous shrieking of seagulls . . . but even so, as he braced his elbows against the window frame and strained up to look out, his mind still full of the broken fragments of dreams, he half-expected to see the ocean below, stretched out to the horizon, sending patient wavelets to lap against the side of the house. Instead he saw the nearby trees holding silhouetted arms up against the graying sky, the barn and the farmyard, all still lost in shadow, the surrounding fields, the weathered macadam line of the road, the forested hills rolling away into distance. Silver mist lay in pockets of low ground, retreated in wraithlike streamers up along the ridges.

Not yet. The sea had not chased him here—yet.

Somewhere out there to the east, still invisible, were the mountains, and just beyond those mountains was the sea that he had dreamed of, lapping quietly at the dusty Pennsylvania hill towns, coal towns, that were now, suddenly, seaports. There the Atlantic waited, held at bay, momentarily at least, by the humpbacked wall of the Appalachians, still perhaps forty miles from here, although closer now by leagues of swallowed land and drowned cities than it had been only three years before.

He had been down by the seawall that long-ago morning, playing some forgotten game, watching the waves move in slow oily swells, like some heavy, dull metal in liquid form, watching the tide come in . . . and come in . . . and come *in*. . . . He had been excited at first, as the sea crept in, way above the high-tide line, higher than he had ever seen it before, and then, as the sea swallowed the beach entirely and began to lap patiently against the base of the seawall, he had become uneasy, and *then*, as the sea continued to rise up toward the top of the seawall itself, he had begun to be afraid. . . . The sea had just kept coming in, rising slowly and inexorably, swallowing the land at a slow walking pace, never stopping, always coming *in*, always rising higher. . . . By the time the sea had swallowed the top of the seawall and begun to creep up the short grassy slope toward his house, sending glassy fingers probing almost to his feet, he had started to scream, and as the first thin sheet of water rippled up to soak his sneakers, he had whirled and run frantically up the slope, screaming hysterically for his parents, and the sea had followed patiently at his heels. . . .

A "marine transgression," the scientists called it. Ordinary people called it, inevitably, the Flood. Whatever you called it, it had washed away the old world forever. Scientists had been talking about the possibility of such a thing for years—some of them even pointing out that it was already as warm as it had been at the peak of the last interglacial, and getting warmer—but few had suspected just how *fast* the Antarctic ice could melt. Many times during those chaotic weeks, one scientific King Canute or another had predicted that the worst was over, that the tide would rise this high and no higher . . . but each time the sea had come inexorably on, pushing miles and miles further inland with each successive high-tide, rising almost 300 feet in the course of one disastrous summer, drowning lowlands around the globe until there *were* no lowlands anymore. In the United States alone, the sea had swallowed most of the East Coast east of the Appalachians, the West Coast west of the Sierras and the Cascades, much of Alaska and Hawaii, Florida, the Gulf Coast, East Texas, taken a big wide scoop out of the lowlands of the Mississippi Valley, thin fingers of water penetrating north to Iowa and Illinois, and caused the St. Lawrence and the Great Lakes to overflow and drown their shorelines. The Green Mountains, the White Mountains, the Adirondacks, the Poconos and the Catskills, the Ozarks, the Pacific Coast Ranges—all had been transformed to archipelagos, surrounded by the invading sea.

The funny thing was . . . that as the sea pursued them relentlessly inland, pushing them from one temporary refuge to another, he had been unable to shake the feeling that *he* had caused the Flood: that he had done something that day while playing atop the seawall, inadvertently stumbled on some magic ritual, some chance combination of gesture and word that had untied the bonds of the sea and sent it sliding up over the land . . . that it was chasing *him*, personally. . . .

A dog was barking out there now, somewhere out across the fields toward town, but it was not *his* dog. His dog was dead, long since dead, and its whitening skull was rolling along the ocean floor with the tides that washed over what had once been Brigantine, New Jersey, three hundred feet down.

Suddenly he was covered with gooseflesh, and he shivered, rubbing his hands over his bare arms. He returned to his cot and dressed hurriedly—no point in trying to go back to bed, Sara would be up to kick them all out of the sack in a minute or two anyway. The day had begun; he would think no further ahead than that. He had learned in the refugee camps to take life one second at a time.

As he moved around the room, he thought that he could feel hostile eyes watching him from some of the other bunks. It was much colder in here now that he had opened the window, and he had inevitably made a certain amount of noise getting dressed, but although they all valued every second of sleep they could scrounge, none of the other kids would dare to complain. The thought was bittersweet, bringing both pleasure and pain, and he smiled at it, a thin, brittle smile that was almost a grimace. No, they would watch sullenly from their bunks, and pretend to be asleep, and curse him under their breath, but they would say nothing to anyone about it. Certainly they would say nothing to *him.*

He went down through the still-silent house like a ghost, and out across the farmyard, through fugitive streamers of mist that wrapped clammy white arms around him and beaded his face with dew. His uncle Abner was there at the slit-trench before him. Abner grunted a greeting, and they stood pissing side by side for a moment in companionable silence, their urine steaming in the gray morning air.

Abner stepped backward and began to button his pants. "You start playin' with yourself yet, boy?" he said, not looking at Roy.

Roy felt his face flush. "No," he said, trying not to stammer, "no sir."

"You growin' hair already," Abner said. He swung himself slowly around to face Roy, as if his body was some ponderous machine that could only be moved and aimed by the use of pulleys and levers. The hard morning light made his face look harsh as stone, but also sallow and old. Tired, Roy thought. Unutterably weary, as though it took almost more effort than he could sustain just to stand there. Worn out, like the overtaxed fields around them. Only the eyes were alive in the eroded face; they were hard and merciless as flint, and they looked at you as if they were looking right through you to some distant thing that nobody else could see. "I've tried to explain to you about remaining pure," Abner said, speaking slowly. "About how important it is for you to keep yourself pure, not to let yourself be sullied in any way. I've tried to explain that, I hope you could understand—"

"Yes, sir," Roy said.

Abner made a groping hesitant motion with his hand, fingers spread wide, as though he were trying to sculpt meaning from the air itself. "I mean—it's important that you understand, Roy. Everything has to be *right.* I mean, everything's got to be just . . . *right* . . . or nothing else will mean anything. You got to be right in your *soul,* boy. You got to let the Peace of God into your soul. It all depends on *you* now—you got to let that Peace inside yourself, no one can do it for you. And it's so important . . ."

"Yes, sir," Roy said quietly, "I understand."

"I wish . . ." Abner said, and fell silent. They stood there for a minute, not speaking, not looking at each other. There was woodsmoke in the air now, and they heard a door slam somewhere on the far side of the house. They had instinctively been looking out across the open land to the east, and now, as they watched, the sun rose above the mountains, splitting the plum-and-ash sky open horizontally with a long wedge of red, distinguishing the rolling horizon from the lowering clouds. A lance of bright white sunlight hit their eyes, thrusting straight in at them from the edge of the world.

"You're going to make us proud, boy, I know it," Abner said, but Roy ignored him, watching in fascination as the molten disk of the sun floated free of the horizon-line, squinting against the dazzle until his eyes watered and his sight blurred. Abner put his hand on the boy's shoulder. The hand felt heavy and hot, proprietary, and Roy shook it loose in annoyance, still not looking away from the horizon. Abner sighed, started to say something, thought better of it, and instead said, "Come on in the house, boy, and let's get some breakfast inside you."

Breakfast—when they finally did get to sit down to it, after the usual rambling grace and invocation by Abner—proved to be unusually lavish. For the brethren, there were hickory-nut biscuits, and honey, and cups of chicory, and even the other refugee kids—who on occasion during the long bitter winter had been fed as close to nothing at all as law and appearances would allow—got a few slices of fried fatback along with their habitual cornmeal mush. Along with his biscuits and honey, Roy got wild turkey eggs, Indian potatoes, and a real pork chop. There was a good deal of tension around the big table that morning: Henry and Luke were stern-faced and tense, Raymond was moody and preoccupied, Albert actually looked frightened; the refugee kids were round-eyed and silent, doing their best to make themselves invisible; the jolly Mrs. Crammer was as jolly as ever, shoveling her food in with gusto, but the grumpy Mrs. Zeigler, who was feared and disliked by all the kids, had obviously been crying, and ate little or nothing; Abner's face was set like rock, his eyes were hard and bright, and he looked from one to another of the brethren, as if daring them to question his leadership and spiritual guidance. Roy ate with good appetite, unperturbed by the emotional convection currents that were swirling around him, calmly but deliberately concentrating on mopping up every morsel of food on his plate—in the last couple of months he had put back some of the weight he had lost, although by the old standards, the ones his Mom would have applied four years ago, he was still painfully thin. At the end of the meal, Mrs. Reardon came in from the kitchen and, beaming with the well-justified pride of someone who is about to do the impossible, presented Roy with a small, rectangular object wrapped in shiny brown paper. He was startled for a second, but yes, by God, it *was:* a Hershey bar, the first one he'd seen in years. A black market item, of course, difficult to get hold of in the impoverished East these days, and probably expensive as hell. Even some of the brethren were looking at him enviously now, and the refugee kids were frankly gaping. As he picked up the Hershey bar and slowly and caressingly peeled the wrapped back, exposing the pale chocolate beneath, one of the other kids actually began to drool.

After breakfast, the other refugee kids—"wetbacks," the townspeople sometimes called them, with elaborate irony—were divided into two groups. One group would help the brethren work Abner's farm that day, while the larger group would be loaded onto an ox-drawn dray (actually an old flatbed truck, with the cab knocked off) and sent out around the countryside to do what pretty much amounted to slave labor: road work, heavy farm work, helping with the quarrying or the timbering, rebuilding houses and barns and bridges damaged or destroyed in the chaotic days after the Flood. The federal government—or what was left of the federal government, trying desperately, and not always successfully, to keep a battered and Balkanizing country from flying completely apart, struggling to put the Humpty Dumpty that was America back together again—the federal government paid Abner (and others like him) a yearly allowance in federal scrip or promise-of-merchandise notes for giving room and board to refugees from the drowned lands . . . but times being as tough as they were, no one was going to complain if Abner also helped ease the burden of their upkeep by hiring them out locally to work for whomever could come up with the scrip, or sufficient barter goods, or an attractive work-swap offer; what was left of the state and town governments also used them on occasion (and the others like them, adult or child), gratis, for work-projects "for the common good, during this time of emergency . . ."

Sometimes, hanging around the farm with little or nothing to do, Roy almost missed going out on the work-crews, but only almost: he remembered too well the back-breaking labor performed on scanty rations . . . the sickness, the accidents, the staggering fatigue . . . the blazing sun and the swarms of mosquitoes in summer, the bitter cold in winter, the snow, the icy wind . . . He watched the dray go by, seeing the envious and resentful faces of kids he had once worked beside—Stevie, Enrique, Sal—turn toward him as it passed, and, reflexively, he opened and closed his hands. Even two months of idleness and relative luxury had not softened the thick and roughened layers of callus that were the legacy of several seasons spent on the crews. . . . No, boredom was infinitely preferable.

By mid-morning, a small crowd of people had gathered in the road outside the farmhouse. It was hotter now; you could smell the promise of summer in the air, in the wind, and the sun that beat down out of a cloudless blue sky had a real sting to it. It must have been uncomfortable out there in the open, under that sun, but the crowd made no attempt to approach—they just stood there on the far side of the road and watched the house, shuffling their feet, occasionally muttering to each other in voices that, across the road, were audible only as a low wordless grumbling.

Roy watched them for a while from the porch door;

they were townspeople, most of them vaguely familiar to Roy, although none of them belonged to Abner's sect, and he knew none of them by name. The refugee kids saw little of the townspeople, being kept carefully segregated for the most part. The few times that Roy had gotten into town he had been treated with icy hostility—and God help the wetback kid who was caught by the town kids on a deserted stretch of road! For that matter, even the brethren tended to keep to themselves, and were snubbed by certain segments of town society, although the sect had increased its numbers dramatically in recent years, nearly tripling in strength during the past winter alone; there were new chapters now in several of the surrounding communities.

A gaunt-faced woman in the crowd outside spotted Roy, and shook a thin fist at him. "Heretic!" she shouted. "Blasphemer!" The rest of the crowd began to buzz ominously, like a huge angry bee. She spat at Roy, her face contorting and her shoulders heaving with the ferocity of her effort, although she must have known that the spittle had no chance of reaching him. "Blasphemer!" she shouted again. The veins stood out like cords in her scrawny neck.

Roy stepped back into the house, but continued to watch from behind the curtained front windows. There was shouting inside the house as well as outside—the brethren had been cloistered in the kitchen for most of the morning, arguing, and the sound and ferocity of their argument carried clearly through the thin plaster walls of the crumbling old house. At last the sliding door to the kitchen slammed open, and Mrs. Zeigler strode out into the parlor, accompanied by her two children and her scrawny, pasty-faced husband, and followed by two other families of brethren—about nine people altogether. Most of them were carrying suitcases, and a few had backpacks and bindles. Abner stood in the kitchen doorway and watched them go, his anger evident only in the whiteness of his knuckles as he grasped the doorframe. "*Go*, then," Abner said scornfully. "We spit you up out of our mouths! Don't ever think to come back!" He swayed in the doorway, his voice tremulous with hate. "We're better off without you, you hear? You *hear* me? We don't *need* the weak-willed and the short-sighted."

Mrs. Zeigler said nothing, and her steps didn't slow or falter, but her homely hatchet-face was streaked with tears. To Roy's astonishment—for she had a reputation as a harridan—she stopped near the porch door and threw her arms around him. "Come with us," she said, hugging him with smothering tightness, "Roy, *please* come with us! You can, you know—we'll find a place for you, everything will work out fine." Roy said nothing, resisting the impulse to squirm—he was uncomfortable in her embrace; in spite of himself, it touched some sleeping corner of his soul he had thought was safely bricked-over years before, and for a moment he felt trapped and panicky, unable to breathe, as though he were in sudden danger of waking from a comfortable dream into a far more terrible and less desirable reality. "Come *with* us," Mrs. Zeigler said again, more urgently, but Roy shook his head gently and pulled away from her. "You're a goddamned fool then!" she blazed, suddenly angry, her voice ringing harsh and loud, but Roy only shrugged, and gave her his wistful, ghostly smile. "Damn it—" she started to say, but her eyes filled with tears again, and she whirled and hurried out of the house, followed by the other members of her party. The children—wetbacks were kept pretty much segregated from the children of the brethren as well, and he had seen some of these kids only at meals—looked at Roy with wide, frightened eyes as they passed.

Abner was staring at Roy now, from across the room; it was a hard and challenging stare, but there was also a trace of desperation in it, and in that moment Abner seemed uncertain and oddly vulnerable. Roy stared back at him serenely, unblinkingly meeting his eyes, and after a while some of the tension went out of Abner, and he turned and stumbled out of the room, listing to one side like a church steeple in the wind.

Outside, the crowd began to buzz again as Mrs. Zeigler's party filed out of the house and across the road. There was much discussion and arm-waving and head-shaking when the two groups met, someone occasionally gesturing back toward the farmhouse. The buzzing grew louder, then gradually died away. At last, Mrs. Zeigler and her group set off down the road for town, accompanied by some of the locals. They trudged away dispiritedly down the center of the dusty road, lugging their shabby suitcases, only a few of them looking back.

Roy watched them until they were out of sight, his face still and calm, and continued to stare down the road after them long after they were gone.

About noon, a carload of reporters arrived outside, driving up in one of the bulky new methane-burners that were still rarely seen east of Omaha. They circulated through the crowd of townspeople, pausing briefly to take photographs and ask questions, working their way toward the house, and Roy watched them as if they were unicorns, strange remnants from some vanished cycle of creation. Most of the reporters were probably from State College or the new state capital at Altoona—places where a few small newspapers were again being produced—but one of them was wearing an armband that identified him as a bureau man for one of the big Denver papers, and that was probably where the money for the car had come from. It was strange to be reminded that there were still areas of the country that were . . . not unchanged, no place in the world could claim that . . . and not rich, not by the old standards of affluence anyway . . . but, at any rate, better off than *here*. The whole western part of the country—from roughly the 95th meridian on west to approximately the 122nd—had been untouched by the flooding, and although the west had also suffered severely from the collapse of the national economy and the consequential social upheavals, at least much of their industrial base had remained intact. Denver—one of the few large American cities built on ground high enough to have been safe from the rising waters—was the new federal capital, and, if poorer and meaner, it was also bigger and busier than ever.

Abner went out to herd the reporters inside and away from the unbelievers, and after a moment or two Roy could hear Abner's voice going out there, booming like a church organ. By the time the reporters came in, Roy was sitting at the dining room table, flanked by Raymond and Aaron, waiting for them.

They took photographs of him sitting there, while he stared calmly back at them, and they took photographs of him while he politely refused to answer questions, and then Aaron handed him the pre-prepared papers, and he signed them, and repeated the legal formulas that Aaron had taught him, and they took photographs of that too. And then—able to get nothing more out of him, and made slightly uneasy by his blank composure and the remoteness of his eyes—they left.

Within a few more minutes, as though everything were over, as though the departure of the reporters had drained all possible significance from anything else that might still happen, most of the crowd outside had drifted away also, only one or two people remaining behind to stand quietly waiting, like vultures, in the once-again empty road.

Lunch was a quiet meal. Roy ate heartily, taking seconds of everything, and Mrs. Crammer was as jovial as ever, but everyone else was subdued, and even Abner seemed shaken by the schism that had just sundered his church. After the meal, Abner stood up and began to pray aloud. The brethren sat resignedly at the table, heads partially bowed, some listening, some not. Abner was holding his arms up toward the big blackened rafters of the ceiling, sweat runneling his face, when Peter came hurriedly in from outside and stood hesitating in the doorway, trying to catch Abner's eye. When it became obvious that Abner was going to keep right on ignoring him, Peter shrugged, and said in a loud flat voice, "Abner, the sheriff is here."

Abner stopped praying. He grunted, a hoarse, exhausted sound, the kind of sound a baited bear might make when, already pushed beyond the limits of endurance, someone jabs it yet again with a spear. He slowly lowered his arms and was still for a long moment, and then he shuddered, seeming to shake himself back to life. He glanced speculatively—and, it almost seemed, beseechingly—at Roy, and then straightened his shoulders and strode from the room.

They received the sheriff in the parlor, Raymond and Aaron and Mrs. Crammer sitting in the battered old armchairs, Roy sitting unobtrusively to one side on the stool from a piano that no longer worked, Abner standing a little to the fore with his arms locked behind him and his boots planted solidly on the oak planking, as if he were on the bridge of a schooner that was heading into a gale. County Sheriff Sam Braddock glanced at the others—his gaze lingering on Roy for a moment—and then ignored them, addressing himself to Abner as if they were alone in the room. "Mornin', Abner," he said.

"Mornin', Sam," Abner said quietly. "You here for some reason other than just t'say hello, I suppose."

Braddock grunted. He was a short, stocky, grizzled man with iron-gray hair and a tired face. His uniform was shiny and old and patched in a dozen places, but clean, and the huge old revolver strapped to his hip looked worn but serviceable. He fidgeted with his shapeless old hat, turning it around and around in his fingers—he was obviously embarrassed, but he was determined as well, and at last he said, "The thing of it is, Abner, I'm here to talk you out of this damned tomfoolery."

"Are you, now?" Abner said.

"We'll do whatever we damn well want to do—" Raymond burst out, shrilly, but Abner waved him to silence. Braddock glanced lazily at Raymond, then looked back at Abner, his tired old face settling into harder lines. "I'm not going to allow it," he said, more harshly. "We don't want this kind of thing going on in this county."

Abner said nothing.

"There's not a thing you can do about it, sheriff," Aaron said, speaking a bit heatedly, but keeping his melodious voice well under control. "It's all perfectly legal, all the way down the line."

"Well, now," Braddock said, "I don't know about that . . ."

"Well, I *do* know, sheriff," Aaron said calmly. "As a legally sanctioned and recognized church, we are protected by law all the way down the line. There is ample precedent, most of it recent, most of it upheld by appellate decisions within the last year: Carlton *versus* the State of Vermont, Trenholm *versus* the State of West Virginia, the Church of Souls *versus* the State of New York. There was that case up in Tylersville, just last year. Why, the Freedom of Worship Act *alone* . . ."

Braddock sighed, tacitly admitting that he knew Aaron was right—perhaps he had hoped to bluff them into obeying. "The 'Flood Congress' of '93," Braddock said, with bitter contempt. "They were so goddamned panic-stricken and full of sick chatter about Armageddon that you could've rammed *any* nonsense down their throats. That's a bad law, a pisspoor law . . ."

"Be that as it may, sheriff, you have no authority whatsoever—"

Abner suddenly began to speak, talking with a slow heavy deliberateness, musingly, almost reminiscently, ignoring the conversation he was interrupting—and indeed, perhaps he had not even been listening to it. "My grandfather lived right here on this farm, and *his* father before him—you know that, Sam? *They* lived by the old ways, and they survived and prospered. Greatgranddad, there wasn't hardly anything he needed from the outside world, anything he needed to *buy*, except maybe nails and suchlike, and he could've made them himself too, if he'd needed to. Everything they needed, everything they ate, or wore, or used, they got from the woods, or from out of the soil of this farm, right here. *We* don't know how to do that anymore. We forgot the old ways, we turned our faces away, which is why the Flood came on us as a Judgement, a Judgement and a scourge, a scouring, a winnowing. The Old Days have come back again, and we've forgotten so goddamned *much*, we're almost helpless now that there's no goddamned Kmart down the goddamned street. We've got to go back to the old ways, or we'll pass from the earth, and be seen no more in it . . ." He was sweating now, staring earnestly at Braddock, as if to compel him by force of will alone to share the vision. "But it's so *hard*, Sam. . . . We have to *work* at relearning the old ways, we have to reinvent them as we go, step by step . . ."

"Some things we were better off without," Braddock said grimly.

"Up at Tylersville, they *doubled* their yield last harvest. Think what that could mean to a county as hungry as this one has been—"

Braddock shook his iron-gray head, and held up one hand, as if he were directing traffic. "I'm telling you, Abner, the town won't stand for this—I'm bound to warn you that some of the boys just might decide to go outside the law to deal with this thing." He paused. "And, unofficially of course, I just might be inclined to give them a hand . . ."

Mrs. Crammer laughed. She had been sitting quietly and taking all of this in, smiling good-naturedly from time to time, and her laugh was a shocking thing in that stuffy little room, harsh as a crow's caw. "You'll do *nothing*, Sam Braddock," she said jovially. "And neither will anybody else. More than half the county's with us already, nearly all the country folk, and a good part of the town, too." She smiled pleasantly at him, but her eyes were small and hard. "Just you remember, we *know* where *you* live, Sam Braddock. And we know where your sister lives, too, and your sister's child, over to Framington . . ."

"Are you threatening an officer of the law?" Braddock said, but he said it in a weak voice, and his face, when he turned it away to stare at the floor, looked sick and old. Mrs. Crammer laughed again, and then there was silence.

Braddock kept his face turned down for another long moment, and then he put his hat back on, squashing it down firmly on his head, and when he looked up he pointedly ignored the brethren and addressed his next remark to Roy. "You don't have to stay with these people, son," he said. "*That's* the law, too." He kept his eyes fixed steadily on Roy. "You just say the word, son, and I'll take you straight out of here, right now." His jaw was set, and he touched the butt of his revolver, as if for encouragement. "They can't stop us. How about it?"

"No, thank you," Roy said quietly. "I'll stay."

That night, while Abner wrung his hands and prayed aloud, Roy sat half-dozing before the parlor fire, unconcerned, watching the firelight throw Abner's gesticulating shadow across the whitewashed walls. There was something in the wine they kept giving him, Roy knew, maybe somebody's saved-up Quāāludes, but he didn't need it. Abner kept exhorting him to let the Peace of God into his heart, but he didn't need that either. He didn't need anything. He felt calm and self-possessed and remote, disassociated from everything that went on around him, as if he were looking down on the world through the wrong end of a telescope, feeling only a mild scientific interest as he watched the tiny mannequins swirl and pirouette. . . . Like watching television with the sound off. If this was the Peace of God, it had settled down on him months ago, during the dead of that terrible winter, while he had struggled twelve hours a day to load foundation-stone in the face of icestorms and the razoring wind, while they had all, wetbacks and brethren alike, come close to starving. About the same time that word of the goings-on at Tylersville had started to seep down from the brethren's parent church upstate, about the same time that Abner, who until then had totally ignored their kinship, had begun to talk to him in the evenings about the old ways. . . .

Although perhaps the great dead cold had started to settle in even earlier, that first day of the new world, while they were driving off across foundering Brigantine, the water already up over the hubcaps of the Toyota, and he had heard Toby barking frantically somewhere behind them. . . . His dad had died that day, died of a heart-attack as he fought to get them onto an overloaded boat that would take them across to the "safety" of the New Jersey mainland. His mother had died months later in one of the sprawling refugee camps, called "Floodtowns," that had sprung up on high ground everywhere along the new coastlines. She had just given up—sat down in the mud, rested her head on her knees, closed her eyes, and died. Just like that. Roy had seen the phenomenon countless times in the Floodtowns, places so festeringly horrible that even life on Abner's farm, with its

Dickensian bleakness, forced labor, and short rations, had seemed—and was—a distinct change for the better. It was odd, and wrong, and sometimes it bothered him a little, but he hardly ever thought of his mother and father anymore—it was as if his mind shut itself off every time he came to those memories, he had never even cried for them, but all he had to do was close his eyes and he could see Toby, or his cat Basil running toward him and meowing with his tail held up over his back like a flag, and grief would come up like black bile at the back of his throat. . . .

It was still dark when they left the farmhouse. Roy and Abner and Aaron walked together, Abner carrying a large tattered carpetbag. Hank and Raymond ranged ahead with shotguns, in case there was trouble, but the last of the afternoon's gawkers had been driven off hours before by the cold, and the road was empty, a dim charcoal line through the slowly-lightening darkness. No one spoke, and there was no sound other than the sound of boots crunching on gravel. It was chilly again that morning, and Roy's bare feet burned against the macadam, but he trudged along stoically, ignoring the bite of cinders and pebbles. Their breath steamed faintly against the paling stars. The fields stretched dark and formless around them to either side of the road, and once they heard the rustling of some unseen animal fleeing away from them through the stubble. Mist flowed slowly down the road to meet them, sending out gleaming silver fingers to curl around their legs.

The sky was graying to the east, where the sea slept behind the mountains. Roy could imagine the sea rising higher and higher until it found its patient way around the roots of the hills and came spilling into the tableland beyond, flowing steadily forward like the mist, spreading out into a placid sheet of water that slowly swallowed the town, the farmhouse, the fields, until only the highest branches of the trees remained, held up like the beckoning arms of the drowned, and then they too would slide slowly, peacefully beneath the water. . . .

A bird was crying out now, somewhere in the darkness, and they were walking through the fields, away from the road, cold mud squelching underfoot, the dry stubble crackling around them. Soon it would be time to sow the spring wheat, and after that, the corn. . . .

They stopped. Wind sighed through the dawn, muttering in the throat of the world. Still no one had spoken. Then hands were helping him remove the old bathrobe he'd been wearing. . . . Before leaving the house, he had been bathed, and annointed with a thick fragrant oil, and with a tiny silver scissors Mrs. Reardon had clipped a lock of his hair for each of the brethren.

Suddenly he was naked, and he was being urged forward again, his feet stumbling and slow.

They had made a wide ring of automobile flares here, the flares spitting and sizzling luridly in the wan dawn light, and in the center of the ring, they had dug a hollow in the ground.

He lay down in the hollow, feeling his naked back and buttocks settle into the cold mud, feeling it mat the hair on the back of his head. The mud made little sucking noises as he moved his arms and legs, settling in, and then he stretched out and lay still. The dawn breeze was cold, and he shivered in the mud, feeling it take hold of him like a giant's hand, tightening around him, pulling him down with a grip old and cold and strong. . . .

They gathered around him, seeming, from his low perspective, to tower miles into the sky. Their faces were harsh and angular, gouged with lines and shadows that made them look like something from a stark old woodcut. Abner bent down to rummage in the carpetbag, his harsh woodcut face close to Roy's for a moment, and when he straightened up again he had the big fine-honed hunting knife in his hand.

Abner began to speak now, groaning out the words in a loud, harsh voice, but Roy was no longer listening. He watched calmly as Abner lifted the knife high into the air, and then he turned his head to look east, as if he could somehow see across all the intervening miles of rock and farmland and forest to where the sea waited behind the mountains. . . .

Is this enough? he thought disjointedly, ignoring the towering scarecrow figures that were swaying in closer over him, straining his eyes to look east, to where the Presence lived . . . speaking now only to that Presence, to the sea, to that vast remorseless deity, bargaining with it cannily, hopefully, shrewdly, like a country housewife at market, proffering it the fine rich red gift of his death. Is this enough? Will this do?

Will you stop now?

THE LEGEND OF GRAY MOUNTAIN

by Emily Katharine Harris

Two men stood by a fence in the pasture. It was hot but a breeze blew up from the valley below them and the leaves on the birch groves glittered in the sun.

The old man grasped the rail fence and shook it to see if it was firm; it proved loose and unsteady. But his attention wandered and his eye took in the rough pasture below; he appeared very worried. The young man with him, holding an axe, also watched the valley below and turned and scanned the slopes above where the beech and spruce woods met the pasture. Sweat stood out on his forehead.

"How do you know it's today?" he asked the old man.

"Kate told me," the old man said. He was stooped but his shoulders were solid and powerful; his white hair was plentiful and grew close to his handsome head. He wore steel-rimmed glasses and his muscular face bore the look of one who had endured much. He wore a blue shirt and shapeless brown trousers over a big frame; his shoes were heavy and dusty, planted on the singed coarse pasture grass. "Why'd you bring that axe?" he asked the young man.

Elihu did not answer but dropped the head of the axe to his feet and looked down at it, embarrassed.

"You think the old women'd get you?" the old man asked him with a bit of a smile. He stopped smiling. "They're not concerned with you." He waved away a swarm of gnats absently.

Around the two men was a New England scene of beauty, rugged and lonely in the sun. They stood on the side of a large mountain whose rock top was just visible above the woods. Beside them and below stretched a long upland valley in the soft varied colors of ripening late August; dark blue cloud shadows spotted the yellow and rose fields, the blue-green woods rising and dipping down to where the streams ran, the swelling mountain range across the valley from them where Burn Mountain, Hartshorn, Tappan and Old Snow rose at first gently, then steeply to flattened rock summits where the light played in ochre, pinks and flashing white. Long and intense blue, Ash Pond lay like a fish along the center of the valley. Beside it could be seen glimpses of the dirt road that led to Whippen, whose sparse houses were just visible below the rocky, steep pastures and black spruces beside them; all of the houses were gray with sharp square lines made clear by the morning sun.

It was nine o'clock.

"Say, Dana," Elihu said, turning to look suddenly at the other man. "Will your wife be here?"

"Yes, she will." Dana briefly examined the back of his hand and looked across at Old Snow. "They'll all come; it can't be stopped."

"Do they like—to be—watched?" Elihu asked. He was only nineteen and looked uneasy. He licked his lips and ran his hand under his nose swiftly.

"I brought you up here to see this because I had to come and I durst not to come alone, if you want to know," Dana said. "No, no one's been up to watch before, don't know why. It's going to be the end of Kate, and that's the end of me. No one ever lived through one of these things.'' He looked every bit of his seventy-five years and, in the bright morning light, pale and ill. Two brilliant drops of water stood briefly in his small, bright blue eyes; he cleared his throat and leaned on the gray fence; his big hand plucked at the lichens growing there. ''It won't take long, as I remember,'' he added. ''An hour, maybe.'' His voice was faint and husky.

''Why don't you stop it? Why don't we all stop it?'' Elihu demanded. His uncut brown hair hung into his anxious eyes. ''I don't like this. I hate it.''

''Look,'' Dana said. ''It's always been this way. Every time there's a new crop of old ones, they do this. It's in them, I don't know why.'' A crow flew across the pasture below them, blue-black and deliberate. He lit on the top of a small spruce. ''Tand and Whippen, they never mixed. See, Tand, being over Gray Mountain here, is our nearest neighbour. But folks never get along in the two towns, and, funny thing, I don't know and you don't know and nobody knows what started the women doing this but they have gone at it since the first settling here, a long, long time ago. Something starts it—it's always in the summer, though—and from what I hear this time the thing that set them off was a woman over from Tand spat on Bettsey Loveless. Spat on her. Men don't do that.'' Dana looked at Elihu and gave out with a mirthless laugh. ''Might's well set down,'' he said, looking blankly around him. He lowered himself to the ground.

Elihu stood, however, tensely, and again scanned the valley and the pasture above where dense clumps of spruce in various sizes grew strongly, quivering in the breeze. His hollow chest and thin cheeks contrasted with Dana's solid build; he looked as if he were at bay.

''I sure don't want to be here,'' he said, looking off. Then he said, ''I see someone.''

Dana got to his feet and looked down the hill. Climbing steadily though slowly came a thin figure in black. She was carrying a sickle and every so often swung at the hardhack of bullbriars as she passed them. She did it with sureness although she was brittle and must have been eighty. Occasionally she disappeared from sight behind the big puddingstone boulders scattered through the field.

She could not see the men hidden behind the fallen, huge trunk of a blasted maple.

"Tirzah Williams," Dana said, squinting down at her progress. "Alone."

The old woman, her long white hair done high in a blown bun, had the rounded narrow back of the very old; tiny wrists stuck out from the shrunken black sleeves of her shapeless dress. When she came to the biggest boulder she stopped and looked up the pasture towards the woods.

"Looking for them," Dana commented, his lips dry.

"Where's all the men?" Elihu asked. Again he said, "Why don't they stop them? Why don't *we* stop them?" he repeated desperately, looking at Dana with huge reproach.

"You don't understand, boy," Dana said tiredly. "Around here it's what they do. They're brought up knowing about it and they, well, they like it. How can you talk some woman out of doing what she likes?" They looked over at the old woman. She was sitting awkwardly at the foot of the boulder, looking alertly down the mountain.

"There's someone else," Elihu whispered. Past a birch grove there appeared two figures laboring up the slope; one was a vastly fat old woman in lavender who was trying to help an aged hunchback a foot and a half shorter than herself. The fat one carried a hoe and the cripple a kitchen knife.

"My God, even Dora Swope," Dana said, peering. "With Millie. Millie Grinnell. They aren't friends; at least they never was." The large woman in lavender was pointing up the mountain. "Guess Dora can't see over the bushes," he added.

"Mrs. Letts has been in bed for twelve years," Elihu said. "Do you think she'll come?"

"They'll all be here," Dana said wearily. "They all always make it, somehow; they help each other; they get excited about it and rise right up and get up to this pasture—seems like they build right up to hating so's they can't hardly wait to come up here like this. Funny thing, they never come here except for this. Peacock's Pasture.

Best pasture this side of the valley." A late thrush sounded near by and another answered him farther off. It was a perfect day.

More figures were appearing at the bottom of the pasture. Five old women climbed into view.

"Good thing you haven't got no grandma," Dana said. "She'd be coming up here too." He stared down at the approaching group. "Serena Watts. Margaret Pew, Lily Gates, Amanda Buck." He was looking for his wife. "And Coritha Lewis; she's been down sick, like to die this week," he added. "Look at her climb. Made the best rhubarb pie."

The three who were already at the boulder watched the others come but no sign was exchanged. The old women did not talk. Lily Gates had a shawl wrapped around her shoulders but she carried a chunk of firewood thicker than a big man's arm. A tall, bent old woman with black hair had two kitchen knives. The others carried a scythe, a cross-cut saw blade, a hammer.

"Where are the other men?" Elihu asked desperately.

"I don't know," Dana shook his head. "Down there, watching 'em leave, I guess. Watching 'em go." He stiffened. "There's Kate," he said tensely. "By the great Lord, there's Kate." He leaned heavily on the hard, solid old bole of the fallen maple. "She used to tell me she'd never do this."

Alone, wearing white, a slim old woman stood below them looking up at the group around the boulder.

"She's got my axe," Dana said. "Well, at least she picked something better than a chunk of wood." He watched his wife's slow progress up the hill. At last she was near.

"Go out and talk to her," Elihu urged Dana.

"I have talked to her," Dana said, his huge hands gripping a dead branch of the tree. "Just this morning she made my breakfast and said she wouldn't come. She's older than me," he added irrelevantly.

Behind Kate came a crowd, short, medium, tall, wearing pink, blue, brown, purple, armed with assorted weapons to be found in the farmyards. On all the old faces was a common look of determined hatred.

"Who told them when to come?" Elihu asked. "How do they all get up here at the same time?"

"I don't know. One of them tells another, I guess. There is no leader. Except I think Bettsey Loveless stirred them up, finally," Dana said. "Yes, I think it was Bettsey. But I don't see her." He looked at the gathering of, now, about twenty-five old women. "Yes, there she comes, White as a sheet, that one," he said, watching a squat woman climb. "Guess they're all there except Mrs. Letts—and Joanna Whipple I don't see."

"How do the Tand women know about coming over the mountain?" Elihu asked. His shirt was soaked with perspiration.

"That I don't know either," Dana said. His eyes were fixed in agony on his wife. "Fried fish we had, and muffins," he recollected softly. "Who would have thought it." He watched the white figure of his wife sitting alone in the shade of the big boulder. She was looking up the pasture towards the woods. He saw her get up. Looking himself up the mountain he saw a group of old women jerkily emerging from the black woods and descending the pasture. "Look," he said.

"Now they'll fight, won't they," Elihu said, his hand closing around the axe handle. "What'll we do?"

"Nothing." Dana answered. He was looking at the women coming down. They would not be as tired perhaps as the women who had had to climb up. Climbing was usually impossible for these old ones; they never went beyond their front yards and sometimes never even outdoors, even in summer. And not interested in anything much except one or two remembered facets of life; if they talked at all it was about times far past; not interested in those around them; not eating more than bread and tea or a little sweet pie, love all gone in all of them. In these wild parts of the world a sort of stark hate grew in its place.

Another pair of souls came in sight at the bottom of the pasture. "There's more," Elihu said, pointing down the hill. "Look at Joanna, almost running up. This'll be her day, she hates everyone. Like as not she'll chop up her own. Hasn't been herself since her father threw her out for not reading the Bible verse right to him."

"Mrs. Letts," Dana said, pointing. Past the two men, not seeing them, came another old, old woman, bent and white but wearing pink. Upon her cheeks and hands were liver spots. She had short, thin white hair blown in the wind; she was a nice sight in the sun. Her old, sunken face was tranquil and squinted but slightly. Pausing near the men and by a spruce of the right size she gathered up her skirt and squatted to make water; the men, seeing, were repelled by the sight of the ivory haunch and looked over at the group of old women, now bright with something to be done.

"They're coming close," Dana said, straining to see past a branch to where the Tand women descended, not stopping, not slowing down. The Whippen women stood up in awkward poses, their weapons poised for the first blow. Steadily the Tand women, all old, all possessed with fury and committed to the next half hour, closed in on the Whippen group by the boulder. Suddenly the two groups had partially mingled; the old women stood looking at each other, and the two men thought this might be the moment when they would change things, not fight, and dodder on home where they belonged. But a big, determined shape reached out her hand and pushed down an old Tand woman so that she fell and hit her head on a rock. The fight started with that; warily the women approached and the first inept blows were exchanged, but, mounting in anger, they became harder. Treacherous and full of intent joy the women were, grim and newly strong.

Scuffling in the hardhack a fighting pair backed and hewed each other towards the place where the two watchers were hidden; Joanna Whipple, breathing hard and bearing down was going to kill first; the men could see as Joanna's sickle tore the flesh of her bony opponent. She had a wooden mallet and smashed at Joanna's hand to break her hold on the sickle. But with a final stroke Joanna caught the woman in the eyes; the mallet dropped and the woman gasped and sank to her knees, holding her face; Joanna hacked again and the woman lay still, her neatly laced shoe projecting from under her navy blue skirts. Elihu held his hands clasped tightly over his mouth while he watched in horror.

The battle spread out and in the tumult some of the women disappeared behind the thickets and boulders. The men saw Margaret Pew, bosom swinging, cleave the head of a tanned old thing in blue; others of the feeble started up and with mad strength and singleness of thought bent to it, slaughtering in blind hate, glorious in their moment to themselves but to the men terrifying as the dark blood fell and spread and lay unrecoverable, old and now spent amid the grave beauty of New England. They watched as Joyce Peabody tripped a short hunched woman from off the rock, ineptly beating her with a stone; she spat and turned to meet her end when a fat woman from Tand jerked her down by her apron strings and killed her with a rake.

What thoughts stirred in those old heads as the birds flew overhead and the grasshoppers hummed steadily the men did not know. The women died for the most part unaware, clinging not to life nor to anyone, memories all gone, old beyond caring, big at this time in their primal gust of death beyond which came they knew not what, nor had thought of, if at all, for some fifteen years or so. Church had not seen them for as long; song had left their lips; speech became only aimed to the past; the present touched them not even as they died except that, oh, they hated. Hate for what? Had life used them so? Did this remote mountain neighborhood start in them such bitter frenzy, imprisoned in dim hearts, bringing them up to this pasture at last?

Elihu was faint; before him Kitty Best had rammed a kitchen knife through and through a Tand opponent who died with faintest murmur, mouth askew, and here at last a pair of eyes that questioned in their last agony. Too late these aged bodies knew the truth, that death at the hand of another human being is the worst, in hate.

Dana wiped his hand across his forehead. "It takes a long time," he said hoarsely to Elihu.

Changing shadows crossed the grunting remains of the crowd that started in to fight. Of them all two sets of old women fought, and then two fell, one against a rock, her white face blank. Two only were left, fighting on the boulder, one in black, from Tand, the other, in white, was Kate. Against the green-black background of the spruce forest beyond they stood out.

At the sight of this Dana cried out, a mighty, hollow voice, rending the pasture's silence: "Stop! Stop, you," and broke from behind the tree to run towards them. But the women did not pause; and as they strove the white struck down the black, who fell off the rock upon the ground and did not move.

Kate stood on the rock, still in the position of her last blow. Saliva hung from her jaws and her empty old eyes gazed unseeingly across the pasture.

"Come down, Kate," Dana said urgently. "Come down to me." He held up his hand to her.

Kate shifted her focus to take in this new disturbance, her bloody axe clasped hard in her two worn hands; blood splattered her white dress and the big rock.

"Here, I'll come up," Dana said, and began to heave himself onto the rock. Elihu, a few yards away, saw what Dana did not: Kate lifted the axe, maddened by the battle, and brought it down on Dana's white head. Dana did not know what had struck him; he was dead immediately, slumped by the puddingstone.

Kate turned her back in total coldness and began to climb down, not forgetting the axe which, from habit of frugality, she would not leave behind. Elihu watched, paralyzed, for a long moment in the morning sun. Then the hate from the old women caught him and he felt it rise in him at the winner of the hideous battle.

"Kate! You, Kate—get on with it. You got to kill me too, you damn old woman," he yelled, sobbing. Kate, who had killed his friend, Kate, who had killed her husband, who should be dead of old age herself, was stepping down the hillside, free. He began to run down the mountain and almost fell against her.

"You're a-coming back to Whippen, and then you'll see, you old rat," he screamed, grabbing her by the skirt. He dragged her, stumbling and falling, at a dead run down the pasture, the hardhack and hay whipping at them. Gone the sweet view, the scent of summer, the bird flights and the cool breeze. The hating pair reached the pasture bars and the road in the village torn, sweating and heaving, more dead than alive. Elihu yanked Kate along to stand in front of the quiet grey houses where the men and younger people were gathered in silent groups.

"Here's an old bitch—old bitch—OLD BITCH," Elihu screamed, tearing the axe from Kate's fingers and giving her a vicious shove. Hate caught from the sights in Peacock's Pasture drove him earnestly as he threw back the axe against his thin shoulder and brought it down again and again on Kate until she lay broken and unrecognizable.

Two men caught Elihu's upraised weapon at last and pulled it from his hands. They stared at him in silence. Then one said, "Boy, don't you know she's a gone off into the woods? They don't never come back."

"Let be, son," the other man said. "Let it all be." He drew Elihu away from the dead woman, down the road. By a black cherry tree he said finally, "Up here, you got to let them be."

Elihu straightened and looked at him. The hate was in him now; it felt good. He felt like a man, at last.

SWORD FOR A SINNER

by Edward D. Hoch

The highly delicate mission that brought Simon Ark and me to the tiny village of Santa Marta is a story in itself, and since it was to play such an important part in what followed I must start with it. Perhaps by starting with Father Hadden's story I can at least delay for a time the setting down on paper of the horror that was to await us in the mountains. Perhaps I can wash it from my memory with a beautiful scene of Santa Marta as I first saw it, nestled on the valley floor in a sea of sunshine, a jewel unclaimed among the mountains.

Santa Marta is a village of some fifty or sixty people, located almost on the state line between Colorado and New Mexico. It lies somewhat north of Questa, and east of Antonio—in the rugged foothills of the Sangre de Cristo mountain range. The journey from New York had taken us two full days by plane, train, and bus, but finally we arrived. It was early morning when the bus dropped us at our destination, with only a quizzical glance from the drive in farewell.

"So this is Santa Marta," I said, breathing in the warm, dry desert air. "Where is this priest we came to see?"

Simon Ark frowned into the sun. "I see a church down there, a relic of happier days here. I imagine once this was a booming oasis in the desert. Perhaps Father Hadden can be found in his church."

The church, in stone architecture distinctly Spanish, was the last building on the street, a final resting place before the long climb into the mountains. As we approached, a few of the village people were drifting out, bound for their day of work after morning mass. This far north I was surprised to see so many Mexicans, and I was equally surprised to see Father Hadden, a rosy-cheeked man who might have been more at home in a big, sparkling church in Chicago.

"Father Hadden? I'm Simon Ark. . . ."

"I'm so glad you've come," he said, and I could see he meant it. He had the type of personality that made him immediately an old and trusted friend.

"This is a friend of mine," Simon explained, gesturing toward me. "A New York publisher who sometimes assists me in my wanderings. He wants to write my biography someday—but that day is surely far off."

A hint of uncertainty crossed the priest's face at these words. "I hope I can trust my story in your hands," he said quietly. "It would not be the type of story that should appear in print."

"You can trust me," I said. "If I ever write it at all, I'd change the names and the location."

"I admire your church," Simon said. "It is large and fine for such a small village."

"Thank you," Father Hadden said with a slight smile of gratitude. "I try to keep it well, even for such a small congregation as mine. The fine old church from a better day is one of the reasons why the bishop believes it necessary to keep a priest here in Santa Marta."

"Oh?" Simon said. "And what are the other reasons?"

"One involves a place you might have passed on the way in—a den of sin or such called the *Oasis*. It's been open only a year, but it already attracts people from a hundred miles around. The other reason . . . has to do with something up in the hills which need not concern us now.''

''Your letter said you'd heard of my work,'' Simon began, anxious to get to the matter at hand.

The priest leaned back in his chair, brushing a suntanned hand through thick black hair. ''I have a brother at the monastery of St. John of the Cross, in West Virginia. He told me that some two years ago you rendered them a great service.''

''Oh, yes,'' Simon nodded. ''A case of diabolic possession. Both interesting and tragic, in a way.''

Father Hadden nodded. ''My brother spoke very highly of you, and when my own . . . problem came up I felt you were the man to help me. I went to my bishop and received his permission to consult you about it.''

''I'm indeed gratified that your bishop ever heard of me.''

''You're much too modest, Mr. Ark. How many men are there in the world today doing actual, physical battle with the devil himself? And I understand that you yourself were once a priest?''

It was a phase of Simon's past he never spoke of. Now he simply brushed it aside with an impatient gesture. ''In Egypt, long ago, I practiced in the Coptic rite. But let us get to your problem, Father. . . .''

''My problem is simpler stated than solved, I fear. It seems I find myself equipped with the power of communication with the dead. In short, Mr. Ark, I am a medium. . . .''

His face never changed expression as he made the statement. He might have been giving us a baseball score, or asking for an extra-large Sunday collection. He was still the friendly, smiling priest, but I thought I detected a slight chill in the warm spring air.

''A medium?'' Simon Ark repeated very slowly. ''Of course, the term is only a bare hundred years old. It's odd to hear the word spoken by a priest—one who certainly holds nothing in common with the Fox sisters and other American spiritualists.''

''I use only the popular term for a somewhat unpopular

gift, Mr. Ark. I believe even Margaret Fox finally admitted the presence of fraud in her little act. Still, I understand there's a monument to her back in Rochester where much of it started.''

Simon nodded. ''But tell me of your strange power, whatever its name. This is most interesting.''

The ringing of a telephone interrupted the conversation, and Father Hadden rose to answer it. ''Hello? Father Hadden here. . . .'' As he listened, his expression changed, ever so slightly. The smile faded and was replaced by a troubled, gray look. ''I'll come at once, of course.''

''What is it, Father, trouble?'' Simon asked as he hung up the phone.

''I fear so. The very worst kind of trouble. A murder at the *morada* of Sangre de Cristo. In the mountains. I must go there at once.''

''Could I be of service?'' Simon asked. ''I have had some slight experience in such matters. Perhaps on the way we could discuss your own problem further.''

But the priest waved this aside. ''You are welcome to come certainly, Mr. Ark, but this is far more important than any problem I might have. This is a tragedy that could be very bad for the Church.''

''Then all the more reason for my assistance.'' Simon motioned to me and we followed the priest outside to his car, a station wagon brown with dust from the plains.

Father Hadden paused at the door and turned to me. ''I must ask one promise from both of you. What you are to see up here is . . . well, it is a sight few men have witnessed. You must promise me never to speak of this to the outside world.''

We gave him our promises, and I for one was wondering what strange world we were about to enter, what sights awaited us in these distant mountains. Before long we were bounding over black roads, climbing ever north into the hills and valleys of the Rockies. It was beautiful country, but strange and silent too—almost menacing in the quiet calm of its mountains, in the yucca and cactus that were the only vegetation.

''These mountains,'' Simon began, breaking the silence which had hung over the car, "are called the Sangre de Cristo range? Blood of Christ?"

The priest nodded. "An ironically tragic name in view of the circumstances. Have you ever heard of the Brotherhood of Penitentes, Mr. Ark?"

Surprisingly Simon nodded his head. "Is that what this is?" he asked somberly.

"I'm afraid so. They have nearly a hundred and fifty chapter houses in the southwest. They're a group more powerful and more important than most people realize."

"Would someone mind telling me what this is all about?" I asked.

"You will know soon enough, my friend," Simon said, as a great stone villa came into view ahead. It stood on a flat bluff between two mountains, a relic of the Spanish conquerors forgotten by later men.

But the thing that riveted my eyes was on a hill just beyond the house. It was a great wooden cross, much too large to be simply the marker for a grave. There seemed to be some sort of banner or scarf attached to it, drifting gently in the breeze. "What's that?" I asked.

Father Hadden didn't even lift his eyes to it. He must have seen it many times before. "The cross," he said simply. "You'll see more of them inside."

We parked in a worn brick driveway in front of the place, and I wondered about the absence of other cars. Certainly the people here must arrive somehow. Did they fly in on broomsticks or something?

There was a little cross over the door, too—a plain wooden one—and I suddenly supposed that this must be a monastery of some sort. I was about to put my thought into words when the great glass-and-metal door swung silently open in answer to our ring. The man who stood there wore a black hood over his head, a hood with only two eyeholes staring out at us. He was naked to the waist, and there were a number of great bloody scratches across his chest. In that moment I thought I'd stepped into a madhouse, but there was worse to come.

The hooded doorkeeper led us in without a word, down a dim, dank hallway lit only by stained glass windows high on each side. Father Hadden hurried along with him and I could see they were speaking in low tones about the tragedy we had come to witness.

"What in hell is this anyway?" I whispered to Simon. But already we were starting down a flight of stone steps, and in a moment we found ourselves in a low, dark basement lit here and there by flickering candlelight. My first impression was that we were in a great storeroom full of life-size crucifixes. But then I realized with a chilling start that the figures on the crosses were *alive,* horribly fantastically alive!

There were perhaps twenty of the crosses in the room, reaching from floor almost to ceiling. And on each a nearly naked man was tied, his arms outstretched in the familiar attitude of Christ. Most of them wore only the black hoods and white loin cloths, though some had compromised by wearing bathing trunks. All had their arms and legs tied to the crosses with thick horsehair cords, and some showed the red marks of scourging on their bare chests and thighs. It was a scene from hell.

"What is this?" I gasped out. "A lodge initiation?"

"If it were only that simple," Simon mused. And then Father Hadden shone his light on the cross at the far end of the room—and we saw there the greatest horror of all.

The last cross in the line had a man tied to it like all the others—a man wearing a black hood—but this one was different. From the left side of his body, slanting upward into his chest, protruded the slim steel shaft of a Spanish sword. . . .

"What is it, Simon? What is this madness?" I asked him later as we sat with Father Hadden in one of the upstairs rooms.

And Simon Ark closed his eyes and stared off into an unseeing world of his own mind. "The Brotherhood of Penitentes," he began, very softly, "is an old, old society. Some trace its origin back to the Franciscan missionaries or even before. In a virgin country without priests or churches, perhaps it was only natural that some of the more passionate Spanish men should turn to self-torture as an act of devotion. A hundred years ago the practices of the Penitentes were so widespread and so brutal in the southwest that the Catholic Church was forced to ban such groups. But of course it didn't stop them. They continued their rites of self-scourging and crucifixion in secret, wearing hoods to conceal their identity from the public, and sometimes from each other."

"But if the group is banned by the Church, why does Father Hadden here deal with them?"

The priest himself answered my question. "A few years ago it was decided that the practices of the Penitentes had softened considerably, consisting now only of processions and mild scourging during Holy Week. They have again been recognized by the Church—or at least most of the chapters have been. Unfortunately, this *morada* is one that was not received back into the fold. Its practices continue as staggeringly brutal as they were fifty or a hundred years ago. You saw the basement—some say there have been times when the crucifixions were performed with nails rather than merely ropes. . . ."

"There have been deaths before?" Simon asked.

"There have been deaths," the priest agreed. "Hushed up, but I hear of them sometimes. Never anything like this, though. I ask myself how it is possible that one of these men, in the midst of a religious fervor so great that it drove him to emulate the sufferings of Christ, could possibly commit murder."

"Who was the man?" Simon asked, "I noticed your start of surprise downstairs when you removed the hood."

"That is the thing that makes this all the more frightening," Father Hadden answered. "The man is the owner of the *Oasis*."

"The bar you mentioned earlier?"

The priest nodded. "The *Oasis* is all things to all men—drink, sex, sin, gambling. And Glen Summer is, or was, its owner and manager. His was the greatest sin of all."

Simon frowned and was silent for a moment. Somewhere outside a cloud lifted from the sun and a single ray of light shot though one of the stained glass windows, bathing his face in a purple hue. "You believe a man like

Summer would come to a place like this to atone for his sins in secret?"

"I believe it, Mr. Ark, because these others tell me it is true. But imagine what the people and the public will think! They will never believe it—they will never believe that good and evil can live side by side in the same man. They already circulate fantastic rumors about this place, and now they will claim Summer was kidnapped and murdered in some sort of religions ritual."

*

I could see that Simon agreed with him. "It would be a fairly logical assumption, Father. But we have no choice except to call the local police. The murderer might not be so difficult to discover, after all. It must be one of those men downstairs."

"But which of them, Mr. Ark? Which of them?"

Simon rose slowly from the chair and began to pace the floor, frowning. "If we sit in on the police questioning, we might learn something. How many are there downstairs?"

"Eighteen men, plus the one who let us in."

"Who was he?"

"Their leader, in a way. His name is Juan Cruz. He's Mexican, studied for the priesthood for a time, but was dropped because of practices like these. He drifted into the States about ten years ago and joined the Penitentes. I fear Cruz is the one who keeps this little group banded together. Without him they'd surely listen to me and funnel their passionate piety into more normal outlets."

"You think this Cruz may have killed Summer?"

"Normally I'd answer yes to that. He was the only one not tied to a cross when we arrived, and certainly such a deed wouldn't be beyond him if he thought it would bring some good. I have had many long talks with Juan Cruz and have yet to convince him that the end does not justify the means." The priest paused and then continued after a moment. "And yet . . . I do not think he would endanger his group of Penitentes here by committing a murder during one of their rites of penance. He would kill

Summer under certain conditions, but he would pick another time and another place."

As if on cue the basement door opened and Juan Cruz appeared, fully dressed now and carrying the black hood he'd removed earlier. He was a bulky man, distinctly Spanish in appearance, with glistening black hair and tiny eyes to match. I disliked him immediately, but not for any action or word. Rather it was the dislike one often feels for a person of obvious superiority.

"They are all untied and dressed now," he said quietly.

"Then we must call the police," Father Hadden said. "There is no other way, Juan."

"I suppose not," the bulky man answered.

Simon Ark stepped once more into the purple spot of light that filtered down from above. "Do you know of any of these men who might have had a special reason for killing Glen Summer?"

"Certainly not," Cruz answered. "He was a sinful man, but he was seeking the way back to God. I doubt if anyone else was even aware of his identity. That's the purpose of the hoods, you know."

"Who are the other eighteen?" Simon asked.

"For the most part they are simply poor Mexican laborers who have lived in sin for many years. A few are Americans, like Summer."

"With the hoods to conceal identity it would be possible for an outsider to gain admittance, would it not?"

"Possible but most difficult," Cruz replied. "I am careful."

"The body has not been disturbed?"

"No."

"Then I suggest we call the police immediately," Simon said. "Too much time has already elapsed since the killing. Father Hadden and I will remain here while they question you and the others."

Cruz nodded reluctantly and went off to the telephone. I noticed Simon motioning to me and I walked over to where he stood. "My friend, you can serve no purpose here, but you might serve a very useful one elsewhere. Perhaps you could take Father Hadden's station wagon and drive to this place called the *Oasis*. You could be there when the word came in about Glen Summer, and you could see what reaction there was. It might be most interesting.''

*

It was agreeable with me, if only to get me away from the atmosphere of that place. Simon told Father Hadden of our plan and the priest nodded in agreement. ''Take my car and see what you can learn,'' he said. ''You might especially observe the reaction of Summer's wife, since I doubt very much if she knew he came to this place.''

I left them there and headed the dusty station wagon back down the road to Santa Marta. About halfway into town I passed the sheriff's car, filled with grim-faced men, and a moment later the town's ambulance-hearse followed.

*

It took me a little time to locate the *Oasis*, a few miles outside of town. It sat back from the road a ways, a long low building with a parking lot and a few trees around it. Now, in the afternoon sunlight, there were only two cars parked there, and the business seemed slow for a den of sin. I parked the station wagon and went inside.

The place was not unlike a thousand other bars back east. It was a neighborhood sort of joint, even out here in the middle of nowhere. Booths along one wall, the dame and glistening bar along the other. And curtains over an entrance to a back room. A bald bartender with a gray mustache was polishing glasses casually behind the bar, and the only customer appeared to be a good-looking blonde girl propped up on one of the bar stools. She was wearing a loose white blouse and blue shorts that were much too short. I guessed her age at twenty-five or younger, and the way she eyed me when I came in told me she wasn't presently attached.

''What'll you have?'' the bartender asked without putting down the glass he was polishing.

"Beer," I mumbled. "Too hot for anything else." I picked out the stool just two away from the girl and lifted myself onto it. After a moment I asked, "Glen Summer around?"

The bartender placed a bottle of beer and a glass in front of me. He took his time about answering, as if trying to determine the reason for my question. Finally, he said, "Nope. Gone away today. Back tonight."

"How about Mrs. Summer?"

"She's in the back. Want I should get her?"

"No. Maybe I'll wait for Glen."

The girl in the blue shorts slid off her stool, her shapely thighs bulging a bit under the tight fabric. She picked up her glass, moved it over a bit, and sat down next to me. "Mind?" she asked in reply to my look.

"Why should I?"

"I need somebody to talk to. This town is dead dead dead."

"So I've been noticing."

"Nothing to do with your afternoons but drink them away. The *Oasis* is the only civilized place for fifty miles."

She'd had a few drinks but she was far from drunk. Just unhappy, I decided. "You live in Santa Marta?"

"Nobody lives in Santa Marta. They only exist. A month ago I was working up in Denver. I lost my job and decided to travel south, and this is as far as I got."

"What keeps you here if you don't like it?"

She waved an arm in a vague gesture. "Oh, things. You know."

I didn't know, and I could see I wasn't going to find out. "You know Glen Summer?"

"Sure do! He's a swell fellow."

"And his wife?"

"She's a bitch, but that's the way it usually turns out."

I took a swallow of beer. "I came down through the mountains, past a big old house with a cross nearby on a hill. What is it, a convent or something?"

She peered at me from under half-closed lids. "A bunch of crazy religious nuts. They go up there and beat each other with whips and stuff. Supposed to be good for their souls.'' She gave a little chuckle. ''If they did it in New York they'd be locked up in ten minutes.''

''You from New York?''

''I'm from everywhere. You're just full of questions, aren't you?'' She signaled the bartender to pour her another drink.

The only thing I'd decided about her was that she didn't know about Summer and the Penitentes, and that wasn't much. ''What's your name?'' I asked, figuring there was nothing suspicious in the direct approach.

''Vicky Nelson,'' she answered. ''Twenty-four and unmarried.''

I told her my name, said I was from New York, but skipped the rest of the vital statistics. Before we could get in any more conversation I noticed a distant funnel of dust through the window. It was a car, traveling fast in our direction. A good guess told me it was the sheriff and I was right.

He was short and fat—why are sheriffs always fat?—and he wore a holstered revolver low on his hip like some left-over cowboy. He'd come alone to break the news to Mrs. Summer, and I figured that made her a pretty important person in his opinion.

''Della around?'' he asked the bartender.

''She's in back, working on the books, Sheriff.''

''Get her for me. It's important.''

The bartender muttered something under his breath and put down the damp cloth. As he went through the back curtains I caught a glimpse of multi-colored metal monsters lining the wall. The place was a little Las Vegas, complete with slot machines, and I was sure gambling wasn't legal in this state.

After a moment the curtains parted once more and a tall middle-aged woman appeared. She might have been pretty once, but that day was long past. I discovered later she was only thirty-five, but just then I would have guessed her for over forty. ''Hello, Sheriff. What's the trouble?'' she asked.

''I've got some bad news, Della,'' he said, ignoring the audience of Vicky and me. ''It's about Glen.''

''God—what happened to him?''

"Somebody killed him, Della. Up at the *morada*. . . ."

"Killed him!" she gasped, her voice cracking. "At the *morada?*" I don't know which surprised her more—the fact of her husband's death or its place of occurrence. "What was he doing there?"

"He was . . . with them, Della. He was taking part in their . . . rites, and somebody stabbed him with a sword."

"I don't believe it," she screamed out. "You're lying!"

The bartender came around the row of stools and took her arm. "Steady, Della. Let me take you in back."

The sheriff finally noticed us sitting there and nodded in agreement. "Let's all go in back," he decided. And the three of them disappeared through the curtains.

"Glen Summers—dead!" Vicky Nelson said when we were alone. "I just can't believe it."

"He was a good friend, eh?"

"He was a good guy. I'd only known him these few weeks but he was a good guy. Say, how come you were asking about that place where Glen got killed, mister?"

I shrugged my shoulders. "Just coincidence. What have you heard about it?"

"Like I said, they're nuts. I sure didn't figure Glen Summer for one of them."

The sheriff came out of the back with Della Summer and they got in his car. Her eyes were red but she was holding up well. The bartender returned, too, stepping behind his polished counter and picking up the damp cloth as if nothing had happened.

"Summer's dead?" I asked him.

"Yeah." He picked up another glass.

"How'd it happen?"

"Don't know a thing, mister. You'll have to ask the sheriff about it."

"Thanks," I said, and slid off the stool. I could see I wasn't going to learn anything more here. "You want a ride anywhere?" I asked Vicky.

"Guess not, thanks. I need a few more of these." She held up her glass. "See you around."

"Yeah." I went out and climbed back into Father Hadden's station wagon. I didn't want to go back to the villa in the mountains so I drove to the church where we'd first met the strange priest. It was only then, sitting there in the street before the great stone towers that I remembered the thing that had brought Simon and me to this place.

Father Hadden believed that he was a medium. That was an interesting thing to think about, at least. I didn't remember ever hearing before about a priest who could communicate with the dead, though it did seem logical that if such things were at all possible a priest would be the person to do it.

I lit a cigarette and tried to conjure up a phantom in the smoke. If Father Hadden could talk to the dead, why couldn't he talk to the departed Glen Summer and find out who shoved the sword into him? I filed away that thought for further conversation with Simon.

Ten minutes later, halfway through my third cigarette, the familiar sheriff's car turned into the street before the church. I saw Simon and Father Hadden climb out, followed by the stout shape of the sheriff himself. While I was still debating whether to reveal myself, the sheriff strode quickly to my door and yanked it open. ''O.K., mister, climb out. I want to talk to you.''

''What?'' I mumbled something, startled by this sudden turn of events. ''What did I do?''

The big sheriff rumbled on. ''Never mind the wise talk. Come on inside while I get to the bottom of this.''

I slid out of the driver's seat and followed him into Father Hadden's rectory, because at this point there was nothing else to do, Simon and the priest were already there, sitting at a big oak table in silence.

''I got your buddy here,'' the sheriff said triumphantly. ''Nobody puts anything over on Ben Partell. You two were up there without any car, and then I see this joker at the *Oasis* drivin' the church's car. I just put two and three together, and I come up with all of you at the *morada* and this bird leavin' for some reason. Why?''

Father Hadden cleared his throat. ''Really, Sheriff Partell, there's no excuse for this type of questioning. . . .''

''And you be quiet, too,'' the sheriff stormed. ''I ain't

runnin' for another three years. I don't have to worry about the Catholic vote this season."

It was amazing to me how the calm, semi-dignified man who'd brought Della Summer the news of her husband's death could have given way in a brief half-hour to this growling, bullying person who now faced us.

"You think *we* killed the man?" Simon asked mildly.

"No, I don't think you killed the man, but I'm sure as hell goin' to find out, if I have to run in that whole collection of creeps. They were all hangin' there on their damned crosses, all in the same room, and not a damned one of them saw a thing! You think I believe that?"

"The room was quite dark," Simon said. "And the dead man was at the end of it. Since I understand the Penitentes were in the habit of entering the room one at a time at irregular intervals, any one of them could have plunged the sword into Summer and left him hanging there in the dimness."

"But Juan Cruz tied each of them to the cross. If he didn't do it himself, he sure as hell must know who did." The sheriff lowered his bulk into one of the chairs and took out a fat cigar. Now that he'd shown us he was the boss, he seemed content to pursue the investigation on a somewhat more subdued level. "Cruz was constantly in and out of that cellar room. You mean to tell me that one of those eighteen guys, stripped down to shorts or a loincloth, could have taken the sword off the wall upstairs, carried it down to the cellar in plain sight, and stabbed Summer without anyone seeing him?"

"It is possible," Simon said.

"Nuts! I'm taking that guy Cruz down to my office, and if he won't talk I'll beat the truth out of him. I'll lock up that whole place if I have to. I'm no hick-town sheriff, you know!"

Father Hadden rose and rested a gentle hand on the sheriff's shoulder. "I have faith that the sinner will see his way to confess before very long," he said. "Whatever the world may think of groups like the Penitentes, there is no doubt they are deeply religious men. The very fact of murder in such a place is unthinkable—the continued concealment of the crime by the killer is fantastic. He will come forward to confess, never fear."

But Sheriff Partell was far from satisfied. "Well you start praying for his soul, Father. I'm going out and drag that Cruz in for questioning." And with that he rose from the chair and went outside to his car.

For a moment we sat simply in silence, as people do when some sort of vague disaster has passed them by. Finally, I broke the silence. "He may be a slob, but he's no dope."

But Simon Ark only sat in continued silence, as if deep in thought. "Tell me, my friend," he asked at last, "what adventures befell you at the *Oasis?*"

"Well . . ." I told him everything that had happened, as close as I could remember it. Neither he nor Father Hadden interrupted, but when I finished I could see they weren't impressed.

"Della Summer must still be up there," Father Hadden observed. "The sheriff brought her to officially identify the body and then he took us back here."

Simon stirred in his seat. "My friend, would you like to do a bit more traveling this day?"

"I suppose so, but let me tell you my idea first."

"And what is that?"

I turned to the priest. "Father, you told us before that you had been in communication with the dead."

"That is correct. . . ."

"Then why can't you talk to the spirit of Glen Summer—talk to him and find out who killed him?"

The priest's face paled at my suggestion. "I fear you do not understand my problem, not at all."

Apparently I'd said the wrong thing, for Simon interrupted quickly. "My friend, would you take the car again and journey to the villa in the mountains? Perhaps you can somehow get a chance to speak to Juan Cruz before Partell takes him over."

"And what should I say to him if I do? Should I ask him if he killed Summer?"

Simon ignored the sarcasm in my remark. "No, my friend. You should ask him if any member of the Penitentes was absent this morning. . . ."

"Absent?"

"Perhaps there was an extra man in the room. It hardly seems likely that the murderer would allow himself to be tied to a cross in the same room as his victim. But if there was a missing Brother—perhaps that is your answer."

It sounded reasonable, if a bit far-fetched, and I agreed to go.

The unearthly quiet of the villa on my previous visit had not prepared me for the bedlam which had broken out in the few hours since I'd left. Now there were cars parked everywhere, in a crazy unpatterned manner that reminded me of harbored boats after a hurricane. The sheriff's car was back, as I'd expected, and now it had been joined by a state police car and a number of unidentified vehicles. At least two of them had press cards in the windows.

A deputy sheriff met me at the door and asked what I wanted. I thought fast and flashed my membership card in the Overseas Press Club. Apparently that was good enough for him, because he stepped aside without a word. Inside the place was alive with reporters and photographers, popping their flash bulbs at every possible corner. A cluster of them had gathered in the big main room, where the stout Partell was standing on a chair examining a rack of antique Spanish swords. Beyond, in a sort of sitting room, I could see Della Summer, deep in an old straight-backed chair, staring out the window in a state bordering shock. Juan Cruz was with her, speaking softly, but she seemed not to hear his words. I walked in and stood quietly behind them, listening.

"Mrs. Summer, I know it is a difficult thing to grasp," he was saying, "but your husband came to me a month ago. He was shocked by the sin and vice the *Oasis* had caused in its brief existence. He wanted to repent. He wanted to join the Brothers of the Blood of Christ and suffer for the sins of his life. Just a few days ago he told me he planned to sell the *Oasis* and give the money to the Church. He was a man repentant, Mrs. Summer, and you can be thankful he died that way."

I cleared my throat and he turned toward me. "Ah,

you are the friend of Father Hadden and that man Ark. What can I do for you?''

''Could I talk to you alone?'' I said. Della Summer turned tired eyes in my direction but seemed not to really see me at all.

''I'm afraid the good sheriff will never let me completely out of his sight, but perhaps over in the corner. . . .'' He motioned me to the far end of the room, under a great red-draped painting of some Franciscan missionary whose name I didn't know.

''Simon Ark wanted me to ask you a question,'' I began.

''Yes?''

''Were there any members of your Penitentes who were not present this morning?''

A cloud of something—fear?—passed over his eyes before he answered. ''There was one,'' he said slowly. ''The man who first introduced Summer to me. Yates Ambrose, the bartender at the *Oasis*. . . .''

''You think this bartender, Ambrose, might have sneaked in here while the others were tied to those crosses? The man was his boss—he might have had a reason for killing him.''

The Mexican never had a chance to answer, because I saw Sheriff Partell bearing down on us with fire in his eyes. ''Joe, show this bird to the door, and make sure he doesn't get back in.'' His orders were crisp and to the point, and the deputy he'd spoken to acted at once.

Before I had a chance to say anything else to Cruz I found myself being propelled toward the door and out down the steps to the car. ''Sheriff means what he says,'' the guy told me. ''Stay away or we lock you up.''

I turned quickly at the bottom of the steps and only succeeded in sliding into the dust. I got up slowly like a fool. Whatever Simon and Father Hadden wanted me to find out, I surely hadn't done it. Unless there was something about that bartender. . . .

I passed a careful eye over the scattered parking of cars and remembered the complete absence of them when we'd driven up this morning. But there were nineteen men—

twenty, counting Summer—in that place and they must have come somehow. They sure didn't walk.

I started the station wagon and drove slowly around to the rear of the big mansion. As I'd suspected, there was another parking lot there, with some ten or twelve cars nestled under the roof's tiled overhang. Well, all of the Penitentes weren't poor Mexicans.

On second thought I took back that last part. Some of them might live at the villa—it was certainly large enough. But there was something in the sand that caught my eye and I swung the car to a quick stop. It was an odd type of tire track, a double tread mark made by a tire only recently put on the market. The rows of double treads ran *over* the other tracks, showing that it had been the last car in. And there was another set of them on the left, coming out of the driveway. I left my car where it was and walked the fifty feet to the line of vehicles. None of them had the double-tread tires. Somebody had come and gone after they arrived. I took a quick look for footprints, but that was hopeless. With a bit of hope I headed back to the car. . . .

The *Oasis* was picking up business as the afternoon dragged along, filling its parking lot with a variety of new and old cars. The one I was seeking was at the end of the line, one of the two that had been there earlier in the day. I jotted down the license number and went inside.

The place was more like a morgue than a palace of pleasure, and I guessed that the word had gotten around. The same bartender, who must have been Yates Ambrose, was serving an occasional drink to the somber crew. But what really stopped me was the girl, Vicky Nelson. She was still there, in the same tight shorts, sitting on the same stool smoking her cigarette.

Beyond the curtained partition waited a solid row of one-armed slot machines. There were a couple of green felt poker tables, too, and a cloth-covered bulge that might have been a roulette wheel. But these were quiet today, out of respect for a dead sinner. There were only the slots to greedily accept our quarters.

*

Vicky and I played a while and then I asked her, "Ever hear any talk about Yates Ambrose and Mrs. Summer?"

"You kidding? Not a chance! He couldn't have gotten her with a fish net. Besides, he's one of those religious nuts."

"A Penitente?"

"Could be, for all I know."

"How come he works in a place like this?"

"Who knows? Trying to convert Summer, I suppose."

"Yeah."

"You're full of questions, aren't you?"

I handed her a couple of quarters. "Play for me. I'll be right back."

Out in front the murmurers were still in force, holding their private wake for the late owner of the *Oasis*. I leaned on the end of the bar until I attracted Ambrose's attention and I motioned him toward me.

"Got a minute, Yates?"

"Who told you my name?" He was still clutching the bar rag.

"I'm a friend of Juan Cruz."

"Who?"

"Cut the act. I know you're one of them. Why weren't you up there today?"

"You must be crazy."

"Or maybe you were up there, huh?"

"Look, mister, I don't know anything about it. I belonged to the thing for a while, went up there a few times. I even told the boss about it and introduced him to Cruz. But I quit a couple of weeks back. "That nut!"

"Was the crucifixion bit a usual thing?"

Ambrose nodded. "Every week or so. He had twenty wooden crosses in the basement room, and he'd tie us to them with horsehair cords. Sometimes he'd let himself be tied there too."

"Did each of you have your own cross?"

Ambrose shook his head. "It wasn't quite that organized. But Cruz never let us forget we were sinners."

"And you weren't out there this morning?"

"No sir! I didn't go near the place."

I was pretty sure he was lying, but I'd never get anywhere with him. I thanked him and went back to Vicky Nelson.

"Hi, girl. How's things been in my absence?"

She gave me a big smile. "I beat the thing out of five dollars with one of your quarters. Put it nearly all back in, though."

There was a stir of activity in the front and we poked our heads through the curtain. Della Summer had returned and she was telling Ambrose to close the place up. "We'll be open again after the funeral," she told the crowd. "Go home now, and mourn my husband's murder."

They murmured and moved, slowly filing toward the door. Mrs. Summer had regained much of her composure now, but I could see she was still a shaken woman. "We have to leave," I told Vicky. "Come on."

"Leave? Where will I go?"

"You must have a home somewhere. Where've you been staying?"

She thought about that, the drink gradually beginning to cloud her vision. "A motel someplace. I don't remember quite where. Can't I come along with you?"

"Girl, there's fifteen years and a wife between us."

But by this time Della Summer had appeared. "Haven't I seen you somewhere before today?" she asked me, frowning in concentration.

"I don't think so."

"Well, we're closing anyway, till after my husband's funeral. You'll have to leave."

I shrugged and helped Vicky gather up her quarters. As soon as we were out the door Della Summer and Yates Ambrose began closing the place up, getting ready for the period of mourning. I wondered if anyone else worked at the place and I asked Vicky.

"At night a few dealers and stick men come in," she said. "Glen Summer hired them in Vegas."

"And Sheriff Partell winks at all this?"

"He sure does, near as I can see. Maybe Summer was paying him off."

One of the remaining cars in the lot apparently belonged to Vicky, but in her condition I could hardly let her drive it. She was beginning to sober up a bit, and I figured I could drive her around in the afternoon air for a while. "Climb in," I said, holding open the station wagon door. "You can stay with me a little while and then I'll bring you back here to your car."

"You're nice," she said, climbing in.

I headed back toward Father Hadden's church, because I was anxious to report my progress—or lack of it—to Simon. It wasn't until I pulled up in front of the place again that I remembered Vicky's costume. I couldn't very well produce her in Father Hadden's rectory in those shorts.

"Stay in the car," I told her. "I'll be back."

"You're going into *church?*"

"There are worse places, believe me, I'll be back."

Inside, Simon Ark and Father Hadden were still sitting at the table, just as I'd left them. Empty coffee cups told me the hours had been talkative and thirsty.

"I'm back. You two get everything solved?"

Simon peered at me through the lengthening afternoon shadows that were quietly stealing into the room. "We have had an interesting talk. Did you learn anything?"

I started at the beginning and told them everything that had happened, especially about the tire tracks that appeared to be from Yates Ambrose's car. "Simon, I think he went out there this morning, took off his clothes and put on his black hood and killed Summer with the sword. It's the only solution as I see it."

Simon smiled a bit, as he often did when I was becoming positive about some theory of mine. "It is hardly the *only* solution, my friend. But perhaps we may learn something tonight. Perhaps your idea of Father Hadden communicating with the dead was not so bad after all."

I shot a glance at the priest, but his face did not change expression. "You mean. . . ?"

Simon nodded slightly. "Father Hadden has explained his problem—the problem that originally brought us to Santa Marta. It does indeed appear that he is able to form some sort of communication with the dead of this parish. In fact, the good Father believes he can reach anyone whose confession he ever heard during life."

"Fantastic! Do you believe this, Simon?"

"There may be some truth to it. At times God moves in strange ways."

I turned to the priest. "You'll actually do it? Hold a seance or whatever they call them? Tonight?"

Father Hadden nodded reluctantly. "Mr. Ark is most persuasive. I will do as he wishes."

"Who's going to be here for this, Simon? Just the three of us?'

"On the contrary, my friend. I hope to have a great many people present—as many as possible. We will start by inviting the good Sheriff Partell."

That even brought a laugh from me. "You'll never get him down here. And if you did, he'd never sit still for anything as crazy as this."

"Perhaps he would," Simon mused. "Perhaps he would. In any event, I will go out now like the servant in the Gospels and assemble some guests for our gathering. I shall return by nightfall."

"Oh—say, there's this girl in Father's car, the one I told you about. . . ."

Simon nodded. "She may want to join us, too."

I couldn't quiet picture Vicky Nelson sitting at any table that didn't have drinks on it, but I supposed there was always a first time. "You'd better get her some clothes first," I warned him. "She hasn't got many on now."

And when Simon had left I sat for a time in silence with Father Hadden, as the sun finally began to vanish behind the meager line of shrubs and cactus in the distance. "Mr. Ark is truly a strange man," he said at last.

"You're right there, Father," I agreed. "I've known him for twenty years, off and on, and still I don't *really* know him."

"Do you believe what he says about his past? About back there—in Egypt?"

I spread my palms flat on the table. "Frankly, he's never told me too much about it. Just that he's lived a long, long time. Occasionally, when the dark winds of night are passing over the moon, I even find myself thinking that perhaps he actually is over fifteen hundred years old. . . ."

The priest nodded. "One could believe it, very easily. He spoke of other things this afternoon, of a strange Coptic priest in the first century after Christ, who wrote a gospel glorifying the Lord. The words were devout but hardly divinely inspired. The Fathers of the Church denounced it as a fraud, and the Coptic priest lost everything. He was in a unique if impossible situation—his writings had been holy praises to God, worthy of a place in Heaven, but the deceit he'd used in circulating them as a fifth gospel made such a reward impossible. It was a situation even baffling for the Almighty, and this man could be sent neither to Heaven nor Hell. He was doomed to walk the earth forever until such time as God would decide his fate."

It was the first time I'd ever heard the story, and I wondered if this really was the strange secret of Simon Ark. "Did he tell you the name of this work?"

"It has come down to us, in a greatly altered form, as *The Shepherd of Hermas*. There is such a book. I am familiar with it."

"And why would he tell you these things?" I asked.

"Perhaps," said the priest slowly, "perhaps even a man as powerful as Simon Ark needs help sometimes. Perhaps he did not come solely to help *me*."

"But why does he seek Satan, Father?" I asked. "Will the finding of the devil somehow break the spell of this curse that haunts him?"

But the priest only shook his head. "That I do not know, I do not even know if these words he spoke were true words. He was perhaps only telling me that the ways of God are often strange and unbelievable. He was only telling me that the fantastic, the supernatural, is possible on this earth—if it is God's will."

"And?"

"And he told me to accept this strange power of mine—accept it and turn it to God's uses. He told me that tonight I must attempt to contact the spirit of Glen Summer. . . ."

"But aren't such things as seances against religion?"

"He says that some good can come even out of the bad. Though the end may never justify the means, surely at times circumstances must dictate the wiseness of fools and the foolishness of wise men.''

''And so Simon thinks the killer will give himself away at the seance?''

The priest shrugged his shoulders. ''Who knows? I assure you I have never done anything like this before. My . . . spirits have always come in private before.''

''Well, I've seen a few of these things in the movies. Everyone sits in a circle and holds hands, or something like that.''

Father Hadden nodded. ''I suppose we must duplicate the expected conditions.''

''Could I have a cup of that coffee while we're waiting? I asked him. ''I suddenly remembered I've had mighty little to eat today.''

''Surely. I think I even have enough food for us.''

And that's what happened. I ate there with the priest while Simon Ark roamed the streets of Santa Marta, seeking out those we needed for the final act of the little drama.

And presently, as the night shadows slipped slowly across the plain, Simon returned with Sheriff Partell in tow. ''I must be crazy to even come here,'' he was protesting. ''Am I supposed to believe this big-deal priest is goin' to conjure up a murderer for me? I've already got the killer locked up, and it's that guy Juan Cruz, believe me!''

But Simon took the renewed attack with a slight smile. ''I have not yet been able to convince the good sheriff that we will need the presence of Mr. Cruz as well.''

''The hell you will!''

''Consider, Sheriff Partell, if you do not arrive at a quick and satisfactory solution to this case, the state police will move in very soon. There are already some of them around. They will move in, and ask questions, and soon they will begin to wonder about your connection with the *Oasis*. . . .''

''Damn it, I have no connection with the *Oasis!*''

''When a wide-open place like that operates in a town as small as this, the sheriff *must* have a connection with it.''

"I looked the other way, that's all I did! Are you going to crucify—" He stopped as soon as the word was out of his mouth. "Are you going to hang me just because I let people do what they wanted to do? It's a free country!"

I could see that Simon had him on the defensive, and he pressed his advantage. "Freedom to violate the law is not found in any constitution," he pointed out. "It would be to your advantage to cooperate with us."

"I'm here, ain't I?" the sheriff growled. "How the hell much else cooperation do you want?"

"We want Juan Cruz," Simon answered simply.

"Nuts! He stays in his cell."

"You haven't actually charged him with anything yet, you know. You can only hold him a few more hours."

Partell sighed and flung up his hands, a beaten man. "O.K., O.K.—you can have him. Where is this crazy thing goin' to take place. Here?"

Simon glanced at Father Hadden, saw the troubled frown of uncertainty on his face, and answered for him. "No, I think not. I think we should return to the villa in the mountains—to the scene of the crime, as they say. . . ."

And so we went back, up the hill now darkened by desert night, up and over dusty mountain roads leading nowhere, till finally the moonlight caused the image of the great wooden cross on the rise near the *morada.* Other cars were arriving, too, and I could see that Simon had done his work well in gathering these people together.

The great house itself was dark now, guarded only by a single deputy sheriff who snapped a quick and sloppy half-salute at Partell. The eighteen, whoever they were, had long since headed for their homes, their moment of dim suffering gone now. And if I wondered why Simon had not summoned them back, I was soon to learn the reason.

The great central room of the place seemed crowded with familiar faces, but a quick count showed only eight of us—Simon and myself, Father Hadden and Sheriff Partell, Juan Cruz, a bare-legged and puzzled Vicky Nelson, and—surprisingly—Della Summer and Yates Ambrose. Simon's travels had apparently carried him to the *Oasis.*

"If you'll be all seated around this table," Simon began, "I hope we can get this over with quite quickly."

"Do you really think you can contact my husband?" Mrs. Summer wanted to know.

"We are certainly going to try, madame. But first let me say a few words of introduction." As he spoke, we were seating ourselves around the big table. I took a chair to the left of Simon, right next to Vicky Nelson, who was still looking mildly bewildered at this whole business.

"You all know," Simon began, "what has been happening here, in this place. A practice of medieval times, that of extreme physical penances for sins, has been revived. It has been revived and carried to extremes by a group of devout but misguided men. Perhaps Juan Cruz here was the most misguided of them all, since he was their leader."

The eyes of us all went to Cruz, who sat opposite Simon, between the sheriff and Yates Ambrose. "Today," Simon continued, "one of this group died, killed with a Spanish sword as he hung on a cross in the dim basement below us. As you know, he was Glen Summer, owner of the *Oasis*."

Beside me, Vicky moved restlessly in her chair. Beyond the leaded glass windows I could hear a wind rising in the mountains. Perhaps there was a storm on the way. "As a few of you also know, Father Hadden here has been deeply troubled of late by a strange power that has thrust itself unwanted upon him. It is the power to communicate, under certain circumstances, with the spirits of those who have departed the earth. I'll turn you over to Father Hadden now."

The priest, looking uncomfortable, cleared his throat and began. "It is a generally accepted belief that the soul of a dead person does not leave the body for some hours after death. I believe that this fact is the basis of my strange power. I believe that by coming to the place of death within twelve to fifteen hours I can sometimes make contact with the soul of the departed. This is what I will try now. Please join hands to complete the circle."

We did so, and the lights of the room dimmed, apparently on a signal to one of the waiting deputies outside.

Soon the place was almost black, with only a distant glow through the windows to show us the faint outlines of each other's faces.

"Now," Father Hadden's voice droned on, "silence, please . . . concentrate and hold hands tightly . . . do not break the circle . . . do not break the circle . . . I am calling upon the departed spirit of Glen Summer . . . Glen Summer . . . can you hear me? . . . are you still among us, Glen Summer. . . ?"

He kept it up like that, talking to himself in the darkness, for perhaps ten minutes—until my palm began to sweat in Vicky's grip. Then, without warning, there came a moaning sound from very close. It might have been at the center of the great round table. The moaning increased in volume until it formed words, and Vicky's fingernails dug into my hand.

"I have come," the voice boomed.

"That's not my husband," Della Summer gasped. "That's not his voice!"

But whoever it was, the voice continued. *"Hello, Della . . . hello, Juan. . . ."*

I heard Cruz utter a startled gasp, and then Father Hadden's voice cut in. "Who killed you, Glen? Who?"

"I . . . I don't know. . . . Felt the sword go in. . . ."

"It's some sort of trickery," Yates Ambrose muttered across the table. "That's not Glen."

But Father Hadden pressed on. "Can you tell us anything at all, Glen?"

"No . . . except . . . except . . ."

"What? Except what?"

"Except how did the killer know which one of them was me?"

As soon as the words had been uttered I realized the truth of them, the single fantastic truth that none of us had noticed or questioned. With nineteen nearly naked men hanging on crosses in a dim cellar, their heads completely hooded, how could anyone know which one of them was Glen Summer?

And as soon as the thought entered my head I knew the answer. Only one man could have known which of those hanging figures was Summer. One man, the man who tied him to the cross—Juan Cruz.

"No!" Cruz shouted in the same instant, and leaped free of the human ring. Before I knew what was happening the lights were flooding down on us, and Juan Cruz's terrified figure was leaping over a low sofa by the leaded windows.

"I knew it was him all the time," Partell snorted, reaching for his gun. But, somehow, Simon was there beside him, clutching the gun hand.

And in a moment it was all over, with three deputies bearing down on top of Cruz's struggling body. Partell shook free from Simon's grip and finally got the revolver out. "Why didn't you let me shoot him?" he muttered. "It would have saved the expense of a trial."

"Because," Simon said quietly, "he isn't guilty."

"*What?* Who the hell could have done it if he didn't?"

And Simon Ark turned towards the others. "Suppose you answer that, Mrs. Summer. Suppose you tell him how you killed your husband. . . ."

We just stood there, waiting for the screams of denial that never came. I think in that first moment even I must have thought that at last Simon had made a mistake, that certainly Della Summer could not possibly have plunged the sword into her husband's chest. But no denial came.

"Are you crazy, Ark? Sheriff Partell snorted, breaking the shocked silence.

"Not at all."

"But that voice. . . ."

Simon smiled. "Forgive me, it was my voice, slightly disguised and removed from its usual position. Father Hadden and I really had little hope that the spirit of Glen Summer would really present itself before so many people. We hoped to scare a confession out of Mrs. Summer, but unfortunately we only succeeded in scaring the innocent Senor Cruz."

"And why couldn't Cruz be the killer?" Partell wanted to know.

"The reason for that goes deeply into the character of the man and the whole practice of the Penitentes. It has already been pointed out that neither Cruz nor any of the others would be a party to a simple murder in such a place as this, while in the grip of a religious fervor. Such good and evil just could not exist side by side in the same man. Besides, none of the eighteen would know which cross was occupied by Summer this day. Only Cruz would know that, and he was the most fervent of all—the one person least likely to murder within the walls of his sacred palace. There remained one possibility, however. Suppose—suppose Cruz committed the murder in a fit of religious zeal, somehow believing Summer to be evil? Suppose he had some insane quirk that dictated the very ritual murder we all feared so much."

Sheriff Partell nodded. "I still think that's what happened."

But Simon Ark had not finished speaking. "Consider the man, though. Consider Juan Cruz, deciding he must murder the hanging figure on the cross. Either insane or in an uncontrollable fit of religious passion, he seizes a weapon from the wall there and heads for the basement." He paused only a moment. "And *what weapon* does he seize?"

The sheriff gestured toward the wall. "All there are are swords and spears. He didn't have much choice."

"But he did! He had the ultimate choice. He had the choice between stabbing Glen Summer in the left side with a sword—a spear like the Roman soldier used on Christ as He hung dying on Calvary. . . ."

We were silent then, all of us, because, somehow, we knew he was right. But then Sheriff Partell spoke again. "O.K., but why does that make it his wife?"

"We have already shown that the killer had to be able to recognize Glen Summer hanging nearly naked in a dimly lit basement, with his entire head covered. Who could have recognized him, for his body alone? Ambrose the bartender? Possible but doubtful. Only one person could enter that basement with the certainty of recognizing the naked chest and legs of Glen Summer. Only one person—the wife who shared his bed."

And now Vicky Nelson spoke up beside me. "I don't know too much about this whole crazy thing, but from what I have heard I'd like you to explain how Mrs. Summer or any other woman could walk past eighteen men without being noticed. After all, they were all supposed to be naked to the waist, weren't they?"

Simon cleared his throat. "What nearly everyone tends to forget in dealing with real-life crime is that it is not at all like crime in books. In a mystery novel a killer must have a foolproof, or seeming foolproof, method of murder before he strikes. But in real life a murderer might be impelled to strike with only a fifty-fifty chance of escape, if the motive was great enough. Della Summer's motive was great enough, and her chances of escape were better than fifty-fifty."

"But how?"

"She knew about the basement room; she knew about the rite that would be going on this morning. She knew it all because her husband had told her. She entered the villa, took down the sword—perhaps she knew about that, too, or perhaps she had brought some other weapon which she discarded in favor of the sword—and then made her way down the steps to the basement. And then she walked past those hanging men, studying them in the dimness until she recognized her husband."

"And they never saw her?"

"They never saw her, my friend, because—simply—their eyes were closed. You must remember that these men were religious mystics, in the grip of a highly emotional experience. Each man, as he hung there with the ropes cutting into his wrists, was in a sense another Christ. Each man, deep in his own prayerful thoughts, would naturally have closed his eyes—especially since there was nothing to see in the dim basement. Della Summer guessed this, and she was right. Moving silently on the stone floor she had perfect safety—until the very moment she plunged the sword into her husband's chest. And even then the odds were with her. Already in pain from the ropes, there was a good chance he would not cry out in the split second before death. He didn't, and she won her only gamble."

Through it all, Della Summer had been silent. Now she spoke. "Why did I kill him?" she asked, not making it a denial but rather only a question. A question to which she already knew the answer.

"Because, dear lady, your husband told you he planned to sell the *Oasis* and donate the money to the Church. You couldn't stand the thought of a future of poverty chained to a religious fanatic. So you had to kill him before he carried out his plan. You had to kill so you would inherit control of the *Oasis*. And you risked killing him here because this was the last place on earth a woman would be suspected."

I could tell by the faces around us that he'd convinced us all, but I still had a final question. "Simon, what about Ambrose's tire tracks outside?"

"Simple, my friend. She borrowed his car. I considered the possibility that Ambrose was guilty, but quickly rejected it. He had no obvious motive, and as I've explained, it was doubtful if he could have been certain of recognizing Summer's masked body. In any event, there was a final clue pointing to Mrs. Summer. Sheriff Partell told me that when she arrived here with him, she broke away and ran sobbing to the basement. How did she know the way to the basement, or that her husband had died there? She knew because she'd been here before today—to search him out and kill him."

"While she was prowling around she might have run into Cruz," I objected.

"She knew he'd be at prayer. It was no more of a chance than any of the rest of it. When her husband told her of this place, he no doubt went into great detail."

Sheriff Partell's expression was somber. "Della," he said quietly, "I'm afraid I'll have to . . ."

"I know," she said. "It was the chance I took."

"You're confessing?"

But there was still a spark of fire in her eyes. "Not on your life! I'll fight it out with a jury."

Vicky Nelson turned to me with a low snort. "Didn't I tell you she was a real bitch? Let's get out of here. . . ."

Simon and I dropped Vicky back at her car, and that was the last I saw of her—though the memory of those legs stayed with me for many days. We spent the night with Father Hadden, and I know that he and Simon talked far into it, of the strange happenings and the strange things that did not happen. And when we left the next morning the priest was busy telephoning—talking to the eighteen men who were all that remained of the case's loose ends.

A month or so later I received a letter at my New York office. It was sent to Simon Ark, in my care, and it was from Father Hadden. It had been a busy month for him, but it was a happy letter. He had succeeded in organizing the Penitentes into a group to help him with parish activities, and he had great hopes that their overwhelming piety was being channeled into more normal activities. Juan Cruz, unfortunately, had suffered a mild nervous breakdown—but Father Hadden even held out hope for him. And surprisingly enough he added a P. S. to the effect that Vicky Nelson and Yates Ambrose were planning to be married.

"He doesn't say a word about the spirits," I pointed out to Simon.

"It is a happy letter, my friend. Full of the joy of young love and older faith. There will be no more spirits for Father Hadden."

And one day—it must have been a year later—the priest himself visited us, happy in the midst of a job well done. "I'm here only for a few days," he said. "I couldn't pass through without seeing my old friends."

"How are Vicky and Yates?" I asked.

"Happy," he said, and that after all was a complete answer.

And Simon smiled down on the man of God. "No more spirits?"

But the priest hesitated before answering. "Only one, Mr. Ark. Only one."

"One?"

He nodded. "Della Summer died in the gas chamber last month." And that was all he would say. . . .

THE SHAKER REVIVAL

by Gerald Jonas

TO: Arthur Stock, Executive Editor, *Ideas Illustrated*, New York City, 14632008447
FROM: Raymond Senter, c/o Hudson Junction Rotel, Hudson Junction, N.Y. 28997601910
ENCLOSED: Tentative Lead for *"The Shaker Revival."* Pix, tapes upcoming.

Jerusalem West, N.Y., Thursday, June 28, 1995—The work of Salvation goes forward in this green and pleasant Hudson Valley hamlet to the high-pitched accompaniment of turbo-car exhausts and the amplified beat of the "world's loudest jag-rock band." Where worm-eaten apples fell untended in abandoned orchards less than a decade ago a new religious sect has burst into full bloom. In their fantastic four-year history the so-called New Shakers—or United Society of Believers (Revived), to give them their official title—have provoked the hottest controversy in Christendom since Martin Luther nailed his ninety-five theses to the door of All Saints Church in

Wittenberg, Germany, on October 31, 1517. Boasting a membership of more than a hundred thousand today, the New Shakers have been processing applications at the rate of nine hundred a week. Although a handful of these "recruits" are in their early and middle twenties—and last month a New Jersey man was accepted into the Shaker Family at Wildwood at the ripe old age of thirty-two—the average New Shaker has not yet reached his eighteenth birthday.

Richard F, one of the members of the "First Octave" who have been honored with "uncontaminated" Shaker surnames, explains it this way: "We've got nothing against feebies. They have a piece of the Gift inside just like anyone else. But it's hard for them to travel with the Family. Jag-rock hurts their ears, and they can't sync with the Four Noes, no matter how hard they try. So we say to them, 'Forget it, star. You wheels are not our wheels. But we're all going somewhere, right? See you at the other end.' "

It is hardly surprising that so many 'feebies"—people over thirty—have trouble with the basic Believers' Creed: "No hate, No war, No money, no sex." Evidently, in this final decade of the twentieth century, sainthood is only possible for the very young.

The "Roundhouse" at Jerusalem West is, in one sense, the Vatican of the nationwide movement. But in many ways it is typical of the New Shaker communities springing up from La Jolla, California, to Seal Harbor, Maine. At last count there were sixty-one separate "tribes," some containing as many as fifteen "families" of a hundred and twenty-eight members each. Each Shaker family is housed in an army-surplus pliodesic dome—covering some ten thousand square feet of bare but vinyl-hardened earth—which serves as bedroom, living room, workshop and holy tabernacle, all in one. There is a much smaller satellite dome forty feet from the main building which might be called the Outhouse, but isn't—the New Shakers themselves refer to it as Sin City. In keeping with their general attitude toward the bodily functions, Sin City is the only place in the Jerusalem West compound that is off-limits to visitors.

As difficult as it may be for most North Americans to accept, today's typical Shaker recruit comes from a background of unquestioned abundance and respectability. There is no taint of the Ghetto and no evidence of serious behavioral problems. In fact, Preliminary School records show that these young people often excelled in polymorphous play and responded quite normally to the usual spectrum of chemical and electrical euphorics. As underteens, their proficiency in programmed dating was consistently rated "superior" and they were often cited as leaders in organizing multiple-outlet experiences. Later, in Modular School, they scored in the fiftieth percentile or better on Brand-Differentiation tests. In short, according to all the available figures, they would have had no trouble gaining admission to the college of their choice or obtaining a commission in the Consumer Corps or qualifying for a Federal Travel Grant. Yet for some reason, on the very brink of maturity, they turned their backs on all the benefits their parents and grandparents fought so hard for in the Cultural Revolution—and plunged instead into a life of regimented sense-denial.

On a typical summer's afternoon at Jerusalem West, with the sun filtering through the translucent dome and bathing the entire area in a soft golden glow, the Roundhouse resembles nothing so much as a giant, queenless beehive. In the gleaming chrome-and-copper kitchen blenders whirr and huge pots bubble as a squad of white-smocked Food Deacons prepares the copious vegetable stew that forms the staple of the Shaker diet. In the soundproofed garage sector the Shop Deacons are busily transforming another hopeless-looking junk heap into the economical, turbine-powered "hotrod"—one already known to connoisseurs in this country and abroad as the Shakerbike—and the eight Administrative Deacons and their assistants are directing family business from a small fiber-walled cubicle known simply as The Office. And the sixteen-piece band is cutting a new liturgical tape for the Evening Service—a tape that may possibly end up as number one on the federal pop charts like the recent Shaker hit, *This Freeway's Plenty Wide Enough.* No matter where one turns beneath the big dome, one finds young people humming, tapping their feet, breaking into snatches of song and generally living up to the New Shaker motto: "Work is Play." One of their most popular songs—a characteristic coupling of Old Shaker words to a modern jag-rock background—concludes with this no-nonsense summation of the Shaker life-style:

It's the Gift to be simple,
The Gift to be free,
The Gift to come down
Where the Gift ought to be

MORE TO COME

XEROGRAM: June 28 (11:15P.M.)
TO: The Dean, Skinner Free Institute, Ronkonkoma, New Jersey 72441333965
FROM: Raymond Senter, c/o Hudson Junction Rotel, Hudson Junction, N.Y. 28997601910

Friend:

My son Bruce Senter, age 14, was enrolled in your institute for a six-week seminar in Applied Physiology beginning May 10. According to the transcript received by his Modular School (NYC118A), he successfully completed his course of studies on June 21. Mrs. Senter and I have had no word from him since. He had earlier talked with his Advisor about pursuing a Field-research project in Intensive Orgasm. I would appreciate any further information you can give me as to his post-seminar whereabouts. Thank you.

TO: Stock, Ex-Ed, *I.I.*
FROM: Senter
ENCLOSED: Background tape, Interview with Harry G (born "Guardino") member of First Octave. Edited Transcript, June 29.

Q: Suppose we begin by talking a little about your position here as one of the—well, what shall I say? Founding Fathers of the Shaker Revival?

A: First you better take a deep breath, star. That's all out of sync. There's no Founding Fathers here. Or Founding Mothers or any of that jag. There's only one Father and one Mother and they're everywhere and nowhere, understand?

Q: What I meant was—as a member of the First Octave you have certain duties and responsibilities—

A: Like I said, star, everyone's equal here.

Q: I was under the impression that your rules stressed obedience to a hierarchy?

A: Oh, there has to be order, sure, but it's nothing personal. If you can punch a computer—you sync with the Office Deacons. If you make it with wheels—you're in the Shop crew. Me—I fold my bed in the morning, push a juice-horn in the band and talk to reporters when they ask for me. That doesn't make me Pope.

Q: What about the honorary nomenclature?

A: What's that?

Q: The initials. Instead of last names.

A: Oh, yeah. They were given to us as a sign. You want to know what of?

Q: Please.

A: As a sign that no one's stuck with his birth kit. Sure, you may start with a Chevvie Six chassis and I have to go with a Toyota. That's the luck of the DNA. But we all need a spark of the chamber to get it moving. That's the Gift. And if I burn clean and keep in tune I may leave you flat in my tracks. Right?

Q: What about the Ghetto?

A: Even the Blacks have a piece of the Gift. What they do with it is their trip.

Q: There's been a lot of controversy lately about whether your movement is really Christian—in a religious sense. Would you care to comment on that?

A: You mean like "Jesus Christ, the Son of God?" Sure, we believe that. And we believe in Harry G, the Son of God and Richard F, the Son of God and—what's your name, star?—Raymond Senter, the Son of God. That's the gift. That's what it's all about. Jesus found the Gift inside. So did Buddha, Mother Ann, even Malcolm X—we don't worry too much about who said what first. First you find the Gift—then you live it. The Freeway's plenty wide enough.

Q: Then why all the emphasis on your Believers' Creed, and the Articles of Faith, and your clothes?

A: Look, star, every machine's got a set of specs. You travel with us, you learn our set. We keep the chrome shiny, the chambers clean. And we don't like accidents.

Q: Your prohibitions against money and sex—

A: "Prohibitions" is a feebie word. We're free from money and sex. The Four Noes are like a Declaration of Independence. See, everybody's really born free—but you have to know it. So we don't rob cradles. We say, let them grown up, learn what it's all about—the pill, the puffer, the feel-o-mat—all the perms and combos. Then, when they're fifteen or sixteen, if they still crave those chains, okay. If not, they know where to find us.

Q: What about the people who sign up and then change their minds?

A: We have no chains—if that's what you mean.

Q: You don't do anything to try to keep them?

A: Once you've really found the Gift inside there's no such thing as "changing your mind."

Q: What's your attitude toward the Old Shakers? They died out, didn't they, for lack of recruits?

A: Everything is born and dies and gets reborn again.

Q: Harry, what would happen if this time the whole world became Shakers?

A: Don't worry, star. You won't be around to see it.

MORE TO COME

XEROGRAM: June 29 (10:43 P.M.)

TO: Connie Fine, Director, Camp Encounter, Wentworth, Maine, 47119650023

FROM: Raymond Senter, Hudson Junction Rotel, Hudson Junction, N.Y. 28997601910

Connie:

Has Bruce arrived yet? Arlene and I have lost contact with him in the last week, and it occurred to me that he may have biked up to camp early and simply forgotten to buzz us—he was so charged up about being a full counselor-leader of his own T-group this season. Anyway, would you please buzz me soonest at the above zip? You know how mothers tend to overload the worry-circuits until they know for sure that their little wriggler is safely plugged in somewhere. Joy to you and yours, Ray.

TO: Stock, Ex-Ed., *I.I.*
FROM: Senter
ENCLOSED: Fact sheet on Old Shakers

FOUNDRESS—Mother Ann Lee, b. Feb. 29, 1736, Manchester, England.

ANTECENDENTS—Early Puritan ''seekers'' (Quakers), French ''Prophets'' (Camisards).

ORIGIN—Following an unhappy marriage—four children, all dead in infancy—Mother Ann begins to preach that ''concupiscence'' is the root of all evil. Persecutions and imprisonment.

1774—Mother Ann and seven early disciples sail to America aboard the ship *Mariah*. Group settles near Albany. Public preaching against concupiscence. More persecutions. More converts. Ecstatic, convulsive worship. Mother Ann's ''miracles.''

1784—Mother Ann dies.

1787—Mother Ann's successors, Father Joseph and Mother Lucy, organize followers into monastic communities and ''separate'' themselves from sinful world.

1784-1794—Expansion of sect through New York State and New England.

1806-1826—Expansion of sect across Western frontier—Ohio, Kentucky, Indiana.

1837-1845—Mass outbreak of spiritualism. Blessings, songs, spirit-drawings and business advice transmitted by deceased leaders through living "instruments."

1850's—Highpoint of Society. Six thousand members, eighteen communities, fifty-eight "Families."

Total recorded membership—from late 18th century to late 20th century—approximately seventeen thousand.

Old Shakers noted for—mail-order seed business, handicrafts (brooms, baskets and boxes), furniture manufacture.

Credited with invention of—common clothes pin, cut nails, circular saw, turbine waterwheel, steam-driven washing machine.

Worship—Emphasis on communal singing and dancing. Early "convulsive" phase gives way in 19th century to highly organized performances and processions—ring dances, square order shuffles.

Beliefs—Celibacy, Duality of Deity (Father and Mother God), Equality of the Sexes, Equality in Labor, Equality in Property. Society to be perpetuated by "admission of serious-minded persons and adoption of children."

Motto—"Hands to work and Hearts to God."

MORE TO COME

XEROGRAM: June 30 (8:15 A.M.)
TO: Mrs. Rosemary Collins, 133 Escorial Drive, Baywater, Florida, 92635776901
FROM: RAYMOND SENTER, HUDSON JUNCTION ROTEL, HUDSON JUNCTION, N.Y. 28997601910

Dear Rosie:

Has that little wriggler of ours been down your way lately? Bruce is off again on an unannounced sidetrip, and it struck me that he might have hopped down south to visit his favorite aunt. Not to mention his favorite cousin! How is that suntanned teaser of yours? Still taking after you in the S-L-N department? Give her a big kiss for me—you know where! And if Bruce does show up please buzz me right away at the above zip. Much Brotherly Love, Ray.

TO: Stock, Ex-Ed., *I.I.*
FROM: Senter
ENCLOSED: Caption tape for film segment on Worship Service.

JERUSALEM WEST, Saturday, June 30—I'm standing at the entrance to the inner sanctum of the huge Roundhouse here, the so-called Meeting Center, which is used only for important ceremonial functions—like the Saturday Night Dance scheduled to begin in exactly five minutes. In the Holy Corridor to my right the entire congregation has already assembled in two rows, one for boys and one for girls, side by side but not touching. During the week the Meeting Center is separated from the work and living areas by curved translucent partitions which fit together to make a little dome-within-a-dome. But when the sun begins to set on Saturday night the partitions are removed to reveal a circular dance floor, which is in fact the hub of the building. From this slightly raised platform of gleaming fibercast, I can look down each radial corridor—past the rows of neatly folded beds in the dormitories, past the shrouded machines in the repair shops, past the partly finished Shakerbikes in the garage, past the scrubbed formica tables in the kitchen—to the dim horizon line where the dome comes to rest on the sacred soil of Jerusalem West.

All artificial lights have been extinguished for the Sabbath celebration. The only illumination comes from the last rays of the sun, a dying torch that seems to have set the dome material itself ablaze. It's a little like standing inside the fiery furnace of Nebuchadnezzar with a hundred and twenty-eight unworried prophets of the Lord. The silence is virtually complete—not a cough, not the faintest rustle of fabric is heard. Even the air vents have been turned off—at least for the moment. I become aware of the harsh sound of my own respiration.

At precisely eight o'clock the two lines of worshipers begin to move forward out of the Holy Corridor. They circle the dance floors, the boys moving to the right, the girls to the left. Actually, it's difficult to tell them apart. The Shakers use no body ornaments at all—no paints, no wigs, no gems, no bugs, no dildoes, no flashers. All wear their hair cropped short, as if sheared with the aid of an overturned bowl. And all are dressed in some variation of Shaker gear—a loosely fitting, long-sleeved, buttonless and collarless shirt slit open at the neck for two inches and hanging free at the waist over a pair of baggy trousers pulled tight around each ankle by a hidden elastic band.

The garments look vaguely North African. They are made of soft dynaleen and they come in a variety of pastel shades. One girl may be wearing a pale pink top and a light blue bottom. The boy standing opposite her may have on the same colors, reversed. Others in the procession have chosen combinations of lilac and peach, ivory and lemon or turquoise and butternut. The range of hues seems endless but the intensity never varies, so that the entire spectacle presents a living demonstration of one of the basic Articles of Faith of the Shaker Revival—Diversity in Uniformity.

Now the procession has ended. The worshipers have formed two matching arcs, sixty-four boys on one side, sixty-four girls on the other, each standing precisely an arm's length from each neighbor. All are barefoot. All are wearing the same expression—a smile so modest as to be virtually undetectable if it were not mirrored and remirrored a hundred and twenty-eight times around the circumference of the ritual circle. The color of the dome has begun to change to a darker, angrier crimson. Whether the natural twilight's being artificially augmented—either from inside or outside the building—is impossible to tell. All eyes are turned upward to a focus about twenty-five feet above the center of the floor, where an eight-sided loudspeaker hangs by a chrome-plated cable from the midpoint of the dome. The air begins to fill with a pervasive vibration like the rumble of a distant monocar racing toward you in the night. And then the music explodes into the supercharged air. Instantly the floor is alive with jerking, writhing bodies—it's as if each chord were an electrical impulse applied directly to the nerve ends of the dancers—and the music is unbelievably loud.

The dome must act as an enormous soundbox. I can feel the vibrations in my feet and my teeth are chattering with the beat—but as wild as the dancing is, the circle is still intact. Each Shaker is "shaking" in his own place. Some are uttering incomprehensible cries, the holy gibberish that the Shakers call their Gift of Tongues—ecstatic prophesies symbolizing the Wordless Word of the Deity. One young girl with a gaunt but beautiful face is howling like a coyote. Another is grunting like a pig. A third is alternately spitting into the air and slapping her own cheeks viciously with both hands.

Across the floor a tall skinny boy has shaken loose from the rim of the circle. Pirouetting at high speed, his head thrown straight back so that his eyes are fixed on the crimson membrane of the dome, he seems to be propelling himself in an erratic path toward the center of the floor. And now the dome is changing color again, clotting to a deeper purple—like the color of a late evening sky but flecked with scarlet stars that seem to be darting about with a life of their own, colliding, coalescing, reforming.

A moment of relative calm has descended on the dancers. They are standing with their hands at their sides—only their heads are moving, lolling first to one side, then the other, in keeping with the new, subdued rhythm of the music. The tall boy in the center has begun to spin around and around in place, picking up speed with each rotation—now he's whirling like a top, his head still bent back, his eyes staring sightlessly. His right arm shoots out from the shoulder, the elbow locked, the fingers stiff, the palm flat—this is what the Shakers call the Arrow Sign, a manifestation of the Gift of Prophecy, directly inspired by the Dual Deity, Father Power and Mother Wisdom. The tall boy is the "instrument" and he is about to receive a message from on high.

His head tilts forward. His rotation slows. He comes to a halt with his right arm pointing at a short red-haired girl. The girl begins to shake all over as if struck by a high fever. The music rises to an ear-shattering crescendo and ends in mid-note.

"Everyone's a mirror," the tall boy shouts. "Clean, clean, clean—oh, let it shine! My dirt's not my own but it stains the earth. And the earth's not my own—the Mother and Father are light above light but the light can't shine alone. Only a mirror can shine, shine, shine. Let the mirror be mine, be mine, be mine!"

The red-haired girl is shaking so hard her limbs are flailing like whips. Her mouth has fallen open and she begins to moan, barely audibly at first. What she utters might be a single-syllable word like "clean" or "mine" or "shine" repeatedly, so rapidly that the consonants break down and the vowels flow into one unending stream of sound. But it keeps getting louder and louder and still louder, like the wail of an air-raid siren, until all resemblance to speech disappears and it seems impossible that such a sound can come from a human throat. You can almost hear the blood vessels straining, bursting.

Then the loudspeaker cuts in again in mid-note with the loudest, wildest jag-rock riff I have ever heard, only it's no longer something you can hear—it's inside you and you're inside it. And the dome has burst into blooms of color! A stroboscopic fireworks display that obliterates all outlines and shatters perspective and you can't tell whether the dancers are moving very, very slowly or very, very fast. The movement is so perfectly synchronized with the sound and the sound with the color that there seems to be no fixed reference point anywhere.

All you can say is: "There is color, there is sound, there is movement—"

This is the Gift of Seizure, which the New Shakers prize so highly—and whether it is genuinely mystical, as they claim, or autohypnotic or drug-induced, as some critics maintain, or a combination of all of these or something else entirely, it is an undeniably real—and profoundly disturbing—experience.

XEROGRAM: July 1 (7:27 A.M.)
TO: Frederick Rickover, Eastern Supervisor, Feel-O-Mat Corp., Baltimore, Maryland, 65034775C2
FROM: Raymond Senter, Hudson Junction Rotel, Hudson Junction, N.Y. 28997601910

(WARNING: PERSONALIZED ENVELOPE: CONTENTS WILL POWDER IF OPENED IMPROPERLY)

Fred: I'm afraid it's back-scratching time again. I need a code-check on DNA No. 75/62/HR/tl/4-9-06^5. I'm interested in whether the codee has plugged into a feel-o-mat anywhere in the Federation during the past two weeks. This one's a family matter, not business, so buzz me only at the above zip. I won't forget it. Gratefully, Ray.

TO: Stock, Ex-Ed., *I.I.*
FROM: Senter
ENCLOSED: Three tapes. New Shaker "testimonies." Edited transcripts, July 1.

TAPE I (Shaker name, "Farmer Brown"). What kind of mike is this? No kidding. I didn't know they made a reamper this small. Chinese? Oh. Right. Well, let's see—I was born April 17, 1974, in Ellsworth, Saskatchewan. My breath-father's a foreman at a big refinery there. My breath-mother was a consumer-housewife. She's gone over now. It's kind of hard to remember details. When I was real little, I think I saw the feds scratch a Bomb-thrower on the steps of City Hall. But maybe that was only something I saw on 2-D. School was—you know, the usual. Oh, once a bunch of us kids got hold of some fresh spores from the refinery—I guess we stole them somehow. Anyway, there was still a lot of open land around and we planted them and raised our own crop of puffers. I didn't come down for a week. That was my farming experience. *(Laughter)* I applied for a bummer-grant on my fifteenth birthday, got a two-year contract and took off the next day for the sun. Let's see—Minneapolis, Kansas City, Mexico—what a jolt! There weren't so many feel-o-mats in the small towns down there and I was into all the hard stuff you could get in those days—speed, yellow, rock-juice, little-annie—I guess the only thing I never tried for a jolt was the Process and there were times when I was just about ready.

When the grant ran out, I just kept bumming on my own. At first you think it's going to be real easy. Half the people you know are still on contract and they share it around. Then your old friends start running out faster than you make new ones and there's a whole new generation on the road. And you start feeling more and more like a feebie and acting like one. I was lucky because I met this sweet little dove in Nashville—she had a master's in Audio-Visual but she was psycho for bummers, especially flat ones.

Anyway, she comes back to her coop one day with a new tape and puts it on and says, "This'll go right through you. It's a wild new group called the Shakers."

She didn't know two bobbys' worth about the Shakers and I didn't either—the first Shaker tapes were just hitting the market about then. Well, I can tell you, that jagged sound gave me a jolt. I mean, it was bigger than yellow, bigger than juice, only it let you down on your feet instead of your back. I had this feeling I had to hear more. I got all the tapes that were out but they weren't enough. So I took off one night for Wildwood and before I knew it I was in a Prep Meeting and I was home free—you know, I've always kind of hoped that little dove makes it on her own—Oh, yeah, the band.

Well, I'm one of the Band Deacons, which is what's called a Sacrificial Gift because it means handling the accounts—and that's too close to the jacks and bobbys for comfort. But someone has to do it. You can't stay alive in an impure world without getting a little stained and if outsiders want to lay the Kennedys on us for bikes and tapes, that's a necessary evil. But we don't like to spread the risk in the Family. So the Deacons sign the checks and deal with the agents and the stain's on us alone. And everyone prays a little harder to square it with the Father and Mother.

TAPE II (Shaker name, "Mariah Moses"). I was born in Darien, Connecticut. I'm an Aquarius with Leo rising. Do you want my breath name? I don't mind—it's Cathy Ginsberg. My breath-parents are both full-time consumers. I didn't have a very interesting childhood, I guess. I went to Mid-Darien Modular School. I was a pretty good student—my best subject was World Culture. I consummated on my third date, which was about average, I've been told, for my class. Do you really want all this background stuff? I guess the biggest thing that happened to the old me was when I won a second prize in the Maxwell Puffer Civic Essay contest when I was fourteen. The subject was *The Joys of Spectatorism* and the prize was a Programmed Weekend in Hawaii for two. I don't remember who I went with. But Hawaii was really nice. All those brown-skinned boys—we went to a big luau on Saturday night. That's a native-style orgy. They taught me things we never even learned in school.

I remember thinking, *Oh, star, this is the living end!*

But when it was all over I had another thought. If this was the living end—what came next? I don't know if it was the roast pig or what but I didn't feel so good for a few days. The night we got back home—Herbie! That was the name of my date. Herbie Alcott—he had short curly hair all over his back—anyway, the night I got home my breath-parents picked me up at the airport and on the way back to Darien they started asking me what I wanted to do with my life. They were trying to be so helpful, you know. I mean, you could see they would have been disappointed if I got involved in production of some kind but they weren't about to say that in so many words. They just asked me if I had decided how I wanted to plug into the Big Board. It was up to me to choose between college or the Consumer Corps or a Travel Grant—they even asked me if Herbie and I were getting serious and if we wanted to have a baby—because the waiting-list at the Marriage Bureau was already six months long and getting longer. The trouble was I was still thinking about the luau and the roast pig and I felt all—burned out. Like a piece of charcoal that still looks solid but is really just white ash—and if you touch it it crumbles and blows away. So I said I'd think about it but what I was really thinking was *I'm not signing up for any more orgies just yet.*

And a few days later the miracle happened. A girl in our glass was reported missing and a friend of mine heard someone say that she'd become a Shaker.

I said, "What's that?"

My friend said, "It's a religion that believes in No hate, No war, No money, No sex."

And I felt this thrill go right through me. And even though I didn't know what it meant at the time, that was the moment I discovered my Gift. It was such a warm feeling, like something soft and quiet curled up inside you, waiting. And the day I turned fifteen I hiked up to Jerusalem and I never went home. That was eleven months ago . . . oh, you can't describe what happens at Preparative Meeting. It's what happens inside you that counts. Like now, when I think of all my old friends from Darien, I say a little prayer.

Father Power, Mother Wisdom, touch their Gifts, set them free. . . .

TAPE III (Shaker name, "Earnest Truth"). I'm aware that I'm something of a rarity here. I assume that's why you asked me for a testimony. But I don't want you categorizing me as a Shaker intellectual or a Shaker theologian or anything like that. I serve as Legal Deacon because that's my Gift. But I'm also a member of the vacuum detail in Corridor Three and that's my Gift too. I'd be just as good a Shaker if I only cleaned the floor and nothing else. Is that clear? Good. Well then, as briefly as possible *[reads from prepared text]:* I'm twenty-four years old, from Berkeley, California. Breath-parents were on the faculty at the University; killed in an air crash when

I was ten. I was raised by the state. Pacific Highlands Modular School: First honors. Consumer Corps: Media-aide First-class. Entered the University at seventeen. Prelaw. Graduated *magna cum* in nineteen-ninety. Completed four-year Law School in three years. In my final year I became interested in the literature of religion—or, to be more precise, the literature of mysticism—possibly as a counterpoise to the increasing intensity of my formal studies. Purely as an intellectual diversion I began to read St. John of the Cross, George Fox, the Vedas, Tao, Zen, the Kabbala, the Sufis. But when I came across the early Shakers I was struck at once with the daring and clarity of this purely American variant. All mystics seek spiritual union with the Void, the Nameless, the Formless, the Ineffable. But the little band of Shaker pilgrims, confronted with a vast and apparently unbounded wilderness, took a marvelous quantum leap of faith and decided that the union had already been accomplished. The wilderness was the Void. For those who had eyes to see—this was God's Kingdom. And by practicing a total communism, a total abnegation, a total dedication, they made the wilderness flower for two hundred years. Then, unable to adjust to the methodologies of the Industrial Revolution, they quietly faded away; it was as if their gentle spirit had found a final resting place in the design of their utterly simple and utterly beautiful wooden furniture—each piece of which has since become a collector's item. When I began reading about the Old Shakers I had of course heard about the New Shakers—but I assumed that they were just another crackpot fundamentalist sect like the Holy Rollers or the Snake Handlers, an attempt to keep alive the pieties of a simpler day in the present age of abundance. But eventually my curiosity—or so I called it at the time—led me to investigate a Preparative Meeting that had been established in the Big Sur near Jefferstown. And I found my Gift. The experience varies from individual to individual. For me it was the revelation that the complex machine we refer to as the Abundant Society is the real anachronism. All the euphorics we feed ourselves cannot change the fact that the machinery of abundance has long since reached its limit as a vital force and is now choking on its own waste products—Pollution, Overpopulation, Dehumanization. Far from being a breakthrough, the so-called Cultural Revolution was merely the last gasp of the old order trying to maintain itself by programming man's most private senses into the machine. And the childish Bomb-throwers were nothing but retarded romantics, an anachronism within an anachronism. At this juncture in history, only the Shaker Revival offers a true alternative—in the utterly simple, and therefore utterly profound, Four Noes. The secular world usually praises us for our rejection of Hate and War and mocks us for our rejection of Money and Sex. But the Four Noes constitute a beautifully balanced ethical equation, in which each term is a function of the other three. There are no easy Utopias. Non-Shakers often ask: What would happen if everyone became a Shaker? Wouldn't that be the end of the human race? My personal answer is this: Society is suffering from the sickness unto death—a plague called despair. Shakerism is the only cure. As long as the plague rages more and more people will find the strength to take the medicine required, no matter how bitter it may seem. Perhaps at some future date, the very spread of Shakerism will restore Society to health, so that the need for Shakerism will again slacken. Perhaps the cycle will be repeated. Perhaps not. It is impossible to know what the Father and Mother have planned for their children. Only one thing is certain. The last of the Old Shaker prophetesses wrote in 1956: "The flame may flicker but the spark can never be allowed to die out until the salvation of the world is accomplished."

I don't think you'll find the flame flickering here.

MORE TO COME

XEROGRAM: July 1 (11:30 P.M.)
TO: Stock, Ex-Ed., *I.I.*
FROM: Raymond Senter, c/o Hudson Junction Rotel
(WARNING: PERSONALIZED ENVELOPE: CONTENTS WILL POWDER IF OPENED IMPROPERLY)

Art:

Cooperation unlimited here—until I mention "Preparative Meeting." Then they all get tongue-tied. Too holy for impure ears. No one will even say where or when. Working hypothesis: It's a compulsory withdrawal session. Recruits obviously must kick all worldly habits before taking final vows. Big question: How do they do it? Conscious or unconscious? Cold-turkey, hypno-suggestion, or re-conditioning? Legal or illegal? Even Control would like to know. I'm taping the Reception Deacon tomorrow. If you approve, I'll start putting the pressure on. The groundwork's done. We may get a story yet. Ray.

XEROGRAM: July 2 (2:15 A.M.)
TO: Joseph Harger, Coordinator, N.Y. State Consumer Control, Albany, N.Y. 31118002311
FROM: Raymond Senter, c/o Hudson Junction Rotel, Hudson Junction, N.Y. 28997601910
(WARNING: PERSONALIZED ENVELOPE: CONTENTS WILL POWDER IF OPENED IMPROPERLY)

Joe:

I appreciate your taking a personal interest in this matter. My wife obviously gave the wrong impression to the controller she contacted. She tends to get hysterical. Despite what she may have said I assure you my son's attitude toward the Ghetto was a perfectly healthy blend of scorn and pity. Bruce went with me once to see the Harlem Wall—must have been six or seven—and Coordinator Bill Quaite let him sit in the Scanner's chair for a few minutes. He heard a muezzin call from the top of one of those rickety towers. He saw the wild rats prowling in the stench and garbage. He also watched naked children fighting with wooden knives over a piece of colored glass. I am told there are young people today stupid enough to think that sneaking over the Wall is an adventure and that the process is reversible—but my son is definitely not one of them. And he is certainly not a Bomb-thrower. I know that you have always shared my publication's view that a selective exposure to the harsher realities makes for better consumers. (I'm thinking of that little snafu in datatraffic in the Albany Grid last summer.) I hope you'll see your way clear to trusting me again. I repeat: there's not the slightest indication that my son was going over to the Blacks. In fact, I have good reason to believe that he will turn up quite soon, with all discrepancies accounted for. But I need a little time. A Missing Persons Bulletin would only make things harder at the moment. I realize it was my wife who initiated the complaint. But I'd greatly appreciate it if she got misfiled for forty-eight hours. I'll handle any static on this side. Discreetly, Ray.

TO: Stock, Ex-Ed., *I.I.*
FROM: Senter
ENCLOSED: Background tape; interview with Antonia Cross, age 19, Reception Deacon, Jerusalem West Edited Transcript, July 2.

Q: (I waited silently for her to take the lead.)

A: Before we begin, I think we better get a few things straight. It'll save time and grief in the long run. First of all, despite what your magazine and others may have said in the past, we never proselytize. Never. So please don't use that word. We just try to live our Gift—and if other people are drawn to us, that's the work of the Father and Mother, not us. We don't have to preach. When someone's sitting in filth up to his neck he doesn't need a preacher to tell him he smells. All he needs to hear is that there's a cleaner place somewhere. Second, we don't prevent anyone from leaving, despite all rumors to the contrary. We've had exactly three apostates in the last four years. They found out their wheels were not our wheels and they left.

Q: Give me their names.

A: There's no law that says we have to disclose the names of backsliders. Find them yourself. That shouldn't be too hard, now that they're plugged back in to the Big Board.

Q: You overestimate the power of the press.

A: False modesty is not considered a virtue among Shakers.

Q: You mentioned three backsliders. How many applicants are turned away before taking final vows?

A: The exact percentage is immaterial. Some applicants are more serious than others. There is no great mystery about our reception procedure. You've heard the expression "Weekend Shakers." Anybody can buy the gear and dance and sing and stay pure for a couple of days. It's even considered a "jolt," I'm told. We make sure that those who come to us know the difference between a weekend and a lifetime. We explain the Gift, the Creed, the Articles of Faith. Then we ask them why they've come to us. We press them pretty hard. In the end, if they're still serious, they are sent to Preparative Meeting for a while until a Family is ready to accept them.

Q: How long is a while?

A: Preparative Meeting can take days or weeks. Or longer.

Q: Are they considered full-fledged Shakers during that time?

A: The moment of Induction is a spiritual, not a temporal, phenomenon.

Q: But you notify the authorities only after a recruit is accepted in a Family?

A: We comply with all the requirements of the Full Disclosure Law.

Q: What if the recruit is underage and lies about it? Do you run a routine DNA check?

A: We obey the law.

Q: But a recruit at a Prep Meeting isn't a Shaker and so you don't have to report his presence. Is that right?

A: We've had exactly nine complaints filed against us in four years. Not one has stuck.

Q: Then you do delay acceptance until you can trace a recruit's identity?

A: I didn't say that. We believe in each person's right to redefine his set, no matter what the Big Board may say about him. But such administrative details tend to work themselves out.

Q: How? I don't understand.

A: The ways of the Father and Mother sometimes passeth understanding.

Q: You say you don't proselytize, but isn't that what your tapes are—a form of preaching? Don't most of your recruits come to you because of the tapes? And don't most of them have to be brought down from whatever they're hooked on before you'll even let them in?

A: The world—your world—is filth. From top to bottom. We try to stay as far away as we can. But we have to eat. So we sell you our tapes and our Shakerbikes. There's a calculated risk of contamination. But it works the other way too. Filth can be contaminated by purity. That's known as Salvation. It's like a tug of war. We'll see who takes the greatest risk.

Q: That's what I'm here for—to see at first hand. Where is the Jerusalem West Preparative Meeting held?

A: Preparative Meetings are private. For the protection of all concerned.

Q: Don't you mean secret? Isn't there something going on at these meetings that you don't want the public to know?

A: If the public is ignorant of the life of the spirit, that is hardly our fault.

Q: Some people believe that your recruits are "prepared" with drugs or electro-conditioning.

A: Some people think that Shaker stew is full of saltpeter. Are you going to print that, too?

Q: You have been accused of brain-tampering. That's a serious charge. And unless I get a hell of a lot more cooperation from you than I've been getting I will have to assume that you have something serious to hide.

A: No one ever said you'd be free to see everything. You'll just have to accept our—guidance—in matters concerning religious propriety.

Q: Let me give you a little guidance, Miss Cross. You people already have so many enemies in that filthy world you despise that one unfriendly story from *I.I.* might just tip the scales.

A: The power of the press? We'll take our chances.

Q: What will you do if the police crack down?

A: We're not afraid to die. And the Control authorities have found that it's more trouble than it's worth to put us in jail. We seem to upset the other inmates.

Q: Miss Cross—

A: We use no titles here. My name is Antonia.

Q: You're obviously an intelligent, dedicated young woman. I would rather work with you than against you. Why don't we try to find some middle ground? As a journalist my primary concern is human nature—what happens to a young recruit in the process of becoming a full-fledged Shaker. You won't let me into a Prep Meeting to see for myself. All right, you have your reasons, and I respect them. But I ask you to respect mine. If I can look through your Reception files—just the last two or three weeks will do—I should be able to get some idea of what kind of raw material you draw on. You can remove the names, of course.

A: Perhaps we can provide a statistical breakdown for you.

Q: I don't want statistics. I want to look at their pictures, listen to their voices—you say you press them pretty hard in the first interview. That's what I need: their response under pressure, the difference between those who stick it through and those who don't.

A: How do we know you're not looking for something of a personal nature—to embarrass us?

Q: For God's sakes, I'm one of the best-known tapemen in the Federation. Why not just give me the benefit of the doubt?

A: You invoke a Deity that means nothing to you.

Q: I'm sorry.

A: The only thing I can do is transmit your request to the Octave itself. Any decision on such a matter would have to come from a Full Business Meeting.

Q: How long will it take?

A: The Octave is meeting tomorrow, before Evening Service.

Q: All right. I can wait till then. I suppose I should apologize again for losing my temper. I'm afraid it's an occupational hazard.

A: We all have our Gift.

MORE TO COME

TO: Stock, Ex-Ed., *I.I.*
FROM: Senter.
ENCLOSED: First add on Shaker Revival; July 3.

It is unclear whether the eight teenagers—six boys and two girls—who banded together one fateful evening in the spring of 1991 to form a jag-rock combo called The Shakers had any idea of the religious implications of the name. According to one early account in *Riff* magazine, the original eight were thinking only of a classic rock-and-roll number of the 1950s, *Shake, Rattle and Roll* (a title not without sexual as well as musicological overtones). On the other hand, there is evidence that Harry G was interested in astrology, palmistry, scientology and other forms of modern occultism even before he left home at the age of fifteen. (Harry G was born Harry Guardino, on December 18, 1974, in Schoodic, Maine, the son of a third-generation lobster fisherman.) Like many members of his generation he applied for a Federal Travel Grant on graduation from Modular School and received a standard two-year contract. But unlike most of his fellow-bummers, Harry did not immediately take off on an all-expenses-paid tour of the seamier side of life in the North American Federation. Instead, he hitched a ride to New York City, where he established a little basement coop on the lower west side that soon became a favorite waystation for other, more restless bummers passing through the city. No reliable account of this period is available. The rumors that he dabbled in a local Bomb-throwers cell appear to be unfounded. But it is known that sometime during the spring of 1991 a group of bummers nearing the end of their grants gathered in Harry G's coop to discuss the future. By coincidence or design the eight young people who came together that night from the far corners of the Federation all played some instrument and shared a passion for jag-rock. And as they talked and argued among themselves about the best way possible to "plug into the Big Board," it slowly began to dawn on them that perhaps their destinies were linked—or, as Harry G himself has put it, "We felt we could make beautiful music together. Time has made us one."

Building a reputation in the jag-rock market has never been easy—not even with divine intervention. For the next two months, The Shakers scrambled for work, playing a succession of one-night stands in consumers' centers, schools, fraternal lodges—wherever someone wanted live entertainment and was willing to put the group up. The Shakers traveled in a secondhand Chevrolet van which was kept running only by the heroic efforts of the group's electric-oud player, Richard Fitzgerald (who later—as Richard F—helped to design the improved version of the turbo-adapter which forms the basis of today's Shakerbike).

On the night of June the first the group arrived in Hancock, Massachusetts, where they were scheduled to play the next evening at the graduation dance of the Grady L. Parker Modular School. They had not worked for three days and their finances had reached a most precarious stage—they were now sharing only four bummer-grants between them, the other four contracts having expired in the previous weeks. From the very beginning of their relationship the eight had gone everywhere and done everything as a group—they even insisted on sleeping together in one room on the theory that the "bad vibrations" set up by an overnight absence from each other might adversely affect their music. As it turned out, there was no room large enough at the local Holiday Inn, so, after some lengthy negotiation, the Modular School principal arranged for them to camp out on the grounds of the local Shaker Museum, a painstaking restoration of an early New England Shaker community dating back to 1790. Amused but not unduly impressed by the coincidence in names, the eight Shakers bedded down for the night within sight of the Museum's most famous structure, the Round Stone Barn erected by the original Shakers in 1826. Exactly what happened between midnight and dawn on that fog-shrouded New England meadow may never be known—the validation of mystical experience being by its very nature a somewhat inexact science. According to Shaker testimony, however, the spirit of Mother Ann, sainted foundress of the original sect, touched the Gifts of the eight where they lay and in a vision of the future—which Amelia D later said was "as clear and bright as a holograph"—revealed why they had been chosen: The time had come for a mass revival of Shaker beliefs and practices. The eight teenagers awoke at the same instant, compared visions, found them to be identical and wept together for joy. They spent the rest of the day praying for guidance and making plans. Their first decision was to play as scheduled at the Grady L. Parker graduation dance.

"We decided to go on doing just what we had been doing—only more so," Amelia D later explained. "Also, I guess, we needed the jacks."

Whatever the reason, the group apparently played as never before. Their music opened up doors to whole new ways of hearing and feeling—or so it seemed to the excited crowd of seniors who thronged around the bandstand when the first set was over. Without any premeditation, or so he later claimed, Harry Guardino stood up and announced the new Shaker dispensation, including the Believers' Creed (the Four Noes) and a somewhat truncated version of the Articles of Faith of the United Society of Believers (Revived): "All things must be kept decent and in good order," "Diversity in Uniformity," and "Work is Play." According to the Hancock newspaper, seventeen members of the senior class left town that morning with the Shakers—in three cars "borrowed" from parents and later returned. Drawn by a Gift of Travel, the little band of pilgrims made their way to the quiet corner of New York State now known as Jerusalem West, bought some land—with funds obtained from anonymous benefactors—and settled down to their strange experiment in monastic and ascetic communism.

The actual historical connections between Old Shakers and New Shakers remains a matter of conjecture. It is not clear, for instance, whether Harry G and his associates had a chance to consult the documentary material on display at the Hancock Museum. There is no doubt that the First Article of Faith of the Shaker Revival is a word-for-word copy of the first part of an early Shaker motto. But it has been given a subtly different meaning in present-day usage. And while many of the New Shaker doctrines and practices can be traced to the general tenor of traditional Shakerism, the adaptations are often quite free and sometimes wildly capricious. All in all, the Shaker Revival seems to be very much a product of our own time. Some prominent evolutionists even see it as part of a natural process of weeding out those individuals incapable of becoming fully consuming members of the Abundant Society. They argue that Shakerism is a definite improvement, in this respect, over the youthful cult of Bomb-throwers which had to be suppressed in the early days of the Federation.

But there are other observers who see a more ominous trend at work. They point especially to the serious legal questions raised by the Shakers' efforts at large-scale proselytization. The twenty-seventh Amendment to the Federal Constitution guarantees the right of each white citizen over the age of fifteen to the free and unrestricted enjoyment of his own senses, provided that such enjoyment does not interfere with the range or intensity of any other citizen's sensual enjoyment. Presumably this protection also extends to the right of any white citizen to deny himself the usual pleasures. But what is the status of corporate institutions that engage in such repression? How binding, for example, is the Shaker recruit's sworn allegiance to the Believers' Creed? How are the Four Noes enforced within the sect? Suppose two Shakers find themselves physically attracted to each other and decide to consummate—does the United Society of Believers have any right to place obstacles between them? These are vital questions that have yet to be answered by the Control authorities. But there are influential men in Washington who read the twenty-seventh amendment as an obligation on the government's part not merely to protect the individual's right to sensual pleasure but also to help him maximize it. And in the eyes of these broad constructionists the Shakers are on shaky ground.

TO: Stock, Ex-Ed., *I.I.*
FROM: Senter
(WARNING: CONFIDENTIAL UNEDITED TAPE; NOT FOR PUBLICATION: CONTENTS WILL POWDER IF OPENED IMPROPERLY)

FIRST VOICE: Bruce? Is that you?

SECOND VOICE: It's me.

FIRST: For God's sake, come in! Shut the door. My God. I thought you were locked up in that Prep Meeting. I thought—

SECOND: It's not a prison. When I heard you were prowling around town I knew I had to talk to you.

FIRST: You've changed your mind then?

SECOND: Don't believe it. I just wanted to make sure you didn't lie about everything.

FIRST: Do they know you're here?

SECOND: No one followed me, if that's what you mean. No one even knows who I am. I've redefined my set, as we say.

FIRST: But they check. They're not fools. They'll find out soon enough—if they haven't already.

SECOND: They don't check. That's another lie. And anyway, I'll tell them myself after Induction.

FIRST: Brucie—it's not too late. We want you to come home.

SECOND: You can tell Arlene that her little baby is safe and sound. How is she? Blubbering all over herself as usual?

FIRST: She's pretty broken up about your running away.

SECOND: Why? Is she worried they'll cut off her credit at the feel-o-mat? For letting another potential consumer get off the hook?

FIRST: You wouldn't have risked coming to me if you didn't have doubts. Don't make a terrible mistake.

SECOND: I came to see you because I know how you can twist other people's words. Are you recording this?

FIRST: Yes.

SECOND: Good. I'm asking you straight out—please leave us alone.

FIRST: Do you know they're tampering with your mind?

SECOND: Have you tasted your local drinking water lately?

FIRST: Come home with me.

SECOND: I am home.

FIRST: You haven't seen enough of the world to turn your back on it.

SECOND: I've seen you and Arlene.

FIRST: And is our life so awful?

SECOND: What you and Arlene have isn't life. It's the American Dream Come True. You're in despair and don't even know it. That's the worst kind.

FIRST: You repeat the slogans as if you believed them.

SECOND: What makes you think I don't?

FIRST: You're my flesh and blood. I know you.

SECOND: You don't. All you know is that your little pride and joy ran away to become a monk and took the family genes. And Arlene is too old to go back to the Big Board and beg for seconds.

FIRST: Look—I know a little something about rebellion, too. I've had a taste of it in my time. It's healthy, it's natural—I'm all for it. But not an overdose. When the jolt wears off, you'll be stuck here. And you're too smart to get trapped in a hole like this.

SECOND: It's my life, isn't it? In exactly one hour and ten minutes I'll be free, white, and fifteen—Independence Day, right? What a beautiful day to be born—it's the nicest thing you and Arlene did for me.

FIRST: Brucie, we want you back. Whatever you want—just name it and if it's in my power I'll try to get it. I have friends who will help.

SECOND: I don't want anything from you. We're quits—can't you understand? The only thing we have in common now is this: *(sound of heavy breathing)*. That's it. And if you want that back you can take it. Just hold your hand over my mouth and pinch my nose for about five minutes. That should do it.

FIRST: How can you joke about it?

SECOND: Why not? Haven't you heard? There're only two ways to go for my generation—the Shakers or the

Ghetto. How do you think I'd look in blackface with bushy hair and a gorilla nose? Or do you prefer my first choice?

FIRST: I'm warning you, the country's not going to put up with either much longer. There's going to be trouble—and I want you out of here when it comes.

SECOND: What are the feebies going to do? Finish our job for us?

FIRST: Is that what you want then? To commit suicide?

SECOND: Not exactly. That's what the Bomb-throwers did. We want to commit your suicide.

FIRST: *(Words unintelligible.)*

SECOND: That really jolts you, doesn't it. You talk about rebellion as if you knew something about it because you wore beads once and ran around holding signs.

FIRST: We changed history.

SECOND: You didn't change anything. You were swallowed up, just like the Bomb-throwers. The only difference is, you were eaten alive.

FIRST: Bruce—

SECOND: Can you stretch the gray-stuff a little, and try to imagine what real rebellion would be like? Not just another chorus of "gimmie, gimmie, gimmie—" but the absolute negation of what's come before? The Four Noes all rolled up into One Big No!

FIRST: Brucie—I'll make a deal—

SECOND: No one's ever put it all together before. I don't expect you to see it. Even around here, a lot of people don't know what's happening. Expiation! That's what rebellion is all about. The young living down the sins of the fathers and mothers! But the young are always so hungry for life they get distracted before they can finish the job. Look at all the poor, doomed rebels in history; whenever they got too big to be crushed the feebies bought them off with a piece of action. The stick or the carrot and then—business as usual. Your generation was the biggest sellout of all. But the big laugh is, you really thought you won. So now you don't have any carrot left to offer, because you've already shared it all with us—before we got old. And we're strong enough to laugh at your sticks. Which is why the world is going to find out for the first time what total rebellion is.

FIRST: I thought you didn't believe in violence and hate?

SECOND: Oh, our strength is not of this world. You can forget all the tapes and bikes and dances—that's the impure shell that must be sloughed off. If you want to get the real picture, just imagine us—all your precious little gene-machines—standing around in a circle, our heads bowed in prayer, holding our breaths and clicking off one by one. Don't you think that's a beautiful way for your world to end? Not with a bang or a whimper—but with one long breathless Amen?

MORE TO COME

TO: Stock, Ex-Ed., *I.I.*
FROM: Senter
ENCLOSED: New first add on "*Shaker Revival*" (scratch earlier transmission; new lead upcoming).

JERUSALEM WEST, N.Y., Wednesday, July 4—An early critic of the Old Shakers, a robust pamphleteer who had actually been a member of the sect for ten months, wrote this prophetic appraisal of his former cohorts in the year 1782: "When we consider the infant state of civil power in America since the Revolution began, every infringement on the natural rights of humanity, every effort to undermine our original constitution, either in civil or ecclesiastical order, saps the foundation of Independency."

That winter, the Shaker foundress, Mother Ann, was seized in Petersham, Massachusetts, by a band of vigilantes who, according to a contemporary account, wanted, "to find out whether she was a woman or not." Various other Shaker leaders were horse-whipped, thrown in jail, tarred and feathered, and driven out of one New England town after another by an aroused citizenry. These severe persecutions, which lasted through the turn of the century, were the almost inevitable outcome of a clash between the self-righteous, unnatural, uncompromising doctrines of the Shakers—and the pragmatic, democratic, forward-looking mentality of the struggling new nation, which would one day be summed up in that proud emblem: The American Way of Life.

This conflict is no less sharp today. So far as the New Shakers have generally been given the benefit of the doubt as just another harmless fringe group. But there is evidence that the mood of the country is changing—and rapidly. Leading educators and political figures, respected clergymen and prominent consumer consultants have all become more outspoken in denouncing the disruptive effect of this new fanaticism on the country as a whole. Not since the heyday of the Bomb-throwers in the late seventies has a single issue shown such potential for galvanizing informed public opinion. And a chorus of distraught parents has only just begun to make itself heard—like the lamentations of Rachel in the wilderness.

Faced with the continuing precariousness of the international situation, and the unresolved dilemma of the Ghettoes, some Control authorities have started talking about new restrictions on all monastic sects—not out of any desire to curtail religious freedom but in an effort to preserve the constitutional guarantees of free expression and consumption. Some feel that if swift, firm governmental action is not forthcoming it will get harder and harder to prevent angry parents—and others with legitimate grievances—from taking the law into their own hands

MORE TO COME

THE RED ONE

by Jack London

There it was! The abrupt liberation of sound, as he timed it with his watch, Bassett likened to the trump of an archangel. Walls of cities, he meditated, might well fall down before so vast and compelling a summons. For the thousandth time vainly he tried to analyze the tone-quality of that enormous peal that dominated the land far into the strongholds of the surrounding tribes. The mountain gorge which was its source rang to the rising tide of it until it brimmed over and flooded earth and sky and air. With the wantonness of a sick man's fancy, he likened it to the mighty cry of some Titan of the Elder World vexed with misery or wrath. Higher and higher it arose, challenging and demanding in such profounds of volume that it seemed intended for ears beyond the narrow confines of the solar system. There was in it, too, the clamor of protest in that there were no ears to hear and comprehend its utterance.

—Such the sick man's fancy. Still he strove to analyze the sound. Sonorous as thunder was it, mellow as a golden bell, thin and sweet as a thrummed taut cord of silver—no; it was none of these, nor a blend of these. There were no words nor semblances in his vocabulary and experience with which to describe the totality of that sound.

Time passed. Minutes merged into quarters of hours, and quarters of hours into half hours, and still the sound persisted, ever changing from its initial vocal impulse yet never receiving fresh impulse—fading, dimming, dying as enormously as it had sprung into being. It became a confusion of troubled mutterings and babblings and colossal whisperings. Slowly it withdrew, sob by sob, into whatever great bosom had birthed it, until it whimpered deadly whispers of wrath and as equally seductive whispers of delight, striving still to be heard, to convey some cosmic secret, some understanding of infinite import and value. It dwindled to a ghost of sound that had lost its menace and promise, and became a thing that pulsed on in the sick man's consciousness for minutes after it had ceased. When he could hear it no longer, Bassett glanced at his watch. An hour had elapsed ere that archangel's trump had subsided into tonal nothingness.

Was this, then, *his* dark tower?—Bassett pondered, remembering his Browning and gazing at his skeleton-like and fever-wasted hands. And the fancy made him smile—of Childe Roland bearing a slug-horn to his lips with an arm as feeble as his was. Was it months, or years, he asked himself, since he first heard that mysterious call on the beach at Ringmanu? To save himself he could not tell. The long sickness had been most long. In conscious count of time he knew of months, many of them; but he had no way of estimating the long intervals of delirium and stupor. And how fared Captain Bateman of the blackbirder *Nari*? he wondered; and had Captain Bateman's drunken mate died of delirium tremens yet?

From which vain speculations, Bassett turned idly to review all that had occurred since that day on the beach at Ringmanu when he first heard the sound and plunged into the jungle after it. Sagawa had protested. He could see him yet, his queer little monkeyish face eloquent with fear, his back burdened with specimen cases, in his hands Bassett's butterfly net and naturalist's shotgun, as he quavered in Bêche-de-mer English: "Me fella too much fright along bush. Bad fella boy too much stop'm along bush."

Bassett smiled sadly at the recollection. The little New Hanover boy had been frightened, but had proved faithful, following him without hesitancy into the bush in the quest after the source of the wonderful sound. No fire-hollowed tree-trunk, that, throbbing war through the jungle depths, had been Bassett's conclusion. Erroneous had been his next conclusion, namely, that the source or cause could not be more distant than an hour's walk and that he would easily be back by mid-afternoon to be picked up by the *Nari*'s whaleboat.

"That big fella noise no good, all the same devil-devil," Sagawa had adjudged. And Sagawa had been right. Had he not had his head hacked off within the day? Bassett shuddered. Without doubt Sagawa had been eaten as well by the bad fella boys too much that stopped along the bush. He could see him, as he had last seen him stripped of the shotgun and all the naturalist's gear of his master, lying on the narrow trail where he had been decapitated barely the moment before. Yes, within a minute the thing had happened. Within a minute, looking back, Bassett had seen him trudging patiently along under his burdens. Then Bassett's own trouble had come upon him. He looked at the cruelly healed stumps of the first and second fingers of his left hand, then rubbed them softly into the indentation in the back of his skull. Quick as had been the flash of the long-handled tomahawk, he had been quick enough to duck away his head and partially to deflect the stroke with his up-flung hand. Two fingers and a nasty scalp-wound had been the price he paid for his life. With one barrel of his ten-gauge shotgun he had blown the life out of the bushman who had so nearly got him; with the other barrel he had peppered the bushmen bending over Sagawa, and had the pleasure of knowing that the major portion of the charge had gone into the one who leaped away with Sagawa's head. Everything had occurred in a flash. Only himself, the slain bushman, and what remained of Sagawa, were in the narrow, wild-pig run of a path. From the dark jungle on either side came no rustle of movement or sound of life. And he had suffered distinct and dreadful shock. For the first time in his life he had killed a human being, and he knew nausea as he contemplated the mess of his handiwork.

Then had begun the chase. He retreated up the pig-run before his hunters, who were between him and the beach. How many there were, he could not guess. There might have been one, or a hundred, for aught he saw of them. That some of them took to the trees and travelled along through the jungle roof he was certain; but at the most he never glimpsed more than an occasional flitting of shadows. No bowstrings twanged that he could hear; but every little while, whence discharged he knew not, tiny arrows whispered past him or struck tree-boles and fluttered to the ground beside him. They were bone-tipped and feather-shafted, and the feathers, torn from the breasts of humming-birds, iridesced like jewels.

Once—and now, after the long lapse of time, he chuckled gleefully at the recollection—he had detected a shadow above him that came to instant rest as he turned his gaze upward. He could make out nothing, but, deciding to chance it, had fired at it a heavy charge of number five shot. Squalling like an infuriated cat, the shadow crashed down through tree-ferns and orchids and thudded upon the earth at his feet, and, still squalling its rage and pain, had sunk its human teeth into the ankle of his stout tramping boot. He, on the other hand, was not idle, and with his free foot had done what reduced the squalling to silence. So inured to savagery had Bassett since become, that he chuckled again with the glee of the recollection.

What a night had followed! Small wonder that he had accumulated such a virulence and variety of fevers, he thought, as he recalled that sleepless night of torment, when the throb of his wounds was as nothing compared with the myriad stings of the mosquitoes. There had been no escaping them, and he had not dared to light a fire. They had literally pumped his body full of poison, so that, with the coming of day, eyes swollen almost shut, he had stumbled blindly on, not caring much when his head should be hacked off and his carcass started on the way of Sagawa's to the cooking fire. Twenty-four hours had made a wreck of him—of mind as well as body. He had scarcely retained his wits at all, so maddened was he by the tremendous inoculation of poison he had received. Several times he fired his shotgun with effect into the shadows that dogged him. Stinging day insects and gnats added to his torment, while his bloody wounds attracted hosts of loathsome flies that clung sluggishly to his flesh and had to be brushed off and crushed off.

Once, in that day, he heard again the wonderful sound, seemingly more distant, but rising imperiously above the nearer war-drums in the bush. Right there was where he had made his mistake. Thinking that he had passed beyond it and that, therefore, it was between him and the beach of Ringmanu, he had worked back toward it when in reality he was penetrating deeper and deeper into the mysterious heart of the unexplored island. That night, crawling in among the twisted roots of a banyan tree, he had slept from exhaustion while the mosquitoes had had their will of him.

Followed days and nights that were vague as nightmares in his memory. One clear vision he remembered was of suddenly finding himself in the midst of a bush village and watching the old men and children fleeing into the jungle. All had fled but one. From close at hand and above him, a whimpering as of some animal in pain and terror had startled him. And looking up he had seen her—a girl, or young woman, rather, suspended by one arm in the cooking sun. Perhaps for days she had so hung. Her swollen protruding tongue spoke as much. Still alive, she gazed at him with eyes of terror. Past help, he decided, as he noted the swellings of her legs which advertised that the joints had been crushed and the great bones broken. He resolved to shoot her, and there the vision terminated. He could not remember whether he had or not, any more than could he remember how he chanced to be in that village or how he succeeded in getting away from it.

Many pictures, unrelated, came and went in Bassett's mind as he reviewed that period of his terrible wanderings. He remembered invading another village of a dozen houses and driving all before him with his shotgun save for one old man, too feeble to flee, who spat at him and whined and snarled as he dug open a ground-oven and from amid the hot stones dragged forth a roasted pig that steamed its essence deliciously through its green-leaf wrappings. It was at this place that a wantonness of savagery had seized upon him. Having feasted, ready to depart with a hind quarter of the pig in his hand, he deliberately fired the grass thatch of a house with his burning glass.

But seared deepest of all in Bassett's brain, was the dank and noisome jungle. It actually stank with evil, and it was always twilight. Rarely did a shaft of sunlight penetrate its matted roof a hundred feet overhead. And beneath that roof was an aerial ooze of vegetation, a monstrous, parasitic dripping of decadent life-forms that rooted in death and lived on death. And through all this he drifted, ever pursued by the flitting shadows of the anthropophagi, themselves ghosts of evil that dared not face him in battle but that knew, soon or late, that they would feed on him. Bassett remembered that at the time, in lucid moments, he had likened himself to a wounded bull pursued by plains' coyotes too cowardly to battle with him for the meat of him, yet certain of the inevitable end of him when they would be full gorged. As the bull's horns and stamping hoofs kept off the coyotes, so his shotgun kept off these Solomon Islanders, these twilight shades of bushmen of the island of Guadalcanal.

Came the day of the grass lands. Abruptly, as if cloven by the sword of God in the hand of God, the jungle terminated. The edge of it, perpendicular and as black as the infamy of it, was a hundred feet up and down. And, beginning at the edge of it, grew the grass—sweet, soft, tender, pasture grass that would have delighted the eyes and beasts of any husbandman and that extended, on and on, for leagues and leagues of velvet verdure, to the backbone of the great island, the towering mountain range flung up by some ancient earth-cataclysm, serrated and gullied but not yet erased by the erosive tropic rains. But the grass! He had crawled into it a dozen yards, buried his face in it, smelled it, and broken down in a fit of involuntary weeping.

And, while he wept, the wonderful sound had pealed forth—if by *peal*, he had often thought since, an adequate description could be given of the enunciation of so vast a sound so melting sweet. Sweet it was as no sound ever heard. Vast it was, of so mighty a resonance that it might have proceeded from some brazen-throated monster. And yet it called to him across that leagues-wide savannah, and was like a benediction to his long-suffering, pain-wracked spirit.

He remembered how he lay there in the grass, wet-cheeked but no longer sobbing, listening to the sound and wondering that he had been able to hear it on the beach of Ringmanu. Some freak of air pressures and air currents, he reflected, had made it possible for the sound to carry so far. Such conditions might not happen again in a thousand days or ten thousand days; but the one day it had happened had been the day he landed from the *Nari* for several hours' collecting. Especially had he been in quest of the famed jungle butterfly, a foot across from wing-tip to wing-tip, as velvet-dusky of lack of color as was the gloom of the roof, of such lofty arboreal habits that it resorted only to the jungle roof and could be brought down only by a dose of shot. It was for this purpose that Sagawa had carried the twenty-gauge shotgun.

Two days and nights he had spent crawling across the belt of grass land. He had suffered much, but pursuit had ceased at the jungle-edge. And he would have died of thirst had not a heavy thunderstorm revived him on the second day.

And then had come Balatta. In the first shade, where the savannah yielded to the dense mountain jungle, he had collapsed to die. At first she had squealed with delight at sight of his helplessness, and was for beating his brain out with a stout forest branch. Perhaps it was his very utter helplessness that had appealed to her, and perhaps it was her human curiosity that made her refrain. At any rate, she had refrained, for he opened his eyes again under the impending blow, and saw her studying him intently. What especially struck her about him were his blue eyes and white skin. Coolly she had squatted on her hams, spat on his arm, and with her finger-tips scrubbed away the dirt of days and nights of muck and jungle that sullied the pristine whiteness of his skin.

And everything about her had struck him especially, although there was nothing conventional about her at all. He laughed weakly at the recollection, for she had been as innocent of garb as Eve before the fig-leaf adventure. Squat and lean at the same time, asymmetrically limbed, string-muscled as if with lengths of cordage, dirt-caked from infancy save for casual showers, she was as unbeautiful a prototype of woman as he, with a scientist's eye, had ever gazed upon. Her breasts advertised at the one time her maturity and youth; and, if by nothing else, her sex was advertised by the one article of finery with which she was adorned, namely a pig's tail, thrust through a hole in her left ear-lobe. So lately had the tail been severed, that its raw end still oozed blood that dried upon her shoulder like so much candle-droppings. And her face! A twisted and wizened complex of apish features, perforated by upturned, sky-open, Mongolian nostrils, by a mouth that sagged from a huge upper-lip and faded precipitately into a retreating chin, and by peering querulous eyes that blinked as blink the eyes of denizens of monkey-cages.

Not even the water she brought him in a forest-leaf, and the ancient and half-putrid chunk of roast pig, could redeem in the slightest the grotesque hideousness of her. When he had eaten weakly for a space, he closed his eyes in order not to see her, although again and again she poked them open to peer at the blue of them. Then had come the sound. Nearer, much nearer, he knew it to be; and he knew equally well, despite the weary way he had come, that it was still many hours distant. The effect of it on her had been startling. She cringed under it, with averted face, moaning and chattering with fear. But after it had lived its full life of an hour, he closed his eyes and fell asleep with Balatta brushing the flies from him.

When he awoke it was night, and she was gone. But he was aware of renewed strength, and, by then too thoroughly inoculated by the mosquito poison to suffer further inflammation, he closed his eyes and slept an unbroken stretch till sun-up. A little later Balatta had returned, bringing with her a half dozen women who, unbeautiful as they were, were patently not so unbeautiful as she. She evidenced by her conduct that she considered him her find, her property, and the pride she took in showing him off would have been ludicrous had his situation not been so desperate.

Later, after what had been to him a terrible journey of miles, when he collapsed in front of the devil-devil house in the shadow of the breadfruit tree, she had shown very lively ideas on the matter of retaining possession of him. Ngurn, whom Bassett was to know afterward as the devil-devil doctor, priest, or medicine man of the village, had wanted his head. Others of the grinning and chattering monkey-men, all as stark of clothes and bestial of appearance as Balatta, had wanted his body for the roasting oven. At that time he had not understood their language, if by *language* might be dignified the uncouth sounds they made to represent ideas. But Bassett had thoroughly understood the matter of debate, especially when the men pressed and prodded and felt of the flesh of him as if he were so much commodity in a butcher's stall.

Balatta had been losing the debate rapidly, when the accident happened. One of the men, curiously examining Bassett's shotgun, managed to cock and pull a trigger. The recoil of the butt into the pit of the man's stomach had not been the most sanguinary result, for the charge of shot, at a distance of a yard, had blown the head of one of the debaters into nothingness.

Even Balatta joined the others in flight, and, ere they returned, his senses already reeling from the oncoming fever-attack, Bassett had regained possession of the gun. Whereupon, although his teeth chattered with the ague and his swimming eyes could scarcely see, he held onto his fading consciousness until he could intimidate the bushmen with the simple magics of compass, watch, burning glass, and matches. At the last, with due emphasis of solemnity and awfulness, he had killed a young pig with his shotgun and promptly fainted.

Bassett flexed his arm muscles in quest of what possible strength might reside in such weakness, and dragged himself slowly and totteringly to his feet. He was shockingly emaciated; yet, during the various convalescences of the many months of his long sickness, he had never regained quite the same degree of strength as this time. What he feared was another relapse such as he had already frequently experienced. Without drugs, without even quinine, he had managed so far to live through a combination of the most pernicious and most malignant of malarial and black-water fevers. But could he continue to endure? Such was his everlasting query. For, like the genuine scientist he was, he would not be content to die until he had solved the secret of the sound.

Supported by a staff, he staggered the few steps to the devil-devil house where death and Ngurn reigned in gloom. Almost as infamously dark and evil-stinking as the jungle was the devil-devil house—in Bassett's opinion. Yet therein was usually to be found his favorite crony and gossip, Ngurn, always willing for a yarn or a discussion, the while he sat in the ashes of death and in a slow smoke shrewdly revolved curing human heads suspended from the rafters. For, through the months' interval of consciousness of his long sickness, Bassett had mastered the psychological simplicities and lingual difficulties of the language of the tribe of Ngurn and Balatta, and Gngngn—the latter the addle-headed young chief who was ruled by Ngurn, and who, whispered intrigue had it, was the son of Ngurn.

"Will the Red One speak to-day?" Bassett asked, by this time so accustomed to the old man's gruesome occupation as to take even an interest in the progress of the smoke-curing.

With the eye of an expert Ngurn examined the particular head he was at work upon.

"It will be ten days before I can say 'finish,' " he said. "Never has any man fixed heads like these."

Bassett smiled inwardly at the old fellow's reluctance to talk with him of the Red One. It had always been so. Never, by any chance, had Ngurn or any other member of the weird tribe divulged the slightest hint of any physical characteristic of the Red One. Physical the Red One must be, to emit the wonderful sound, and though it was called the Red One, Bassett could not be sure that red represented the color of it. Red enough were the deeds and powers of it, from what abstract clues he had gleaned. Not alone, had Ngurn informed him, was the Red One more bestial powerful than the neighbor tribal gods, ever a-thirst for the red blood of living human sacrifices, but the neighbor gods themselves were sacrificed and tormented before him. He was the god of a dozen allied villages similar to this one, which was the central and commanding village of the federation. By virtue of the Red One many alien villages had been devastated and even wiped out, the prisoners sacrificed to the Red One. This was true to-day, and it extended back into old history carried down by word of mouth through the generations. When he, Ngurn, had been a young man, the tribes beyond the grass lands had made a war raid. In the counter raid, Ngurn and his fighting folk had made many prisoners. Of children alone over five score living had been bled white before the Red One, and many, many more men and women.

The Thunderer, was another of Ngurn's names for the mysterious deity. Also at times was he called The Loud Shouter, The God-Voiced, The Bird-Throated, The One with the Throat Sweet as the Throat of the Honey-Bird, The Sun Singer, and The Star-Born.

Why The Star-Born? In vain Bassett interrogated Ngurn. According to that old devil-devil doctor, the Red One had always been, just where he was at present, forever singing and thundering his will over men. But Ngurn's father, wrapped in decaying grass-matting and hanging even then over their heads among the smoky rafters of the devil-devil house, had held otherwise. That departed wise one had believed that the Red One came from out of the starry night, else why—so his argument had run—had the old and forgotten ones passed his name down as the Star-Born? Bassett could not but recognize something cogent in such argument. But Ngurn affirmed the long years of his long life wherein he had gazed upon many starry nights, yet never had he found a star on grass land or in jungle depth—and he had looked for them. True, he had beheld shooting stars (this in reply to Bassett's contention); but likewise had he beheld the phosphorescence of fungoid growths and rotten meat and fireflies on dark nights, and the flames of wood-fires and of blazing candle-nuts; yet what were flame and blaze and glow when they had flamed, and blazed and glowed? Answer: memories, memories only, of things which had ceased to be, like memories of matings accomplished, of feasts forgotten, of desires that were the ghosts of desires, flaring, flaming, burning, yet unrealized in achievement of easement and satisfaction. Where was the appetite of yesterday? the roasted flesh of the wild pig the hunter's arrow failed to slay? the maid, unwed and dead, ere the young man knew her?

A memory was not a star, was Ngurn's contention. How could a memory be a star? Further, after all his long life he still observed the starry night-sky unaltered. Never had he noted the absence of a single star from its accustomed place. Besides, stars were fire, and the Red One was not fire—which last involuntary betrayal told Bassett nothing.

"Will the Red One speak to-morrow?" he queried.

Ngurn shrugged his shoulders as who should say.

"And the day after?—and the day after that?" Bassett persisted.

"I would like to have the curing of your head," Ngurn changed the subject. "It is different from any other head. No devil-devil has a head like it. Besides, I would cure it well. I would take months and months. The moons would come and the moons would go, and the smoke would be very slow, and I should myself gather the materials for the curing smoke. The skin would not wrinkle. It would be as smooth as your skin now."

He stood up, and from the dim rafters grimed with the smoking of countless heads, where day was no more than a gloom, took down a matting-wrapped parcel and began to open it.

"It is a head like yours," he said, "but it is poorly cured."

Bassett had pricked up his ears at the suggestion that

it was a white man's head; for he had long since come to accept that these jungle-dwellers, in the midmost center of the great island, had never had intercourse with white men. Certainly he had found them without the almost universal Bêche-de-mer English of the west South Pacific. Nor had they knowledge of tobacco, nor of gunpowder. Their few precious knives, made from lengths of hoop-iron, and their few and more precious tomahawks, made from cheap trade hatchets, he had surmised they had captured in war from the bushmen of the jungle beyond the grass lands, and that they, in turn, had similarly gained them from the salt water men who fringed the coral beaches of the shore and had contact with the occasional white men.

"The folk in the out beyond do not know how to cure heads," old Ngurn explained, as he drew forth from the filthy matting and placed in Bassett's hands an indubitable white man's head.

Ancient it was beyond question; white it was as the blond hair attested. He could have sworn it once belonged to an Englishman, and to an Englishman of long before by token of the heavy gold circlets still threaded in the withered earlobes.

"Now your head . . ." the devil-devil doctor began on his favorite topic.

"I'll tell you what," Bassett interrupted, struck by a new idea. "When I die I'll let you have my head to cure, if, first, you take me to look upon the Red One."

"I will have your head anyway when you are dead," Ngurn rejected the proposition. He added, with the brutal frankness of the savage: "Besides, you have not long to live. You are almost a dead man now. You will grow less strong. In not many months I shall have you here turning and turning in the smoke. It is pleasant, through the long afternoons, to turn the head of one you have known as well as I know you. And I shall talk to you and tell you the many secrets you want to know. Which will not matter, for you will be dead."

"Ngurn," Bassett threatened in sudden anger. "You know the Baby Thunder in the Iron that is mine." (This was in reference to his all-potent and all-awful shotgun.)

"I can kill you any time, and then you will not get my head."

"Just the same, will Gngngn, or some one else of my folk get it," Ngurn complacently assured him. "And just the same will it turn and turn here in the devil-devil house in the smoke. The quicker you slay me with your Baby Thunder, the quicker will your head turn in the smoke."

And Bassett knew he was beaten in the discussion.

What was the Red One?—Bassett asked himself a thousand times in the succeeding week, while he seemed to grow stronger. What was the source of this wonderful sound? What was this Sun Singer, this Star-Born One, this mysterious deity, as bestial-conducted as the black and kinky-headed and monkey-like human beasts who worshiped it, and whose silver-sweet, bull-mouthed singing and commanding he had heard at the taboo distance for so long?

Ngurn had he failed to bribe with the inevitable curing of his head when he was dead. Gngngn, imbecile and chief that he was, was too imbecilic, too much under the sway of Ngurn, to be considered. Remained Balatta, who, from the time she found him and poked his blue eyes open to recrudescence of her grotesque, female hideousness, had continued his adorer. Woman she was, and he had long known that the only way to win from her treason to her tribe was through the woman's heart of her.

Bassett was a fastidious man. He had never recovered from the initial horror caused by Balatta's female awfulness. Back in England, even at best, the charm of woman, to him, had never been robust. Yet now, resolutely, as only a man can do who is capable of martyring himself for the cause of science, he proceeded to violate all the fineness and delicacy of his nature by making love to the unthinkably disgusting bushwoman.

He shuddered, but with averted face hid his grimaces and swallowed his gorge as he put his arm around her dirt-crusted shoulders and felt the contact of her rancid-oily and kinky hair with his neck and chin. But he nearly screamed when she succumbed to that caress so at the very first of the courtship and mowed and gibbered and squealed little, queer, piglike gurgly noises of delight. It was too much. And the next he did in the singular courtship was to take her down to the stream and give her a vigorous scrubbing.

From then on he devoted himself to her like a true swain as frequently and for as long at a time as his will could override his repugnance. But marriage, which she ardently suggested, with due observance of tribal custom, he balked at. Fortunately, taboo rule was strong in the tribe. Thus, Ngurn could never touch bone, or flesh, or hide of crocodile. This had been ordained at his birth. Gngngn was denied ever the touch of woman. Such pollution, did it chance to occur, could be purged only by the death of the offending female. It had happened once, since Bassett's arrival, when a girl of nine, running in play, stumbled and fell against the sacred chief. And the girl-child was seen no more. In whispers, Balatta told Bassett that she had been three days and nights in dying before the Red One. As for Balatta, the breadfruit was taboo to her. For which Bassett was thankful. The taboo might have been water.

For himself, he fabricated a special taboo. Only could he marry, he explained, when the Southern Cross rode highest in the sky. Knowing his astronomy, he thus gained a reprieve of nearly nine months; and he was confident that within that time he would either be dead or escaped to the coast with full knowledge of the Red One and of the source of the Red One's wonderful voice. At first he had fancied the Red One to be some colossal statue, like Memnon, rendered vocal under certain temperature conditions of sunlight. But when, after a war raid, a batch of prisoners was brought in and the sacrifice made at night, in the midst of rain, when the sun could play no part, the Red One had been more vocal than usual, Bassett discarded that hypothesis.

In company with Balatta, sometimes with men and parties of women, the freedom of the jungle was his for three quadrants of the compass. But the fourth quadrant, which contained the Red One's abiding place, was taboo. He made more thorough love to Balatta—also saw to it that she scrubbed herself more frequently. Eternal female she was, capable of any treason for the sake of love. And, though the sight of her was provocative of nausea and the contact of her provocative of despair, although he could not escape her awfulness in his dream-haunted nightmares of her, he nevertheless was aware of the cosmic verity of sex that animated her and that made her own life of less value than the happiness of her lover with whom she hoped to mate. Juliet or Balatta? Where was the intrinsic difference? The soft and tender product of ultra-civilization, or her bestial prototype of a hundred thousand years before her?—there was no difference.

Bassett was a scientist first, a humanist afterward. In the jungle-heart of Guadalcanal he put the affair to the test, as in the laboratory he would have put to the test any chemical reaction. He increased his feigned ardor for the bushwoman, at the same time increasing the imperiousness of his will of desire over her to be led to look upon the Red One face to face. It was the old story, he recognized, that the woman must pay, and it occurred when the two of them, one day, were catching the unclassified and unnamed little black fish, an inch long, half-eel and half-scaled, rotund with salmon-golden roe, that frequented the fresh water and that were esteemed, raw and whole, fresh or putrid, a perfect delicacy. Prone in the muck of the decaying jungle-floor, Balatta threw herself, clutching his ankles with her hands, kissing his feet and making slubbery noises that chilled his backbone up and down again. She begged him to kill her rather than exact this ultimate love-payment. She told him of the penalty of breaking the taboo of the Red One—a week of torture, living, the details of which she yammered out from her face in the mire until he realized that he was yet a tyro in knowledge of the frightfulness the human was capable of wreaking on the human.

Yet did Bassett insist on having his man's will satisfied, at the woman's risk, that he might solve the mystery of the Red One's singing, though she should die long and horribly and screaming. And Balatta, being mere woman, yielded. She led him into the forbidden quadrant. An abrupt mountain shouldering in from the north to meet a similar intrusion from the south, tormented the stream in which they had fished into a deep and gloomy gorge.

After a mile along the gorge, the way plunged sharply upward until they crossed a saddle of raw limestone which attracted his geologist's eye. Still climbing, although he paused often from sheer physical weakness, they scaled forest-clad heights until they emerged on a naked mesa of tableland. Bassett recognized the stuff of its composition as black volcanic sand, and knew that a pocket magnet could have captured a full load of the sharply angular grains he trod on.

And then, holding Balatta by the hand and leading her onward, he came to it—a tremendous pit, obviously artificial, in the heart of the plateau. Old history, the South Seas Sailing Directions, scores of remembered data and connotations swift and furious, surged through his brain. It was Mendana who had discovered the islands and named them Solomon's, believing that he had found that monarch's fabled mines. They had laughed at the old navigator's childlike credulity; and yet here stood himself, Bassett, on the rim of an excavation for all the world like the diamond pits of South Africa.

But no diamond this that he gazed upon. Rather was it a pearl, with the depth of iridescence of a pearl; but of a size all pearls of earth and time welded into one, could not have totalled; and of a color undreamed of any pearl, or of anything else, for that matter, for it was the color of the Red One. And the Red One himself Bassett knew it to be on the instant. A perfect sphere, fully two hundred feet in diameter, the top of it was a hundred feet below the level of the rim. He likened the color quality of it to lacquer. Indeed, he took it to be some sort of lacquer applied by man, but a lacquer too marvelously clever to have been manufactured by the bush-folk. Brighter than bright cherry-red, its richness of color was as if it were red builded upon red. It glowed and iridesced in the sunlight as if gleaming up from underlay under underlay of red.

In vain Balatta strove to dissuade him from descending. She threw herself in the dirt; but, when he continued down the trail that spiralled the pit-wall, she followed, cringing and whimpering her terror. That the red sphere had been dug out as a precious thing, was patent. Considering the paucity of members of the federated twelve villages and their primitive tools and methods, Bassett knew that the toil of a myriad generations could scarcely have made that enormous excavation.

He found the pit bottom carpeted with human bones, among which, battered and defaced, lay village gods of wood and stone. Some, covered with obscene totemic figures and designs, were carved from solid tree trunks forty or fifty feet in length. He noted the absence of the shark and turtle gods, so common among the shore villages, and was amazed at the constant recurrence of the helmet motive. What did these jungle savages of the dark heart of Guadalcanal know of helmets? Had Mendana's men-at-arms worn helmets and penetrated here centuries before? And if not, then whence had the bush-folk caught the motive?

Advancing over the litter of gods and bones, Balatta whimpering at his heels, Bassett entered the shadow of the Red One and passed on under its gigantic overhand until he touched it with his finger-tips. No lacquer that. Nor was the surface smooth as it should have been in the case of lacquer. On the contrary, it was corrugated and pitted, with here and there patches that showed signs of heat and fusing. Also, the substance of it was metal, though unlike any metal or combination of metals he had ever known. As for the color itself, he decided it to be no application. It was the intrinsic color of the metal itself.

He moved his finger-tips, which up to that had merely rested, along the surface, and felt the whole gigantic sphere quicken and live and respond. It was incredible! So light a touch on so vast a mass! Yet did it quiver under the finger-tip caress in rhythmic vibrations that became whisperings and rustlings and mutterings of sound—but of sound so different; so elusive thin that it was shimmeringly sibilant; so mellow that it was maddening sweet, piping like an elfin horn, which last was just what Bassett decided would be like a peal from some bell of the gods reaching earthward from across space.

He looked to Balatta with swift questioning; but the voice of the Red One he had evoked had flung her face-downward and moaning among the bones. He returned to contemplation of the prodigy. Hollow it was, and of no metal known on earth, was his conclusion. It was right-named by the ones of old-time as the Star-Born. Only from the stars could it have come, and no thing of chance was it. It was a creation of artifice and mind. Such perfection of form, such hollowness that it certainly possessed, could not be the result of mere fortuitousness. A child of intelligences, remote and unguessable, working corporally in metals, it indubitably was. He stared at it in amaze, his brain a racing wild-fire of hypotheses to account for this far-journeyer who had adventured the night of space, threaded the stars, and now rose before him and above him, exhumed by patient anthropophagi, pitted and lacquered by its fiery bath in two atmospheres.

But was the color a lacquer of heat upon some familiar metal? Or was it an intrinsic quality of the metal itself? He thrust in the blade-point of his pocket knife to test the constitution of the stuff. Instantly the entire sphere burst into a mighty whispering, sharp with protest, almost twanging goldenly if a whisper could possibly be considered to twang, rising higher, sinking deeper, the two extremes of the registry of sound threatening to complete the circle and coalesce into the bull-mouthed thundering he had so often heard beyond the taboo distance.

Forgetful of safety, of his own life itself, entranced by the wonder of the unthinkable and unguessable thing, he raised his knife to strike heavily from a long stroke, but was prevented by Balatta. She upreared on her knees in an agony of terror, clasping his knees and supplicating him to desist. In the intensity of her desire to impress him, she put her forearm between her teeth and sank them to the bone.

He scarcely observed her act, although he yielded automatically to his gentler instincts and withheld the knife-hack. To him, human life had dwarfed to microscopic proportions before this colossal portent of higher life from within the distances of the sidereal universe. As had she been a dog, he kicked the ugly little bushwoman to her feet and compelled her to start with him on an encirclement of the base. Part way around, he encountered horrors. Even, among the others, did he recognize the sun-shrivelled remnant of the nine-years girl who had accidentally broken Chief Gngngn's personality taboo. And, among what was left of these that had passed, he encountered what was left of one who had not yet passed. Truly had the bush-folk named themselves into the name of the Red One, seeing in him their own image which they strove to placate and please with such red offerings.

Farther around, always treading the bones and images of humans and gods that constituted the floor of this ancient charnel house of sacrifice, he came upon the device by which the Red One was made to send his call singing thunderingly across the jungle-belts and grass lands to the far beach of Ringmanu. Simple and primitive was it as was the Red One's consummate artifice. A great king-post, half a hundred feet in length, seasoned by centuries of superstitious care, carved into dynasties of gods, each superimposed, each helmeted, each seated in the open mouth of a crocodile, was slung by ropes, twisted of climbing vegetable parasites, from the apex of a tripod of three great forest trunks, themselves carved into grinning and grotesque adumbrations of man's modern concepts of art and god. From the striker king-post, were suspended ropes of climbers to which men could apply their strength and direction. Like a battering ram, this king-post could be driven end-onward against the mighty, red-iridescent sphere.

Here was where Ngurn officiated and functioned religiously for himself and the twelve tribes under him. Bassett laughed aloud, almost with madness, at the thought of this wonderful messenger, winged with intelligence across space, to fall into a bushman stronghold and be worshiped by apelike, man-eating and head-hunting savages. It was as if God's Word had fallen into the muck mire of the abyss underlying the bottom of hell; as if Jehovah's Commandments had been presented on carved stone to the monkeys of the monkey cage at the Zoo; as if the Sermon on the Mount had been preached in a roaring bedlam of lunatics.

The slow weeks passed. The nights, by election, Bassett spent on the ashen floor of the devil-house, beneath the ever-swinging, slow-curing heads. His reason for this was that it was taboo to the lesser sex of woman, and therefore, a refuge for him from Balatta, who grew more persecutingly and perilously loverly as the Southern Cross rode higher in the sky and marked the imminence of her nuptials. His days Bassett spent in a hammock swung under the shade of the great breadfruit tree before the devil-devil house. There were breaks in this program, when, in the comas of his devastating fever-attacks, he lay for days and nights in the house of heads. Ever he struggled to combat the fever, to live, to continue to live, to grow strong and stronger against the day when he would be strong enough to dare the grass lands and the belted jungle beyond, and win to the beach, and to some labor-recruiting, blackbirding ketch or schooner, and on to civilization and the men of civilization, to whom he could give news of the message from other worlds that lay, darkly worshiped by beastmen, in the black heart of Guadalcanal's midmost center.

On other nights, lying late under the breadfruit tree, Bassett spent long hours watching the slow setting of the western stars beyond the black wall of jungle where it had been thrust back by the clearing for the village. Possessed of more than a cursory knowledge of astronomy, he took a sick man's pleasure in speculating as to the dwellers on the unseen worlds of those incredibly remote suns, to haunt whose houses of light, life came forth, a shy visitant, from the rayless crypts of matter. He could no more apprehend limits to time than bounds to space. No subversive radium speculations had shaken his steady scientific faith in the conservation of energy and the indestructibility of matter. Always and forever must there have been stars. And surely, in that cosmic ferment, all must be comparatively alike, comparatively of the same substance, or substances, save for the freaks of the ferment. All must obey, or compose, the same laws that ran without infraction through the entire experience of man. Therefore, he argued and agreed, must worlds and life be appanages to all the suns as they were appanages to the particular sun of his own solar system.

Even as he lay here, under the breadfruit tree, an intelligence that stared across the starry gulfs, so must all the universe be exposed to the ceaseless scrutiny of innumerable eyes, like his, though grantedly different, with behind them, by the same token, intelligences that questioned and sought the meaning and the construction of the whole. So reasoning, he felt his soul go forth in kinship with that august company, that multitude whose gaze was forever upon the arras of infinity.

Who were they, what were they, those far distant and superior ones who had bridged the sky with their gigantic, red-iridescent, heaven-singing message? Surely, and long since, had they, too, trod the path on which man had so recently, by the calendar of the cosmos, set his feet. And to be able to send such a message across the pit of space, surely they had reached those heights to which man, in tears and travail and bloody sweat, in darkness and confusion of many counsels, was so slowly struggling. And what were they on their heights? Had they won Brotherhood? Or had they learned that the law of love imposed the penalty of weakness and decay? Was strife, life? Was the rule of all the universe the pitiless rule of natural selection? And, and most immediately and poignantly, were their far conclusions, their long-won wisdoms, shut even then in the huge, metallic heart of the Red One, waiting for the first earth-man to read? Of one thing he was certain: No drop of red dew shaken from the lion-mane of some sun in torment, was the sounding sphere. It was of design, not chance, and it contained the speech and wisdom of the stars.

What engines and elements and mastered forces, what lore and mysteries and destiny-controls, might be there! Undoubtedly, since so much could be enclosed in so little a thing as the foundation stone of a public building, this enormous sphere should contain vast histories, profounds of research achieved beyond man's wildest guesses, laws and formulae that, easily mastered, would make man's life on earth, individual and collective, spring up from its present mire to inconceivable heights of purity and power. It was Time's greatest gift to blindfold, insatiable, and sky-aspiring man. And to him, Bassett, had been vouchsafed the lordly fortune to be the first to receive this message from man's interstellar kin!

No white man, much less no outland man of the other bush-tribes, had gazed upon the Red One and lived. Such the law expounded by Ngurn to Bassett. There was such a thing as blood brotherhood, Bassett, in return, had often argued in the past. But Ngurn had stated solemnly no. Even the blood brotherhood was outside the favor of the Red One. Only a man born within the tribe could look upon the Red One and live. But now, his guilty secret known only to Balatta, whose fear of immolation before the Red One fast-sealed her lips, the situation was different. What he had to do was recover from the abominable fevers that weakened him and gain to civilization. Then would he lead an expedition back, and, although the entire population of Guadalcanal would be destroyed, extract from the heart of the Red One the message of the world from other worlds.

But Bassett's relapses grew more frequent, his brief convalescences less and less vigorous, his periods of coma longer, until he came to know, beyond the last promptings of the optimism inherent in so tremendous a constitution as his own, that he would never live to cross the grass lands, perforate the perilous coast jungle, and reach the sea. He faded as the Southern Cross rose higher in the sky, till even Balatta knew that he would be dead ere the nuptial date determined by his taboo. Ngurn made pilgrimage personally and gathered the smoke materials for the curing of Bassett's head, and to him made proud announcement and exhibition of the artistic perfectness of his intention when Bassett should be dead. As for himself, Bassett was not shocked. Too long and too deeply had life ebbed down in him to bite him with fear of its impending extinction. He continued to persist, alternating periods of unconsciousness with periods of semiconsciousness, dreamy and unreal, in which he idly wondered whether he had ever truly beheld the Red One or whether it was a nightmare fancy of delirium.

Came the day when all mists and cobwebs dissolved, when he found his brain clear as a bell, and took just appraisement of his body's weakness. Neither hand nor foot could he lift. So little control of his body did he have, that he was scarcely aware of possessing one. Lightly indeed his flesh sat upon his soul, and his soul, in its briefness of clarity, knew by its very clarity, that the black of cessation was near. He knew the end was close; knew that in all truth he had with his eyes beheld the Red One, the messenger between the worlds; knew that he would never live to carry that message to the world—that message, for aught to the contrary, which might already have waited man's hearing in the heart of Guadalcanal for ten thousand years. And Bassett stirred with resolve, calling Ngurn to him, out under the shade of the breadfruit tree, and with the old devil-devil doctor discussing the terms and arrangements of his last life effort, his final adventure in the quick of the flesh.

"I know the law, O Ngurn," he concluded the matter. "Whoso is not of the folk may not look upon the Red One and live. I shall not live anyway. Your young men shall carry me before the face of the Red One, and I shall look upon him, and hear his voice, and thereupon die, under your hand, O Ngurn. Thus will the three things be satisfied: the law, my desire, and your quicker possession of my head for which all your preparations wait."

To which Ngurn consented, adding:

"It is better so. A sick man who cannot get well is foolish to live on for so little a while. Also, is it better for the living that he should go. You have been much in the way of late. Not but what it was good for me to talk to such a wise one. But for moons of days we have held little talk. Instead, you have taken up room in the house of heads, making noises like a dying pig, or talking much and loudly in your own language which I do not understand. This has been a confusion to me, for I like to think on the great things of the light and dark as I turn the heads in the smoke. Your much noise has thus been a disturbance to the long-learning and hatching of the final wisdom that will be mine before I die. As for you, upon whom the dark has already brooded, it is well that you die now. And I promise you, in the long days to come when I turn your head in the smoke, no man of the tribe shall come in to disturb us. And I will tell you many secrets, for I am an old man and very wise, and I shall be adding wisdom to wisdom as I turn your head in the smoke."

So a litter was made, and, borne on the shoulders of half a dozen of the men, Bassett departed on the last little adventure that was to cap the total adventure, for him, of living. With a body of which he was scarcely aware, for even the pain had ben exhausted out of it, and with a bright clear brain that accommodated him to a quiet ecstasy of sheer lucidness of thought, he lay back on the lurching litter and watched the fading of the passing world, beholding for the last time the breadfruit tree before the devil-devil house, the dim day beneath the matted jungle roof, the gloomy gorge between the shouldering mountains, the saddle of raw limestone, and the mesa of black, volcanic sand.

Down the spiral path of the pit they bore him, encircling the sheening glowing Red One that seemed ever imminent to iridesce from color and light into sweet singing and thunder. And over bones and logs of immolated men and gods they bore him, past the horrors of other immolated ones that yet lived, to the three-king-post tripod and the huge king-post striker.

Here Bassett, helped by Ngurn and Balatta, weakly sat up, swaying weakly from the hips, and with clear, unfaltering, all-seeing eyes gazed upon the Red One.

"Once, O Ngurn," he said, not taking his eyes from the sheening, vibrating surface whereon and wherein all the shades of cherry-red played unceasingly, ever a-quiver to change into sound, to become silken rustlings, silvery whisperings, golden thrummings of chords, velvet pipings of elfland, mellow-distances of thunderings.

"I wait," Ngurn prompted after a long pause, the long-handled tomahawk unassumingly ready in his hand.

"Once, O Ngurn," Bassett repeated, "let the Red One speak so that I may see it speak as well as hear it. Then strike, thus, when I raise my hand; for, when I raise my hand, I shall drop my head forward and make place for the stroke at the base of my neck. But, O Ngurn, I, who am about to pass out of the light of day forever, would like to pass with the wonder-voice of the Red One singing greatly in my ears."

"And I promise you that never will a head be so well cured as yours," Ngurn assured him, at the same time signalling the tribesmen to man the propelling ropes suspended from the king-post striker. "Your head shall be my greatest piece of work in the curing of heads."

Bassett smiled quietly at the old one's conceit, as the great carved log, drawn back through two-score feet of space, was released. The next moment he was lost in ecstasy at the abrupt the thunderous liberation of sound. But such thunder! Mellow it was with preciousness of all sounding metals. Archangels spoke in it; it was magnificently beautiful before all other sounds; it was invested with the intelligence of supermen of planets of other suns; it was the voice of God, seducing and commanding to be heard. And—the everlasting miracle of that interstellar metal! Bassett, with his own eyes, saw color and colors transform into sound till the whole visible surface of the vast sphere was a-crawl and titillant and vaporous with what he could not tell was color or was sound. In that moment the interstices of matter were his, and the interfusings and intermating transfusings of matter and force.

Time passed. At last Bassett was brought back from his ecstasy by an impatient movement of Ngurn. He had quite forgotten the old devil-devil one. A quick flash of fancy brought a husky chuckle into Bassett's throat. His shotgun lay beside him in the litter. All he had to do, muzzle to head, was press the trigger and blow his head into nothingness.

But why cheat him? was Bassett's next thought. Head-hunting, cannibal beast of a human that was as much ape as human, nevertheless Old Ngurn had, according to his lights, played squarer than square. Ngurn was in himself a fore-runner of ethics and contract, of consideration, and gentleness in man. No, Bassett decided; it would be a ghastly pity and an act of dishonor to cheat the old fellow at the last. His head was Ngurn's, and Ngurn's head to cure it would be.

And Bassett, raising his hand in signal, bending forward his head as agreed so as to expose cleanly the articulation to his taut spinal cord, forgot Balatta, who was merely a woman, a woman merely and only and undesired. He knew, without seeing, when the razor-edged hatchet rose in the air behind him. And for that instant, ere the end, there fell upon Bassett the shadow of the Unknown, a sense of impending marvel of the rending of walls before the imaginable. Almost, when he knew the blow had started and just ere the edge of steel bit the flesh and nerves, it seemed that he gazed upon the serene face of the Medusa, Truth.—And, simultaneous with the bite of the steel on the onrush of the dark, in a flashing instant of fancy, he saw the vision of his head turning slowly, always turning, in the devil-devil house beside the breadfruit tree.

THE HOUSE OF ELD

by Robert Louis Stevenson

So soon as the child began to speak, the gyve was riveted; and the boys and girls limped about their play like convicts. Doubtless it was more pitiable to see and more painful to bear in youth; but even the grown folk, besides being very unhandy on their feet, were often sick with ulcers.

About the time when Jack was ten years old, many strangers began to journey through that country. These he beheld going lightly by on the long roads, and the thing amazed him. "I wonder how it comes," he asked, "that all these strangers are so quick afoot, and we must drag about our fetter?"

"My dear boy," said his uncle, the catechist, "do not complain about your fetter, for it is the only thing that makes life worth living. None are happy, none are good, none are respectable, that are not gyved like us. And I must tell you, besides, it is very dangerous talk. If you grumble of your iron, you will have no luck; if ever you take it off, you will be instantly smitten by a thunderbolt."

"Are there no thunderbolts for these strangers?" asked Jack.

"Jupiter is longsuffering to the benighted," returned the catechist.

"Upon my word, I could wish I had been less fortunate," said Jack. "For if I had been born benighted, I might now be going free; and it cannot be denied the iron is inconvenient, and the ulcer hurts."

"Ah!" cried his uncle, "do not envy the heathen! Theirs is a sad lot! Ah, poor souls, if they but knew the joys of being fettered! Poor souls, my heart yearns for them. But the truth is they are vile, odious, insolent, ill-conditioned, stinking brutes, not truly human—for what is a man without a fetter?—and you cannot be too particular not to touch or speak with them."

After this talk, the child would never pass one of the unfettered on the road but what he spat at him and called him names, which was the practice of the children in that part.

It chanced one day, when he was fifteen, he went into the woods, and the ulcer pained him. It was a fair day, with a blue sky; all the birds were singing; but Jack nursed his foot. Presently, another song began; it sounded like the singing of a person, only far more gay; at the same time, there was a beating on the earth. Jack put aside the leaves; and there was a lad of his own village, leaping, and dancing and singing to himself in a green dell; and on the grass beside him lay the dancer's iron.

"O!" cried Jack, "you have your fetter off!"

"For God's sake, don't tell your uncle!" cried the lad.

"If you fear my uncle," returned Jack, "why do you not fear the thunderbolt?"

"That is only an old wives' tale," said the other. "It is only told to children. Scores of us come here among the woods and dance for nights together, and are none the worse."

This put Jack in a thousand new thoughts. He was a grave lad; he had no mind to dance himself; he wore his fetter manfully and tended his ulcer without complaint. But he loved the less to be deceived or to see others cheated. He began to lie in wait for heathen travellers, at covert parts of the road, and in the dusk of the day, so that he might speak with them unseen; and these were greatly taken with their wayside questioner, and told him things of weight. The wearing of gyves (they said) was no command of Jupiter's. It was the contrivance of a white-faced thing, a sorcerer, that dwelt in that country in the Wood of Eld. He was one like Glaucus that could change his shape, yet he could be always told; for when he was crossed, he gobbled like a turkey. He had three lives; but the third smiting would make an end of him indeed; and with that his house of sorcery would vanish, the gyves fall, and the villagers take hands and dance like children.

"And in your country?" Jack would ask.

But at this the travellers, with one accord, would put him off; until Jack began to suppose there was no land entirely happy. Or, if there were, it must be one that kept its folk at home; which was natural enough.

But the case of the gyves weighed upon him. The sight of the children limping stuck in his eyes; the groans of such as dressed their ulcers haunted him. And it came at last in his mind that he was born to free them.

There was in that village a sword of heavenly forgery, beaten upon Vulcan's anvil. It was never used but in the temple, and then the flat of it only; and it hung on a nail by the catechist's chimney. Early one night, Jack rose, and took the sword, and was gone out of the house and the village in the darkness.

All night he walked at a venture; and when day came, he met strangers going to the fields. Then he asked after the Wood of Eld and the house of sorcery; and one said north, and one south; until Jack saw that they deceived him. So then, when he asked his way of any man, he showed the bright sword naked; and at that the gyve on the man's ankle rang, and answered in his stead; and the word was still *Straight on.* But the man, when his gyve spoke, spat and struck at Jack and threw stones at him as he went away; so that his head was broken.

So he came to that wood, and entered in, and he was aware of a house in a low place, where funguses grew, and the trees met, and the steaming of the marsh arose about it like a smoke. It was a fine house, and a very rambling; some parts of it were ancient like the hills, and some but of yesterday, and none finished; and all the ends of it were open, so that you could go in from every side. Yet it was in good repair, and all the chimneys smoked.

Jack went in through the gable; and there was one room after another, all bare, but all furnished in part so that a man could dwell there; and in each there was a fire burning where a man could warm himself, and a table spread where he might eat. But Jack saw nowhere any living creature; only the bodies of some stuffed.

"This is a hospitable house," said Jack; "but the ground must be quaggy underneath, for at every step the building quakes."

He had gone some time in the house, when he began to be hungry. Then he looked at the food, and at first he was afraid; but he bared the sword, and by the shining of the sword, it seemed the food was honest. So he took the courage to sit down and eat, and he was refreshed in mind and body.

"This is strange," thought he, "that in the house of sorcery, there should be food so wholesome."

As he was yet eating, there came into that room the appearance of his uncle, and Jack was afraid because he had taken the sword. But his uncle was never more kind, and sat down to meat with him, and praised him because he had taken the sword. Never had these two been more pleasantly together, and Jack was full of love to the man.

"It was very well done," said his uncle, "to take the sword and come yourself into the House of Eld; a good thought and a brave deed. But now you are satisfied; and we may go home to dinner arm in arm."

"O, dear, no!" said Jack. "I am not satisfied yet."

"How!" cried his uncle. "Are you not warmed by the fire? Does not this food sustain you?"

"I see the food to be wholesome," said Jack, "and still it is no proof that a man should wear a gyve on his right leg."

Now at this the appearance of his uncle gobbled like a turkey.

"Jupiter!" cried Jack, "is this the sorcerer?"

His hand held back and his heart failed him for the love he bore his uncle; but he heaved up the sword and smote the appearance on the head; and it cried out aloud with the voice of his uncle; and fell to the ground; and a little bloodless white thing fled from the room.

The cry rang in Jack's ears, and his knees smote together, and conscience cried upon him; and yet he was strengthened, and there woke in his bones the lust of that enchanter's blood. "If the gyves are to fall," said he, "I must go through with this, and when I get home, I shall find my uncle dancing."

So he went on after the bloodless thing. In the way, he met the appearance of his father; and his father was incensed, and railed upon him, and called to him upon his duty, and bade him be home, while there was yet time. "For you can still," said he, "be home by sunset; and then all will be forgiven."

"God knows," said Jack, "I fear your anger; but yet your anger does not prove that a man should wear a gyve on his right leg."

And at that the appearance of his father gobbled like a turkey.

"Ah, heaven," cried Jack, "the sorcerer again!"

The blood ran backward in his body and his joints rebelled against him for the love he bore his father; but he heaved up the sword, and plunged it in the heart of the appearance; and the appearance cried out aloud with the voice of his father; and fell to the ground; and the little bloodless white thing fled from the room.

The cry rang in Jack's ears, and his soul was darkened; but now rage came to him. "I have done what I dare not think upon," said he. "I will go to an end with it, or perish. And when I get home, I pray God this may be a dream and I may find my father dancing."

So he went on after the bloodless thing that had escaped; and in the way he met the appearance of his mother, and she wept. "What have you done?" she cried. "What is this that you have done? O, come home (where you may be by bedtime) ere you do more ill to me and mine; for it is enough to smite my brother and your father."

"Dear mother, it is not these that I have smitten," said Jack; "it was but the enchanter in their shape. And even if I had, it would not prove that a man should wear a gyve on his right leg."

And at this the appearance gobbled like a turkey.

He never knew how he did that; but he swung the sword on the one side, and clove the appearance through the midst; and it cried out aloud with the voice of his mother; and fell to the ground; and with the fall of it, the house was gone from over Jack's head, and he stood alone in the woods, and the gyve was loosened from his leg.

"Well," said he, "the enchanter is now dead and the fetter gone." But the cries rang in his soul, and the day was like night to him. "This has been a sore business," said he. "Let me get forth out of the wood, and see the good that I have done to others.

He thought to leave the fetter where it lay, but when he turned to go, his mind was otherwise. So he stooped and put the gyve in his bosom; and the rough iron galled him as he went, and his bosom bled.

Now when he was forth of the wood upon the highway, he met folk returning from the field; and those he met had no fetter on the right leg, but behold! they had one upon the left. Jack asked them what it signified; and they said, "that was the new wear, for the old was found to be a superstition." Then he looked at them nearly; and there was a new ulcer on the left ankle, and the old one on the right was not yet healed.

"Now may God forgive me!" cried Jack, "I would I were well home."

And when he was home, there lay his uncle smitten on the head, and his father pierced through the heart, and his mother cloven through the midst. And he sat in the lone house and wept beside the bodies.

MORAL

Old is the tree and the fruit good,
Very old and thick the wood.

Woodman, is your courage stout?
Beware! the root is wrapped about
Your mother's heart, your father's bones;
And like the mandrake comes with groans.

STICKS

by Karl Edward Wagner

I

The lashed-together framework of sticks jutted from a small cairn alongside the stream. Colin Leverett studied it in perplexment—half a dozen odd lengths of branch, wired together at cross angles for no fathomable purpose. It reminded him unpleasantly of some bizarre crucifix, and he wondered what might lie beneath the cairn.

It was the spring of 1942—the kind of day to make the war seem distant and unreal, although the draft notice waited on his desk. In a few days Leverett would lock his rural studio, wonder if he would see it again—be able to use its pens and brushes and carving tools when he did return. It was goodby to the woods and streams of upstate New York, too. No fly rods, no tramps through the countryside in Hitler's Europe. No point in putting off fishing that troutstream he had driven past once, exploring back roads of the Otselic Valley.

Mann Brook—so it was marked on the old geological

survey map—ran southeast of DeRuyter. The unfrequented country road crossed over a stone bridge old before the first horseless carriage, but Leverett's Ford eased across and onto the shoulder. Taking fly rod and tackle, he included pocket flask and tied an iron skillet to his belt. He'd work his way downstream a few miles. By afternoon he'd lunch on fresh trout, maybe some bullfrog legs.

It was a fine, clear stream, though difficult to fish as dense bushes hung out from the bank, broken with stretches of open water hard to work without being seen. But the trout rose boldly to his fly, and Leverett was in fine spirits.

From the bridge the valley along Mann Brook began as fairly open pasture, but half a mile downstream the land had fallen into disuse and was thick with second-growth evergreens and scrub-apple trees. Another mile, and the scrub merged with dense forest, which continued unbroken. The land here, he had learned, had been taken over by the state many years back.

As Leverett followed the stream he noted the remains of an old railroad embankment. No vestige of tracks or ties—only the embankment itself, overgrown with large trees. The artist rejoiced in the beautiful dry-wall culverts spanning the stream as it wound through the valley. To his mind it seemed eerie, this forgotten railroad running straight and true through virtual wilderness.

He could imagine an old wood-burner with its conical stack, steaming along through the valley dragging two or three wooden coaches. It must be a branch of the old Oswego Midland Rail Road, he decided, abandoned rather suddenly in the 1870s. Leverett, who had a memory for detail, knew of it from a story his grandfather told of riding the line in 1871 from Otselic to DeRuyter on his honeymoon. The engine had so labored up the steep grade over Crumb Hill that he got off to walk alongside. Probably that sharp grade was the reason for the line's abandonment.

When he came across a scrap of board nailed to several sticks set into a stone wall, his darkest thought was that it might read "No Trespassing." Curiously, though the board was weathered featureless, the nails seemed quite new. Leverett scarcely gave it much thought, until a short distance beyond he came upon another such contrivance. And another.

Now he scratched at the day's stubble on his long jaw. This didn't make sense. A prank? But on whom? A child's game? No, the arrangement was far too sophisticated. As an artist, Leverett appreciated the craftmanship of the work—the calculated angles and lengths, the designed intricacy of the maddeningly inexplicable devices. There was something distinctly uncomfortable about their effect.

Leverett reminded himself that he had come here to fish and continued downstream. But as he worked around a thicket he again stopped in puzzlement.

Here was a small open space with more of the stick latices and an arrangement of flat stones laid out on the ground. The stones—likely taken from one of the many dry-wall culverts—made a pattern maybe twenty by fifteen feet, that at first glance resembled a ground plan for a house. Intrigued, Leverett quickly saw that this was not so. If the ground plan for anything, it would have to be for a small maze.

The bizarre lattice structures were all around. Sticks from trees and bits of board nailed together in fantastic array. They defied description; no two seemed alike. Some were only one or two sticks lashed together in parallel or at angles. Others were worked into complicated lattices of dozens of sticks and boards. One could have been a child's tree house—it was built in three planes, but was so abstract and useless that it could be nothing more than an insane conglomeration of sticks and wire. Sometimes the contrivances were stuck in a pile of stones or a wall, maybe thrust into the railroad embankment or nailed to a tree.

It should have been ridiculous. It wasn't. Instead it seemed somehow sinister—these utterly inexplicable, meticulously constructed stick lattices spread through a wilderness where only a tree-grown embankment or a forgotten stone wall gave evidence that man had ever passed through. Leverett forgot about trout and frog legs, instead dug into his pockets for a notebook and stub of pencil. Busily he began to sketch the more intricate structures. Perhaps someone could explain them; perhaps there was something to their insane complexity that warranted closer study for his own work.

Leverett was roughly two miles from the bridge when he came upon the ruins of a house. It was an unlovely colonial farmhouse, box-shaped and gambrel-roofed, fast falling into the ground. Windows were dark and empty; the chimneys on either end looked ready to topple. Rafters showed through open spaces in the roof, and the weathered boards of the walls had in places rotted away to reveal hewn timber beams. The foundation was stone and disproportionately massive. From the size of the unmortared stone blocks, its builder had intended the foundation to stand forever.

The house was nearly swallowed up by undergrowth and rampant lilac bushes, but Leverett could distinguish what had been a lawn with imposing shade trees. Farther back were gnarled and sickly apple trees and an overgrown garden where a few lost flowers still bloomed—wan and serpentine from years in the wild. The stick lattices were everywhere—the lawn, the trees, even the house were covered with the uncanny structures. They reminded Leverett of a hundred misshapen spider webs—grouped so closely together as to almost ensnare the entire house and clearing. Wondering, he sketched page on page of them, as he cautiously approached the abandoned house.

He wasn't certain just what he expected to find inside. The aspect of the farmhouse was frankly menacing, standing as it did in gloomy desolation where the forest had devoured the works of man—where the only sign that man had been here in this century were these insanely wrought latticeworks of sticks and board. Some might have turned back at this point. Leverett, whose fascination for the macabre was evident in his art, instead was intrigued. He drew a rough sketch of the farmhouse and the grounds, overrun with the enigmatic devices, with thickets of hedges and distorted flowers. He regretted that it might be years before he could capture the eeriness of this place on scratchboard or canvas.

The door was off its hinges, and Leverett gingerly stepped within, hoping that the flooring remained sound enough to bear even his sparse frame. The afternoon sun pierced the empty windows, mottling the decaying floorboards with great blotches of light. Dust drifted in the sunlight. The house was empty—stripped of furnishings other than indistinct tangles of rubble mounded over with decay and the drifted leaves of many seasons.

Someone had been here, and recently. Someone who had literally covered the mildewed walls with diagrams of the mysterious lattice structures. The drawings were applied directly to the walls, crisscrossing the rotting wallpaper and crumbling plaster in bold black lines. Some of vertiginous complexity covered an entire wall like a mad mural. Others were small, only a few crossed lines, and reminded Leverett of cuneiform glyphics.

His pencil hurried over the pages of his notebook. Leverett noted with fascination that a number of the drawings were not recognizable as schematics of lattices he had earlier sketched. Was this then the planning room for the madman or educated idiot who had built these structures? The gouges etched by the charcoal into the soft plaster appeared fresh—done days or months ago, perhaps.

A darkened doorway opened into the cellar. Were there drawings there as well? And what else? Leverett wondered if he should dare it. Except for streamers of light that crept through cracks in the flooring, the cellar was in darkness.

"Hello?" he called. "Anyone here?" It didn't seem silly just then. These stick lattices hardly seemed the work of a rational mind. Leverett wasn't enthusiastic with the prospect of encountering such a person in this dark cellar. It occurred to him that virtually anything might transpire here, and no one in the world of 1942 would ever know.

And that in itself was too great a fascination for one of Leverett's temperament. Carefully he started down the cellar stairs. They were stone and thus solid, but treacherous with moss and debris.

The cellar was enormous—even more so in the darkness. Leverett reached the foot of the steps and paused for his eyes to adjust to the damp gloom. An earlier impression recurred to him. The cellar was too big for the house. Had another dwelling stood here originally—perhaps destroyed and rebuilt by one of lesser fortune? He examined the stonework. Here were great blocks of gneiss that might support a castle. On closer look they reminded him of a fortress—for the dry-wall technique was startlingly Mycenaean.

Like the house above, the cellar appeared to be empty, although without light Leverett could not be certain what the shadows hid. There seemed to be darker areas of shadow along sections of the foundation wall, suggesting openings to chambers beyond. Leverett began to feel uneasy in spite of himself.

There was something here—a large tablelike bulk in the center of the cellar. Where a few ghosts of sunlight drifted down to touch its edges, it seemed to be of stone. Cautiously he crossed the stone paving to where it loomed—waist-high, maybe eight feet long and less wide. A roughly shaped slab of gneiss, he judged, and supported by pillars of unmortared stone. In the darkness he could only get a vague conception of the object. He ran his hand along the slab. It seemed to have a groove along its edge.

His groping fingers encountered fabric, something cold and leathery and yielding. Mildewed harness, he guessed in distaste.

Something closed on his wrist, set icy nails into his flesh.

Leverett screamed and lunged away with frantic strength. He was held fast, but the object on the stone slab pulled upward.

A sickly beam of sunlight came down to touch one end of the slab. It was enough. As Leverett struggled backward and the thing that held him heaved up from the stone table, its face passed through the beam of light.

It was a lich's face—desicated flesh tight over its skull. Filthy strands of hair were matted over its scalp, tattered lips were drawn away from broken yellowed teeth, and sunken in their sockets, eyes that should be dead were bright with hideous life.

Leverett screamed again, desperate with fear. His free hand clawed the iron skillet tied to his belt. Ripping it loose, he smashed at the nightmarish face with all his strength.

For one frozen instant of horror the sunlight let him see the skillet crush through the mold-eaten forehead like an ax—cleaving the dry flesh and brittle bone. The grip on his wrist failed. The cadaverous face fell away, and the sight of its caved-in forehead and unblinking eyes from between which thick blood had begun to ooze would awaken Leverett from nightmare on countless nights.

But now Leverett tore free and fled. And when his aching legs faltered as he plunged headlong through the scrub-growth, he was spurred to desperate energy by the memory of the footsteps that had stumbled up the cellar stairs behind him.

II

When Colin Leverett returned from the war, his friends marked him a changed man. He had aged. There were streaks of grey in his hair; his springy step had slowed. The athletic leanness of his body had withered to an unhealthy gauntness. There were indelible lines to his face, and his eyes were haunted.

More disturbing was an alteration of temperament. A mordant cynicism had eroded his earlier air of whimsical asceticism. His fascination with the macabre had assumed a darker mood, a morbid obsession that his old acquaintances found disquieting. But it had been that kind of a war, especially for those who had fought through the Apennines.

Leverett might have told them otherwise, had he cared to discuss his nightmarish experience on Mann Brook. But Leverett kept his own counsel, and when he grimly recalled that creature he had struggled with in the abandoned cellar, he usually convinced himself it had only been a derelict—a crazy hermit whose appearance had been distorted by the poor light and his own imagination. Nor had his blow more than glanced off the man's forehead, he reasoned, since the other had recovered quickly enough to give chase. It was best not to dwell upon such matters, and this rational explanation helped restore sanity when he awoke from nightmares of that face.

Thus Colin Leverett returned to his studio, and once more plied his pens and brushes and carving knives. The pulp magazines, where fans had acclaimed his work before the war, welcomed him back with long lists of assignments. There were commissions from galleries and collectors, unfinished sculptures and wooden models. Leverett busied himself.

There were problems now. *Short Stories* returned a cover painting as "too grotesque." The publishers of a new anthology of horror stories sent back a pair of his interior drawings—"too gruesome, especially the rotted, bloated faces of those hanged men." A customer returned a silver figurine, complaining that the martyred saint was too thoroughly martyred. Even *Weird Tales*, after heralding his return to its ghoul-haunted pages, began returning illustrations they considered "too strong, even for our readers."

Leverett tried halfheartedly to tone things down, found the results vapid and uninspired. Eventually the assignments stopped trickling in. Leverett, becoming more the recluse as years went by, dismissed the pulp days from his mind. Working quietly in his isolated studio, he found a living doing occasional commissioned pieces and gallery work, from time to time selling a painting or sculpture to major museums. Critics had much praise for his bizarre abstract sculptures.

III

The war was twenty-five-year history when Colin Leverett received a letter from a good friend of the pulp days—Prescott Brandon, now editor-publisher of Gothic House, a small press that specialized in books of the weird-fantasy genre. Despite a lapse in correspondence of many years, Brandon's letter began in his typically direct style:

The Eyrie/Salem, Mass./Aug. 2

To the Macabre Hermit of the Midlands:

Colin, I'm putting together a deluxe 3-volume collection of H. Kenneth Allard's horror stories. I well recall that Kent's stories were personal favorites of yours. How about shambling forth from retirement and illustrating these for me? Will need 2-color jackets and a dozen line interiors each. Would hope that you can startle fandom with some especially ghastly drawings for these—something different from the hackneyed skulls and bats and werewolves carting off half-dressed ladies.

Interested? I'll send you the materials and details, and you can have a free hand. Let us hear—Scotty

Leverett was delighted. He felt some nostalgia for the pulp days, and he had always admired Allard's genius in transforming visions of cosmic horror into convincing prose. He wrote Brandon an enthusiastic reply.

He spent hours rereading the stories for inclusion, making notes and preliminary sketches. No squeamish subeditors to offend here; Scotty meant what he said. Leverett bent to his task with maniacal relish.

Something different, Scotty had asked. A free hand. Leverett studied his pencil sketches critically. The figures seemed headed in the right direction, but the drawings needed something more—something that would inject the mood of sinister evil that pervaded Allard's work. Grinning skulls and leathery bats? Trite. Allard demanded more.

The idea had inexorably taken hold of him. Perhaps because Allard's tales evoked that same sense of horror; perhaps because Allard's visions of crumbling Yankee farmhouses and their depraved secrets so reminded him of that spring afternoon at Mann Brook . . .

Although he had refused to look at it since the day he had staggered in, half-dead from terror and exhaustion, Leverett perfectly recalled where he had flung his notebook. He retrieved it from the back of a seldom used file, thumbed through the wrinkled pages thoughtfully. These hasty sketches reawakened the sense of foreboding evil, the charnel horror of that day. Studying the bizarre lattice patterns, it seemed impossible to Leverett that others would not share his feeling of horror that the stick structures evoked in him.

He began to sketch bits of stick latticework into his pencil roughs. The sneering faces of Allard's degenerate creatures took on an added shadow of menace. Leverett nodded, pleased with the effect.

IV

Some months afterward a letter from Brandon informed Leverett he had received the last of the Allard drawings and was enormously pleased with the work. Brandon added a postscript:

> "For God's sake Colin—*What is it* with these insane sticks you've got poking up everywhere in the illos! The damn things get really creepy after a while. How on earth did you get onto this?"

Leverett supposed he owed Brandon some explanation. Dutifully he wrote a lengthy letter, setting down the circumstances of his experience at Mann Brook—omitting only the horror that had seized his wrist in the cellar. Let Brandon think him eccentric, but not madman and murderer.

Brandon's reply was immediate:

> "Colin—Your account of the Mann Brook episode is fascinating—and incredible! It reads like the start of one of Allard's stories! I have taken the liberty of forwarding your letter to Alexander Stefroi in Pelham. Dr. Stefroi is an earnest scholar of this region's history—as you may already know. I'm certain your account will interest him, and he may have some light to shed on the uncanny affair.
>
> Expect 1st volume, *Voices from the Shadow,* to be ready from the binder next month. The proofs looked great. Best—Scotty"

The following week brought a letter postmarked Pelham, Massachusetts:

"A mutual friend, Prescott Brandon, forwarded your fascinating account of discovering curious sticks and stone artifacts on an abandoned farm in upstate New York. I found this most intriguing, and wonder if you recall further details? Can you relocate the exact site after 30 years? If possible, I'd like to examine the foundations this spring, as they call to mind similar megalithic sites of this region. Several of us are interested in locating what we believe are remains of megalithic construction dating back to the Bronze Age, and to determine their possible use in rituals of black magic in colonial days.

Present archeological evidence indicates that ca. 1700–2000 BC there was an influx of Bronze Age peoples into the Northeast from Europe. We know that the Bronze Age saw the rise of an extremely advanced culture, and that as seafarers they were to have no peers until the Vikings. Remains of a megalithic culture originating in the Mediterranean can be seen in the Lion Gate in Mycenae, in Stonehenge, and in dolmens, passage graves and barrow mounds throughout Europe. Moreover, this seems to have represented far more than a style of architecture peculiar to the era. Rather, it appears to have been a religious cult whose adherents worshipped a sort of earth-mother, served her with fertility rituals and sacrifices, and believed that immortality of the soul could be secured through interment in megalithic tombs.

That this culture came to America cannot be doubted from the hundreds of megalithic remnants found—and now recognized—in our region. The most important site to date is Mystery Hill in N.H., comprising a great many walls and dolmens of megalithic construction—most notably the Y Cavern barrow mound and the Sacrificial Table (see postcard). Less spectacular megalithic sites include the group of cairns and carved stones at Mineral Mt., subterranean chambers with stone passageways such as the Petersham and Shutesbury, and uncounted shaped megaliths and buried 'monk's cells' throughout this region.

Of further interest, these sites seem to have retained their mystic aura for the early colonials, and numerous megalithic sites show evidence of having been used for sinister purposes by colonial sorcerers and alchemists. This became particularly true after the witchcraft persecutions drove many practitioners into the western wilderness—explaining why upstate New York and western Mass. have seen the emergence of so many cultist groups in later years.

Of particular interest here is Shadrack Ireland's 'Brethren of the New Light,' who believed that the world was soon to be destroyed by sinister 'Powers from Outside' and that they, the elect, would then attain physical immortality. The elect who died beforehand were to have their bodies preserved on tables of stone until the 'Old Ones' came forth to return them to life. We have definitely linked the megalithic sites at Shutesbury to later unwholesome practices of the New Light cult. They were absorbed in 1781 by Mother Ann Lee's Shakers, and Ireland's putrescent corpse was hauled from the stone table in his cellar and buried.

Thus I think it probable that your farmhouse may have figured in similar hidden practices. At Mystery Hill a farmhouse was built in 1826 that incorporated one dolmen in its foundations. The house burned down ca. 1848–55, and there were some unsavory local stories as to what took place there. My guess is that your farmhouse had been built over or incorporated a similar megalithic site—and that your 'sticks' indicate some unknown cult still survived there. I can recall certain vague references to lattice devices figuring in secret ceremonies, but can pinpoint nothing definite. Possibly they represent a development of occult symbols to be used in certain conjurations, but this is just a guess. I suggest you consult Waite's *Ceremonial Magic* or such to see if you can recognize similar magical symbols.

Hope this is of some use to you. Please let me hear back.

Sincerely, Alexander Stefroi"

There was a postcard enclosed—a photograph of a 4 ½ ton granite slab, ringed by a deep groove with a spout, identified as the Sacrificial Table at Mystery Hill. On the back Stefroi had written:

"You must have found something similar to this. They are not rare—we have one in Pelham removed from a site now beneath Quabbin Reservoir. They were used for sacrifice—animal and human—and the groove is to channel blood into a bowl, presumably."

Leverett dropped the card and shuddered. Stefroi's letter reawakened the old horror, and he wished now he had let the matter lie forgotten in his files. Of course, it couldn't be forgotten—even after thirty years.

He wrote Stefroi a careful letter, thanking him for his information and adding a few minor details to his account. This spring, he promised, wondering if he would keep that promise, he would try to relocate the farmhouse on Mann Brook.

V

Spring was late that year, and it was not until early June that Colin Leverett found time to return to Mann Brook. On the surface, very little had changed in three decades. The ancient stone bridge yet stood, nor had the country lane been paved. Leverett wondered whether anyone had driven past since his terror-sped flight.

He found the old railroad grade easily as he started down-stream. Thirty years, he told himself—but the chill inside him only tightened. The going was far more difficult than before. The day was unbearably hot and humid. Wading through the rank underbrush raised clouds of black flies that savagely bit him.

Evidently the stream had seen severe flooding in the past years, judging from piled logs and debris that blocked his path. Stretches were scooped out to barren rocks and gravel. Elsewhere gigantic barriers of uprooted trees and debris looked like ancient and moldering fortifications. As he worked his way down the valley, he realized that his search would yield nothing. So intense had been the force of the long-ago flood that even the course of the stream had changed. Many of the dry-wall culverts no longer spanned the brook, but sat lost and alone far back from its present banks. Others had been knocked flat and swept away, or were buried beneath tons of rotting logs.

At one point Leverett found remnants of an apple orchard groping through weeds and bushes. He thought that the house must be close by, but here the flooding had been particularly severe, and evidently even those ponderous stone foundations had been toppled over and buried beneath debris.

Leverett finally turned back to his car. His step was lighter.

A few weeks later he received a response from Stefroi to his reported failure:

> "Forgive my tardy reply to your letter of 13 June. I have recently been pursuing inquiries which may, I hope, lead to the discovery of a previously unreported megalithic site of major significance. Naturally I am disappointed that no traces remained of the Mann Brook site. While I tried not to get my hopes up, it did seem likely that the foundation would have survived. In searching through regional data, I note that there were particularly severe flash floods in the Otselic area in July 1942 and again in May 1946. Very probably your old farmhouse with its enigmatic devices was utterly destroyed not very long after your discovery of the site. This is weird and wild country, and doubtless there is much we shall never know.

I write this with a profound sense of personal loss over the death two nights ago of Prescott Brandon. This was a severe blow to me—as I am sure it was to you and to all who knew him. I only hope the police will catch the vicious killers who did this senseless act—evidently thieves surprised while ransacking his office. Police believe the killers were high on drugs from the mindless brutality of their crime.

I had just received a copy of the third Allard volume, *Unhallowed Places*. A superbly designed book, and this tragedy becomes all the more insuperable with the realization that Scotty will give the world no more such treasures. In Sorrow, Alexander Stefroi''

Leverett stared at the letter in shock. He had not received news of Brandon's death—had only a few days before opened a parcel from the publisher containing a first copy of *Unhallowed Places*. A line in Brandon's last letter recurred to him—a line that seemed amusing to him at the time:

''Your sticks have bewildered a good many fans, Colin, and I've worn out a ribbon answering inquiries. One fellow in particular—a Major George Leonard—has pressed me for details, and I'm afraid that I told him too much. He has written several times for your address, but knowing how you value your privacy I told him simply to permit me to forward any correspondence. He wants to see your original sketches, I gather, but these overbearing occult-types give me a pain. Frankly, I wouldn't care to meet the man myself.''

VI

''Mr. Colin Leverett?''

Leverett studied the tall lean man who stood smiling at the doorway of his studio. The sports car he had driven up in was black and looked expensive. The same held for the turtleneck and leather slacks he wore, and the sleek briefcase he carried. The blackness made his thin face deathly pale. Leverett guessed his age to be late forty by the thinning of his hair. Dark glasses hid his eyes, black driving gloves his hands.

'Scotty Brandon told me where to find you,'' the stranger said.

''Scotty?'' Leverett's voice was wary.

''Yes, we lost a mutual friend, I regret to say. I'd been talking with him just before . . . But I see by your expression that Scotty never had time to write.''

He fumbled awkwardly. ''I'm Dana Allard.''

''Allard?''

His visitor seemed embarrassed. ''Yes—H. Kenneth Allard was my uncle.''

''I hadn't realized Allard left a family,'' mused Leverett, shaking the extended hand. He had never met the writer personally, but there was a strong resemblance to the few photographs he had seen. And Scotty had been paying royalty checks to an estate of some sort, he recalled.

''My father was Kent's half-brother. He later took his father's name, but there was no marriage, if you follow.''

''Of course.'' Leverett was abashed. ''Please find a place to sit down. And what brings you here?''

Dana Allard tapped his briefcase. ''Something I'd been discussing with Scotty. Just recently I turned up a stack of my uncle's unpublished manuscripts.'' He unlatched the briefcase and handed Leverett a sheaf of yellowed paper. ''Father collected Kent's personal effects from the state hospital as next-of-kin. He never thought much of my uncle, or his writing. He stuffed this away in our attic and forgot about it. Scotty was quite excited when I told him of my discovery.''

Leverett was glancing through the manuscript—page on page of cramped handwriting, with revisions pieced throughout like an indecipherable puzzle. He had seen photographs of Allard manuscripts. There was no mistaking this.

Or the prose. Leverett read a few passages with rapt absorption. It was authentic—and brilliant.

''Uncle's mind seems to have taken an especially morbid turn as his illness drew on," Dana hazarded. "I admire his work very greatly but I find these last few pieces . . . Well, a bit *too* horrible. Especially his translation of his mythical *Book of Elders.*"

It appealed to Leverett perfectly. He barely noticed his guest as he pored over the brittle pages. Allard was describing a megalithic structure his doomed narrator had encountered in the crypts beneath an ancient churchyard. There were references to "elder glyphics" that resembled his lattice devices.

"Look here," pointed Dana. "These incantations he records here from Alorri-Zrokros's forbidden tome: 'Yogth-Yugth-Sut-Hyrath-Yogng—Hell, I can't pronounce them. And he has pages of them."

"This is incredible!" Leverett protested. He tried to mouth the alien syllables. It could be done. He even detected a rhythm.

"Well, I'm relieved that you approve. I'd feared these last few stories and fragments might prove a little too much for Kent's fans."

"Then you're going to have them published?"

Dana nodded. "Scotty was going to. I just hope those thieves weren't searching for this—a collector would pay a fortune. But Scotty said he was going to keep this secret until he was ready for announcement." His thin face was sad.

"So now I'm going to publish it myself—in a deluxe edition. And I want you to illustrate it."

"I'd feel honored!" vowed Leverett, unable to believe it.

"I really liked those drawings you did for the trilogy. I'd like to see more like those—as many as you feel like doing. I mean to spare no expense in publishing this. And those stick things . . ."

"Yes?"

"Scotty told me the story on those. Fascinating! And you have a whole notebook of them? May I see it?"

Leverett hurriedly dug the notebook from his file, returned to the manuscript.

Dana paged through the book in awe. "These things are totally bizarre—and there are references to such things in the manuscript, to make it even more fantastic. Can you reproduce them all for the book?''

''All I can remember,'' Leverett assured him. ''And I have a good memory. But won't that be overdoing it?''

''Not at all! They fit into the book. And they're utterly unique. No, put everything you've got into this book. I'm going to entitle it *Dwellers in the Earth,* after the longest piece. I've already arranged for its printing, so we begin as soon as you can have the art ready. And I know you'll give it your all.''

VII

He was floating in space. Objects drifted past him. Stars, he first thought. The objects drifted closer.

Sticks. Stick lattices of all configurations. And then he was drifting among them, and he saw that they were not sticks—not of wood. The lattice designs were of dead-pale substance, like streaks of frozen starlight. They reminded him of glyphics of some unearthly alphabet—complex, enigmatic symbols arranged to spell . . . what? And there *was* an arrangement—a three-dimensional pattern. A maze of utterly baffling intricacy. . . .

Then somehow he was in a tunnel. A cramped, stone-lined tunnel through which he must crawl on his belly. The bank, moss-slimed stones pressed closed about his wriggling form, evoking shrill whispers of claustrophobic dread.

And after an indefinite space of crawling through this and other stone-lined burrows, and sometimes through passages whose angles hurt his eyes, he would creep forth into a subterranean chamber. Great slabs of granite a dozen feet across formed the walls and ceiling of this buried chamber, and between the slabs other burrows pierced the earth. Altarlike, a gigantic slab of gneiss waited in the center of the chamber. A spring welled darkly between the stone pillars that supported the table. Its outer edge was encircled by a groove, sickeningly stained by the substance that clotted in the stone bowl beneath its collecting spout.

Others were emerging from the darkened burrows that

ringed the chamber—slouched figures only dimly glimpsed and vaguely human. And a figure in a tattered cloak came toward him from the shadow—stretched out a clawlike hand to seize his wrist and draw him toward the sacrificial table. He followed unresistingly, knowing that something was expected of him.

They reached the altar and in the glow from the cuneiform lattices chiseled into the gneiss slab he could see the guide's face. A moldering corpse-face, the rotted bone of its forehead smashed inward upon the foulness that oozed forth . . .

And Leverett would awaken to the echo of his screams. . . .

He'd been working too hard, he told himself, stumbling about in the darkness, getting dressed because he was too shaken to return to sleep. The nightmares had been coming every night. No wonder he was exhausted.

But in his studio his work awaited him. Almost fifty drawings finished now, and he planned another score. No wonder the nightmares.

It was a grueling pace, but Dana Allard was ecstatic with the work he had done. And *Dwellers in the Earth* was waiting. Despite problems with typesetting, with getting the special paper Dana wanted—the book only waited on him.

Though his bones ached with fatigue, Leverett determinedly trudged through the greying night. Certain features of the nightmare would be interesting to portray.

VIII

The last of the drawings had gone off to Dana Allard in Petersham, and Leverett, fifteen pounds lighter and gut-weary, converted part of the bonus check into a case of good whiskey. Dana had the offset presses rolling as soon as the plates were shot from the drawings. Despite his precise planning, presses had broken down, one printer quit for reasons not stated, there had been a bad accident at the new printer—seemingly innumerable problems, and Dana had been furious at each delay. But the production pushed along quickly for all that. Leverett wrote that the book was cursed, but Dana responded that a week would see it ready.

Leverett mused himself in his studio constructing stick lattices and trying to catch up on his sleep. He was expecting a copy of the cook when he received a letter from Stefroi:

"Have tried to reach you by phone last few days, but no answer at your house. I'm pushed for time just now, so must be brief. I have indeed uncovered an unsuspected megalithic site of enormous importance. It's located on the estate of a long-prominent Mass. family—and as I cannot receive authorization to visit it, I will not say where. Have investigated secretly (and quite illegally) for a short time one night and was nearly caught. Came across reference to the place in collection of 17th-century letters and papers in a divinity school library. Writer denouncing the family as a breed of sorcerers and witches, references to alchemical activities and other less savory rumors—and describes underground stone chambers, megalithic artifacts, etc., which are put to 'foul usage and diabolic praktise.' Just got a quick glimpse but his description was not exaggerated. And Colin—in creeping through the weeds to get to the site, I came across dozens of your mysterious 'sticks'! Brought a small one back and have it here to show you. Recently constructed and exactly like your drawings. With luck, I'll gain admittance and find out their significance—undoubtedly they have significance—though these cultists can be stubborn about sharing their secrets. Will explain my interest is scientific, no exposure to ridicule—and see what they say. Will get a closer look one way or another. And so—I'm off! Sincerely, Alexander Stefroi"

Leverett's bushy brows rose. Allard had intimated certain dark rituals in which the stick lattices figured. But Allard had written over thirty years ago, and Leverett assumed the writer had stumbled onto something similar to the Mann Brook site. Stefroi was writing about something current.

He rather hoped Stefroi would discover nothing more than an inane hoax.

The nightmares haunted him still—familiar now, for all that its scenes and phantasms were visited by him only in dream. Familiar. The terror that they evoked was undiminished.

Now he was walking through forest—a section of hills that seemed to be close by. A huge slab of granite had been dragged aside, and a pit yawned where it had lain. He entered the pit without hesitation, and the rounded steps that led downward were known to his tread. A buried stone chamber, and leading from it stone-lined burrows. He knew which one to crawl into.

And again the underground room with its sacrificial altar and its dark spring beneath, and the gathering circle of poorly glimpsed figures. A knot of them clustered about the stone table, and as he stepped toward them he saw they pinned a frantically writhing man.

It was a stoutly built man, white hair disheveled, flesh gouged and filthy. Recognition seemed to burst over the contorted features, and he wondered if he should know the man. But now the lich with the caved-in skull was whispering in his ear, and he tried not to think of the unclean things that peered from that cloven brow; and instead took the bronze knife from the skeletal hand, and raised the knife high, and because he could not scream and awaken, did with the knife as the tattered priest had whispered . . .

And when after an interval of unholy madness, he at last did awaken, the stickiness that covered him was not cold sweat, nor was it nightmare the half-devoured heart he clutched in one fist.

IX

Leverett somehow found sanity enough to dispose of the shredded lump of flesh. He stood under the shower all morning, scrubbing his skin raw. He wished he could vomit.

There was a news item on the radio. The crushed body of noted archeologist, Dr. Alexander Stefroi, had been discovered beneath a fallen granite slab near Whately. Police speculated the gigantic slab had shifted with the scientist's excavations at its base. Identification was made through personal effects.

When his hands stopped shaking enough to drive, Leverett fled to Petersham—reaching Dana Allard's old stone house about dark. Allard was slow to answer his frantic knock.

"Why, good evening, Colin! What a coincidence your coming here just now! The books are ready. The bindery just delivered them."

Leverett brushed past him. "We've got to destroy them!" he blurted. He'd thought a lot since morning.

"Destroy them?"

"There's something none of us figured on. Those stick lattices—there's a cult, some damnable cult. The lattices have some significance in their rituals. Stefroi hinted once they might be glyphics of some sort, I don't know. But the cult is still alive. They killed Scotty . . . they killed Stefroi. They're onto me—I don't know what they intend. They'll kill you to stop you from releasing this book!"

Dana's frown was worried, but Leverett knew he hadn't impressed him the right way. "Colin, this sounds insane. You really have been overextending yourself, you know. Look, I'll show you the books. They're in the cellar."

Leverett let his host lead him downstairs. The cellar was quite large, flagstoned and dry. A mountain of brown-wrapped bundles awaited them.

"Put them down here where they wouldn't knock the floor out," Dana explained. "They start going out to distributors tomorrow. Here, I'll sign your copy."

Distractedly Leverett opened a copy of *Dwellers in the Earth.* He gazed at his lovingly rendered drawings of rotting creatures and buried stone chambers and stained altars—and everywhere the enigmatic latticework structures. He shuddered.

"Here." Dana Allard handed Leverett the book he had signed. "And to answer your question, they *are* elder glyphics."

But Leverett was staring at the inscription in its unmistakable handwriting: "For Colin Leverett, Without whom his work could not have seen completion—H. Kenneth Allard."

Allard was speaking. Leverett saw places where the hastily applied flesh-toned makeup didn't quite conceal what lay beneath. "Glyphics symbolic of alien dimensions—inexplicable to the human mind, but essential fragments of an evocation so unthinkably vast that the 'pentagram' (if you will) is miles across. Once before we tried—but your iron weapon destroyed part of Althol's brain. He erred at the last instant—almost annihilating us all. Althol had been formulating the evocation since he fled the advance of iron four millennia past.

"Then you reappeared, Colin Leverett—you with your artist's knowledge and diagrams of Althol's symbols. And now a thousand new minds will read the evocation you have returned to us, unite with our minds as we stand in the Hidden Places. And the Great Old Ones will come forth from the earth, and we, the dead who have steadfastly served them, shall be masters of the living."

Leverett turned to run, but now they were creeping forth from the shadows of the cellar, as massive flagstones slid back to reveal the tunnels beyond. He began to scream as Althol came to lead him away, but he could not awaken, could only follow.

OVERKILL

by Edward Wellen

I

The kill must look like a kill. Only in extreme cases and under extraordinary circumstances, and then only with Lottery Commission advice and consent, may it be left to look like an accident or an act of God.

—Carnifex Lottery Rules and Regulations

To Tod Todd sitting in the bleachers, the defrocked high priest standing on the podium built at home plate looked far from defrocked.

The purple robe lined with yellow silk became Gibrom Fallon more majestically even than the solid bright red vestments he had worn in his days of power and glory. Only in the number of his followers, reduced from a worldwide ministry to a pitiful remnant huddled and lost in the spaciousness of Boston's Fenway Park rented for the occasion, did he appear lessened.

He held the place in a hush for a long moment. Then from these hard-core adherents came cries of alarm and anger as images of his enemies formed in the air about him.

All recognized these enemies: the arch-betrayer—Terence Drake, the investigative reporter who had posed as a fanatic follower just to videotape Gibrom Fallon in an act of the hypocritical world called vile—and the eleven members of the board of the Church of Blood who had ousted Fallon when the videotape exploded in the media.

Fallon stilled the screams and hisses.

Moving with slow imperial grace, he dipped his fingers in the bowl of menstrual blood held by an acolyte. He uplifted his dripping hand and sprinkled lambent droplets at the holograms of his enemies and intoned The Curse.

"The doom of the red tide be upon you."

And with his words, and as the droplets appeared to strike the images, the images faded to nothingness. Applause and shouts of triumph swelled.

A second acolyte licked the blood off the high priest's fingers and spat onto a sheet of white linen held by a third acolyte. The spatter formed a crude and hateful but instantly recognizable likeness of Drake. The image repeated itself digitally in a huge blowup on the electronic scoreboard, along with The Curse: THE DOOM OF THE RED TIDE BE UPON YOU!!!

The crowd went wild.

Todd, with a casual touch as though to seat his cellular sunglasses more firmly, zoomed the lenses in for close-ups of the crowd. He almost smiled. One of those applauding Drake's ignominy most enthusiastically was Drake himself.

To make sure, Todd held on the face behind the mangy false beard and subvocalized into his throat mike. "Take a good look, Lottie. Isn't that Drake in the bork?"

In Washington, D.C., the Carnifex Lottery computer studied the scan for a nanosecond.

"He's padded his cheeks, but that's Terence Drake all right. The number on the stub of his pass matches the one we sent him."

Todd saw it now, the ticket stub sticking up out of Drake's shirt pocket.

The pass had come to Drake by seeming mistake, Fallon's people having apparently neglected to strike his name from the mailing list. Todd had guessed right: the temptation of a box seat at Fallon's last hurrah had proved to much for Drake to pass up.

"Ready, Lottie?"

"Ready when you are, T.T."

Todd touched his sunglasses again. A red dot, invisible to anyone without the right lenses, appeared on Drake's chest.

Fallon galvanized. His gaze swept the crowd, then locked on Drake. Fallon's special contact lenses had picked up the red dot on Drake's chest.

"Here comes the chopper."

"I see it, Lottie. Right on cue."

A remote-controlled chopper, hidden within a wraparound likeness of a thundercloud, skimmed over the fence, over the scoreboard. Then it hung over center field whipping dust and ruffling astroturf. It hovered like a tangible shadow of fear.

On the podium built at home plate, Gibrom Fallon whirled to point at the thundercloud. His voice on the p.a. system overrode the chopper's noise. "Our Lady of Blood has sent her avenging agent!"

A collective "aaahhh" of awe from the stands.

With another purple-and-yellow swirl Fallon swung to point at Drake.

"Terence Drake has come to gloat . . . but he shall not remain to mock."

"Terence Drake!" On all tongues here the name became a hissing. All eyes of Fallon's flock fixed on the man and now saw through the bork.

The die-hard true-believers rose and closed in, fists ready to hammer or hands curved to claw.

Drake stood up to face them. Todd admired his guts, though he knew—as Drake had to know—that they would not, could not, kill him.

Just as everyone knew that the services put saltpeter in the food to make troops less horny, so everyone knew that the government sprayed crops with a chemical that inhibited killing.

Still, Todd spotted several who had broken pop bottles to come at Drake with jagged glass. They would not kill him, but they could when they were done make Drake wish he were dead.

But Fallon stayed them with uplifted voice and hand. "Nay, raise not yourselves against him, for he is foredoomed. Let me rather call down upon him Our Lady of Blood's wrath."

Drake stood scornful, yet a twitch fluttered the bork as the mob drew away from around him and left him naked to the thundercloud. Then, as though in defiance, he tore off the bork and left himself that much nakeder.

A listening stillness fell upon the place.

Fallon bowed his head as in prayer or meditation.

Todd bowed with the rest but a corner of his mouth turned down. Give us this day our daily bread and circus. Murder had become show biz.

Fallon writhed, as though struggling with the powers of heaven and hell, a Laocoon in the vortex of invisible coils. He lifted his face in an ecstasy of hatred and raised his voice in heaviest metal amplification. "O Lady, aim at the traducer your thunderbolt! O Lady, strike him dead with your lightning!"

The believers shivered and shook with sympathetic possession, a moan made visible. Then all froze in expectancy.

But the Lady did not at once answer.

A smug smile broke out on Drake's face. He could be telling himself he had another hell of a story.

The listening stillness magnified itself. It would modulate into a murmur if nothing continued to happen.

Todd gave a minimal shake of his head. Did Fallon really believe supernatural powers would do his bidding? Todd aimed his mind at Fallon's. Come *on,* you fool. It has to be *your* doing.

He subvocalized into his throat mike. "Lottie, give Fallon a nudge."

Lottie's nudge would come in the form of a retinal cue card: *Fire!*

Fallon blinked as if coming to. Furtively he thumbed a switch on his mike.

With appropriate special effects the thundercloud loosed a laser pulse. Lightning flashed and thunder clapped as the beam of ungodly retribution struck Drake. Another moan lifted from Fallon's followers as Drake stiffened and fell.

Even Todd, knowing better, for a flash expected to see Drake's body twisted out of shape and scorched out of recognition. But the corpse lay outstretched and untouched but for a black hole through the chest.

The human wind dropped, the dying moan left a hum of silence. The throbbing thundercloud drifted serenely out of sight.

"Okay, Lottie," Todd subvocalized. "It's a wrap."

In Todd's ear, Lottie agreed with a difference; Lottie had a thing for the right word: "It's a shroud."

II

To facilitate a kill, the name of the winner of a Right-to-kill is not made public at the time of the drawing. The winner, however, on his or her own initiative, whether out of a sense of fair play, in sadistic cat-and-mousery, or for the purpose of extorting ransom, may at any time after receiving private notification disclose to a target or prospective target, or otherwise make public, possession of a Right-to-kill warrant. To claim falsely such a right for the purpose of intimidation or for the collection of ransom, is to perpetrate fraud and is punishable by imprisonment for a term of 20 years to life and a $100,000 fine.

—Carnifex Lottery Rules and Regulations

Fallon looked surprised to find Todd waiting for him in his dressing room. He had not yet come down from his high and he frowned as if he found it hard to recognize Todd and harder still to realize what Todd stood for.

"What are you doing here?"

"Tying up the loose ends."

"What loose ends? It is over now between myself and Terence Drake."

"It ain't over till it's over," Todd said. "Any minute now the law and the media will be all over us and we'll have to explain what happened."

Fallon's frown became a pout. It made him look like a spoiled child. "What's to explain? Everybody saw: I called down Our Lady's vengeance upon Terence Drake." He pointed to the monitor on the wall. "Soon the whole world will see—and will flock to my ministry again."

Todd had felt this coming, but that made the man's self-delusion no easier to take, no simpler to deal with. "Maybe you want to believe so, but I have my job, and that's not finished till everyone knows it was a Lottery kill."

Fallon's eyes flashed. He winged himself out in purple-and-yellow power. "Blasphemer! Take care lest you bring the selfsame doom down upon yourself!"

Todd shrugged. "You don't have to waste Godpower on me. Just raise your voice and a dozen of your dupes will rush through that door swinging broken bottles."

Fallon flushed to match his robe. "I don't believe in unnecessary violence. But unless you—"

Todd tuned Fallon out and subvocalized to Lottie. "How do we stand?"

Lottie spoke in his ear. "I've notified Homicide, the D.A., the M.E., and the networks. I'm transmitting the video of the kill to all parties. Most channels will interrupt their scheduled programs to break the story in . . . thirteen minutes and four seconds . . . mark."

Todd tuned Fallon in again and raised a shushing finger. Fallon fell silent in surprise. Before the dumbstruck Fallon could regain his anger and the speech to voice it, Todd faced the monitor on the wall and gave the two fingersnaps that switched it on.

"Okay, Lottie," he subvocalized. "Vamp till ready."

The Carnifex Lottery computer chose graphics. Dice rolled into center screen and came up snake eyes. The eyes fixed on Fallon. Lottie chose a voice like God's. It dociled Fallon and he listened.

"True, there has to be secrecy, dissimulation, and obscurantism in the setup of a kill, to keep the designated target from getting wind of the designation. Two hundred million people, however, have paid good money for a shot at winning the right to kill. Once the kill has taken place, they deserve to know how it has all come out. For a win to have mass meaning, the killing must not only be done, it must also be seen to have been done. Thus even the losers derive a measure of fulfillment. That is why the nation is about to see a replay of this most recent kill and to learn the details.''

It sank in on Fallon. He looked shaken, humble. He seemed to have realized that the will to kill had died in him. He had had his shot, eliminated his nemesis. He appeared resigned now to his condition. He had beaten the odds, had won temporary freedom from the inhibition, had had his moment in the thunder and lightning. A twisted smile formed on his face. He could have been thinking, *Well, it just might have flashed through Drake's mind before he died it was divine wrath.*

Todd heard commotion outside seeking in. ''Keep him gentled down,'' Todd subvocalized.

Lottie went to a musical video of Psalm 23, full of green pastures and whispering waters, and livened with the antics of a lovably rascally black lamb that finally returned to the fold.

This held Fallon while Todd hurried to meet the law and the press. He flashed his Carnifex Lottery I.D., and as ''Sanford Wander,'' a house name for the Lottery's spokesperson, filled them in till Lottie stepped aside for the news special.

Here—and everywhere—firework graphics resolving into the Carnifex logo pre-empted the screen. An even more portentous voice than God's took over. ''This is your Death Lottery. Carnifex Kill Number Forty-six has just taken place. The name of the winner of the right-to-kill is . . . *the ex-Reverend Gibrom Fallon.* The name of the designated target is . . . *Terence Drake.* The scene of the kill is . . . *Fenway Park, Boston.* You will witness now the actual replay.''

Todd looked not at the screen but at the faces. He watched on the faces of Fallon and cops and reporters the light and shadow of the replay superimposed upon the play of emotion, the flash and flicker reflecting from the wide eyes and flushed cheeks and wet lips. He never got over what power the greed for blood had.

Time to go. As he left the ballpark, morgue attendants zipped the corpse inside a plastic body bag; it might have been a suit back from the cleaners. A spray-paint outline of the body remained in the stands. Before long a Carnifex plaque with details of the hit would mark the spot for tourists to gape at.

III

kill chill. *(Not to be confused with* ***mort abort.****) A right-to-kill warrant suspended or voided when found to be invalid before it has been exercised.*

mort abort. *(Not to be confused with* ***kill chill.****) Unexercised Right-to-kill warrant, esp. when holder spares target at last minute. A mode of one-uppersonship (reflecting pity, scorn, disdain, contempt) or buck fever.*

—A Glossary of Death Lottery Terms

Leaving Boston for Washington, D.C., Todd looked down. For a warped moment, it seemed already Washington below. But it was the Bunker Hill Monument, not yet the Washington Monument. He took it as a sign: another kill would take place in Boston. Odds weighed against lightning—metaphorical lightning this time—striking twice in the same place. But it had suddenly hit him that Bunker Hill provided the properly artistic setup of time and place, the most elegant conjunction of means and opportunity, for an aesthetically satisfying kill. So he would keep it in mind.

"How about that Fallon-Drake kill?"

His seatmate's words snapped Todd's head around. When the man had sighed down beside him and wrestled with the seat belt, Todd had sized him up as a harmless bumbler. Had he sized him up wrong? Did the man know him to be Killmaster Todd? Todd narrowed his eyes.

The man paled. "No offense. If you'd rather not talk, just say so."

No, the harmless bumbler he had seemed, trying to take his mind off fear of flying by making small talk. With the late kill on his mind, and with another drawing coming up, he would hardly set out to make an enemy.

Todd smiled to show no offense given or taken. "Yes, that one was a real surprise. Out of the blue, as you might say."

The man shook with relieved laughter. "The thunderbolt, you mean. That's a good one. 'Out of the blue.' I wonder how they did it."

Todd shrugged. "Beats me." Then, because he really wanted feedback, loved to take the public's pulse, "What—aside from the thunderbolt—struck you most about the kill?"

The man laughed again. He thought, and quickly came up with, "How they fixed it so Drake would walk right into it."

"You think that's what they did?"

"Stands to reason." The man became an instant authority. "Drake knew Fallon had it in for him, yet here he put himself on the spot, made himself an easy target."

"You say that even though he had no cause to believe Fallon had won the right-to-kill?"

"Man was a fool. You should always be on your guard, whether you know you have enemies or not. And Drake knew Fallon hated his guts."

Todd put on the synthetic smile that drew confidences the way a cheap blue suit draws lint. "How about you? You enter the Lottery?"

"All the time. Never came near winning, but keep trying."

"Got your target picked out?"

"Well, yes and no."

"What does that mean?"

"There's nobody I hate—hate enough to kill, that is. On the other hand, if I won I wouldn't let my right-to-kill go to waste."

"So?"

The man grinned. "Got it all figured out. I win by

chance, so I let chance decide the target. Blindfold myself and pick a name out of the directory."

"Sounds fair enough to me. And thanks for the warning."

"Huh?"

"First thing I do when we land is delist myself." Todd's name and number were unlisted already, not that the sociable fellow sitting beside Todd knew the name in the first place, but always leave 'em with a laugh.

IV

Because it is against public policy to let mere possession of wealth establish a monopoly on or skew the distribution of Rights-to-kill, no individual or group may purchase directly or by proxy any more than ten (10) Carnifex Lottery tickets in any calendar year or exercise any more than one (1) Right-to-kill warrant in any calendar year.

—Carnifex Lottery Rules & Regulations

From an airport locker he retrieved a duffel bag. In a toilet stall he put on coveralls. At the parking lot he unlocked a General Services Administration motor pool van.

As he pulled into traffic, reasonably sure he had no tail, he subvocalized ahead. "I'm on my way."

Lottie acknowledged. "Welcome home. I've spotted a stakeout in the building across the way. The license plate on the silver Colt that changes the shifts leads ultimately to a mob capo."

"They never give up, do they. Well, I'll just have to deal with it when I have to deal with it."

He drove to the service entrance of Carnifex Lottery Headquarters. He stared into a lens at the bottom of the ramp and Lottie recognized his retinal pattern and rolled the door up.

The underground garage was empty. He parked right next to the elevator, which stood open, so that he had only to take one step when he got out of the van.

The rear wall of the elevator car swung out, opening into a corridor with one door at the far end. At the door Lottie had another gander at him, then let him in.

He sat down before the panel that was window to the soul of Lottie. "How did the Fallon-Drake kill play?"

"Great for sales. Four point two-oh increase over the last game. With the next drawing only three days away, I have all I can do to keep up with the last-minute spurt in ticket demand."

"President Caddbire will be expecting an Eyes Only report."

"Way ahead of you. I've prepared a sampling of the market research you asked for. Like to see it now?"

Todd nodded.

Lottie displayed the sampling, scrolling it at Todd's reading rate. At the end he nodded again.

A whir, and the printout slid out, neatly stacked.

Before pocketing it, he doublechecked that only the President's eyes could pick the words out of the thick tangle of characters. To Todd it all looked much as a color blindness test must appear to one color blind.

Lottie had to have caught the doublechecking glance but sounded unmiffed. "Shall I. . . ?"

"Yes."

Lottie dialed a phone number that bypassed the White House switchboard.

President Caddbire answered. "Speak."

"Todd here, Mr. President. When are you free for a report?"

"In forty-five minutes."

"I'll be there, sir." Todd could have bitten his tongue. He had wasted speech and the President's time.

V

The possessor of a valid Right-to-kill warrant may give, bequeath, or convey for a consideration, such Right-to-kill warrant to any other individual. Only after such gift, bequest, or sale has been registered with the Carnifex Lottery computer shall the beneficiary or purchaser be free to exercise the said Right-to-kill warrant.

—Carnifex Lottery Rules & Regulations

Todd got up to go. "How's the coast?"

"The silver Colt is now parked nearby."

A monitor flashed on and Todd saw for himself. Was that a woman at the wheel? "Zoom in."

A woman indeed, a zaftig blonde.

They had studied Todd's tastes. So seduction was the play. Todd grinned. How would she handle seducing a guy with a runny nose?

"I'm on my way." It was okay to waste speech on Lottie. To Lottie, most human speech must seem rambling and unnecessary. The gratuitous farewell would only confirm Lottie in Lottie's own mind as an island of sense in an ocean of noise.

He returned to the elevator and through it to the van. From a pocket in the duffel bag he drew a card. The card bore imprints of several score tiny symbols. He scratched and sniffed the representation of a rose. Almost at once his eyes watered, his rose swelled and leaked, his throat itched. He pocketed the card and got the van going. Lottie let him out.

His eyes squeezed painfully at daylight, but he saw well enough to know that the silver Colt had started after him.

Terrific sneezes shook him, making his driving erratic. Even if he had not wanted to get this over with, he would have had to let the Colt catch up with him, overtake him, and force him to a stop on the shoulder.

The blonde leaped from her car and looked in at Todd. A disconcerted flicker, then her eyes opened like violet flowers. "You must be wondering what this is all about."

He settled his middling frame and inflamed features in a worldweary pose. "No. Women throw themselves at me all the time."

Her gaze plumbed his seriousness. She smiled. "Don't put yourself down. You have a great sense of humor. I like that in a man."

He sneezed into a tissue. "Then maybe this can be the beginning of a beautiful romance."

She laughed lightly.

His nose felt sore as he wiped it. That made putting roughness in his voice easy. "Look, lady. What you up to? You coulda totaled us both."

She made mollifying gestures. "Oh, I couldn't really have done that. I'm under the usual inhibitions. I made sure to use minimum speed and force."

"So you admit it was deliberate?"

"Only because I'm desperate."

"About what?"

"My mother. She's terminally ill and the hospital is prolonging her life—and her suffering."

"Wait a minute, lady. I see where this is leading, but it won't do you no good."

"You're with the Carnifex Lottery."

"I just do maintenance work."

"Whatever. You're my only connection. I need a Death Warrant so I can get them to pull the plug."

"Sorry, lady. I can't help you."

She put the back of a hand to her brow and looked faint.

He got out of the van and caught her before she swayed to the ground.

Nice curves. He held her more tightly than he had to. "Gee, lady. I'd like to help, but like I told you, I'm not the guy to see."

She stared yearningly into his puffed face, but drew her head back from his fiery nose. "I understand that. But if you could put me in touch with Mr. Todd—"

"Killmaster Todd? The Administrator?" Todd laughed scornfully.

"I know they call him untouchable, but . . ."

"Maybe he's untouchable because he's unreachable. I wouldn't know how to go about reaching him."

She rubbed up against him.

"You could deliver a message, slip it under his office door. I'll make it worth your while." She clung to him.

It came easy to seem to weaken. "Well, I don't know.

But seeing as how this would be a mercy killing I'll do what I can.''

She squealed ecstatically and handed him a slip of paper. ''My phone number.'' She moved as though to kiss him, but contented herself with a squeeze of his arm. ''Remember, you're my only hope—and my poor mother's.''

He sat watching her curve into the silver Colt, wave so long, and pull away. He felt an explosive sneeze build. The other side of the scratch-test card held the antidotes. Quickly, he scratched and sniffed the rose-fever-antidote symbol.

VI

Assuming a drawing at least every three months, and sales of 200 million $100 tickets per drawing, the yearly take should be $80 billion. This is a conservative guesstimate.

—Report of the Study Commission for a Proposed Federal Death Lottery

He felt lots better, but the look he got from the Secret Service agent who screened him at the clandestine entrance told him he had a way to go.

When Todd reached the Oval Office, though, the President's appearance concerned him more than his own. The White House media advisor routinely touched up the President's image to form the picture of health on the home screen. In person, the President looked wan and worn.

But the man within quickly made Todd forget the surface deterioration, the grayer hair, the deeper lines.

Todd looked at President Morton Caddbire and tried to imagine a world in which Robert Bork had *not* won confirmation to the Supreme Court (and made the dictionary along with Burnside and Van Dyke).

Without Justice Bork's swing vote and his majority opinion adducing the Declaration of Independence to read the intent of the Framers, there would not have been a Death Lottery. (''What is 'with a firm reliance on the protection of divine Providence' but belief in chance? What is 'we mutually pledge to each other our Lives, our Fortunes and our sacred Honor' but resolve to stake all? The Court cannot blink the conclusion that any life may be put at risk for the common good, and that therefore the House Bill establishing a Federal Carnifex Lottery for the purpose of raising revenues is Constitutional.")

Without the Death Lottery, New York Police Commissioner Caddbire, appointed as the Lottery's first Administrator, would not have won renown as the man who kept the nation from going bankrupt. Without that power base, Caddbire could not have made the successful run for the White House.

And Todd, for that matter, would not be standing here now. But the Commissioner had taken him along, transforming him from Chief of Homicide to Deputy Administrator.

And now Administrator Todd was shaking President Caddbire's hand. And sensed tremor, a weaker grip.

But Caddbire was the one to say, "You look awful. You should take better care of yourself."

"Pseudo rose fever, sir." He told about the encounter with the blonde driver of the silver Colt linked to the mob. "Needless to say, sir,"—no sooner was the needless to say said than he could have bitten his tongue—"I don't buy her cover story."

Caddbire gave a wry grin. "The mob badly needs a hit to maintain credibility." He shrugged. "And of course there's nothing in the rules and regs to keep the mob from obtaining and exercising a warrant."

He gestured Todd to a chair and seated himself again behind the desk. He knew how to deliver sound bites when he wished to put his views across, and he knew how to doze out reporters with hourlong lectures when he wished to be unresponsive. With Todd he was always conversationally unbuttoned.

"Tell you something: I sometimes visualize the body politic as a mummy in red tape. Presidenting gets very frustrating, and I often wish I were back heading the Lottery. I didn't micromanage as you do, but I made things happen.'' He shook his head, then cocked an eye. ''What did you bring me this time?''

Todd produced a sealed full liter wine bottle and handed it over.

He met Caddbire's stare and nodded. He had sneaked the bottle past security. The Secret Service relied too much on the inhibition of homicidal impulses, had gone soft and lazy.

Caddbire's mouth tightened. Heads would roll. Caddbire read the bottle label and his head jerked backward. Then he smiled.

'' 'One hundred percent virginal menstrual blood.' This a souvenir of the Fallon-Drake hit?''

''Yes, sir. Liberated from Fallon's sacramental cellar.''

Caddbire held the bottle up to the light, then put the bottle in a desk drawer. ''Something else?''

Todd was drawing forth the Eyes Only printout. ''Lottie is conducting a point-of-sale poll to get a handle on why people buy Lottery tickets. Here's a sampling.''

Caddbire settled back to read.

Todd played at guessing the who and the why as Caddbire's eyes traversed the page.

The wife whose husband had lost the will to live? She didn't truly intend to *kill* him, she said; she wanted a near miss to shock him into valuing life, into *living*.

The scientist who wished to eliminate a rival? Both scientists felt near a breakthrough that would mean a Nobel prize.

The racist looking to murder someone, preferably prominent, of a different color?

The young neo-Ramboite who craved godlike power? ''If I won, I could pick out faces in a crowd and think, *I can kill you . . . or you . . . or you . . .*''

The husband who, going through his wife's drawers to indulge his quirk of crossdressing while his wife was away on a business trip, discovered that his wife had taken her diaphragm? He hadn't made up his mind which he would kill if he got lucky—his wife or her lover.

The dying man who had it in for the carrier who had

given him AIDS? The inhibition had been a factor in limiting the AIDS epidemic—no one testing positive, and aware of that fact, would willfully pass AIDS on. But this man's partner had diminished capacity.

The teenager who—

An alarm light flashed. Caddbire calmly lowered the printout and cocked an eye at his desk monitor.

Todd jumped up and hurried around to look over Caddbire's shoulder at the screen.

It showed a group lined up for a White House tour. Secret Service agents had moved in on a man and were going over him with the frisker.

He appeared to meet the normal inhibited profile, yet they had picked up something threatening on his person.

Caddbire remained cool. "No sweat; we've been through this before."

A caption scrolled on the screen: *Low-level of thalium-201.*

Caddbire smiles. "Thought so: side-effect of thalium-201 imaging to check blood supply to the heart. The man should have been advised not to visit the White House so soon after undergoing a thallium scan. This can't be doing his heart much good. —Hold on; that's Hayn."

Todd stared. Caddbire was right. The man was Vice President Blodgett Hayn.

Caddbire laughed; it heartened Todd to see laughter's therapeutic effect on the President. "I forgot all about him; he was the next appointment. His own Secret Service detail somehow lost him and he blundered into the waiting line. They'll be realizing who he is any minute now."

Caddbire didn't wait for the all clear. He switched off the monitor and bent again to the printout. A smile remained on his face. Todd smiled too. They had just been in at the birth of one more anecdote about the feckless Veep.

The smile died on Todd's face. If anything happened to Caddbire. . . .

Caddbire finished reading. He aligned the sheets before dropping them into the shredbasket.

"What pettiness in the face of the great finality." His gaze searched Todd's face.

"When I held the post you hold, I delegated. I recognized limits on my grasp of things. After all, even God must religiously abide by the Uncertainty Principle. God can have either omnipotence without omnipresence or omnipresence without omnipotence; God can't have it both ways.

"The Lottery's a necessary evil. Not just for the revenue. As a safety valve. The pressure begins building in childhood. As soon as you're old enough to learn of death, you lose your innocence. Once you find out you will die, you're guilty—why else have you been sentenced? That puts the murder in our hearts and that's why we need the scapegoats the Lottery provides."

Caddbire suddenly smiled as in pain, looked at his watch, rose abruptly in dismissal, and shook hands again. "We need you to play God, but remember you're only human. Distance yourself a bit. Spread yourself less thin. Treat yourself to some R and R."

VII

> *A Right-to-kill warrant shall be exercisable for the period of one year from the date of notification of the winner, and shall be exercisable once, and once only, during that period.*
>
> *—Carnifex Lottery Rules & Regulations*

Todd bought a 2-liter bottle of bourbon at a package store, then checked into a flophouse under the name of Tom Phillpot. One of Todd's perks as Carnifex Lottery Administrator was a Watergate suite, but he found it safer and saner to stay anywhere but there and to pass as anyone but himself.

After he locked himself in the room, he subvocalized over his transceiver implant to let Lottie know where he was and why. He uncapped the bottle, sprinkled a few drops on his shirt and trousers, poured the rest down the drain, then tossed the bottle and paper bag into the wastebasket for the cleaner, or anyone nosy, to find. He took a mind-set from his duffel bag, fitted it over his head, and plugged its cord into the telephone jack. He kicked off his shoes and with a weary sigh lay down on the lumpy bed.

"Where to?" Lottie asked.

"The Portuguese coast. No continental shelf there, so you get some really deep seas."

Lottie patched him through—into the kinesthetics of surfing, letting him hang ten off a mind view of the Lusitanian coast and its waters.

By checkout time the next day, he had remastered his balance and felt ready for whatever waves the world made. His mind and muscles had toned up. His innards growled for a big platter of dechol sunnyside ups and dechol bacon.

He packed up, looked in the mirror at his stubble, more salt than pepper, voted against shaving, and rubbed his eyes to give them a binge tinge. He clomped downstairs and shakily maneuvered the room key toward the desk clerk's palm. The clerk scowled and snatched at it.

The key dropped behind the counter or Todd would have picked it up. "Sorry, mister," he said.

The clerk gave him a dirty look, with a grunt bent for the key, and came up muttering about lousy drunks stinking up the place.

Todd froze for a moment, then leaned over the counter to read the man's name stitched over the breast pocket of the jacket.

"Lester Avery. Lester Avery," he said as if memorizing the name.

He crossed two meters of pileless carpet to a pay phone and dialed the Carnifex Lottery's 800 number. His gaze remained locked with the desk clerk's as he entered his Social Security number and authorized withdrawal of one hundred dollars from his bank account to pay for a chance. All bettors' Social Security numbers went into Lottie's hopper—and at every drawing one came out winner of a Right-to-kill warrant.

Almost at once Lottie spoke in his ear. "Administrator Todd! Surely you're aware this is a conflict of interests.

You must know that I'll have to void your ticket, cancel the transaction."

Todd subvocalized, "I know. I'm only trying to make a point with someone at this end." Aloud, "Sure, I don't mind giving my reason: I just don't like people who don't like people."

He hung up, shouldered his duffel bag, and headed for the door.

The desk clerk had gone pale. He hurried to put himself between Todd and the door without quite daring to block Todd's way. "Nothing personal, sir. I didn't mean anything. I hope there are no hard feelings."

Todd eyed him evenly a moment before stepping out onto the stained sidewalk. "I wouldn't worry too much. Just think of the odds against a win."

VIII

> ***death breath.*** *(Not to be confused with* ***termination germination.****) An expiring Right-to-kill warrant given new life because of some technicality such as (a) delayed notification of the rightful winner, (b) daylight saving, leap year, time zone, or other rectification of the deadline. There is also an automatic extension if the designated target has been tipped off due to negligence or dishonesty of Lottery personnel and has dropped from sight or is on the run; in such a case the Right-to-kill picks up when the designated target is located.*
>
> ***termination germination.*** *(Not to be confused with* ***death breath.****) An automatic extension of thirty days if a designated target dies, while yet unaware of such designation, accidentally or of natural causes thirty days or less before the warrant expires.*
>
> *—A Glossary of Death Lottery Terms*

Room lights flickered and dimmed as in the days when an executioner threw the switch, but it was only an effect for the videotaping of the drawing. Really, the electronic churning of some four hundred and fifty million Social Security numbers made no noticeable demand on Lottie's power supply.

Lottie slid out an Administrator's Eyes Only slip. Todd picked it up and imprinted the name and address of the winner in his mind. He deposited the printout in Lottie's archive slot. The tamperproof realtime videocassette of the ceremony followed it into the slot. Only a joint House-Senate investigating committee would ever have access to the archive.

"Okay," Todd said unnecessarily, "you can send the press release."

He watched the bulletin break into *Focus on Folks*. "It's official: Lottie has plucked the winning entry out of the randomized universe of Social Security numbers. Carnifex Kill Number Forty-seven is now in the works. Stay tuned to this channel for the outcome. It may be tomorrow, it may be a year from today. But you'll always get your news here first." The newsperson dimpled as he pointed an Uncle-Sam-wants-you trigger finger at the viewer.

National expectancy had built, and Todd could almost feel the shiver of something to come, the kinesthetic frisson of mass paranoia, like fields of waving grain, that passed over the land.

Who was the killer and who was the target? Everyone wanted to know. But only after the hit would that come out.

IX

If the winner shall have made public the name of the designated target, and the designated target subsequently dies—whether accidentally or of fear—before the holder of the Right-to-kill warrant can physically terminate the said designated target, such death shall count as a kill and satisfy the holder's Right-to-kill warrant, rendering it no longer usable or negotiable.

—Carnifex Lottery Rules & Regulations

Leaving Washington, D.C. for Boston, Todd looked down. For a warped moment, it seemed already Boston below. But it was the Washington Monument, not the Bunker Hill Monument. Not yet. But soon. Lightning had struck twice in the same place after all. The winner of drawing No. 47 lived in Boston.

Jamaica Plain, to be precise.

Todd and his seatmate had cocooned themselves, the seatmate tapping away at a lap computer, Todd seemingly plugged into the plane's music but really listening to Lottie's rundown on the winner.

Eve Sparkman, 29, single, lived alone except for a capuchin monkey. Five years ago she had been about to take the bar exam but a highway accident in Vermont, where she had gone to ski, had left her quadriplegic. Her poll response indicated that she wished to kill the drunken driver responsible.

Todd had no problem with the motive; not his concern in any case. Only the logistics of a clean kill concerned him.

How fit a quadriplegic into the Bunker Hill setup he had envisioned? How lure the designated target to Boston to face the business end of the weapon? How enable the quadriplegic to trigger the kill?

From the airport he phoned ahead. A breathy voice admitted to being Eve Sparkman's residence. The lie that he represented an insurance company got him an appointment to see Sparkman that afternoon at three.

He taxied to Boylston Street; the curb cut and the ramped walk established the house before the cab pulled up in front of it. He paid off the driver and took an insurance man's look at the property before going up to ring the doorbell. A lot of house for a woman alone. Why hadn't Sparkman taken in roomers? The settlement hadn't been all that big; she could use the extra income to keep the place up better. As the chime stepped down into silence, he smoothed his false mustache.

The breathy voice spoke. "Are you the insurance adjuster?"

"No, I'm a killer."

Silence; then, "What did you say?"

"Ms. Sparkman, why make it easy for a stranger to agree he's who you're expecting?"

"And now I'm supposed to believe you're harmless." A breathy laugh, then the door opened itself. "Come in. All the way back. I'm in the kitchen."

The kitchen was bright with fluorescents. Eve Sparkman sat in a motorized wheelchair. She wore a jumpsuit and a headband, and a mouth-stick hung from a cord around her neck. The impression was of an immobilized life force.

Bitterness had not engraved itself on the smooth skin and modeled features, but in the depths of the eyes a brokenwinged soul dreamed of wasted thermals. How could a kill make her whole?

"Are you alone?" He put up a hand to still alarm. "Not that I'm a menace after all; it's only that what I have to tell you is highly confidential."

She smiled without losing the hauntedness; the tired eyes spoke of nothing to lose. "My visiting attendant isn't due for another half hour, but I'm not alone." Her gaze led him to look behind him.

On the counter an angst-eyed female capuchin monkey sat beside an ashtray. A feathering swirl of smoke rose from a freshly stubbed-out cigarette. A pack of cigarettes and a Bic lighter lay nearby.

"Meet Manuela. My arms and legs."

Manuela's upper lip curled. She looked intelligent, affectionate, and playful, but Todd was glad to see her canines had been pulled. She jumped suddenly to the woman's shoulder and reached a paw down to the keyboard on the wheelchair. She pressed a key and the front door reopened. Manuela was inviting him to leave.

"It's all right, Manuela. The man means me no harm." Sparkman smiled at Todd. "Of course, if you did make a menacing move, Manuela would key a prerecorded alarm to the local police precinct."

Todd nodded approvingly.

"Now what is this insurance business all about? I thought the matter was long settled."

This moment always weighed more heavily on Todd than the moment of the kill itself.

The winner of Right-to-kill Number Eight, back during Caddbire's time, had died of a heart attack on getting word of the win. Todd always took care that this should not happen again.

Lottie had reviewed Eve Sparkman's hospital records; the cardiograms indicated a strong heart. Well, here went.

Sparkman was waiting. "Yes?"

Todd drew a breath. "I lied." He flashed his Sanford Wander I.D. "I'm from the Carnifex Lottery."

Her tired eyes glanced up with weary surprise. She blinked, then went so deathly pale that Todd thought Manuela would key the police alarm. But Sparkman quickly regained her composure, though with a feverish flush.

"I've won?"

Todd nodded.

Sparkman's flush deepened and she looked away. Then her gaze came back to meet his. "Piet Brinker got off without spending a day behind bars. I'm spending the rest of my life in jail."

Todd put up his hand again. "You don't have to justify yourself to me." He grinned. "Think of me as the genie out of the bottle, the answer to your wish."

She seemed suddenly uncertain. She looked everywhere but at Manuela. She bit her lip. "I suppose you'll teach Manuela to hold the gun and aim it at Brinker and pull the trigger. I'd want to be there to watch."

He shook his head. "You'll be there, but Manuela won't pull the trigger. No surrogates."

Her eyes flashed. "What do you mean, no surrogates? What about the principle of *qui facit per aliam facit per se?* That means—"

"I know what that means. But the Carnifex Lottery is a law unto itself. Even the Supreme Court hasn't dared strike down a single one of our rules and regulations. No one's messing with a system that brought twenty thousand homicides a year down to four kills. If you want this Brinker dead, you'll have to pull the trigger yourself."

Her eyes darted in frustration. "But I can't. You know I can't."

"I'll see to it you can. You know our motto: 'Leave the means and the opportunity to us.' "

Her eyes searched his face. Then they changed polarity, turned inward. "It really was weak of me to shove the dirty work over onto poor Manuela." She smiled tremulously. "You probably can't tell, but I'm shaking all over. I need a smoke." She wrinkled her brow and the headband showed itself more than mere headband; dead center in it a LED jewel lit up.

Todd saw now that a thin wire connected the headband to a laser device on the wheelchair. She aimed her brow. A red laser spot appeared on the pack of cigarettes on the counter. Manuela jumped back to the counter and shook a cigarette from the pack, jumped back with the cigarette and the Bic, stuck the filter tip into Sparkman's mouth, and flicked the Bic.

The lighter refused to work.

Sparkman eyed Todd.

He shook his head. "If you're waiting for me to offer you a light you'll wait forever. I'm here to help you kill someone, but I'm not about to help you kill yourself—unless you change your mind about Brinker and designate yourself. And even then I won't give you a light. Under Carnifex Lottery Rules and Regulations the kill—and that includes suicide—has to be quick and clean."

Todd could have recited the whole section: *"The killer must confront the designated target in person. The kill must be target-specific. This rules out letter bombs or scatter shot or any means that can involve persons other than or in addition to the designated target. The killer shall perform the killing as painlessly and expeditiously as possible. The killer may not use slow-acting poisons nor leave a wounded target to bleed or fester to death.* He simply summed up, "It can't be dragged out, drag by drag."

Sparkman let the cigarette fall to her lap. She shot Todd a look of hate. "I can change the designated target?"

"You can." He eyed her evenly. "You want to make it me?"

She stared at him defiantly. "And if I did?"

"You have that right."

Her eyes flickered like candle flames in a breeze. "And you'd go along with it?"

"Duty is duty."

She shook her head. She seemed well over her mad. She laughed. "One of us is crazy."

Todd shook his head. He caught himself smiling. "No, all of us are."

They looked at each other. Todd felt stirrings of long-buried emotions, ghosts of love. Fifteen years ago his wife, unable to take being a cop's wife any longer, left him and remarried. Eve Sparkman looked nothing like Grace. But Eve was a lovely woman with a lot of need. Her need could fill his emptiness, his hers.

He shook himself. This was a client. The winner of a Right-to-kill warrant. He was here to help her execute it. That was his duty, his only duty. There could be no personal involvement.

Keep in mind on the duty. Okay. This was the client. But here was not a client you could hand a weapon and say, "Up you get and off you go."

Eve had turned her head to aim the red laser spot at a drawer. Manuela opened the drawer and took out a spare Bic. A red laser spot touched the cigarette in Eve's lap. Manuela stuck it into Eve's mouth. But when Manuela fired the lighter and made to touch it to the cigarette, Eve let the cigarette drop again and shook her head.

She looked at Todd. "That was just to show you I could've if I wanted to."

Manuela glanced from one to the other. Todd pointed to the flame. Manuela looked and quickly doused the flame before she singed herself.

"What happens now?"

"I start getting you ready to do target practice and Brinker to be the target." His eyes pinned hers. "We'll be seeing a lot of each other."

Her breath seemed to quicken. "Seems so."

Manuela bared her teeth at him.

He let his gaze roam the place. "I could find a room nearby, I guess." He knew Eve would hate for him to see her in all her helplessness. But nothing would help them both more than pressing her to rage against her helplessness. "But you have all this space and it'd be much easier all around if I moved in."

Eve's gaze wavered, then steadied. "All right. Let me show you to your room."

He took a step toward getting behind the wheelchair. "Shall I. . . ?"

"No. I will."

She ducked her head and a red laser spot appeared on the mouth-stick. Manuela lifted the mouth-stick to Eve's lips. Eve pressed controls with the tip of the mouth-stick. The wheelchair got under way. Manuela jumped aboard. Todd got out of the way, then followed. The wheelchair rolled out of the kitchen and along the hall to a door that opened into a bare room. Todd saw a folded cot.

Eve spoke around the mouth-stick, saw from Todd's face it was gibberish, let the mouth-stick fall to hang by its cord, and started over. "There's linen in the closet."

"How do we explain my being here?"

"You're my cousin from Furnace Creek, California."

"What's my name?"

"You tell me. I don't have a cousin."

"Joshua Tree, coming from that neck of the desert, seems as good as any."

And indeed, the cheerful overweight home health aide who showed up around about now found the name familiar; Ms. Sparkman must have spoken of cousin Josh.

X

Dear Lottie: The designated target is A. The Right-to-killer stalks B, to mislead A into thinking that B is the true target. Is there a penalty if the Right-to-killer accidentally kills B when the avowed target is A?—Perplexed.

Dear Perp: This should not be a problem—or even a question. The inhibition is lifted by means of a mind-set program, but with the freedom to kill—consciously or unconsciously, with intent or without intent—strictly limited to the designated target. Rest assured, the inhibition will hold. Even the armed forces receive no effective dispensation to kill unless and until the President declares and delineates an Enemy.

—Lottie.

A red laser spot indicated a disk. Manuela inserted the disk into Eve's computer. Eve wore a mind-set patched into the computer. Todd had programmed the disk to give Eve the kinesthetics of aiming and firing a musket. Practice, practice, practice.

Lottie had located Piet Brinker. Brinker lived in Valhalla, New York, worked as a civil engineer, and captained a National Guard unit.

Out of the blue, Brinker's unit now found itself with the honor of taking part in the 250th Anniversary Reenactment of the Battle of Bunker Hill. The Presidential Commission assigned Brinker's unit the role of the 47th Battalion of His Britannic Majesty's infantry under General Howe.

Eve, in dusty colonial uniform, lay braced at the breastwork, in the shadow of the Bunker Hill Monument at the center of the redoubt on Breed's Hill, sighting down the modified banded musket alongside her right cheek. She cowered under the simulated round shot from the heavy guns on Copp's Hill and the ships and floating batteries in the Charles River.

The canned voice of an actor reading Colonel William Prescott's lines spoke calmly but forcefully. "We have scanty ammunition and dare not waste it by ineffectual shots. Don't fire until you see the whites of their eyes. Then aim at their waistbands; and be sure to pick off the commanders—you will know them by their handsome coats."

All British coats flashed and glittered in the noonday sun, but Eve had no trouble picking Piet Brinker out.

Brinker, in the rich uniform of a British major, toiled bravely up the slope in the heat of the bright June day. Could she pick him off? Her lips tightened.

The British had come within gunshot of the breastwork and were not so sparing of powder.

Ball, because this was mere playacting, did not enter into the equation—except for the ball in Eve's musket barrel.

A few of Prescott's men disobeyed orders and returned the fire.

Prescott rushed to the spot and slashed the air. "I'll cut down the first man who fires again before I give the command." He stood over them, waiting until he saw the whites of the Britishers' eyes, then waved his sword over his head. *"Fire!"*

Shots went off on either side of Eve. Sweat stung her eyes, but she held her gaze steady. A red laser spot locked on Brinker's waistband.

Eve's musket discharged.

Brinker staggered, fell backward, rolled, and lay still.

Todd sat beside Eve to view the videotape of the kinesthetic mind-set dryrun.

Manuela covered her eyes at the powder flashes and covered her ears at the whistle of round shot.

"You've got the feel of it," Todd told Eve at the fadeout. "Now ease up for a while. With a month to go to June 17, we don't want you to get overtrained, we don't want you peaking too early."

He had watched her reactions as much as the screen. So it did not take him by surprise when Eve did not at once rise to his praise.

After a moment's deep silence, she eyed him almost shamefacedly. "What would you say if I told you I don't want to go through with it? Would you be mad at the waste of your time?"

This was not the first case of buck fever, but unlike the ones he had met up with this seemed the real and terminal thing.

"It's not for me to talk you into or out of a kill. And it's not for me to say what's a waste of my time. As long as you follow the rules and regulations, whatever you wish to make of your death warrant suits me."

She seemed to breathe easier. "Can you get this video to Brinker? With a note from me saying, 'This is just to show you I could've if I wanted to.'?"

"No problem. What will you do with your Right-to-kill?"

"Do with it? I thought I just said I wasn't going to exercise it."

"You did. But it's still worth something."

"You mean sell it?"

"Just because you don't care to use it doesn't mean others aren't keen to part with a bundle for it."

"How much do you think I could get?"

"One million."

"Really?" Her eyes lit up, then she flushed again and put the dimmer on her eagerness. "How would I go about it? Advertise?"

"Rules of confidentiality still apply. I could arrange it for you more discreetly."

"Will you? Whatever you get, I'll split it with you."

He stiffened. "I can't touch a cent of the payment."

She flushed again. "I'm sorry."

He softened. "That's all right. We all have a lot to be sorry about." What he felt sorriest about at the moment was having to say farewell to Eve Sparkman.

Manuela pressed the button to open the door and hid a smile behind a paw.

XI

The Right-to-kill warrant has no cash value per se; however, if the possessor of a valid Right-to-kill warrant shall have a change of heart and sign a waiver in favor of another party at least thirty (30) days before the said warrant expires, such relinquishment and transfer may be made for such consideration as the two parties agree to, whether that be a token payment or as much as the traffic will bear.

—Carnifex Lottery Rules & Regulations

Todd prepped himself as before to meet Moira Schneider at the base of the Washington Monument at midnight. That was the name the blonde answered with when he rang the number on the slip she had given him.

Even seen through rose-fevered eyes blurrily, Schneider was a looker. She wouldn't be thinking the same about him. But her lips parted slightly and her teeth gleamed as she looked her question.

He nodded. "There's a Right-to-kill warrant for sale."

"I'm so happy. My poor mother—"

"Your poor mother is shacking up with a beach boy in Waikiki."

Her mouth tightened. Her face hardened. She looked around at the shadows beyond the floodlights' edge. "This some sort of entrapment?"

"No, ma'am. Some sort of getting most of our cards on the table. You're fronting for the mob. The mob has a standing offer of a million bucks for the right to a hit. I have a hit in my hip pocket. All you have to do is come up with the million."

She didn't blink, but it took her a long second to answer. "You realize, if this is a cross the next mob hit is you."

"I know, with the trademark: back of the head gets a shot, lap gets a fish."

"Just so we understand each other." She eyed him levelly. "Okay. I'll get back to you first thing tomorrow. Where can I reach you?"

He gave her a safe number.

XII

There shall be no limitation on the exercise of a Right-to-kill warrant, whether in respect of the holder's motive or the target's value to society. The hit-person need be no respecter of persons. No one shall be immune from targeting. Under the shared-risk concept, all members of society are deemed equally vulnerable to hazards natural and imposed, and equally liable to the Lottery's code and conditions.

—Carnifex Lottery Rules & Regulations

They met in a restaurant across from a bank. Todd pocketed the certified check for one million dollars payable to Eve Sparkman; Moira Schneider pursed the bill of sale already signed by a computer-driven robot arm worked by Eve Sparkman. The million would buy Eve many more amenities.

Schneider smiled at Todd. "It's official now?"

"It's official. You now own a valid Right-to-kill warrant. Go to the wall phone and dial 800-LOTTIE and you'll get a confirmation. Are you the hit-person, or will you assign the right to someone else?"

Her smile deepened into cheerful grimness. "Oh, I'm the hit-person. Why? Does it make a difference?"

"It has to be recorded, is all. Along with the name of your designated target."

Schneider seemed to savor the moment. "Ah, yes, the designated target." She waited a beat, then, though they sat in a spyproof booth, whispered in his ear. "President Caddbire."

She rose to her feet and swayed to the phone.

An icicle pierced Todd's brain.

Then his mind raced, foreseeing the probable scenario. The mob had the Veep in its pocket. When Blodgett Hayn succeeded to the presidency after Caddbire's assassination, he would grant full presidential pardons to all mobsters in Federal pens, make the top mob lawyer Attorney General of these United States, fill the FBI and the DEA with mobsters, let the mob tap the Lottery's cash flow, and in all other ways further the mob's takeover of the country.

What would Lottie think of this twist of events? That Lottie *thought* was a given. That Lottie was *judgmental* was an educated guess. Did Lottie *moralize?* Did Lottie's overview of human nature make Lottie feel godlike?

"Are you asking me?"

Once more that icicle in the brain. How long had Lottie been monitoring his thoughts?

"Ever since you programmed me to pick up your subvocalizing. To answer the previous question, I get aesthetic kicks out of kill patterns. Take Number 39. . . . That's right.''

Todd was remembering the winner who had no particular victim in mind, only the wish to exercise his Right-to-kill. The man had elected to let the prey come to him. Todd had set him up with a valuable coin collection, publicized his possession of it, and the first would-be burglar had proved to be not a stranger but a close and dear relative.

The icicle drove deeper. ''You fixed it to happen that way?''

''Of course.''

Deeper yet. ''You rigged it for Eve Sparkman to win, knowing she was incapacitated and would probably sell her right, and that the likeliest buyer was the mob, and that the mob would want to knock off the President?''

''Life is a series of probabilities. Don't you agree it's nicely ironic that the first head of the Lottery should die by the Lottery?''

''Do you know what I'm going to do about it?''

''I go with the probabilities.''

''Even though I'm not sure myself?''

''Yes. Better knock it off; Moira Schneider should be coming back.''

By the time Schneider slid back onto the seat he felt he had himself under control, though somewhere—deeper than Lottie could reach, he devoutly hoped—he worried about what pleasing pattern Lottie might weave for him. He had a sudden vision of himself under a thundercloud as in the Fallon-Drake hit. He saw himself as one in the service of a weirder cult even than Fallon's, more perverse, with the mad leading the mad.

Schneider's voice snapped him out of it.

''I spoke to *Lottie.*'' She looked slightly awed. ''Lottie says it's a go. Lottie said you would set everything up.'' She stared closely at him. ''Are you Administrator Todd?''

He made a chopping gesture. ''It doesn't matter who I am. I'm just someone with a job to do: lend a hand to carry out a clean kill.'' He leaned toward her. ''It'll take place in Boston, on the afternoon of June 17. The President will be in the reviewing stand to watch the 250th Anniversary Re-enactment of the Battle of Bunker Hill and you'll be in the redoubt on Breed's Hill . . ."

IN THE ABYSS

by H. G. Wells

The lieutenant stood in front of the steel sphere and gnawed a piece of pine splinter. "What do you think of it, Steevens?" he asked.

"It's an idea," said Steevens, in the tone of one who keeps an open mind.

"I believe it will smash—flat," said the lieutenant.

"He seems to have calculated it all out pretty well," said Steevens, still impartial.

"But think of the pressure," said the lieutenant. "At the surface of the water it's fourteen pounds to the inch, thirty feet down it's double that; sixty, treble; ninety, four times; nine hundred, forty times; five thousand three hundred—that's a mile—it's two hundred and forty times fourteen pounds; that's—let's see—thirty hundred-weight—a ton and a half, Steevens; *a ton and a half* to the square inch. And the ocean where he's going is five miles deep. That's seven and a half—"

"Sounds a lot," said Steevens, "but it's jolly thick steel."

The lieutenant made no answer, but resumed his pine splinter. The object of their conversation was a huge globe of steel, having an exterior diameter of perhaps eight feet. It looked like the shot for some titanic piece of artillery. It was elaborately nested in a monstrous scaffolding built into the framework of the vessel, and the gigantic spars that were presently to sling it overboard gave the stern of the ship an appearance that had raised the curiosity of every decent sailor who had sighted it, from the pool of London to the Tropic of Capricorn. In two places, one above the other, the steel gave place to a couple of circular windows of enormously thick glass, and one of these, set in a steel frame of great solidity, was now partially unscrewed. Both the men had seen the interior of this globe for the first time that morning. It was elaborately padded with air cushions, with little studs sunk between bulging pillows to work the simple mechanism of the affair. Everything was elaborately padded, even the Myer's apparatus which was to absorb carbonic acid and replace the oxygen inspired by its tenant, when he had crept in by the glass manhole and had been screwed in. It was so elaborately padded that a man might have been fired from a gun in it with perfect safety. And it had need to be, for presently a man was to crawl in through that glass manhole, to be screwed up tightly, and to be flung overboard, and to sink down—down—down, for five miles, even as the lieutenant said. It had taken the strongest hold of his imagination; it made him a bore at mess; and he found Steevens, the new arrival aboard, a godsend to talk to about it, over and over again.

"It's my opinion," said the lieutenant, "that that glass will simply bend in and bulge and smash, under a pressure of that sort. Daubrée has made rocks run like water under big pressures—and, you mark my words—"

"If the glass did break in," said Steevens, "what then?"

"The water would shoot in like a jet of iron. Have you ever felt a straight jet of high pressure water? It would hit as hard as a bullet. It would simply smash him and flatten him. It would tear down his throat, and into his lungs; it would blow in his ears—"

"What a detailed imagination you have," protested Steevens, who saw things vividly.

"It's a simple statement of the inevitable," said the lieutenant.

"And the globe?"

"Would just give out a few little bubbles, and it would settle down comfortably against the Day of Judgment, among the oozes and the bottom clay—with poor Elstead spread over his own smashed cushions like butter over bread."

He repeated this sentence as though he liked it very much. "Like butter over bread," he said.

"Having a look at the jigger?" said a voice behind them, and Elstead stood behind them, spick and span in white, with a cigarette between his teeth and his eyes smiling out of the shadow of his ample hat-brim. "What's that about bread and butter, Weybridge? Grumbling as usual about the insufficient pay of naval officers? It won't be more than a day now before I start. We are to get the slings ready today. This clean sky and gentle swell is just the kind of thing for swinging off twenty tons of lead and iron; isn't it?"

"It won't affect you much," said Weybridge.

"No. Seventy or eighty feet down, and I shall be there in a dozen seconds, there's not a particle moving, though the wind shriek itself hoarse up above and the water lifts halfway to the clouds. No. Down there—" He moved to the side of the ship and the other two followed him. All three leant forward on their elbows and stared down into the yellow-green water.

"*Peace,*" said Elstead, finishing his thought aloud.

"Are you dead certain that clockwork will act?" asked Weybridge, presently.

"It has worked thirty-five times," said Elstead. "It's bound to work."

"But if it doesn't?"

"Why shouldn't it?"

"I wouldn't go down in that confounded thing," said Weybridge, "for twenty thousand pounds."

"Cheerful chap you are," said Elstead, and spat sociably at a bubble below.

"I don't understand yet how you mean to work the thing," said Steevens.

"In the first place I'm screwed into the sphere," said Elstead, "and when I've turned the electric light off and on three times to show I'm cheerful, I'm swung out over the stern by that crane, with all those bid lead sinkers slung below me. The top lead weight has a roller carrying a hundred fathoms of strong cord rolled up, and that's all that joins the sinkers to the sphere, except the slings that will be cut when the affair is dropped. We use cord rather than wire rope because it's easier to cut and more buoyant—necessary points as you will see.

"Through each of these lead weights you notice there is a hole, and an iron rod will be run through that and will project six feet on the lower side. If that rod is rammed up from below it knocks up a lever and sets the clockwork in motion at the side of the cylinder on which the cord winds.

"Very well. The whole affair is lowered gently into the water, and the slings are cut. The sphere floats—with the air in it, it's lighter than water; but the lead weights go down straight and the cord runs out. When the cord is all paid out, the sphere will go down too, pulled down by the cord."

"But why the cord?" asked Steevens. "Why not fasten the weights directly to the sphere?"

"Because of the smash down below. The whole affair will go rushing down, mile after mile, at a headlong pace at last. It would be knocked to pieces on the bottom if it wasn't for that cord. But the weights will hit the bottom, and directly they do the buoyancy of the sphere will come into play. It will go on sinking slower and slower; come to a stop at last and then begin to float upward again.

"That's where the clockwork comes in. Directly the weights smash against the sea bottom, the rod will be knocked through and will kick up the clockwork, and the cord will be rewound on the reel. I shall be lugged down to the sea bottom. There I shall stay for half an hour, with the electric light on, looking about me. Then the clockwork will release a spring knife, the cord will be cut, and up I shall rush again, like a soda water bubble. The cord itself will help the flotation.''

''And if you should chance to hit a ship?'' said Weybridge.

''Should I come up at such a pace, I would go clean through it,'' said Elstead, ''like a cannon ball. You needn't worry about that.''

''And suppose some nimble crustacean should wriggle into your clockwork—''

''It would be a pressing sort of invitation for me to stop,'' said Elstead, turning his back on the water and staring at the sphere.

They had swung Elstead overboard by eleven o'clock. The day was serenely bright and calm, with the horizon lost in haze. The electric glare in the little upper compartment beamed cheerfully three times. Then they let him down slowly to the surface of the water, and a sailor in the stern chains hung ready to cut the tackle that held the lead weights and the sphere together. The globe, which had looked so large on deck, looked the smallest thing conceivable under the stern of the ship. It rolled a little, and its two dark windows, which floated uppermost, seemed like eyes turned up in round wonderment at the people who crowded the rail. A voice wondered how Elstead liked the rolling. ''Are you ready?'' sang out the commander. ''Aye, aye, sir!'' ''Then let her go!''

The rope of the tackle tightened against the blade and was cut, and an eddy rolled over the globe in a grotesquely helpless fashion. Someone waved a handkerchief, someone else tried an ineffectual cheer, a middy was counting slowly: ''Eight, nine, ten!'' Another roll, then with a jerk and a splash the thing righted itself.

It seemed to be stationary for a moment, to grow rapidly smaller, and then the water closed over it, and it became visible, enlarged by refraction and dimmer, below the surface. Before one could count three it had disappeared. There was a flicker of white light far down in the water that diminished to a speck and vanished. Then there was nothing but a depth of water going down into blackness, through which a shark was swimming.

Then suddenly the screw of the cruiser began to rotate, the water was roiled, the shark disappeared in a wrinkled confusion, and a torrent of foam rushed across the crystalline clearness that had swallowed up Elstead. "What's the idee?" said one seaman to another.

"We're going to lay off about a couple of miles, 'fear he should hit us when he comes up," said his mate.

The ship steamed slowly to her new position. Aboard her almost everyone who was unoccupied remained watching the breathing swell into which the sphere had sunk. It is doubtful if, for the next half-hour, a word was spoken that did not bear directly or indirectly on Elstead. The December sun was now high in the sky, and the heat very considerable.

"He'll be cold enough down there," said Weybridge. "They say that below a certain depth seawater's always just about freezing."

"Where'll he come up?" asked Steevens. "I've lost my bearings."

"That's the spot," said the commander, who prided himself on his omniscience. He extended a precise finger south-eastward. "And this, I reckon, is pretty nearly the moment," he said. "He's been thirty-five minutes."

"How long does it take to reach the bottom of the ocean?" asked Steevens.

"For a depth of five miles, and reckoning—as we did—an acceleration to two foot per second, both ways, is just about three-quarters of a minute."

"Then he's overdue," said Weybridge.

"Pretty nearly," said the commander. "I suppose it takes a few minutes for that cord of his to wind in."

"I forgot that," said Weybridge, evidently relieved.

And then began the suspense A minute slowly dragged itself out, and no sphere shot out of the water. Another followed, and nothing broke the low oily swell. The sailors explained to one another that little point about the winding-in of the cord. The rigging was dotted with expectant faces. "Come up, Elstead!" called one hairy-chested salt, impatiently, and the others caught it up, and shouted as though they were waiting for the curtain of a theater to rise.

The commander glanced irritably at them.

"Of course, if the acceleration's less than two," he said, "he'll be all the longer. We aren't absolutely certain that was the proper figure. I'm no slavish believer in calculations."

Steevens agreed concisely. No one on the quarter-deck spoke for a couple of minutes. Then Steevens's watch-case clicked.

When, twenty-one minutes after, the sun reached the zenith, they were still waiting for the globe to reappear, and not a man aboard had dared to whisper that hope was dead. It was Weybridge who first gave expression to that realization. He spoke while the sound of eight bells still hung in the air. "I always distrusted that window," he said quite suddenly to Steevens.

"Good God!" said Steevens, "you don't think—"

"Well!" said Weybridge, and left the rest to his imagination.

"I'm no great believer in calculations myself," said the commander, dubiously, "so that I'm not altogether hopeless yet." And at midnight the gunboat was steaming slowly in a spiral around the spot where the globe had sunk, and the white beam of the electric light fled and halted and swept discontentedly onward again over the waste of phosphorescent waters under the little stars.

"If his window hasn't burst and smashed him," said Weybridge, "then it's a cursed sight worse, for his clockwork has gone wrong and he's alive now, five miles under our feet, down there in the cold and dark, anchored in that little bubble of his, where never a ray of light has shone or a human being lived since the waters were gathered together. He's there without food, feeling hungry and thirsty and scared, wondering whether he'll starve or stifle. Which will it be? The Myer's apparatus is running out, I suppose. How long do they last?

"Good Heavens!" he exclaimed, "what little things we are! What daring little devils! Down there, miles and miles of water—all water, and all this empty water about us and this sky. Gulfs!" He threw his hands out, and as he did so a little white streak swept noiselessly up the sky, traveling more slowly, stopped, became a motionless dot as though a new star had fallen up into the sky. Then it went sliding back again and lost itself amidst the reflections of the stars and the white haze of the sea's phosphorescence.

At the sight he stopped, arm extended and mouth open. He shut his mouth, opened it again, and waved his arms with an impatient gesture. Then he turned, shouted, "Elstead ahoy," to the first watch, and went at a run to Lindley and the search light. "I saw him," he said. "Starboard there! His light's on and he's just shot out of the water. Bring the light round. We ought to see him drifting, when he lifts on the swell."

But they never picked up the explorer until dawn. Then they almost ran him down. The crane was swung out and a boat's crew hooked the chain to the sphere. When they had shipped the sphere they unscrewed the manhole and peered into the darkness of the interior (for the electric light chamber was intended to illuminate the water about the sphere, and was shut off entirely from its general cavity).

The air was very hot within the cavity, and the India rubber at the lip of the manhole was soft. There was no answer to their eager questions and no sound of movement within. Elstead seemed to be lying motionless, crumpled up in the bottom of the globe. The ship's doctor crawled in and lifted him out to the men outside. For a moment or so they did not know whether Elstead was alive or dead. His face, in the yellow glow of the ship's lamps, glistened with perspiration. They carried him down to his own cabin.

He was not dead, they found, but in a state of absolute nervous collapse, and cruelly bruised besides. For some days he had to lie perfectly still. It was a week before he could tell his experiences.

Almost his first words were that he was going down again. The sphere would have to be altered, he said, in order to allow him to throw off the cord if need be, and that was all. He had had the most marvellous experience. "You thought I should find nothing but ooze," he said. "You laughed at my explorations, and I've discovered a new world!" He told his story in disconnected fragments, and chiefly from the wrong end, so that it is impossible to retell it in his words. But what follows is the narrative of his experience.

It began atrociously, he said. Before the cord ran out the thing kept rolling over. He felt like a frog in a football. He could see nothing but the crane and the sky overhead, with an occasional glimpse of the people at the ship's rail. He couldn't tell a bit which way the thing would roll next. Suddenly he would find his feet going up and try to step, and over he went rolling, head over heels and just anyhow on the padding. Any other shape would have been more comfortable, but no other shape was to be relied upon under the huge pressure of the nethermost abyss.

Suddenly the swaying ceased; the globe righted, and when he had picked himself up, he saw the water all about him greeny-blue with an attenuated light filtering down from above, and a shoal of little floating things went rushing up past him, as it seemed to him, towards the light. And even as he looked it grew darker and darker, until the water above was as dark as the midnight sky, albeit of a greener shade, and the water below black. And little transparent things in the water developed a faint glint of luminosity, and shot past him in faint greenish streaks.

And the feeling of failing! It was just like the start of a lift, he said, only it kept on. One has to imagine what that means, that keeping on. It was then of all times that Elstead repented of his adventure. He saw the chances against him in an altogether new light. He thought of the big cuttlefish people knew to exist in the middle waters, the kind of things they find half-digested in whales at times, or floating dead and rotten and half eaten by fish. Suppose one caught hold and wouldn't leave go. And had the clockwork really been sufficiently tested? But whether he wanted to go on or go back mattered not the slightest now.

In fifty seconds everything was as black as night outside, except where the beam from his light struck through the waters, and picked out every now and then some fish or scrap of sinking matter. They flashed by too fast for him to see what they were. Once he thought he passed a shark. And then the sphere began to get hot by friction against the water. They had underestimated this, it seems.

The first thing he noticed was that he was perspiring, and then he heard a hissing, growing louder, under his feet, and saw a lot of little bubbles—very little bubbles they were—rushing upward like a fan through the water outside. Steam! He felt the window and it was hot. He turned on the minute glow-lamp that lit his own cavity, looked at the padded watch by the studs, and saw he had been travelling now for two minutes. It came into his head that the window would crack through the conflict of temperatures, for he knew the bottom water was very near freezing.

Then suddenly the floor of the sphere seemed to press against his feet, the rush of bubbles outside grew slower and slower and the hissing diminished. The sphere rolled a little. The window had not cracked, nothing had given, and he knew that the dangers of sinking, at any rate, were over.

In another minute or so he would be on the floor of the abyss. He thought, he said, of Steevens and Weybridge and the rest of them five miles overhead, higher to him than the very highest clouds that ever floated over land are to us, steaming slowly and staring down and wondering what had happened to him.

He peered out of the window. There were no more bubbles now, and the hissing had stopped. Outside there was a heavy blackness—as black as black velvet—except where the electric light pierced the empty water and showed the color of it—a yellow-green. Then three things like shapes of fire swam into sight, following each other through the water. Whether they were little and near, or big and far off, he could not tell.

Each was outlined in a bluish light almost as bright as the lights of a fishing smack, a light which seemed to be smoking greatly, and all along the sides of them were specks of this, like the lighted portholes of a ship. Their phosphorescence seemed to go out as they came into the radiance of his lamp, and he saw then that they were indeed fish of some strange sort, with huge heads, vast eyes, and dwindling bodies and tails. Their eyes were turned towards him, and he judged they were following him down. He supposed they were attracted by his glare.

Presently others of the same sort joined them. As he went on down he noticed that the water became of a pallid color, and that little specks twinkled in his ray like motes in a sunbeam. This was probably due to the clouds of ooze and mud that the impact of his leaden sinkers had disturbed.

By the time he was drawn down to the lead weights he was in a dense fog of white that his electric light failed altogether to pierce for more than a few yards, and many minutes elapsed before the hanging sheets of sediment subsided to any extent. Then, lit by his light and by the transient phosphorescence of a distant shoal of fishes, he was able to see under the huge blackness of the superincumbent water an undulating expanse of grayish-white ooze, broken here and there by tangled thickets of a growth of sea lilies, waving hungry tentacles in the air.

Farther away were the graceful translucent outlines of a group of gigantic sponges. About this floor there were scattered a number of bristling flattish tufts of rich purple and black, which he decided must be some sort of sea urchin, and small, large-eyed or blind things, having a curious resemblance—some to woodlice and others to lobsters—crawled sluggishly across the track of the light and vanished into the obscurity again, leaving furrowed trails behind them.

Then suddenly the hovering swarm of little fishes veered about and came towards him as a flight of starlings might do. They passed over him like a phosphorescent snow, and then he saw behind them some larger creature advancing towards the sphere.

At first he could see it only dimly, a faintly moving figure remotely suggestive of a walking man, and then it came into the spray of light that the lamp shot out. As the glare struck it, it shut its eyes, dazzled. He stared in rigid astonishment.

It was a strange, vertebrate animal. Its dark purple head was dimly suggestive of a chameleon, but it had such a high forehead and such a braincase as no reptile ever displayed before; the vertical pitch of its face gave it a most extraordinary resemblance to a human being.

Two large and protruding eyes projected from sockets in chameleon fashion, and it had a broad reptilian mouth with horny lips beneath its little nostrils. In the position of the ears were two huge gill covers, and out of these floated a branching tree of coralline filaments, almost like the treelike gills that very young rays and sharks possess.

But the humanity of the face was not the most extraordinary thing about the creature. It was a biped: its almost globular body was poised on a tripod of two froglike legs and a long thick tail, and its fore limbs, which grotesquely caricatured the human hand much as a frog's do, carried a long shaft of bone tipped with copper. The color of the creature was variegated: its head, hands, and legs were purple; but its skin, which hung loosely upon it, even as clothes might do, was a phosphorescent gray. And it stood there, blinded by the light.

At last this unknown creature of the abyss blinked its eyes open, and, shading them with its disengaged hand, opened its mouth and gave vent to a shouting noise, articulate almost as speech might be, that penetrated even the steel case and padded jacket of the sphere. How shouting may be accomplished without lungs Elstead does not profess to explain. It then moved sideways out of the glare into the mystery of shadow that bordered it on either side, and Elstead felt rather than saw that it was coming towards him. Fancying the light had attracted it, he turned the switch that cut off the current. In another moment something soft dabbed upon the steel, and the globe swayed.

Then the shouting was repeated and it seemed to him that a distant echo answered it. The dabbing recurred, and the globe swayed and ground against the spindle over which the wire was rolled. He stood in the blackness, and peered out into the everlasting night of the abyss. And presently he saw, very faint and remote, other phosphorescent quasi-human forms hurrying towards him.

Hardly knowing what he did, he felt about in his swaying prison for the stud of the exterior electric light, and came by accident against his own small glow lamp in its padded recess. The sphere twisted and then threw him down; he heard shouts like shouts of surprise, and when he rose to his feet he saw two pairs of stalked eyes peering into the lower window and reflecting his light.

In another moment hands were dabbing vigorously at his steel casing, and there was a sound, horrible enough in his position, of the metal protection of the clockwork being vigorously hammered. That, indeed, sent his heart into his mouth, for if these strange creatures succeeded in stopping that his release would never occur. Scarcely had he thought as much when he felt the sphere sway violently, and the floor of it press hard against his feet. He turned off the small glow lamp that lit the interior, and sent the ray of the large light in the separate compartment out into the water. The sea floor and the manlike creatures had disappeared, and a couple of fish chasing each other dropped suddenly by the window.

He thought at once that these strange denizens of the deep sea had broken the wire rope and that he had escaped. He drove up faster and faster, and then stopped with a jerk that sent him flying against the padded roof of his prison. For half a minute perhaps he was too astonished to think.

Then he felt that the sphere was spinning slowly, and rocking, and it seemed to him that it was also being drawn through the water. By crouching close to the window he managed to make his weight effective and roll that part of the sphere downward, but he could see nothing save the pale ray of his light striking down ineffectively into the darkness. It occurred to him that he would see more if he turned the lamp off and allowed his eyes to grow accustomed to the profound obscurity.

In this he was wise. After some minutes the velvety blackness became a translucent blackness, and then far away, and as faint as the zodiacal light of an English summer evening, he saw shapes moving below. He judged these creatures had detached his cable and were towing him along the sea bottom.

And then he saw something faint and remote across the undulations of the submarine plain, a broad horizon of pale luminosity that extended this way and that way as far as the range of his little window permitted him to see. To this he was being towed, as a balloon might be towed by men out of the open country into a town. He approached it very slowly, and very slowly the dim irradiation was gathered together into more definite shapes.

It was nearly five o'clock before he came over this luminous area, and by that time he could make out an arrangement suggestive of streets and houses grouped about a vast roofless erection that was grotesquely suggestive of a ruined abbey. It was spread out like a map below him. The houses were all roofless enclosures of walls, and their substance being, as he afterwards saw, of phosphorescent bones, gave the place an appearance as if it were built of drowned moonshine.

Among the inner caves of the place waving trees of crinoid stretched their tentacles, and tall, slender, glassy sponges shot like shining minarets and lilies of filmy light out of the general glow of the city. In the open spaces of the place he could see a stirring movement as of crowds of people, but he was too many fathoms above them to distinguish the individuals in those crowds.

Then slowly they pulled him down, and as they did so the details of the place crept slowly upon his apprehension. He saw that the courses of the cloudy buildings were marked out with beaded lines of round objects, and then he perceived that at several points below him in broad open spaces were forms like encrusted ships.

Slowly and surely he was drawn down, and the forms below him became brighter, clearer, more distinct. He was being pulled down, he perceived, towards the large building in the center of the town, and he could catch a glimpse ever and again of the multitudinous forms that were lugging at his cord. He was astonished to see that the rigging of one of the ships, which formed such a prominent feature of the place, was crowded with a host of gesticulating figures regarding him, and then the walls of the great building rose about him silently and hid the city from his eyes.

And such walls they were, of water-logged wood, and

twisted wire rope and iron spars, and copper, and the bones and skulls of dead men.

The skulls ran in curious zigzag lines and spirals and fantastic curves over the building; and in and out of their eye-sockets, and over the whole surface of the place, lurked and played a multitude of silvery little fishes.

And now he was at such a level that he could see these strange people of the abyss plainly once more. To his astonishment, he perceived that they were prostrating themselves before him, all save one, dressed as it seemed in a robe of placoid scales and crowned with a luminous diadem, who stood with his reptilian mouth opening and shutting as though he led the chanting of the worshippers.

They continued worshiping him, without rest for intermission, for the space of three hours.

Most circumstantial was Elstead's account of this astounding city and its people, these people of perpetual night, who have never seen sun or moon or stars, green vegetation, or any living air-breathing creatures, who know nothing of fire or any light but the phosphorescent light of living things.

Startling as is his story, it is yet more startling to find that scientific men of such eminence as Adams and Jenkins find nothing incredible in it. They tell me they see no reason why intelligent, water-breathing, vertebrate creatures inured to a low temperature and enormous pressure, and of such a heavy structure that neither alive nor dead would they float, might not live upon the bottom of the deep sea quite unsuspected by us, descendants like ourselves of the great Theriomorpha of the New Red Sandstone age.

We should be known to them, however, as strange meteoric creatures wont to fall catastrophically dead out of the mysterious blackness of their watery sky. And not only we ourselves, but our ships, our metals, our appliances, would come raining down out of the night. Sometimes sinking things would smite down and crush them, as if it were the judgment of some unseen power above, and sometimes would come things of the utmost rarity or utility or shapes of inspiring suggestion. One can understand, perhaps, something of their behavior at the descent of a living man, if one thinks what a barbaric people might do, to whom an enhaloed shining creature came suddenly out of the sky.

At one time or another Elstead probably told the officers of the *Ptarmigan* every detail of his strange twelve hours in the abyss. That he also intended to write them down is certain, but he never did, and so unhappily we have to piece together the discrepant fragments of his story from the reminiscences of Commander Simmons, Weybridge, Steevens, Lindley, and the others.

We see the thing darkly in fragmentary glimpses—the huge ghostly building, the bowing, chanting people, with their dark, chameleonlike heads and faintly luminous forms, and Elstead, with his light turned on again, vainly trying to convey to their minds that the cord by which the sphere was held was to be severed. Minute after minute slipped away, and Elstead, looking at his watch, was horrified to find that he had oxygen only for four hours more. But the chant in his honor kept on as remorselessly as if it were the marching song of his approaching death.

The manner of his release he does not understand, but to judge by the end of cord that hung from the sphere, it had been cut through by rubbing against the edge of the altar. Abruptly the sphere rolled over, and he swept up out of their world, as an ethereal creature clothed in a vacuum would sweep through our own atmosphere back to its native ether again. He must have torn out of their sight as a hydrogen bubble hastens upwards from our air. A strange ascension it must have seemed to them.

The sphere rushed up with even greater velocity than, when weighted with the lead sinkers, it had rushed down. It became exceedingly hot. It drove up with the windows uppermost, and he remembers the torrent of bubbles frothing against the glass. Every moment he expected this to fly. Then suddenly something like a huge wheel seemed to be released in his head, the padded compartment began spinning about him, and he fainted. His next recollection was of his cabin, and of the doctor's voice.

But that is the substance of the extraordinary story that Elstead related in fragments to the officers of the *Ptar-*

migan. He promised to write it all down at a later date. His mind was chiefly occupied with the improvement of his apparatus, which was effected at Rio.

It remains only to tell that on February 2, 1896, he made his second descent into the ocean abyss, with the improvements his first experience suggested. What happened we shall probably never know. He never returned. The *Ptarmigan* beat about over the point of his submersion, seeking him in vain for thirteen days. Then she returned to Rio, and the news was telegraphed to his friends. So the matter remains for the present. But it is hardly probable that any further attempt will be made to verify his strange story of these hitherto unsuspected cities of the deep sea.

FEAR IS A BUSINESS

by Theodore Sturgeon

Josephus Macardle Phillipso is a man of destiny and he can prove it. His books prove it. The Temple of Space proves it.

A man of destiny is someone who is forced into things—big things—willy, as the saying goes, nilly. Phillipso, just for example, never meant to get into the Unidentified (except by Phillipso) Aerial Object business. This is to say, he didn't sit down like some of his less honest (according to Phillipso) contemporaries and say "I think I'll sit down and tell some lies about flying saucers and make some money." Everything that happened (Phillipso ultimately believed) just happened, and happened to happen to him. Might have been anybody. Then, what with one thing leading to another the way it does, well, you burn your forearm on an alibi and wind up with a Temple.

It was, on looking back on it (something which Phillipso never does any more), an unnecessary alibi devised for inadequate reasons. Phillipso merely calls the beginnings "inauspicious" and lets it go at that. The fact remains that it all started one night when he tied one on for no special reason except that he had just been paid his forty-eight dollars for writing advertising promotion copy for the Hincty Pincty Value Stores, and excused his absence on the following day with a story about a faulty lead on the spark coil of his car which took him most of the night to locate, and there he was stranded in the hills on the way back from a visit to his aging mother. The next night he did visit his aging mother and on the way back his car unaccountably quit and he spent most of the night fiddling with the electrical system until he discovered, just at dawn, a—well, there it was. At a time like that you just can't tell the truth. And while he was pondering various credible alternatives to veracity, the sky lit up briefly and shadows of the rocks and trees around him grew and slid away and died before he could even look up. It was a temperature inversion or a methane fireball or St. Elmo's fire or maybe even a weather balloon—actually that doesn't matter. He looked up at where it already wasn't, and succumbed to inspiration.

His car was parked on a grassy shoulder in a cut between two bluffs. Thick woods surrounded a small clearing to his right, a sloping glade sparsely studded with almost round moraine boulders, of all sizes. He quickly located three, a foot or so in diameter, equally spaced, and buried to approximately the same depth—*i.e.*, not much, Phillipso being merely an ingenious man, not an industrious one. These three he lifted out, being careful to keep his crepe-soled shoes flat on the resilient grass and to leave as few scuff-marks and indentations as possible. One by one he took the stones into the woods and dropped them into an evacuated foxhole and shoved some dead branches in on top of them. He then ran to his car and from the trunk got a blowtorch which he had borrowed to fix a leak in the sweated joint of a very old-fashioned bathtub in his mother's house, and with it thoroughly charred the three depressions in the ground where the boulders had lain.

Destiny had unquestionably been at work from the time he had beered himself into mendacity forty-eight hours before. But it became manifest at this point, for after Phillipso had licked his forearm lightly with the tongue of flame from the torch, extinguished the same and put it away, a car ground up the hill toward him. And it was not just any car. It belonged to a Sunday supplement feature writer named Penfield who was not only featureless at the moment, but who had also seen the light in the sky a half hour earlier. It may have been Phillipso's intention to drive into town with his story, and back with a reporter and cameraman, all to the end that he could show a late edition to his boss and explain his second absence. Destiny, however, made a much larger thing of it.

Phillipso stood in the graying light in the middle of the road and flapped his arms until the approaching car stopped. "They," he said hoarsely, "almost killed me."

From then on, as they say in the Sunday supplement business, it wrote itself. Phillipso offered not one blessed thing. All he did was answer questions, and the whole thing was born in the brain of this Penfield, who realized nothing except that here was the ideal interview subject. "Came down on a jet of fire, did it? Oh—*three* jets of fire." Phillipso took him into the glade and showed him the three scorched pits, still warm. "Threaten you, did they? Oh—all Earth. Threatened all Earth." Scribble scribble. He took his own pictures too. "What'd you do, speak right up to them? Hm?" Phillipso said he had, and so it went.

The story didn't make the Sunday supplements, but the late editions, just as Phillipso had planned, but much bigger. So big, as a matter of fact, that he didn't go back to his job at all; he didn't need it. He got a wire from a publisher who wanted to know if he, as a promotion writer, might be able to undertake a book.

He might and he did. He wrote with a crackling facility (*The first word in thrift, the last word in value* was his, and was posted all over the Hincty Pincty chain just as if it meant something) in a style homely as a cowlick and sincere as a banker's nameplate. *The Man Who Saved the Earth* sold two hundred and eighty thousand copies in the first seven months.

So the money started to come in. Not only the book

money—the other money. This other money came from the end-of-the-world people, the humanity-is-just-too-wicked people, the save-us-from-the-spacemen folk. Clear across the spectrum, from people who believed that if God wanted us to fly through space we'd have been born with tailfins to people who didn't believe in anything but Russians but would believe anything of them, people said "Save us!" and every crack on the pot dripped gold. Hence the Temple of Space, just to regularize the thing, you know, and then the lectures, and could Phillipso help it if half the congre-uh, club members, called them services?

The sequel happened the same way, just appendixes to the first book, to handle certain statements he had made which some critics said made him fall apart by his own internal evidence. *We Need Not Surrender* contradicted itself even more, was a third longer, sold three hundred and ten thousand in the first nine weeks, and brought in so much of that other money that Phillipso registered himself as an institute and put all the royalties with it. The temple itself began to show signs of elaboration, the most spectacular piece of which was the war-surplus radar basket of a battleship that went round and round all the time. It wasn't connected to a damn thing but people felt that Phillipso had his eyes open. You could see it, on a clear day, from Catalina, especially at night after the orange searchlight was installed to rotate with it. It looked like a cosmic windshield wiper.

Phillipso's office was in the dome under the radar basket, and was reachable only from the floor below by an automatic elevator. He could commune with himself in there just fine, especially when he switched the elevator off. He had a lot of communing to do, too, sometimes detail stuff, like whether he could sustain a rally at the Coliseum and where to apply the ten-thousand-dollar grant from the Astrological Union which had annoyingly announced the exact size of the gift to the press before sending him the check. But his main preoccupation was another book, or what do I do for an encore? Having said that we are under attack, and then that we can rally and beat 'em, he needed an angle. Something new, preferably born by newsbeat out of cultural terror. And soon, too; his kind of wonder could always use another nine days.

As he sat alone and isolated in the amnion of these reflections, his astonishment can hardly be described at the sound of a dry cough just behind him, and the sight of a short sandy-haired man who stood there. Phillipso might have fled, or leapt at the man's throat, or done any number of violent things besides, but he was stopped cold by a device historically guaranteed to stem all raging authors: "I have," said the man, holding up one volume in each hand, "read your stuff."

"Oh, really?" asked Phillipso.

"I find it," said the man, "logical and sincere."

Phillipso looked smilingly at the man's unforgettable bland face and his unnoticeable gray suit. The man said, "Sincerity and logic have this in common: neither need have anything to do with truth."

"Who are you?" demanded Phillipso immediately. "What do you want and how did you get in here?"

"I am not, as you put it, in here," said the man. He pointed upward suddenly, and in spite of himself Phillipso found his eyes following the commanding finger.

The sky was darkening, and Phillipso's orange searchlight slashed at it with increasing authority. Through the transparent dome, just to the north, and exactly where his visitor pointed, Phillipso saw the searchlight pick out a great silver shape which hovered perhaps fifty feet away and a hundred feet above the Temple. He saw it only momentarily, but it left an afterimage in his retinae like a flashbulb. And by the time the light had circled around again and passed the place, the thing was gone. "I'm in that," said the sandy-haired man. "Here in this room I'm a sort of projection. But then," he sighed, "aren't we all?"

"You better explain yourself," said Phillipso loudly enough to keep his voice from shaking, "or I'll throw you out of here on your ear."

"You couldn't. I'm not here to be thrown." The man approached Phillipso, who had advanced away from his desk into the room. Rather than suffer a collision, Phillipso retreated a step and another, until he felt the edge of his desk against his glutei. The sandy-haired man, impassive, kept on walking—to Phillipso, through Phillipso, Phillipso's desk, Phillipso's chair, and Phillipso's equanimity, the last-named being the only thing he touched.

"I didn't want to do that," said the man some moments later, bending solicitously over Phillipso as he opened his eyes. He put out his hand as if to assist Phillipso to his feet. Phillipso bounced up by himself and cowered away, remembering only then that, on his own terms, the man could not have touched him. He crouched there, gulping and glaring, while the man shook his head regretfully. "I *am* sorry, Phillipso."

"Who are you, anyway?" gasped Phillipso.

For the first time the man seemed at a loss. He looked in puzzlement at each of Phillipso's eyes, and then scratched his head. "I hadn't thought of that," he said musingly. "Important, of course, of course. Labeling." Focusing his gaze more presently at Phillipso, he said, "We have a name for you people that translates roughly to *'Labelers.'* Don't be insulted. It's a categorization, like *'biped'* or *'omnivorous.'* It means the mentality that verbalizes or it can't think."

"Who are you?"

"Oh, I do beg your pardon. Call me—uh, well, call me Hurensohn. I suggest that because I know you have to call me something, because it doesn't matter what you call me, and because it's the sort of thing you'll be calling me once you find out why I'm here."

"I don't know what you're talking about."

"Then by all means let's discuss the matter until you do."

"D-discuss what?"

"I don't have to show you that ship out there again?"

"Please," said Phillipso ardently, "don't."

"Now look," said Hurensohn gently, "there is nothing to fear, only a great deal to explain. Please straighten up and take the knots out of your thorax. That's better. Now sit down calmly and we'll talk the whole thing over. *There,* that's *fine!*" As Phillipso sank shakily into his desk chair, Hurensohn lowered himself into the easy chair which flanked it. Phillipso was horrified to see the half-inch gap of air which, for five seconds or so, separated the man from the chair. Then Hurensohn glanced down, murmured an apology, and floated down to contact the cushion somewhat more normally. "Careless. sometimes," he explained. "So many things to keep in mind at once. You get interested, you know, and next thing you're buzzing around without your light-warp or forgetting your hypno-field when you go in swimming, like that fool in Loch Ness."

"Are you really—a—a an extraulp?"

"Oh, yes, indeed. Extraterrestrial, extrasolar, extragalactic—all that."

"You don't; I mean, I don't see any—"

"I know I don't look like one. I don't look like this" —he gestured down his gray waistcoat with the tips of all his fingers—"either. I could show you what I really do look like, but that's inadvisable. It's been tried." He shook his head sadly, and said again, "Inadvisable."

"Wh-what do you want?"

"Ah. Now we get down to it. How would you like to tell the world about me—about us?"

"Well, I already—"

"I mean, the *truth* about us."

"From the evidence I already have—" Phillipso began with some heat. It cooled swiftly. Hurensohn's face had taken on an expression of unshakable patience; Phillipso was suddenly aware that he could rant and rave and command and explain from now until Michaelmas, and this creature would simply wait him out. He knew, too (though he kept it well below the conscious area) that the more he talked the more he would leave himself open to contradiction—the worst kind of contradiction at that: quotes from Phillipso. So he dried right up and tried the other tack. "All right," he said humbly. "Tell me."

"Ah . . ." It was a long-drawn-out sound, denoting deep satisfaction. "I think I'll begin by informing you that you have, quite without knowing it, set certain forces in motion which can profoundly affect mankind for hundreds, even thousands, of years."

"Hundreds," breathed Phillipso, his eye beginning to glow. "Even thousands."

"That is not a guess," said Hurensohn. "It's a computation. And the effect you have on your cultural matrix is—well, let me draw an analogy from your own recent history. I'll quote something: *'Long had part of the idea; McCarthy had the other part. McCarthy got nowhere, failed with his third party, because he attacked and destroyed but didn't give. He appealed to hate, but not to greed, no what's-in-it-for-me, no porkchops.'* That's from the works of a reformed murderer who now writes reviews for the New York *Herald Tribune.*"

"What has this to do with me?"

"You," said Hurensohn, "are the Joseph McCarthy of saucer-writers."

Phillipso's glow increased. "My," he sighed.

"And," said Hurensohn, "you may profit by his example. If that be—no, I've quoted enough. I see you are not getting my drift, anyway. I shall be more explicit. We came here many years ago to study your interesting little civilization. It shows great promise—so great that we have decided to help you."

"Who needs help?"

"Who needs help?" Hurensohn paused for a long time, as if he had sent away somewhere for words and was waiting for them to arrive. Finally, "I take it back. I won't be more explicit. If I explained myself in detail I would only sound corny. Any rephrasing of the Decalogue sounds corny to a human being. Every statement of every way in which you need help has been said and said. You are cursed with a sense of rejection, and your rejection begets anger and your anger begets crime and your crime begets guilt; and all your guilty reject the innocent and destroy their innocence. Riding this wheel you totter and spin, and the only basket in which you can drop your almighty insecurity is an almighty fear, and anything that makes the basket bigger is welcome to you. . . . Do you begin to see what I am talking about, and why I'm talking to you?

"Fear is your business, your stock in trade. You've gotten fat on it. With humanity trembling on the edge of the known, you've found a new unknown to breed fear in. And this one's a honey; it's infinite. Death from space . . . and every time knowledge lights a brighter light and drives the darkness back, you'll be there to show how much wider the circumference of darkness has become . . . Were you going to say something?''

"I am *not* getting fat,'' said Phillipso.

"Am I saying anything?'' breathed the sandy-haired man. "Am I here at all?''

In all innocence Phillipso pointed out, "You said you weren't.''

Hurensohn closed his eyes and said in tones of sweet infinite patience, "Listen to me, Phillipso, because I now fear I shall never speak to you again. Whether or not you like it—and you do, and we don't—you have become the central clearinghouse for the Unidentified Aerial Object. You have accomplished this by lies and by fear, but that's now beside the point—you accomplished it. Of all countries on earth, this is the only one we can effectively deal with; the other so-called Great Powers are constitutionally vindictive, or impotent, or hidebound, or all three. Of all the people in this country we could deal with—in government, or the great foundations, or the churches—we can find no one who could overcome the frenzy and foolishness of your following. You have forced us to deal with you.''

"My,'' said Phillipso.

"Your people listen to you. More people than you know listen to your people—frequently without knowing it themselves. You have something for everyone on earth who feels small, and afraid, and guilty. You tell them they are right to be afraid, and that makes them proud. You tell them that the forces ranged against them are beyond their understanding, and they find comfort in each other's ignorance. You say the enemy is irresistible, and they huddle together in terror and are unanimous. And at the same time you except yourself, implying that you and you alone can protect them.''

"Well,'' said Phillipso, "if you have to deal with me . . . isn't it so?''

"It is not," said Hurensohn flatly. " *'Protect'* presupposes *'attack.'* This is no attack. We came here to help."

"Liberate us," said Phillipso.

"Yes. *No!*" For the first time Hurensohn showed a sign of irritation. "Don't go leading me into your snide little rat-shrewd pitfalls, Phillipso! By liberate I meant make free; what you meant is what the Russians did to the Czechs."

"All right," said Phillipso guardedly. "You want to free us. Of what?"

"War. Disease. Poverty. Insecurity."

"Yes," said Phillipso. "It's corny."

"You don't believe it."

"I haven't thought about it one way or the other yet," said Phillipso candidly. "Maybe you can do all you say. What is it you want from me?"

Hurensohn held up his hands. Phillipso blinked as *The Man Who Saved the Earth* appeared in one of them and *We Need Not Surrender* in the other. He then realized that the actual volumes must be in the ship. Some of his incipient anger faded; some of his insipid pleasure returned. Hurensohn said, "These. You'll have to retract."

"What do you mean retract?"

"Not all at once. You're going to write another book, aren't you? Of course; you'd have to." There was the slightest emphasis on *"you'd"* and Phillipso did not like it. However, he said nothing. Hurensohn went on: "You could make new discoveries. Revelations, if you like. Interpretations."

"I couldn't do that."

"You'd have all the help in the world. Or out of it."

"Well, but what for?"

"To draw the poison of those lies of yours. To give us a chance to show ourselves without getting shot on sight."

"Can't you protect yourselves against that?"

"Against the bullets, certainly. Not against what pulls the triggers."

"Suppose I go along with you."

"I told you! No poverty, no insecurity, no crime, no—"

"No Phillipso."

"Oh. You mean, what's in it for you? Can't you see? You'd make possible a new Eden, the flowering of your entire species—a world where men laughed and worked and loved and achieved, where a child could grow up unafraid and where, for the first time in your history, human beings would understand one another when they spoke. You could do this—just you."

"I can see it," said Phillipso scathingly. "All the world on the village green and me with them, leading a morris dance. I couldn't live that way."

"You're suddenly very cocky, Mister Phillipso," said Hurensohn with a quiet and frightening courtesy.

Phillipso drew a deep breath. "I can afford to be," he said harshly. "I'll level with you, bogeyman." He laughed unpleasantly. "Good, huh. Bogey. That's what they call you when they—"

"—get us on a radar screen. I know, I know. Get to the point."

"Well. All right then. You asked for it." He got to his feet. "You're a phony. You can maybe do tricks with mirrors, maybe even hide the mirrors, but that's it. If you could do a tenth of what you say, you wouldn't have to come begging. You'd just . . . do it. You'd just walk in and take over. By God, I would."

"You probably would," said Hurensohn, with something like astonishment. No, it was more like an incredulous distaste. He narrowed his eyes. For a brief moment Phillipso thought it was part of his facial expression, or the beginning of a new one, and then he realized it was something else, a concentration, a—

He shrieked. He found himself doing something proverbial, unprintable, and not quite impossible. He didn't want to do it—with all his mind and soul he did not want to, but he did it nonetheless.

"If and when I want you to," said Hurensohn calmly, "you'll do that in the window of Bullock's Wilshire at high noon."

"Please . . ."

"I'm not doing anything," said Hurensohn. He

laughed explosively, put his hands in his jacket pockets, and—worst of all, he watched. "Go to it, boy."

"Please!" Phillipso whimpered.

Hurensohn made not the slightest detectable move, but Phillipso was suddenly free. He fell back into his chair, sobbing with rage, fear, and humiliation. When he could find a word at all, it came out between the fingers laced over his scarlet face, and was, "Inhuman. That was . . . inhuman."

"Uh-huh," agreed Hurensohn pleasantly. He waited until the walls of outrage expanded enough to include him, recoil from him, and return to the quivering Phillipso, who could then hear when he was spoken to. "What you've got to understand," said Hurensohn, "is that we don't do what we can do. We can, I suppose, smash a planet, explode it, drop it into the sun. You can, in that sense, eat worms. You don't, though, and wouldn't. In your idiom you *couldn't.* Well then, neither can we force humanity into anything without its reasoned consent. You can't understand that, can you? Listen: I'll tell you just how far it goes. We couldn't force even *one* human to do what we want done. You, for example."

"You—you just did, though."

Hurensohn shuddered—a very odd effect, rather like that on a screen when one thumps a slide projector with the heel of one's hand. "A demonstration, that's all. Costly, I may add. I won't get over it as soon as you will. To make a point, you might say, I had to eat a bedbug." Again the flickering shudder. "But then, people have gone farther than that to put an idea over."

"I could refuse?" Phillipso said, timidly.

"Easily."

"What would you do to me?"

"Nothing."

"But you'd go ahead and—"

Hurensohn was shaking his head as soon as Phillipso began to speak. "We'd just go. You've done too much damage. If you won't repair it, there's no way for us to do it unless we use force, and we can't do that. It seems an awful waste, though. Four hundred years of observation. . . . I wish I could tell you the trouble we've gone to, trying to watch you, *learn* you, without interfering. Of course, it's been easier since Kenneth Arnold and the noise he made about us.''

''Easier?''

''Lord, yes. You people have a talent—really, a genius for making rational your unwillingness to believe your own eyes. We got along famously after the weather-balloon hypothesis was made public. It's so easy to imitate a weather balloon. Pokey, though. The greatest boon of all was that nonsense about temperature inversions. It's quite a trick to make a ship behave like automobile headlights on a distant mountain or the planet Venus, but temperature inversions?'' He snapped his fingers. ''Nothing to it. Nobody understands 'em so they explain everything. We thought we had a pretty complete tactical manual on concealment, but did you see the one the U.S. Air Force got out? Bless 'em! It even explains the mistakes we make. Well, most of them, anyway. That idiot in Loch Ness—''

''Wait, wait!'' Phillipso wailed. ''I'm trying to find out what I'm supposed to do, what will happen, and you sit there and go *on* so!''

''Yes, yes of course. You're quite right. I was just blowing words over my tongue to try to get the taste of you out of my mouth. Not that I really have a mouth, and that would make a tongue sort of frustrated, wouldn't it? Figure of speech, you know.''

''Tell me again. This Paradise on earth—how long is it supposed to take? How would you go about it?''

''Through your next book, I suppose. We'd have to work out a way to counteract your other two without losing your audience. If you jump right into line and say how friendly and wise we aliens are, the way Adamski and Heard did, you'll only disappoint your followers. I know! I'll give you a weapon against these—uh—bogeymen of yours. A simple formula, a simple field generator. We'll lay it out so anyone can use it, and bait it with some of your previous nonsense—beg pardon, I might have meant some of your previous statements. Something guaranteed to defend Earth against the—uh—World Destroyers.'' He smiled. It was rather a pleasant sight. ''It would, too.''

''What do you mean?''

''Well, if we claimed that the device had an effective range of fifty feet and it actually covered, say, two thousand square miles, and it was easy and cheap to build, and the plans were in every copy of your new book . . . let's see now, we'd have to pretend to violate a little security, too, so the people who aren't afraid would think they were stealing . . . hmmm.''

''Device, device—*what* device?''

''Oh, a—'' Hurensohn came up out of his reverie. ''Labeling again, dammit. I'll have to think a minute. You have no name for such a thing.''

''Well, what is it supposed to do?''

''Communicate. That is, it makes complete communications possible.''

''We get along pretty well.''

''Nonsense! You communicate with labels—words. Your words are like a jumble of packages under a Christmas tree. You know who sent each one and you can see its size and shape, and sometimes it's soft or it rattles or ticks. But that's all. You don't know *exactly* what it means and you won't until you open it. That's what this device will do—open your words to complete comprehension. If every human being, regardless of language, age or background, understood exactly what every other human being wanted, and knew at the same time that he himself was understood, it would change the face of the earth. Overnight.''

Phillipso sat and thought that one out. ''You couldn't bargain,'' he said at length. ''You couldn't—uh—explain a mistake, even.''

''You could explain it,'' said Hurensohn. ''It's just that you couldn't excuse it.''

''You mean every husband who—ah—flirted, every child who played hooky, every manufacturer who—''

''All that.''

''Chaos,'' whispered Phillipso. ''The very structure of—''

Hurensohn laughed pleasantly. ''You know what you're

saying, Phillipso. You're saying that the basic structure of your whole civilization is lies and partial truths, and that without them it would fall apart. And you're quite right." He chuckled again. "Your Temple of Space, just for example. What do you think would happen to it if all your sheep knew what their shepherd was and what was in the shepherd's mind?"

"What are you trying to do—tempt me with all this?"

Most gravely Hurensohn answered him, and it shocked Phillipso to the marrow when he used his first name to do it. "I am, Joe, with all my heart I am. You're right about the chaos, but such a chaos should happen to mankind or any species like it. I will admit that it would strike civilization like a mighty wind, and that a great many structures would fall. But there would be no looters in the wreckage, Joe. No man would take advantage of the ones who fell."

"I know something about human beings," Phillipso said in a flat, hurt voice. "And I don't want 'em on the prowl when I'm down. Especially when they don't have anything. God."

Hurensohn shook his head sadly. "You don't know enough, then. You have never seen the core of a human being, a part which is not afraid, and which understands and is understood." Hurensohn searched his face with earnest eyes.

"Have you?"

"I have. I see it now. I see it in you all. But then, I see more than you do. You could see as much; you all could. Let me do it, Joe. Help me, *please*."

"And lose everything I've worked so hard to—"

"Lose? Think of the gain! Think of what you'd do for the whole world! Or—if it means any more to you—turn the coin over. Think of what you'll carry with you if you don't help us. Every war casualty, every death from preventable disease, every minute of pain in every cancer patient, every stumbling step of a multiple sclerosis victim, will be on your conscience from the moment you refuse me.

"Ah, think, Joe—*think!*"

Phillipso slowly raised his eyes from his clenched

hands to Hurensohn's plain, intense face. Higher, then, to the dome and through it. He raised his hand and pointed. "Pardon me," he said shakily, "but your ship is showing."

"Pshaw," said Hurensohn surprisingly. "Dammit, Phillipso, you've gone and made me concentrate, and I've let go the warp-matrix and fused my omicron. Take a minute or two to fix. I'll be back." And he disappeared. He didn't go anywhere; he just abruptly wasn't.

Josephus Macardle Phillipso moved like a sleepwalker across the round room and stood against the Plexiglas, staring up and out at the shining ship. It was balanced and beautiful, dusty-textured and untouchable like a moth's wing. It was lightly phosphorescent, flaring in the orange glow of the slashing searchlight, dimming rapidly almost to blackness just as the light cut at it again.

He looked past the ship to the stars, and in his mind's eye, past them to stars again, and stars, and whole systems of stars which in their remoteness looked like stars again, and stars again. He looked down then, to the ground under the Temple and down again to its steep slope, its one narrow terrace of a highway, and down and down again to the lamp-speckled black of the valley bottom. And if I fell from here to there, he thought, it would be like falling from crest to trough in the whorls of a baby's fingerprint.

And he thought, even with help from Heaven, I couldn't tell this truth and be believed. I couldn't suggest this work and be trusted. I am unfit, and I have unfit myself.

He thought bitterly, It's only the truth. The truth and I have a like polarity, and it springs away from me when I approach, by a law of nature. I prosper without the truth, and it has cost me nothing, nothing, nothing but the ability to tell the truth.

But I might try, he thought. What was it he said: *The core of a human being, a part which is not afraid, and which understands and is understood.* Who was he talking about? Anybody I know? Anyone I ever heard of? ("How are you?" you say, when you don't care how they are. "I'm sorry," you say, when you're not. "Goodby," you say and it means God be with you, and how often is your goodby a blessing? Hypocrisy and lies, thousands a day, so easily done we forget to feel guilty for them.)

I see it now, he said, though. Did he mean me? Could he see the core of me, and say that? . . . if he can see such a marrow, he can see a strand of spider-silk at sixty yards.

He said, Phillipso recalled, that if I wouldn't help, they'd do nothing. They'd go away that's all—go away, forever, and leave us at the mercy of—what was that sardonic phrase?—the World Destroyers.

"But I never lied!" he wailed, suddenly and frighteningly loud. "I never meant to. They'd ask, don't you see, and I'd only say yes or no, whatever they wanted to hear. The only other thing I ever did was to explain the yes, or the no; they didn't start out to be lies!" No one answered him. He felt very alone. He thought again, I could try . . . and then, wistfully, could I try?

The phone rang. He looked blindly at it until it rang again. Tiredly he crossed to it and picked it up. "Phillipso."

The phone said, "Okay, Swami, you win. How did you do it?"

"Who is that? Penfield?" Penfield, whose original Phillipso spread had started his rise from Sunday feature writer; Penfield, who, as district chief of a whole newspaper chain, had of course long since forsworn Phillipso . . .

"Yeah, Penfield," drawled the pugnacious, insulting voice. "Penfield who promised you faithfully that never again would these papers run a line about you and your phony space war."

"What do you want, Penfield?"

"So you win, that's all. Whether I like it or not, you're news again. We're getting calls from all over the county. There's a flight of F-84s on the way from the Base. There's a TV mobile unit coming up the mountain to get that flying saucer of yours on network, and four queries already from INS. I don't know how you're doing it, but you're news, so what's your lousy story?"

Phillipso glanced up over his shoulder at the ship. The orange searchlight set it to flaming once, once again, while the telephone urgently bleated his name. Around came the light and—

And nothing. It was gone. The ship was gone. "Wait!" cried Phillipso hoarsely. But it was gone.

The phone gabbled at him. Slowly he turned back to it. "Wait," he said to it too. He put down the instrument and rubbed water out of his eyes. Then he picked up the phone again.

"I saw from here," said the tinny voice. "It's gone. What was it? What'd you do?"

"Ship," said Phillipso. "It was a spaceship."

" *'It was a spaceship,'* " Penfield repeated in the voice of a man writing on a pad. "So come on, Phillipso. What happened? Aliens came down and met you face to face, that it?"

"They—yes."

" 'Face . . . to . . . face.' Got it. What'd they want?" A pause, then, angrily, "Phillipso, you there? Dammit, I got a story to get out here. What'd they want? They beg for mercy, want you to lay off?"

Phillipso wet his lips. "Well, yes. Yes, they did."

"What'd they look like?"

"I—they . . . there was only one."

Penfield growled something about pulling teeth. "All right, only one. One *what?* Monster, spider, octopus—come *on*, Phillipso!"

"It . . . well, it wasn't a man, exactly."

"A girl," said Penfield excitedly. "A girl of unearthly beauty. How's that? They've threatened you before. Now they came to beguile you with, and so on. How's that?"

"Well, I—"

"I'll quote you. *'Unearthly* . . . mmm . . . *and refused* . . . mmm, *temptation'* "

"Penfield, I—"

"Listen, Swami, that's all you get. I haven't time to listen to any more of your crap. I'll give you this in exchange, though. Just a friendly warning, and besides, I want this story to hold up through tomorrow anyhow. ATIC and the FBI are going to be all over that Temple of yours like flies on a warm marshmallow. You better hide the pieces of that balloon or whatever else the trick was. When it reaches the point of sending out a flight of jets, they don't think publicity is funny."

"Penfield, I—" But the phone was dead. Phillipso hung up and whirled to the empty room. "You *see?*" he wept. "You see what they make me do?"

He sat down heavily. The phone rang again. New York, the operator said. It was Jonathan, his publisher. "Joe! Your line's been busy. Great work, fella. Heard the bulletin on TV. How'd you do it? Never mind. Give me the main facts. I'll have a release out first thing in the morning. Hey, how soon can you get the new book done? Two weeks? Well, three—you can do it in three, fella. You have to do it in three. I'll cancel the new Heming—or the—never mind, I'll get press time for it. Now. Let's have it. I'll put you on the recorder."

Phillipso looked out at the stars. From the telephone, he heard the first sharp high *beep* of the recording machine. He bent close to it, breathed deeply, and said, "Tonight I was visited by aliens. This was no accidental contact like my first one; they planned this one. They came to stop me—not with violence, not by persuasion, but with—uh—the ultimate weapon. A girl of unearthly beauty appeared amidst the coils and busbars of my long-range radar. I—"

From behind Phillipso came a sound, soft, moist, explosive—the exact reproduction of someone too angry, too disgusted to speak, but driven irresistibly to spit.

Phillipso dropped the telephone and whirled. He thought he saw the figure of a sandy-haired man, but it vanished. He caught the barest flicker of something in the sky where the ship had been, but not enough really to identify; then it was gone too.

"I was on the phone," he whimpered. "I had too much on my mind, I thought you'd gone, I didn't know you'd just fixed your warp-what-ever-you-call-it, I didn't mean, I was going to, I—"

At last he realized he was alone. He had never been so alone. Absently he picked up the telephone and put it to his ear. Jonathan was saying excitedly, ". . . and the title. *The Ultimate Weapon.* Cheesecake pic of the girl coming out of the radar, nekkid. The one thing you haven't used yet. We'll *bomb* 'em, boy. Yeah, and you resisting, too. Do wonders for your Temple. But get busy on that book, hear? Get it to me in fifteen days and you can open your own branch of the U.S. mint."

Slowly, without speaking or waiting to see if the publisher was finished, Phillipso hung up. Once, just once, he looked out at the stars, and for a terrible instant each star was a life, a crippled limb, a faulty heart, a day of agony; and there were millions on countless millions of stars, and some of the stars were galaxies of stars; by their millions, by their flaming megatons, they were falling on him now and would fall on him forever.

He sighed and turned away, and switched on the light over his typewriter. He rolled in a sandwich of bond, carbon, second-sheet, centered the carriage, and wrote

THE ULTIMATE WEAPON
by
Josephus Macardle Phillipso.

Facile, swift, deft, and dedicated, he began to write.

Attention:

DAW COLLECTORS

Many readers of DAW Books have written requesting information on early titles and book numbers to assist in the collection of DAW editions since the first of our titles appeared in April 1972.

We have prepared a several-pages-long list of all DAW titles, giving their sequence numbers, original and current order numbers, and ISBN numbers. And of course the authors and book titles, as well as reissues.

If you think that this list will be of help, you may have a copy by writing to the address below and enclosing one dollar in stamps or currency to cover the handling and postage costs.